TO THE NAVEL OF THE WORLD

TO THE NAVEL OF THE WORLD

YAKS AND UNHEROIC TRAVELS IN NEPAL AND TIBET

by

Peter Somerville-Large

God forbid, thought I, that I should brutalize this innocent
creature; let her go at her own pace, and let me patiently follow.
Robert Louis Stevenson.

You cannot stay for ever on a yak's back.
Chinese proverb.

HAMISH HAMILTON: LONDON

First published in Great Britain 1987
by Hamish Hamilton Ltd
27 Wrights Lane London W8 5TZ

British Library Cataloguing in Publication Data

Somerville-Large, Peter
To the navel of the world: yaks and
unheroic travels in Nepal and Tibet.
1. Nepal — Description and travel
I. Title
915.49'604   DS493.53

ISBN 0-241-12108-6

Typeset by Computerised Typesetting Services Limited,
311 Ballards Lane, Finchley, London N12 8LY

Printed in Great Britain by Butler & Tanner, Frome, Somerset

To Gillian and Caroline

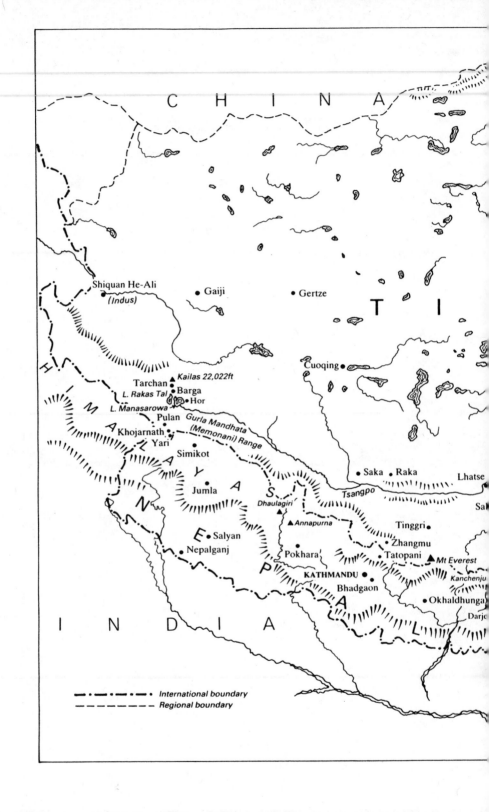

C H I N A

T I

Shiquan He-Ali
(Indus)

• Gaiji   • Gertze

Cuoqing •

Tarchan ▲ Kailas 22,022ft
L. Rakas Tal • Barga
L. Manasarowa • Hor
Pulan   Gurla Mandhata
Khojarnath • (Memonani) Range
Yari
Simikot   • Saka • Raka   Lhatse

Jumla •   Tsangpo   Sa

Dhaulagiri ▲

▲ Annapurna   • Tinggri

• Salyan   • Zhangmu
Nepalganj   Pokhara •   Tatopani ▲ Mt Everest
N   Kanchenju

KATHMANDU •
E   Bhadgaon

P   • Okhaldhunga

A   Darje

I N D I A   L

H

M

A

L

A

Y

A

S

•–•–•–•–• International boundary
– – – – – Regional boundary

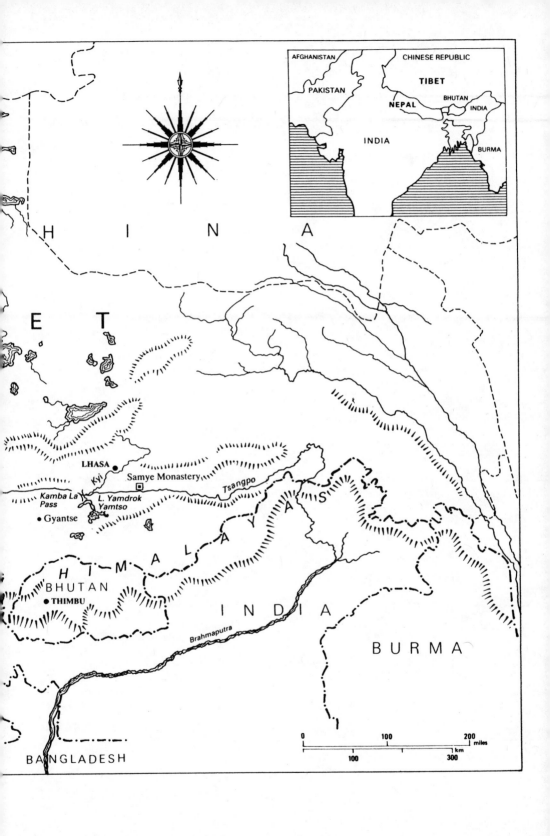

List of illustrations

All the photographs were taken by Caroline Blunden and reproduced with her permission.

CONTENTS

PART ONE – NEPAL

PART TWO – TIBET

PART ONE

NEPAL

CHAPTER 1

Return to Kathmandu

In a restaurant on the Thamel an American girl said, 'Your stools are the only way of finding out the condition of your stomach for sure.' She contrasted diarrhoeic, amoebic and bacillary textures as she ate burnt yak steak, apple strudel and custard. She talked about her trip, nothing out of the ordinary: Bali, via Australia, then Singapore, Bangkok and the poppy fields of upper Thailand. Outside the window a man was selling bamboo flutes which hung down in a circle from a hoop he held like an umbrella over his head. Sometimes he would play one, a thin piping sound against the traffic noises. An illuminated sign flickered on and off. LAB TEST...BLOOD...STOOL...URINE...SPUTUM...SKIN.... I hadn't visited Kathmandu for thirty years, the average lifespan of a Nepali.

When I was last here I had been one of the two tourists. We stayed at the government guesthouse overlooking the grassy expanse of the Tunde Khel because there were no hotels.

I had steeled myself for changes in Nepal since I planned to return. After rereading Robert Louis Stevenson's *Travels with a Donkey* I wondered if a similar journey with a yak would be interesting. Everyone thought 'Travels with a Yak' a charming idea.

A week before in Dublin I had eaten a farewell meal with my women folk whose centrepiece had been a cake with a chocolate yak walking across the frosting. The lady who made the cake sent along a poem by Jack Pielutsny with a note ' . . . food for thought on the ascent.'

> Yickity-yackity, yickity-yak,
> The yak has a scraffity scraffity back,
> Some yaks are brown yaks and some are black . . .

I had found out more. The yak is the highest dwelling mammal in the world. Wild yaks, which rarely come down the mountains to below 14,000 feet, are the size of large bison to which they are related. They are usually covered in long coats of black hair caked in mud. Their horns are immense and their tongues are so harsh that they can scrape the flesh off bones. Tibetan literature is full of legends about fierce wild yak, huge incarnate demons, solitary like abominable snowmen. Ancient battles were fought against them and they were hunted in sacred hunts. Now wild yak have been slaughtered to the edge of extinction; a few lonely creatures survive in the mountains of western Tibet.

I would be seeking out domesticated yak, *bos grunniens* a beast of burden since ancient times, the long-haired bovines still so useful in Nepal, Tibet and other highlands of Central Asia. Their hair and fine wool, plucked at the time they shed their winter coats, are used for weaving blankets and making ropes. Yak hide, dyed scarlet, is made into traditional bags for storage, book ties, and in the old days shaky boats to cross the Tsangpo and other rivers. Yaks provide the butter for Tibetan tea, butter lamps and sacred butter statues. Their beef is good, if tough. Above all they are useful as mountain pack animals. Their large lungs make them immune from the high altitude sickness that can kill horses. In central Nepal their numbers are increasing since they have been engaged in transporting tourists' baggage.

They are bad-tempered and unreliable. Pack animals they may be, but reluctantly. They have been bred down so that they are smaller than their wild cousin (and the Nepalese domesticated yak is smaller than the Tibetan). But they have never lost the notion that they are wild animals doing a job under duress. They must remain in the mountains; they can live in a lower altitude than wild yaks, but cannot come down much below 10,000 feet or they will die.

It had been hard to find areas in Nepal which were suitable for yak travel and at the same time went beyond the usual trekker's routes. Permits were difficult to obtain. I had a pile of correspondence from old Nepali hands.

'I only know the western part of the itinerary you gave me, and if Mustang means any place off the path to Muktinath, then it is certainly 'Forbidden Territory.' The last person who wanted to get off the beaten track to that extent managed to obtain the king's permission, as he was a personal friend of H.M.'

'I believe that Peter Somerville-Large should place no reliance on the Royal Nepalese Embassy and come out to Kathmandu to do battle from scratch, as it were, and be pleasantly pleased if any earlier efforts have borne fruit.'

'I suggest that a mountain pony would be more reliable . . .'

'The best porters are Sherpa women.'

'Don't have anything to do with yaks, my dear Peter. My opinion is that, unless properly treated, they can be false friends.'

I made out routes for yaks across upper Nepal. Caroline would accompany me, taking photographs. Later we would travel in Tibet where she would speak Chinese.

I studied the lists she had sent over from London ' . . . moleskins for your feet . . . thermal underwear, lip salves, ice crampons, flea powder, snow glasses, nylon rope' – that was for tethering yaks – *Playboy* – that was the request of a Nepali friend. 'Have you bought foot alcohol yet? I can't say I altogether approve of it. I don't like tin spoons and forks. Why can't we get something decent?'

Gillian, my wife, said, 'She won't approve of your boots.' I had bought an Irish-made pair, a brand that had been used by the British army in the Falklands. After I had broken them in by walking all over the Wicklow Hills, someone told me about their defects. Water had seeped into their soles on the spongy bogs of Goose Green. Port Stanley was recaptured in spite of them. The firm had thousands of pairs that had been withdrawn on its hands.

Caroline had also written, 'Please let me know what the Chinese Embassy in Dublin says about individual visas to Tibet. There are other ways of getting them if you can't do it in Dublin, but time is short.'

'Don't do anything unwise.' Like everyone else Gillian had been beguiled by the thought of a shaggy little member of the species *bos grunniens* called Modestine with a ring through her nasal septum who would be my travelling companion. She was less thrilled when she learnt that I also planned to be accompanied by a tall, handsome Anglo-Irish girl who insisted on introducing me to everyone as 'Uncle'.

My daughter said, 'What about your teeth?'

'A trek is not a wilderness experience,' warned one of the guidebooks in a gentle reminder about the state of the Omelette Trail and the Toilet Paper Trail to which the majority of travellers in Nepal are confined. 'The term "trekking" denotes an act of travelling on foot with the object of sight-seeing various natural and cultural sites in places where means of transport are not ordinarily available.'

A trek meant more supplies to be obtained in London. A sleeping bag; down or hollow fill? I took the wrong advice. Water filters came in three categories, good, bad or worse. Naturally we chose the best, which made any filthy liquid emerge as pure as holy water. A terrifying list of medicines. Caroline had obtained her own brand of stomach pills from a friend who was an expert in tropical diseases.

People had given her a lot of things. 'Sammy lent me these.' Enormous dark glasses. 'I believe they cost more than a hundred and fifty dollars.' Another friend donated two smart sleeping bags which fitted one inside the other. A zip bag was a present; so were her T-shirts, one with a picture of a glass of Guinness, the other showing Lord Rosse's giant telescope at Birr, which she intended to wear at the base of Everest in order to promote the Castle gardens.

'I wish I had your wide circle of friends.'

'I make it my business to organize things properly, and anyway people like helping me.'

Nhuche greeted me at Kathmandu Airport with his Volkswagen and chauffeur. I had met him in 1955 and had stayed with him at his school in Swayambunath. Last year he came to Ireland and talked about yaks. One had almost killed him while he was travelling in Tibet.

'If a yak was offered to me as a present, Peter, I would not accept it. They have bad natures. Their karma is not good.'

As his chauffeur drove us, I tried to recognize all the places which had been fields when I was last here. The new buildings spread down the valley towards Swayambunath where the school was situated beneath the sacred hill crowned by the famous temple with the four pairs of wavy eyes.

Nhuche is a Newar, a member of the race which has always inhabited the Kathmandu valley. As a young man he went to Tibet to study Buddhism, staying in a house where a woman was married to five brothers. You could tell which brother was in her bedroom by the shoes placed outside the door. When he returned to Nepal he started the little school which has grown big and become well known. This year, 1985, his sixty-fifth, he had opened a sister establishment for orphans on the principle that one school would pay for the other. The rich would help the poor. The new school below the village and monasteries consisted of three buildings, a courtyard and a garden. Above the classrooms the small community prayer room contained a wooden statue of Buddha, a picture of Christ and an altar covered with flowers.

In the evening I walked up the flight of stone steps through trees shivering with monkeys. There were just as many or more as there had been thirty years ago, but now there were beggars as well who waited for prey. A thin arm stretched from a sheet, a boy with a gashed mouth followed me up the steps, two at a time. 'Hello, hello, what is your name?' shouted a wild man running out of a shrine rattling a bowl. A large monkey sat on a stone and masturbated. From the centre of the plinth rose

[6]

a spire composed of thirteen gilded discs, graded in size, symbolizing the thirteen stages of Nirvana, topped by an umbrella-like toren. Blue eyes of a giant beneath the golden topknot gazed four ways complacently above the stylized question marks that represented noses. The four faces of the chaitya may have shown cynicism rather than the all-seeing power of the god-head as they looked down on the antique dealers among the shrines of the five Dyanni Buddhas and the foreigners fluttering prayer wheels. Dirt, stench, monkeys, beggars, tourists, it was still a place where religion was practised among the cares of life. An evening wind stirred the trees as sunset glowed over city and valley. Above the huddle of shrines and buildings the strings of circus-coloured prayer flags crackled and banners stretched round the gold toren. The buildings became alive with movement as the noise of wind drowned out the rattle of prayer wheels and all the hawking and spitting.

In the village at the foot of the steps the hippies came out like crepuscular animals attracted by the last glow of the evening sun. The small sad colony living here had found the combination of squalor and beauty irresistible, particularly when it could also enjoy the Nepali's tolerance and lack of curiosity. They were subdued, almost with an air of somnambulance, the dusty-haired woman carrying a baby on her back, the American saddhu in saffron robes, his hair pulled back in a bun, another man, also with long hair, but long and loose as a fairy princess's complemented by an equally vigorous frosted beard. The hairy men sat on their haunches swallowing little pastries dipped in yellow sauce. They were gaunt compared to the confident Tibetans walking past arrayed in cloaks that fell down to coloured felt boots.

All night dogs yapped and howled, a sound known locally as Kathmandu music. At daybreak Swayambunath was wrapped in haze but, as the sun rose, fields and houses gradually emerged into view and sharp colours took hold – the gold of the toren spiralling above the trees, the glare of blue eyes painted on white, the dark green of the valley and the shining wall of distant snow mountains.

'Good morning, Sar. Good morning, Sar.' Tiny children rushed outside and collected in the garden under the statue of Buddha where lessons would be held among the flowers. Nhuche had funded the building of the school with contributions from all over the world, which he whipped up relentlessly. His other enthusiasms also ranged beyond the valley, and today, after midday, the children would be given a holiday while he held an international peace conference.

Around the gateway leading up to the temple, among the monkeys cavorting in and out of sacred stones, some Tibetans were praying and prostrating beside a line of taxis. A group was straining to turn an enormous prayer wheel. From here it was a short walk down to the river and across the bridge to the centre of the city.

Much was as I remembered in the small area where Kathmandu retains its market squares and temples and manages to preserve a world which tourism has not changed. Thirty years ago I had walked among these rose brick houses with their blackened intricately carved doors and windows and jutting eaves almost touching each other across the lanes and gateways. They were ancient buildings which had survived the earthquake of 1933; Nhuche had memories of undulating ground and crashing masonry. Everything that was wood was carved with robust detail. Below the steps of a temple a pile of fruit and vegetables showed a similar obsession for pattern – an hour must have been spent arraying the onions and brinjals and oranges like a knot garden. A cow snatched at salad heads. Behind latticework the dark interiors of shops and houses swarmed convivially with people like a beehive on a summer's day. Out in the street were other swarms – flies homing in across the sacks of rice and dhal to the trays of sticky cakes.

Here was the same rich mixture of people, Sherpas, Rais and Thamangs, porters loaded down with burdens that would crush a pony, a file of Newari women each with a conical basket roped across her head. Years ago the Tibetans had been nomads; now they had settled and many had become merchants. Past a circle of pedicabs with brightly coloured hoods an elephant strode down to the river with two boys perched on its back.

The traffic clashed with my memories. Even more than the tourists it had changed things; I could recall precisely the special ancient hubbub of a city without motor traffic. Cars pushed their way through the crowds down dark little lanes never meant to accommodate them. A policeman vainly blew his whistle above the infuriated noise of horns as two Australian girls dressed in little more than bikinis argued with a taxi driver about their fare.

It would have been a grand day for sight-seeing, except that it was Holi and the air was full of flying bags of coloured dye. Every child in the city seemed to be armed with powder and lying in wait. The little plastic missiles came plummeting down from rooftop and window or darted straight out of a doorway. Soon my hair was blue and my trousers and jacket were smeared red as if I had been wounded. All day the flying reds, blues, greens and yellows slapped many a tourist so that he resembled

[*8*]

something out of a very young child's colouring book. A Hawaian shirt received a red sunset as the podgy wearer was photographing a woman kneeling beside a small metal shrine with her tray of offerings. Not only tourists – by evening almost everyone in the city had become a painted victim of carnival. The wandering cows were battered with splodges. The elephant must have made a fine target.

Nhuche's Volkswagen, ferrying delegates from the airport, had sustained a few colourful daubs. Otherwise the battles of Holi were excluded from the conference. The school, now decorated with posters showing the effects of man-made destruction, was crowded out with Japanese industrialists, schoolgirls, a middle-aged English woman, Indian Buddhists meditating and pointing out to each other the advantages of peace. Reluctantly I said goodbye to Nhuche. I knew I should be in the centre of the city since the only way to deal with local bureaucracy was to be immediate and available.

I went to the Kathmandu Guest House, a place that makes an instant rapport with any traveller who leaves the crowded streets and finds himself a few minutes later in a lush garden full of flowers nursing a glass of beer. I have met people who, hearing the name, wince with great pleasure. 'Ah yes . . . the Kathmandu Guest House . . .' The food was good and clean, service efficient, terms cheap. The atmosphere evoked a stately past. I sat with my glass surrounded by cannas, arums, ferns and the Corinthian pillars built for the old nobility. Here I could pick up the latest travel news and exchange gossip. Anyone might learn the best route of a mountain top, find out about permits, pack animals and porters, where to meet a male or female partner, acquire cheap tickets or dispose of surplus equipment.

A group of overlanders came in on their way from Australia to London looking like people who had braved desperate odds, after crossing India pinioned in two sweaty lines in the back of a truck. The Guest House offered a short respite, and then on to Karachi. They collected in another corner of the garden, gulping beer and listening to their group leader lecturing them predictably. ' . . . Always buy two toilet rolls at a time if you have the chance . . . Respect the driver, we're all one big family . . . See you later at the bar . . .'

I went over to the notice-board. Meningitis shots available from Tek Hospital free and painless. Deutschbus to Europe, some seats available. Treasury grade lapi lazuli, first quality, direct from Afghanistan . . .

'My dear fellow. How nice to see you after all this time.'

Here was my old friend, Promode, looking encouragingly unchanged.

[*9*]

We talked briefly about the vanished medieval past. I praised the Guest House and mentioned that I understood it had once been a Rana palace.

'Only C class Ranas lived here, I can assure you.' Promode was a former member of that ruling elite, excusing its fall from grace. 'Come. My car is outside.' He escorted me to a Volkswagen even older than Nhuche's. When I had known him before he had owned one of the dozen or so serviceable vehicles in the capital, all of which had been carried up in pieces from India on the backs of porters, across the terai and over the foothills. His had stood out from the other little Model T Fords, a long, low-slung monster with a fish head exhaust and a curving brass horn in the shape of a snake with ruby eyes.

As we drove down past the Thamel, Promode told me about the new Chinese-built road. We made a detour to look at the Tunde Kehl, the open space in the city centre, where, last time I was here, a whole lot of animals were having their heads ceremoniously chopped off. Promode pointed out the statue of Jung Bahadur.

'He survives in such a prominent place because he was related to the king.'

Other Rana statues have been discreetly removed; in one provincial city an ex-Prime Minister presides over the local garbage dump. Meanwhile the king has asserted his position as living ruling divine monarch by pulling down his palace and building a glossy new white model that stands behind wrought-iron railings which evoke Hollywood and soap operas. I remembered the old one, rococo and ramshackle, maintaining six hundred servants, most of them idle.

Promode showed me some of the remaining Rana palaces scattered in a dowdy group in the old compound. They had been fairly down-at-heel thirty years ago, a number of them half-ruined in the earthquake of 1933. Their owners had tended to spend their time visiting their other palaces in Benares or moving on to Calcutta to dispose of lakhs of rupees on wine, women and song. Since the political changes which caused the Ranas to lose their power and priveleges, a good many of their Kathmandu residences had been demolished or taken over by the government or let out. The American Club rented most of the building owned by Promode's cousin, Dermode. Where was the one owned by the cousin who was a field marshal? The baroque extravaganza run by another cousin as a private zoo?

Promode waved a dismissive hand. 'Rented or ruined.'

His own palace was one of the few to remain in private hands, but not without a struggle. In 1955 his chief worry had been how to dismiss his sixty remaining servants and ensure that they wouldn't starve. Now it was how to collect his rents. A sign advertising HAND OCULIST – what on earth could that be? – was stuck in the window of a cavernous room which I remembered being filled with gilt furniture and tigers' heads.

The Hitty Durbar was a white-stuccoed, three-storeyed building which had been designed in the early years of the century by a Japanese architect who had been an admirer of the Graeco-Roman style. Massive balconies whose wrought-iron balustrades alternated with empty niches which had never contained statues were supported by a forest of Corinthian pillars. The exterior retained the air of a Riviera casino. But inside – all utterly changed. All offices and shops.

I indulged in nostalgia, recalling the old decor: the drawing room with its heavy gilt chairs and pink chandeliers; the walls covered with hunting trophies and family portraits of kings and great-uncles among splayed tiger skins and elephant tusks; the lines and lines of sepia photographs of topeed figures squatting beside dead tigers attended by elephants and beaters and soldiers and bearers; how we sat under the dusty chandelier nibbling sugar rice and flicking cigarette ash into silver-mounted elephant's feet, looked down on by maharajas displaying blazing decorations on golden jackets and maharanis prim in Victorian black.

All were gone, the tigers snarling to reveal plaster tongues slotted between finger-length eye teeth, the silver equestrian statue presented to Promode's grandfather by Edward VII, the bird of paradise crown with its plumes and pearls and fringe of emeralds. At least almost all gone – the flat that he retained on the top floor contained a few relics of old decency, ormolu furniture and a Venetian mirror.

He produced snapshots taken long ago. Here was the marquee he had erected in our honour in front of the Corinthian façade. On that day he had led us to an open yard where some pots bubbled over fires, sending out an odour of mutton fat and vegetables fried in ghee.

'You recognize that?' He had been like a schoolboy giggling with excitement as he rushed around stirring the pots. 'It is Irish stew. I know that is the Irish national dish so I asked the cook to prepare it for you.' He had prudently stuck to curry.

Here were pictures of his tiny children who were now middle-aged. Promode and myself were just recognizable.

'Say that we have become elderly persons, Peter, though not old.'

He was horrified by my plans. Like most Nepalese living in Kathmandu he found the idea of moving outside the valley appalling. At one time he had been governor of a remote hill station and had never forgotten

[*11*]

the awful experience. All his sacrifices, his rationalization of his palace, had meant that he could stay in the city.

'It will be such a hard life to spend a number of months in those primitive areas where there are no modern amenities. I pity you with all my heart.'

Nevertheless he helped me in my search for permits and authorizations. I went round the tourist agencies which have proliferated in the boom years of international travel. Tiger Tops, Mountain Travel, Yak and Yeti and numerous others catering for adventure-seekers. You might ski down Everest, float by raft down a river, observe crocodiles and tigers in a game park, study Buddhism or join a queue to climb a mountain. It was all big business. But no one sought adventures with yaks.

'You want to ride one of these dirty animals? I would not advise such a foolish enterprise.'

The Nepalese government tried to restrict the corrosive nature of tourism by keeping the travelling Typhoid Marys to certain well-known routes. Places where yaks flourished were either off limits or presented problems. Taking a yak on any sort of proper journey which avoided a restricted area usually involved a lethal dip into a valley 10,000 feet below. In any case it was extremely difficult to find out which areas were forbidden. What about the route that led across the dreaded Tesi Lapcha Pass, made hideous by glaciers and falling rocks? Was that restricted? No one seemed to know. Nor were they certain about the Rolwaling valley. Certainly it had been out of bounds two years ago, but a number of people had been there since. Rolwaling was a thin wedge of a valley west of Everest running east-west just south of the Tibetan border. It was famous for its yaks and the Abominable Snowman which had left panda-sized prints there quite recently.

With the help of Promode and other influential contacts I continued to make enquiries at government departments and travel agencies.

'I am sorry, Sir. Perhaps if you knew someone to do with the palace? Or a government minister?'

'Of course we have a list of restricted areas. But these can vary.'

'Sir, it is a pity you do not know H.M.'

The owner of Sherpa Travel had an idea. 'Do not worry, Sir. Everything will be all right if you buy a mountain.'

I listened.

'The government charges climbers so much per peak depending on the height. Even if Rolwaling is technically restricted, I can get you a mountain just inside the valley for three hundred pounds.'

[*12*]

Compared to Everest at forty thousand dollars for a permit, this mountain appeared to be a bargain. Its name was Pharchamo and, although I could not find it on any map, I was assured it was there somewhere. When I asked about the regulations governing the procurement of a mountaineering license, I was given a bewildering leaflet which contained thirty-six clauses covering wages for porters, health, insurance, compensation in case of accident or death, and a list of essential equipment. 'A mountaineering expedition,' it said, 'means the act of carrying out a mountaineering expedition by an organized team with the object of reaching the peak of a particular mountain of the Nepalese Himalayan Range.' Could we consider ourselves an organized team?

The process of getting permissions for trekking and climbing is full of hidden dangers and surprises. Foreigners pay the government for a specified trekking permit in certain designated areas or a peak fee for the mountain of their choice which depends on height and importance. Currently there are 87 peaks open to foreign expeditions and 17 more for joint Nepalese–foreign expeditions. While these bits of paper assume enormous importance in Kathmandu, when you get outside the valley, few officials are interested in them. Indeed, if he really wanted to, there is little to stop the mountaineer 'topping out' the peak of his choice without permission. As for trekking, rather than follow the well-trodden tourist trail, it is hardly surprising that many people struggle to escape to a less polluted area.

'Do not worry your head, Sir. If you wish to climb the mountain, that is entirely up to you. There is no necessity. When you have paid the deposit and obtained the licence, then you may enter the Rolwaling valley without delay.'

Everyone said that Pharchamo, wherever it might be, was extraordinarily cheap. Everest had a queue of climbing expeditions stretching out to the end of the century, and other prestigious mountains were also dear, with queues waiting to climb them. There was no interest whatsoever in my insignificant peak. But, even with my receipt, would I be allowed to approach it?

The man at Mountain Travel said, 'I must warn you, Sir, last year we tried to get a permit for a retiring ambassador to enter Rolwaling and without any success. Either an area is restricted or it is not. Which is to be? We ourselves cannot tell.'

Caroline arrived in Kathmandu and within a few hours was installed in a house on the outskirts with cook and servants. Someone had lent it to her.

She had already formulated several plans for us, but rather to my surprise took Pharchamo seriously.

'A mountain for only three hundred pounds – that must be a rock bottom price. We might even climb it.' For a time we toyed with the heady idea of planting the Irish tricolour on top. We could hire a Sherpa guide with mountaineering experience. As novices we would have to learn some elementary techniques of using ropes, pitons and crampons. Perhaps it was not such a good idea.

'It's a question of not straining yourself, Peter. Let's not delude ourselves. I am a lot younger than you and I don't want to be stuck in some God-forsaken place looking after an invalid.'

In any case she was not yet ready to join me. She was off to Lhasa for a quick trip with a friend. Meanwhile I would forget about Pharchamo and the Rolwaling for the time being and go ahead to Namche Bazar to wander along the most popular trail in the Himalayas. And, yaks or no yaks, I wished very much to go to Tibet. The *Rising Sun*, the English newspaper in Kathmandu, announced that the frontier between Nepal and Tibet would be open to foreigners for the first time. The larger tourist agencies had begun their preparations. Brochures appeared.

'Drive through the remote untouched hinterland of Tibet . . . climbing up to 17,600 feet before arriving at Lhasa (11,850 ft), the religious, cultural and economic centre of Tibet. You will have the opportunity to visit the world famous Potala Palace, the Norbulingka, the Dalai Lama's summer palace and innumerable monasteries amidst the pollution-free magnificence of jagged mountain peaks and turquoise blue lakes where an extraordinary tranquillity still pervades . . .'

Caroline had taken visitors to Tibet several times the long way via China. She already had a Hong Kong visa enabling her to enter mainland China of which Tibet was a part. So did her friend. They would get up from Kathmandu to Lhasa, and if this worked well she would try a second trip with me, if possible something more ambitious. But I needed a visa, a cheap one. Enquiries made it clear that the new accord between Tibet and Nepal only benefited people willing to pay a minimum of a hundred and fifty dollars a day.

'I have a friend who lives in Hong Kong who would be able to get you a visa for a small fee.'

'What happens if it doesn't arrive?'

'It will. When I organize something, Peter, I make sure that things work out. It's just a question of efficiency.'

CHAPTER 2

Trekker

While Caroline went on her travels I took the flight to Lukla and trekked up to Namche Bazar. Outside Lukla I paid to enter Mount Sagarmatha National Park, adding to the Nepali income from tourism and receiving a leaflet which included an appeal:

> Let no one say and say it to your shame
> That all was beauty here until you came.

This was an exhortation to the trekker to keep Everest tidy. Sagarmatha, Goddess Mother of the Mountain Snow, is what Nepalis call Everest. The park is one of six created since 1973 by the Nepali government in an attempt to lessen the destruction of the primary forest which has traditionally provided fuel and building materials. In the past thirty years the cut-and-come again custom that controlled the gathering of wood has been put under fatal pressure by a huge increase in population. Nor have the forests been helped by the arrival of visitors from outside Nepal.

During the 1960s big mountain expeditions began invading the Khumbu area with armies of non-Sherpa porters who cut down trees along the trail. Porters, retained for months at the foot of the big peaks, made devastating raids on the juniper forests for firewood. The Sherpas in their turn discarded age-old restrictions on collecting firewood and felling trees. Then after 1959 thousands of land-hungry Tibetan refugees arrived, also needing fuel and space.

The National Park is intended to benefit the Sherpas by preserving what forest remains, restricting the activities of tourists and carrying out some reforestation. But people still largely rely on wood for fuel and old men grumble because of the prohibitions on lifestock. Cattle and zopkiok (cross-bred yaks) are forbidden to graze among newly-planted saplings, while goats, the great changers of landscape, formerly a mainstay of village economy, are not allowed in the park at all. The upper forest teems with pheasants which are a protected species and these birds dart out of the greenery on to the terraced fields looking for potato shoots. There are places where Sherpas have given up cultivation altogether. While the need for preserving the forest is recognized, the hacking away at green timber and removal of forest cover continues inexorably. Looking at denuded hillsides it is hard to grasp that Buddhism holds it a sin to cut down trees except in unavoidable circumstances.

I walked in drizzle among oaks, whitebeam and hemlock buttressed by ivy-dark rhododendrons yet to flower. Further up were Himalayan pines. They had been salvaged in the nick of time. Outside the park the hills were shaved like lamas' heads with here and there the stubble of felled trunks left as a reminder of where the forest had stood.

For a time I was in the company of a couple of Englishmen who had completed a quickie course in Buddhism in a gompa near Kathmandu and were hoping to enlarge their religious experience. Then an Australian.

'I'm buggered. But I wouldn't miss it for worlds.' Above us were the famous snow peaks dotted with mountaineers. Below the trail rushed the milk-white waters of the Dudh Kosi river.

'Where are you going?'

'Base Camp.' His panting was horrible. Each winded visitor contributed to grotesque changes. At present around five thousand trekkers came this way annually, and there were times of the year when there were more visitors than Sherpas in Namche Bazar.

Here was Mountain Travel with its porters, zopkioks and weak-kneed trekkers making the ascent to Namche.

'Where's the luggage, Ted?'

'All the junk is coming up behind. Give the little guys a chance.'

'For God's sake take it easy. We've got the time.'

'I couldn't take it easier, Hon. I'm seventy-two and things can't hurt me any more.'

More and more people – it was like the Grand Trunk Road in *Kim*. As elsewhere in the Himalayas trekkers divided between groups and independent travellers. The guidebooks unhesitatingly recommended group trekking through agencies which kept people all together under control. But the independents persisted in great numbers, trying to be wild and free and to do something a little more remarkable than slogging up the same slope as everyone else. Most carried their own rucksacks, provisions and lavatory paper, and were mean. They drank black tea because it was a rupee less than white, shamelessly badgered the Sherpas for bargains, and tended to discuss prices among themselves rather than great thoughts.

The decision to carry one's own belongings has moral implications as well as financial.

'I'd hate to be reincarnated into a baggage coolie,' said my companion watching another weary tour group plod up followed by the long line of porters steadying the orange and blue luggage with the aid of straps across their foreheads. I was doing my own porterage and regretting it. This was no way to enjoy the forest, the rushing river, the sparkling waterfalls and green moss. I was so weary I could scarcely raise my head to see the mountains.

I passed an Englishwoman with a huge pack on her back, tears streaming down her face. Her husband was far ahead. 'He wouldn't allow me a porter. He said he couldn't bear to see the little fellows carrying so much. He wouldn't listen when I told him he was depriving them of money.'

In the lodge in Namche Bazar I was experiencing for the first time the rich enveloping hospitality of a Sherpa household. It was a place where numbers constantly fluctuated. To father, mother, two sons, two daughters and the odd friend or stray servant were added the trekkers who called in throughout the season, stayed a night or two and moved on. Father, whose name was Passang, was a sick man who rarely got out of bed. Between helping their mother with the housework, the daughters spent their leisure with their school books or brushing her long black hair. From time to time an old man would appear with a puppy thrust into his trousers, the woolly head peering out above his waist band.

The children did their homework for the Hillary School. I helped the youngest with his English. He had written his name in Roman script in the front of his exercise book, Ang Noma Sherpa. Inside: 'Say whether each of these statements is true or false: One. Aesop wrote many stories. Two. It is known that Aesop stole a gold cup from the temple in Delhi.' Aesop has always been popular in the East. In China early translations of his pragmatic fables were far more appreciated than the sombre and puzzling tale of salvation that the missionaries preached. Ang was passionately learning English, the key to prosperity. 'What is a tortoise? What is a hare? What is a dictator, please? How do you spell aeroplane?' He planned to become a guide.

The lodge, which had escaped modernization, was a long two-storey building with a stone terrace in front and a wooden ladder leading upstairs from the bottom rooms which were used for animals. On the second floor the household lived in the main room which ran across the top of the house under a high wooden ceiling. Everything was wooden, floorboards, dresser, beds, benches and shutters cut from the forest.

Glazed windows, the glass carried in by plane and up by porter, were an innovation of the last fifteen years.

The first task of the morning was to light the fire around which life revolved. Guests lay in their sleeping bags watching one of the daughters bring in bundles of sticks and pats of dung, and then kneel down and blow, head on one side, coaxing the first cigarette-end spark into a fierce little fire that would burn all day. There was no chimney and the smoke made its way upwards, nudging the ceiling, which, after decades of smoky caresses, had acquired the sheen of black enamel noted by early Himalayan travellers reclining in similar family rooms.

The other daughter was carrying up the first of the day's relay of water in two plastic containers once used for petrol, and pouring it on to a line of shining copper cauldrons. Apart from the altar set between shelves of religious knick-knacks, these cauldrons were the most precious things in the house.

Namaste. The fire-lighting daughter bent over my sleeping bag with tea and the smile that was part of her, like a limb. Before going to school the girls would continue to bring up water, and then help their mother with the cooking, peeling the endless potatoes, preparing the dishes that would simmer with a tinge of spice all day in pots and dekshis placed around the mud stove. The menu card hanging on the wall, written in neat Hillary School script with prices marked against each item, offered yak steak, momos or Sherpa hamburger, fried potatoes, eggs, porridge, rice and Mustang coffee laced with raki. In between looking after her sick husband, feeding the orphan lamb, seeing the children off to school and keeping an eye on her lodgers, the woman of the house watched pots all day long.

As the sun rose a deep braying came from next door where two young lamas in saffron robes sat on a rooftop bellowing through collapsible Tibetan trumpets. To sound the long wavering notes that rose or fell according to lung power, they rested the nine-foot-long silver-painted horns on an oil drum. Sometimes the noise was a sigh and a whisper; then one of them would blow hard and a note snorted all over the town, a vast raspberry, a piece of grass between giant thumbs, a magnified corncrake. I recalled Madame David-Neel's flattering description of similar horns in Tibet. 'These huge musical instruments, sustaining the harmonious wailing Tibetan hautboys, produced a solemn impressive music which filled the whole valley with deep sonorous voices.'

In the smoke and soot the sleeping bags moved like pupae about to reveal insects. A bearded head poked out, another, a third that hadn't a beard and could have been a woman. Men and women were mixed up. Jacques, for instance, was mixed up with his porters, two smiling Sherpa girls. He sat and glared at the other guests, a pretty moon-faced porter at each shoulder, looking like a Moghul prince dallying with court ladies.

Mine host and hostess (smiling) watched without curiosity as the talk began about Bali, Singapore, Bangkok, Tamil Nadu, Kashmir, Burma – a brief stay in Burma since you are only allowed six days and the Burmese make everything expensive. Sri Lanka was cheap, so was the commune in Kerala. You could last on a hundred dollars a month. The Gilgit trail took you up to Hunza, full of old men who lived to be a hundred on a diet of apricots. Hunza was quite cheap, but during the summer the bazaar tended to run out of soft drinks like Coca Cola. Nepal was cheap. Langtang Manang, Muktinath, Jomsom, Annapurna . . .

The other topic was health, although the only person here who was actually supine and would lie in his sleeping bag all day was an Australian who had dislocated his knee on a piece of Khumbu ice while returning from Base Camp. He seemed quite content to spend his time practising Nepali swear words he had learned from his porter: ass hair, miser, fucker, catch my banana.

The little room off the passage could have been worse for people obsessed with the state of their stomachs. In the gloom they also peered to see if their urine was cloudy or green. Slits in the wooden floor gave a glimpse of dark regions where what went down was mixed with leaves and straw and carried away by yak to fertilize tiny fields.

In surroundings like this, medieval Europeans must have lain and waited in dread for the coming of the Black Death. Now the menace was AMS. 'How's your head?' was the constant question in between the talk of travel and bargains and the checking of pulses. Three people had head-aches, the English architect who had taken off two years ago to see the world, the grey-faced German girl with the unsympathetic boy-friend, and the ginger-bearded Australian who had drunk so much Mustang coffee the night before. Acute Mountain Sickness is said to affect one person in five. Symptoms to watch for at high altitude include wet or dry coughs, abdominal cramps, large amounts of gas after eating, breathless-ness and periodic breathing . . . four or five breaths, and then a frighten-ing period of no breathing at all for as long as ten or fifteen seconds, a pattern that can go on for hours at a time. You must get your porters, or better still, if you can afford it, summon a helicopter to hurry you down from the heights.

So far I had no symptoms apart from spasms of bad temper.

Namche Bazar put me in mind of Babar the Elephant's Celesteville with its rows of simple little houses placed one above the other up the slope, connected by lanes as steep as ladders. Most buildings were new and presented themselves as hotels and shops. They had signboards freshly painted each season, many saying WELCOME. One advertised a new Sherpa Mail Service organized by Rinchon Karna Sherpa. Could his relays of carriers run faster and speed up the time it took communications to reach the outside world from Khumbu? Above another doorway someone had written WE TRUST IN GOD ... INTERNATIONAL FOOTREST. Nearly all the houses had prayer flags stuck on poles on the roof and just below the town God was also receiving messages from the series of prayer wheels turned by the river which kept them spinning away in their little stone huts.

The unending visitors dribbled up and down followed by porters who had given up farming years ago and left the planting of crops to their women-folk. A party of American children were arriving, a group on a tour arranged by an agency called Family Trekking. How could they possibly be enjoying themselves? The tiny children were being carried up in traditional baskets on porters' backs to the dusty slopes where their mothers were looking round for proper lavatories. A line of orange bugs crawled up, Japanese mountaineers, their equipment following in drums and metal boxes that glinted on another chain of porters who unloaded in a dirty lane with an air of achievement while their employers took photographs. The people of Namche are still remarkably tolerant about cameras. They don't ask for money, but smile and smile, the old man showing one long tooth waving a plastic prayer wheel, the child in the long dress and bonnet like an Elizabethan baby – oh, how cute! – the Tibetan woman holding up the kukri which will be purchased and added to the load.

I visited the yaks under the living room of the lodge where I was staying and peered through the gloom at large scowling creatures with thick black hair and plumed tails. Winter had passed in the dark stable, but now there were springtime excursions carrying the muesli of dung and leaves from the lavatory out to Passang's fields to be dumped in smelly brown heaps. Soon there would be ploughing. I made the mistake of trying to stroke the biggest animal who was called Roko, meaning black, and received my first demonstration of yak temperament when, to the accompaniment of orange saliva fountaining from a gaping mouth, curved horns flashed in the darkness.

There were not many other yaks around Namche, which stands at

10,000 feet, just about the lowest limit of their habitat. Occasionally a small convoy of pack animals appeared from above, or I would see a lonely yak or nak or zopkiok grazing in a crazy perpendicular field.

'Too low here for good yak,' I was told. So next day I went up to the livestock farm outside Shyangboche to see more. I set off to the sound of lamas' horns accompanied by Passang's children on their way to the Hillary School at Khumjung. Having already done a morning's work attending to trekkers' needs, they rushed ahead of me, meeting a stream of other children all wearing Western clothes and carrying leather satchels who bounded up the steep hill at the beginning of a journey that would take them an hour. It would take me two.

Most of the early morning movement was centred around the little cross-roads leading to the post office and bank. A Sherpa in a track suit collected a bit of precious dung off the street; an old woman settled in a doorway, preening herself in the first rays of sun. Crows squawked and danced among trekkers' garbage piled behind the ladders that linked the houses and strewn in front of a turnip-shaped chorton.

The day was fine with streamers of cloud that drifted up from the terai looking like prayer scarfs. At the top of the town near a mani wall carved with lettering, figures of Buddha and wheels of life, stood a dilapidated little gompa with an empty courtyard and empty rooms. There were no trees anywhere, and Namche's lines of houses were ranged on steep scorched ground. Gathering firewood was an increasingly punishing task as the forest receded and incursions into the Park were forbidden. The piles of sticks and logs around each house were getting ever more difficult and expensive to obtain since a journey to the nearest forest where fuel was available and the return under the wearisome load took a man two days.

Above the rooftops were a scattering of small terraced fields, thin ledges of ochre-coloured earth scraped clean of rocks and stones. Three girls in long black dresses were planting potatoes, two digging the earth towards them with mattocks, the third carrying a basin of seed potatoes which she deftly threw into each hole made for them. When they caught sight of me their laughter was uproarious. After two decades of tourism each reeling, gasping foreigner was still a good joke. Or was my appearance particularly comical? Children continued to run past, Good morning, Sar. Good morning, Sar. I followed an old woman bearing an immense load in a basket who was putting increased distance between us.

Down in the bowl of the Dudh Kosi valley leading back to Lukla the preserved forest rose and fell in dense different greens, an undulating ridge which reproached the bare brown slopes above and formed a plush foreground for a cold circle of giants – Khumbi Yla, Tawachee, Lhotse, Ama Dablam, Thamserku, Kusuan. And the biggest of the lot.

I climbed to Shyangboche Airstrip, another dusty field a little longer than usual gouged out of the side of a hill. A sign beside the highest airfield in the world said ALTITUDE 3800M. There was only one approach and if the pilot fluffed the landing he hit rock. A decade ago this had happened to a plane belonging to the Royal Nepalese Airways which was one of the reasons why the airfield was so moribund with its control tower half-finished, and a woman herding yaks on the deserted runway.

Shyangboche Airstrip was constructed to provide access to the Everest View Hotel, a vainglorious idea developed by a consortium of Japanese and Nepalese entrepreneurs in 1971. Five-star luxury would look out on the highest mountain. In a place where chimneys were unknown, carpets, curtains, taps and saucepans had to be brought in by porter or flown in. Guests were flown in too, an hour's flight from Kathmandu, and then they were carried by yak from Shyangboche along a track leading above a gorge on an almost perpendicular descent. They were all rich and some were old; clinging to coarse yak hair they hardly had a moment to look up at the peaks overhead. They hadn't time to become acclimatized after the flight, and when they reached the comfortable hotel with the fine view, they tended to get ill and even die. That was in spite of the oxygen breathing apparatus supplied in each room instead of television and Gideon bibles.

The hotel was a low pleasant building in wood and stone surrounded by a parkland of trees. A flight of steps led up to the front door where a notice read 'Hotel Everest View Now Open for Lodge Accommodation Only. With Restaurant and Bar Facilities for All Visitors. Regret any Inconvenience to our Valued Guests.'

After the elegant exterior inside was a shock. I received the impression that a wind had raged through the building knocking down doors and furniture. Or I might be on a sinking liner. The reception hall had coconut matting and little else; there was a desk of sorts, but no chairs. A stone-walled passage led to derelict rooms and a kitchen filled with rusty cookers and fridges. There was no heating. In the big empty cold dining room I sat down at a table and thought of coffee and bacon. The menus said Welcome to the Highest Placed Hotel in the world. To all Best Wishes for the Happy Year of 1985. Thanks. New Management. When a waiter in a padded climbing jacket appeared to serve the only guest, I ordered the cheapest things, tomato soup and egg and chips. The chips took twenty minutes – time to look out on the sharp dark triangle with the ever-present wisp of cloud looming above the sun-lit rooftops of Thyangboche monastery. Incomparable. Forget Khumbi Yla, Kusuan, Lhotse.

The Manager, huddled in an anorak, a woolly hat pulled over his ears, had been working out figures on an adding machine with stiff, cold fingers. Now he came over and sat at my table.

'You have enjoyed your meal? In these days we have a good out-of-season rate. A bargain, Sir. The price of a room is only fifteen dollars.' In bed you could enjoy the view, although the oxygen mask might well be rusty and empty. 'We hope to do many improvements.' He pointed out a hole in the floor, the wave pattern of a leak at the corner of the ceiling, and a crack in the glass which, if you looked with one eye, made a new route up the Goddess Mother.

'The Japanese people have no sense, Sir. How did they not realize that this place is very cold in winter? In summer there is monsoon and rain. The mist is here all the time. It is a cloak, Sir. You cannot see the mountains.'

As I moved off he called after me, 'If you come back in October, Sir, a night will cost you more than a hundred dollars!'

The royal yak farm, just up the trail through an arched wooden gateway, consisted of a few austere buildings and a long, walled enclosure surrounded by trees. There was no sign of any yaks, only a cow. This was a Swiss cow.

'She will be mated to a yak and no doubt will give birth to a satisfactory calf. Swiss cows give better milk,' declared Mr Charad Chandra Nenpane, the Livestock Officer. A graduate from Kathmandu University, this was his first post. We sat in his office with its picture of the royal family and a tapestried cushion on my chair on which was embroidered an ideal yak – noble, handsome, its horns and fur worked in gold thread.

Mr Nenpane told me that, although tourism had generally supplanted farming as the main source of income throughout Sherpa territory, nevertheless the yak and its hybrid offspring were still essential for the well-being of small communities.

The domesticated yak was less than half the size of a wild yak. Yak was strictly the name for the male of the species. Sherpas call the males yak, the females nak. For many thousands of years yak have been crossed with other cattle such as the Tibetan *bosaunus typicus* whose bulls are known as lang. The results are zopkiok and zhum. Zopkiok and zhum can live at lower altitudes; zhum give more milk and are altogether more satisfactory than nak. A good zhum might cost as much as four thousand rupees. Only the female hybrids are fertile. Zopkiok are also fine; cross-bred yaks are reliable pack animals, less aggressive than the pure-breds and easier to handle if they are treated right. So far no name has been devised for the offspring of a yak and a Swiss cow.

Mr Nenpane continued to pour out information. 'Do you know, Mr Peter, a yak's white tail can be worth more than two hundred and fifty rupees?'

'What do they eat . . . grass?'

He threw up his hands. 'And where do you find grass?' We looked out of the window at mountains and shrivelled vegetation. 'At this time of year before the rains there is nothing for these beasts. We give them hay and potatoes and maize flour mixed with water twice a week.' When yaks went trekking on the bare mountain a good proportion of the load they carried had to be their own personal provisions. They got lonely and needed company. They liked to travel in pairs. A lonely yak was a bad-tempered yak.

'What about riding them?'

'Indeed, Mr Peter, they are not meant for riding. You will find it quite difficult to get hold of a riding yak. Saddles, bridles, other essentials – these are very hard to come by. A riding yak must be especially trained. Tell me, in Europe do you go around riding bulls?'

He threw up his hands again. 'I tell you, Mr Peter, that not so long ago some foolish foreigner got killed taking a riding yak across a glacier. The saddle slipped! There was a crevasse! Too bad!'

An assistant came into the room looking worried. Mr Nenpane listened anxiously.

'My friend here tells me some very bad news. A yak has been killed by a wolf.'

'I'm so sorry. Do wolves often attack?'

'Sometimes at this time of year. And we can do nothing. In a national park no wild animal can be trapped or killed. Not even a damned wolf.'

'How can you protect your yaks?'

'It is very difficult, let me assure you. Now we have fifty-six animals. This morning when I awoke we had fifty-seven.'

'Where are they?'

'Most of them are high up on the mountain in a yersa.'

I elicited that a yersa was a stone mountain hut like an Irish booley. The ownership of land in yersa settlements used to be very important among lifestock breeders, and until the advent of tourists whole families would move up to higher pastures during the monsoon months. Since the

[*24*]

keeping of large herds of yaks by Sherpas has declined in the face of tourism, many yersas have fallen into disuse or have been turned into tourist lodges. The few that are occupied by herdsmen during the summer months have become rarities.

Mr Nenpane said, 'I think it would be better if you learn more about yaks. Then, perhaps, we may see about a riding beast.' He sounded like Duveen with a rich, uncouth client, starting him off with something modest and gradually working up to a Gainsborough. 'As it happens I have a convoy which will be bringing up potatoes to my herd. You may accompany it. Come here on Sunday morning at eight o'clock and bring warm clothes.'

Rain spluttered on the small windows of Passang's house, dripped through the black roof, hissed into the fire and fell into the cooking. Outside Namche was covered in mist. Rain fell on the little sloping muddy field where the tents had changed from orange to blue with the arrival of a new group the night before. After dumping their loads the porters had erected them in a line together with the cooking tent from which Sherpa stew was ladled out. On no account were the closely supervised clients of the trekking company allowed to stay in houses where those who shepherded them would have to share profits. Here was a sad sight, the tents side by side pegged down in the mud while the rain bucketed down, and a number of early risers wearing shorts, standing outside under umbrellas. Only a few yards away stood a Sherpa lodge offering smoky hospitality. Guidebooks are full of warnings for the misocapric; in addition the traveller is constantly reminded about dirt, noise and monotonous food and told that camping with a reliable agency is infinitely preferable.

One after another, drifts of clouds spilled up the valley bringing rain and a promise of softness and greenness, a baptism of renewal after arid winter months. Namche was blotted out, the mountains were dissolved and today there would be no view of Everest from the hotel. At the yak farm five animals had been prepared for the journey, three yaks and two zopkioks, male cross breeds, the mules of the Himalayas. They stood outside their stables, hairy silhouettes in the mist, with three attendants who were taking supplies up the yersa.

'Cowboys,' said Mr Nenpane. They were small wiry men in tracksuits and combat caps covered with camouflage markings. In spite of the rain two wore dark glasses. None could speak English. The leader was called Hari Kumar.

The day's trek was a short one to Khumjung where the potatoes were to be loaded. A group of pines stood out against the rocks like a Japanese print as men and animals shot up the track into swirling mist and I tried to keep up. Occasionally far ahead up in cloud I would hear a yak grunting and the patter of stones thrown at it, to hurry it on. The track unfolded eerily, a narrow steep path with flights of stone steps, giant boulders and occasionally the roc's-egg shape of a chorton springing out of the mist. Around one of them I caught a glimpse of a dozen witchy women squatting with baskets and bags, one with a yak skin tied in a bundle on her back, others resting tall conical baskets brimming over with goods. One moment, and then they disappeared in white swirls. So fair and foul a day I have not seen. The mist turned back to rain as I followed down a track transformed into a watercourse brimming with liquid, leading to Khumjung, a village of shadows.

In the rain I was directed to a large house with the familiar stables on the ground floor, the ladder leading up, another smoke-filled room, another smiling cook, more trekkers.

'We come from Hamburg.'

In the morning strokes of sunlight fell on the little altar with its figures of Buddha, the shelf supporting a line of copper bowls, a pair of boots hanging from a nail, a pennant from a mountaineering expedition and a frame of photographs. A rank of Thermos flasks, red, blue and green, complemented the shining bowls. The fire was relit and the small wooden shutter over the window was unlatched to reveal a view. It was strange having my vision restored. There was a gompa and two large chortons. There were the trees and boulders among which I had slithered the day before, now looking beguilingly easy, The mountains had reappeared.

I visited the school. When the headmaster, Mr Shyam, started teaching nearly thirty years ago most people had no formal education at all. He wrote letters for them, distributed iodine tablets and observed TB sufferers. There was no medical care in Khumbu. In 1950 the mountaineer Tom Bourdillon passed a village of some sixty people of whom forty had just died of an unknown illness, perhaps typhus. It is well for anthropologists and people like myself to bewail the jolly old ways that continue in western Nepal far from the trekking crowds, where the old structures of society remain unchanged, goitre pouches are still common and people die young.

The dramatic breakthrough in education in this area was due to the energies of Edmund Hillary. In 1960 his Himalayan Trust built the first classrooms here and today over three hundred children attend the school. George Lowe, a member of the original Everest team, another tall New

Zealander, was on an annual tour of inspection as morning lessons began, signalled by a bell-like note struck on an empty oxygen cylinder. For Lowe and Hillary the twenty-three schools of the Trust scattered through this part of Nepal are linked with the triumph of their youth. The practical and massive thank-you to the Sherpas includes hospitals and health centres where patients are charged a token rupee.

'We have been lucky,' Mr Shyam said. Prosperity was the result of living at the foot of Everest.

Lt. Colonel L. A. Waddell, author of *Lhasa and its Mysteries,* wrote a good precise description of yaks in 1905. 'They are shaggy beasts, in appearance something between the American bison and the cattle of the Scotch Highlands, and their curious grunting call is aptly denoted in their scientific name of "the grunting ox" *(bos grunniens)*. They are noble looking massive animals, especially the bull yaks – in spite of their oddly round and squat appearance. The thick coat of hair which protects them from perishing in the arctic cold of the snows, is longest on their sides and undersides. The tail ends in a great bushy tuft, which serves the same purpose as the bushy tail of the hibernating squirrel, curling over its owner's feet and nose when asleep, like a rug, and thus affording protection against the intense cold of the Himalayan nights. These bushy yak tails are much in demand in India as fly whisks for Indian princes and as royal emblems for the idols in Indian temples.'

The two yaks and three zopkioks were being loaded with sacks of potatoes. This was a job requiring alertness and presence of mind, since each animal was bent on outwitting its groom and if possible sticking a horn in his ribs. You don't stroke yaks, or make any of the discreet signals that calm a nervous horse. You whistle at them and you watch every movement. As sacks were roped together and loaded, the cowboys approaching their charges with the wary care of their Western counterparts approaching a rodeo bull, the awful grunting came regularly, combined with a grinding of teeth. The noise was distressing, with a perpetual suggestion of effort about it and a tinge of pain. The name yak is onomatopoeic.

The zopkioks, two café-au-lait in colour, the third spotted black and white, lacked the blinding fringe and were like sturdy shaggy little cows. The yaks were shining black and a lot more hairy. They were rather like compressed bison, with much less of the broad head, and their shagginess blurred their sturdy outline. They were nearer to the ground than bison, their short legs mostly hidden by a mass of the hair like drapes around

Victorian piano legs. Hair curtained their eyes, thickly covered their flanks and backs and humps, and fell in a petticoat around them. The bushy tails were like foxes' tails, none of the snake-and-tassel appendages of other bovines. Lyre-shaped killer horns protruded from the mass of fur in front; occasionally as a yak tossed its head, moaned, ground its teeth and let fly a spurt of saliva, you caught a glimpse of a big brown eye. They might be impervious to cold, they were great for high mountains, they were sure-footed, but they were wild animals at heart. You could be loading potatoes onto the backs of zebras. All the time you knew they were waiting for some little thing to disturb them and send them galloping off, trying to get rid of their burdens. Suddenly I had great respect for the cowboys arranging three sacks on each back, two on each side, an extra one on top tied together with rope pulleys.

Hari Kumar, a sinewy young man who could run straight up any hill, whistled all the time, not to compensate for the fact that our conversation was limited to 'O.K.', 'Stop', 'Good Morning', but to urge on his charges. Whistling, a counterpoint to the groans, soothed the savage breast. Whistling and throwing stones was the way to drive yaks on.

Leaving Khumjung was like the start of a Grand Prix as yak and zopkiok galloped off with the cowboys running behind, each man loaded with a bag of additional rations. 'What the hell?' called out an angry American as they hurtled past, almost knocking him down. His words were lost in cowboys' laughter as they raced by. Everyone knew that on a narrow trail a loaded yak takes precedence, and you must give way to these hairy juggernauts.

Below the village the potato fields thinned out, and soon we were descending into a narrow boulder-filled valley covered with birch and fir trees. Then we came out above the main gorge of the Dudh Kosi facing ranges of mountains that were so high the mind did not fit them in with the rocks and ice below and the places where the forest still clawed up their lower slopes. They were like clouds. Everywhere you walked there was a bird of prey circling overhead; other signs of life were usually trekkers and their entourages making their way along the grand highway to Everest.

The foliage was luxuriant; a waterfall came spilling from an overhanging rock. I could not see much of this pleasant detail since as we moved the sun dried the rain-soaked mud, and soon the animals ahead were kicking up blinding dust with their hooves and skirts. They galloped along with the three whistling cowboys in perpetual pursuit. If a yak ran too far ahead or turned off the track to graze, they were all after him to stop. They would surround him, shifting his load of potatoes, turning him round until he faced the right way. More whistling and shouting disciplined the other animals to an extent that often they would stop dead and stay put for minutes, Then, when it seemed that nothing on earth would get them moving again, they were suddenly off, making dust.

The small village of Phunki Thanghka lay at the bottom of the valley reached by a long skinny bridge. Each yak faced it and was willed to make the crossing. One by one they took a run at it like the Billy Goats Gruff, and clattered across the undulating wooden boards. There must be times when an animal misses its footing and vanishes into the white river beneath. I hadn't the vocabulary to ask Hari Kumar.

We spent a couple of hours recuperating in a teahouse near a fringe of prayer wheels turned by the river. The roar of water dashing over the rocks echoed in the still air as we consumed white tea and biscuits under a picture of the Dalai Lama and a shelf filled with leftovers from mountaineering expeditions. When I offered Hari Kumar a tin reduced to ten rupees, he studied the bright red picture of a Japanese octopus for a long time before shaking his head.

When we moved on, the sky changed from blue to white as suddenly as if a curtain had been drawn, and a loud wind drowned out the sound of the river, bringing snow with it. Soon my clothes were covered with soft, fluffy flakes, the path under the trees shone white and the yaks turned into moving Christmas cakes. Hari Kumar increased the pace as I struggled to keep up far behind the convoy. The path went up towards the monastery of Thyangboche and its sacred hill from where some lamas were coming down towards us, giving way to our yaks, their robes shrouded in snow-flakes, cowled heads bent down in the face of the blast. We moved past them up to the holy place to yells augmented by a wail of Indian music from the small transistor carried by a cowboy as a precious symbol of the good life.

Through the snow I made out an enclosed gateway, then the outline of the gompa, a dim shape jutting out above the trees. Beside us a line of blue tents from which came gruff German voices was casually pitched on the most sacred site in Khumbu. The cowboys squatted down and smoked cigarettes, and I thought for a glad moment that we might be spending the night here. But no – once again the yaks set off on their constant trot, while I followed miserably. We went down and then we entered forest, trees plastered with snow, giant rhododendrons frozen white. The transistor was switched off – it may have interfered with all the noise directed at the yaks. Between the cries and whistles, other sounds were squeaking boots on snow, animal grunts, the regular note of bells from round their necks and a pad of cloven hooves supporting their loads. All around was a marvellous frozen forest.

The trees ended at another gorge with a suspension bridge where spray from the Imja Khola had stiffened on the moss and lichen that hung lacey-white from branches above the river bed. The yaks stopped, sniffing the cold air, then tripped over one by one. On the other side the forest stopped as if sheared with a knife. It was still snowing hard; for another rest period we found a small shelter in another gateway crossing the track, its walls painted with Buddhas in meditation. More cigarettes while the yaks stood motionless.

Two hours later we came down to Pangboche heralded by chortons and mani walls built in the middle of the path. Even where the snow made it difficult to see, the cowboys followed the Buddhist precept of going around them clockwise, while the yaks went by the more direct route. I followed the yaks. Beyond Pangboche to renewed yells the yaks veered off the track and began climbing up a wilderness of rocks where, in addition to snow, the mountainside was covered with a thick layer of icy mist. Far above me I could hear the cowboys calling and the occasional sharp noise of a bell. It seemed that I had been lost for hours, and then the mist lifted so that I could see a narrow shelf of land with some walled fields and enclosures. Around a group of mountain huts were dozens and dozens of yaks standing in the snow. And here the convoy stopped. It had been travelling for ten hours.

The cowboys just had time before darkness fell to unload the sacks and bring them into the hut, a simple stone building roofed over with sods of turf. There was no room in the small interior for furniture. Sacks of potatoes and pieces of firewood carried up the same long route we had come today were piled against one wall, while beside another were heaped blankets and clothes. Through the smoke I could make out crowds of men in track suits. I slumped down by the fire and was handed a cup of tea. It was heaven.

Each week at this time of year a similar convoy of potatoes was shuttled up to keep the herd going until there was enough grass. Throughout the summer season the herders lived in this hut. One was breaking up wood, while another sliced potatoes for the pot. We ate bowls of potatoes tasting of smoke before lying down on the ground like rows of sausages crowded one beside the other. Some slept under rough blankets made from yak wool; others had sleeping bags acquired from mountaineers. Two men sat up much of the night playing cards by firelight to songs from the transistor.

In the morning light, filtered through holes in the roof and stone walls, the storm was a memory. A man's head lay a few inches from mine. and an extra pair of legs lay across my sleeping bag. The head turned and grinned while someone brought in an armful of juniper and lit the fire which gave off little flames, and an asphyxiating resin-scented smoke. Soon a pot of potatoes was being cooked for breakfast.

The yaks had to be fed first. Herded in a stone enclosure before release on the mountain they were given a ration of grass and two kilos of cooked potatoes to a chorus of moans and grunts that might be interpreted as joy. Then it was our turn. We sat outside eating our potatoes, watching the rising sun turn the mountains fuchsia pink, then luminous orange which slowly bleached to glittering white.

After breakfast everyone relaxed. Someone cut his fingernails, another preened himself in a mirror, others played cards and listened to the transistor. There was one older man, the only one dressed in traditional clothes, a long black coat topped by a fur hat with flaps drooping over his eyes and nose. Unlike the spring dandies in their track suits, he kept himself perpetually busy making small hoops of barkwood for holding ropes and harness. When he had finished that, he passed his time by plucking out strands of coarse wool from around his wrist and spinning it on a little wooden spindle. He spun as automatically as if he was swirling a prayer wheel until he got tired of that and rose to his feet and went after the yaks who were scattered on the mountain snatching at minuscule mouthfuls of food.

I made the mistake of following him. Just behind the yersa compound loomed the peak of Tawachee, a medium-sized Himalayan giant, and it seemed to be that without actually turning into mountaineers and rock climbers we had reached the limit of any negotiable land. I misjudged the ability of fifty yaks to trot up a vertical incline, followed by the old man running up the rocks behind them. He ran away with his yaks, leaving me to gasp and clutch my aching head in front of one of the world's most desolate and intimidating views. The shark's teeth of Ama Dablam were behind my back; in front rose a wave of angry mountains that included Nuptse and Everest. I was alone, listening to my pounding heart, remembering that as you get older the hills get steeper.

CHAPTER 3

Zopkiok

After the yersa Namche seemed a suburb, not a place to linger. The mountains beckoned you, urging you not to stay down here, but to go up even if you were not planning to climb them. The feverish urge to make for the heights was not confined to mountaineers. I would go to Gokyo, which was a beacon for trekkers.

A Dutchman at Passang's lodge told me, 'The place was so cold the toothpaste froze in the tube. Your urine froze solid.'

Mr. Pemajon helped me to find transport. His family had an important position in the town. We sat in the small room of his house high above everything; from the window I peered down over the rooftops loaded with stones to gaze at the passing scene like the Lady of Shalott. I could see each group of trekkers coming up the steep slope from the river, two elderly European women and four porters dripping in perspiration, a party of Nepalese, some Japanese carrying a rising sun flag and coloured paper fish on sticks. The room was cold and Mr Pemajon had a blanket over his shoulders as he crouched by the window pointing out the other houses he owned, together with the crescent of small fields around which Namche was built. He was a little disillusioned by tourists, but inevitably involved.

He recommended a guide for me who lived in Jarkot, the cluster of houses planted between vast rocks overlooking Namche. It appeared that Pemba knew all about yaks and would bring one along tomorrow. He would take it from his brother's field.

Pemba was a Tibetan who had escaped to Nepal as a child before his family went on to Darjeeling. When photographs of refugee Tibetan children were circulated among individuals and charitable organizations throughout the world, he had been adopted by a Belgian priest who took on the responsibility for his education. Every month they exchanged letters, and then one month nothing arrived.

'He was an old man and he die.'

Although Pemba was in the tenth class, he had to leave school. He drifted back to his family which had returned to Nepal and settled in the Khumbu area. Having learned English at school, he found work for a trekking company at 35 rupees a day, the same wage as a porter, and tried to see a future for himself. 'In Europe I might have been a pop star.'

He wore the smart blue jean suit sent to him from Belgium by his adoptive father. His baseball cap was scarlet and white.

The yak, whose name was Nangpa, was a scrawny little animal. I had my rucksack and tent, together with a few provisions. Pemba brought his own small bag and a large burlap sack of hay, and started the business of loading up, balancing everything around the small wooden pack saddle and tying the bundles down with ropes. The hay sack in particular was big and slippery, and kept sliding off. At each delay Nangpa showed increasing signs of impatience, snorting and shying. The operation was watched by jeering trekkers.

'You cannot seriously propose to take that beast to Gokyo,' said the Dutchman. 'You forget what I told you about the cold.'

'It looks real hungry to me,' said an American, 'and you intend to feed it all that distance on one teensy weensy bag of hay?'

The lady of the house got Nangpa going by picking up a stick and belting him.

The day was hot with only a few clouds rolling up the valley. The Namche shopkeepers were arranging their goods on the pavement outside, jewellery, bags of biscuits and sweets, a Tibetan lama's skull trimmed with silver. There were yak blankets, yak skin shoes, yak skin coats, toy yaks. On the wall of one house was a stuffed yak's head. An old woman politely stuck out her tongue and the crows seemed to mock us.

The track went past the police check point where theoretically every tourist was supposed to produce his trekking permits. The three men sitting outside the hut were bored. You want to sign the book? One of them got up stiffly and brought me into the office, yawning. I signed the ledger which keeps everyone satisfied, officials in Kathmandu, the trekkers who have paid. This year 25,000 would be permitted to wander over Nepal.

Nangpa was slothful, stopping on the track every few yards, moving on reluctantly when urged by Pemba's enraged screams and thumps. He would go on for a very short distance and stop again, kicking up dust. He stopped and shied for the tenth time at a group of men who were shouting and throwing stones at two large birds of prey with wings like black fingers. The birds spiralled slowly upwards on a thermal rising from the valley until they became specks. The men continued on their way. Nangpa refused to budge.

'Why don't you lead him?'

'It is done this way, Boss.'

I looked at Nangpa critically. His ears were decorated with red woollen tufts that hung down like earrings. He was piebald like a tinker's pony at home. His little short legs scarcely came up to my knees. His horns were formidable enough, his tail was reasonably bushy, but he lacked substance. I remembered the animals taking potatoes to the yersa, and how for all their melancholy nastiness they kept galloping ahead uphill and out of sight. There had been no stopping them. They had been a lot more handsome. At least – two were handsome, three less so. Nangpa had hardly more hair than a cow.

'Yak?'

'Zopkiok,' Pemba said casually.

'We agreed a yak.'

He looked away at a mountain and there was a long pained silence.

'Zopkiok good as yak. My mother need yak for ploughing.'

The real thing approached from the opposite direction along the trail, a line of proper yaks bearing big loads and hurrying, hurrying. Nangpa was a flawed imitation. You could see the difference as they swept by with their Hovercraft gait, how much hairier they were, altogether bigger, their bison humps distinctive, their massive figures somehow majestic. In comparison Nangpa looked seedy. Sluggish, his head constantly hanging down, he did not even seem to be a good example of a zopkiok.

We continued on the trail in sulky silence, punctuated by Nangpa's spurts of movement. This part of the route was the same I had followed last week, down the deep gorge of the Dudh Kosi. At Phunki Thanghka Nangpa stopped again at the bridge with an air of long practice and began chewing leaves. A long wait during which to observe how the whole valley sparkled with the approach of spring. Light shone on the budding trees, on the cascading stream and the distant water wheels for quite a long time before he could be pursuaded to trot across. Birds were singing. Behind the teahouses half-naked Germans were sunning themselves outside their tents, while a group of French were shrilly objecting to the price the teahouse charged for tea and fried bread.

We stayed for half an hour so that Nangpa could be fed on potatoes to give him strength for the climb up to Thyangboche. We plodded up hill glimpsing through the fir trees a bright blue sky and a snow-caked mountain looming across the valley, its crevices and serrated edge shining like glass. Ahead charged another convoy of yaks weighed down with large boxes of Spenser's Tea and pyramids of eggs. We met people coming down, Sherpas moving at an easy trot under their loads, trekkers looking jaded. An elderly Englishman, his leg bandaged, hobbled down with the aid of a ski stick. He had been to Base Camp.

'It's like Piccadilly Circus. There's a glut of Norwegian and American climbers. What's the weather like in Lukla?'

'Misty when I last heard. People have been waiting for the plane for two days.'

'I have to be back in London by Monday for a directors' meeting.'

Just a little higher up Thyangboche was waiting for us and every other traveller in Khumbu. Last week the snow had blotted out detail and the gompa had been veiled in mist. Today things were more lively. From the small tower built over the main courtyard a line of lamas sounded horns while another rang a bell. I read the notice-board.

Welcome to Thyangboche. Please Step in the Land of Trekkers Paradise for Remote Shelter. We ask Your help to Keep our Place Clean and Collect all Trash.

At one time, and not so long ago that most Sherpas remember, Thyangboche was remote as well as holy. The monastery traces back to Lama Sanga Dorje, the fifth of the reincarnate lamas of the Rong-phu monastery in Tibet. Towards the end of the seventeenth century he brought Buddhism to Khumbu by flying over the high mountains from Tibet and landing at Thyangboche, and later at Pangboche, leaving his sacred footprints at both places. When he died his body evaporated into a rainbow, and his eyes, tongue and heart remained to be placed in a silver casket.

More recently Thyangboche has had its ups and downs. After the gompa was destroyed in the 1933 earthquake, rebuilding took many years. In the 1960s the arrival of mountaineers had a devastating effect on the numbers of monks, many of whom were induced to leave because of the large wages offered to anyone capable of carrying a load at high altitudes. Today the monastery has been enriched by gifts; every Everest expedition includes in its budget a fistful of kafkas and a large donation to be offered to the current Rimpoche. The buildings are restored and the establishment is flourishing, but it is a different place from the holy spot of thirty years ago where nothing disturbed the lamas' meditation except the rustle of wind and the cluck of pheasants. It is bedlam. Some sleep in the crowded dormitory set up by the National Park. Others stay in the

Mountain Travel Guest House which is smart, comfortable and relatively expensive. There is plenty of room for tents.

The Gompa Inn is run on behalf of the monastery by a nierwa released from ritual duties. Trekkers were reading books, eating, complaining or boasting like the Dane who had been up to the Khumbu icefall a dozen times. A haunted-looking German woman had sickened above Pheriche and had to turn back; another German wearing scratched spectacles hoped to study the ecology of Base Camp.

'You could save yourself the trouble by inspecting any old municipal garbage dump,' said one of the three fierce Australian girls who put you in mind of Amazons. A plump American in a T-shirt saying 'When the Going gets Tough the Tough get Going,' carried a copy of *New York Times* not that much out of date. His companion's head was bad.

'I'm sorry, Margaret, you're not handling altitude too well. Everyone going up to the Kalar Pattar is psychopathic. Try some Diomox . . . '

'I have, I have . . . '

'Frankfully and truthfully, there is no need to press it.'

An English girl was dying to meet the Rimpoche. 'Don't we need kafkas?' White scarves are as essential a part of the serious trekker's equipment as stomach pills. Her friend, who was as hairy as a yak, said, 'I've got the bloody kafkas. Anyway it's not that wonderful meeting him. Reincarnate lamas are two a penny in Nepal since they cut down on them in Tibet. You bet the next Dalai Lama will come from Nepal.'

The German with the scratched spectacles gulped a mugful of chang. 'You can time the effects of chang to the exact hour. In thirty-three hours you will get diarrhoea, then severe vomiting. A pity they do not distil the water . . . it is a good drink.' The nierwa brought him more.

When he brought chang for us, together with chappatis and fried potatoes, Pemba became happier.

'I think it will be a good trip, Boss.'

Tourist lodges were scattered around the compound beneath the little knoll on which the main gompa stood. Behind the gateway a little courtyard was surrounded by wooden pillars in the style of a Christian cloister, each pillar having been carried up the mountain trail. Upstairs was the main room with thangkas and images of Buddha; lamas' cells huddled round it, together with a newly-finished library intended to be a major literary source for those wishing to study Mahayana Buddhism – and there were plenty of them around. Nearby were some of the highest latrines in the world; you peed over a drop of a thousand feet.

At dawn I went up to view the mountains by the early light. A track led upwards from the entrance of the monastery past a chorton and a small mani wall with a PLEASE DO NOT DISTURB notice. Higher up the rhododendrons thickened into a piece of forest full of birds. In the woods around Thyangboche life is sacred and you are supposed to be able to see all sorts of fancy pheasants and rose-pink pigeons. The only birds I noticed were the choughs looking for garbage. But my eyes were gazing upward for Sagarmatha, Chomolungma, Qomolangma Feng, Mi-ti Gu-ti Cha-pu Long-na, Everest, old Peak Fifteen.

And the others. Here from a high wooded spur covered with firs and rhododendrons you could look out in every direction at a bewitching selection of snow peaks. Identifying them was like picking out constellations, I found Thamserku, and then Kantega, which the mountaineers describe disparagingly as a 22,000-footer, but is singularly beautiful with its crowned white head and hanging glaciers. Kwangde, Tawachee, Everest, Nuptse, Lhotse, Ama Dablam – saying their names was like reciting a mantra. Lama Sanga Dorje had a purpose similar to that of the early Christian hermits in seeking holiness in a remote place, and it must have been as spiritually uplifting for him to meditate before the great mountains as it was for the monks of Skellig Michael to contemplate the presence of God on the pathless sea.

Pemba, Nangpa and I set off on our travels when the morning air was still crisp, the light is more intense and the mountains have a sheen which they lose as the sun gets higher. Nangpa had been given potatoes, but he looked disgruntled.

'It is the weather, Boss,' Pemba volunteered. 'You hear thunderstorm last night?'

I remembered moonlight.

'Zopkiok and yak not like thunder. Too much noise.' He shook his head as if I was to blame. He had tried to get more potatoes, but the lodges, busy catering for tourists, had none to spare.

We plunged down on the far side of the hill through a wood which was under the care of the monastery. There was no discernible track, just a thick slice of woodland falling down to a river where tendrils of lichen and moss fell over our heads in silver curtains. The other side of the valley was just about bare of trees; once I heard a woodman's axe ringing out another death note. It took holiness to preserve trees in these parts, and the monastery was doing a better job than the park people.

Soon I was experiencing Sherpa's Law number one – in the Himalayas a short run down is invariably followed by a much more difficult ascent. Ahead of me Nangpa was demonstrating Yak's Law – the most lacklustre yak hybrid will occasionally show a frantic burst of speed as if it is being pursued by hornets. While Pemba ran after him whistling in vain, the zopkiok had disappeared upwards and out of sight.

I abandoned any idea of keeping up with them; the day was hot and cloudless and I sat on a ledge looking across the river back to Thyangboche on its wooded hill. The sun shone on the gold toren and caught the wings of a flight of snow pigeons so that they glinted like tinfoil. Far below, the river fell in a deep blue line. I slept and woke and got lost. Here the smaller tracks were nothing more than the imprint of dust between stones, with nothing to indicate where zopkiok and attendant had vanished. By the time I found them, panicking about my tent and provisions, there had been plenty of time for the two of them to sink back into listlessness.

Although Pemba had been unable to obtain potatoes, he had managed to buy two extra sacks of hay which he carried along. They had not impeded him running after his beast, but now brought him down to the same pace. Nangpa, who carried everything else, had long forgotten his hysteria and had returned to his sluggish ways. All the way up over rocks and boulders he had to be prodded, pushed, roared at, shouted at and poked away from the precipice.

Phortse was a lovely little place standing facing Thyangboche on a high shelf of sloping land above the upper reaches of the Dudh Kosi. Chorton, houses and some small fields starred with flowers. Pemba stopped outside a house and began unloading with great haste.

'Good place for camping, Boss. I stay in house. You put up tent.'

In the months to come my tent would be a valued friend, but this was only the second time I had erected it. On the last occasion I had been watched by my applauding family in the garden at home. During his travels with Modestine (a tractable animal compared to Nangpa) Robert Louis Stevenson pointed out the disadvantages that a tent brings to the solitary traveller. 'It is troublesome to pitch, and troublesome to strike again, and even on the path it forms a conspicuous feature of your baggage.' Instead he took along a Victorian sleeping bag that served a double purpose, 'a bed by night and a portmanteau by day.'

Since that time tents have become a lot more compact, but they are still tiresome to erect. Most of Phortse watched me and Pemba struggle. Two husky girls digging in a field lay down their mattocks and ran over to help, chortling and laughing. Then Nangpa stirred into life and walked through the maze of equipment, his sharp little hooves treading on nylon ropes.

Pemba said, 'It is best you put up tent yourself, Boss. That way no one else is to blame.' So I wrestled alone before an audience, and in due course I put up my little green igloo. On the far side of the village another segment of unsullied woodland fell down to the river. From below me came the sound of children singing, where the schoolmaster sat with his pupils in a circle conducting an outdoor lesson. His small mud school with the tin roof built by the Hillary Trust catered for fifty-seven children.

What did they all want to do when they left? Mr Ran Prasad Ray said, 'They want to live in Kathmandu.'

He was gathering them up to take inside as the wind strengthened and the sun vanished in mist. I could see nothing but only hear the sound of mattocks from the girls who had helped me, who were still breaking up the sandy soil, wrapped in a cloud.

My idea of camping had been to be completely independent. But the primus would not light.

Pemba stood outside the tent watching. 'Very difficult stove. Over ten thousand feet no pressure.'

I joined him in the house under which the tent was perched. Upstairs above the hearth fire the Dalai Lama was placed beside a coloured cut-out of Everest, an ice-axe and a rucksack with a certificate dated 1980 from the Eastern Sierra Himalayan Expedition; the usual glass-fronted wooden frame holding precious family photographs. A couple posed resolutely in their best clothes, the man in a Western-style suit a little too big so that the trousers made waves around his ankles, the woman wearing a wonderful patchwork silk apron in scarlet and yellow and a pair of gilded earmuffs that had kinship to a Celtic-torc. Other photos showed the man in snow goggles and a balaclava, the king and queen and a couple of small children.

Here were the children, rather bigger, together with a baby and a whiskery old grandfather. The man of the house, like so many heads of Sherpa families, was away. 'He porter.' After a supper of potatoes taken from the embers and eaten in their skins, I watched the young wife mush a piece of potato in her mouth like a pigeon and give it to the baby. The children drank glasses of chang, the baby cried, a mouse ran across the floor. Then the woman put the baby in a basket on her back and gently rocked it from side to side. From the stable downstairs came the sound of yak bells.

My tent waited below. After I had shivered all night on stony ground, in the morning, as the smell of kerosene failed to heat up water to pour on a tea bag, I could see in the dim light that the fly sheet was frosted over. Up in the house Pemba had slept by the fire near the old man and the children, and while I munched dry muesli he cajoled the woman into cooking him a Sherpa breakfast. Then it was time to strike camp, an operation complicated by Nangpa who was once again dissatisfied with his morning meal.

'I don't think we reach Gokyo today, Boss. He carry big load. He need plenty rest.'

'It's not very far.'

'Distance not important. He still tired from long walk.'

Nangpa was not showing immediate signs of fatigue. He twisted and fought like a rodeo horse as Pemba struggled to tie down bags and sacks.

'Eh . . . eh!' He gave him a clout and another bag fell to the ground. 'Very bad animal.'

'Why don't you let him calm down?' I was holding the nose rope as if I had a swordfish on the end of the line.

'Zopkiok must learn obedience. Must learn I am master. I give it to him, you see.'

A long time later Nangpa surrendered to Pemba's blows and returned to resume his apathetic movement. We were on our way at last, and I felt once again the exhilaration of the Himalayan spring morning, watching the sun hit the mountain tops, touching the high peaks and glaciers, then slowly descending into the valleys towards the dark thumb of land on which Phortse sat. Suddenly the grey stone walls and fields where women were already working became suffused with golden streams of light. Smoke poured out through shingled rooftops as we left the village and walked through another patch of woodland that the axe had spared. As we moved among black velvet shadows, a small deer watched us walk past from a thicket of bushes and trees which blended perfectly with the spotted brown skin. Koileri, Pemba told me, bored. Very common deer.

We were out in the thin sunshine ascending the upper portion of the Dudh Kosi valley, a narrow cleft in the mountains which many people think more beautiful than the conventional grandeurs of the Everest trail. It was still early in the year for sheep and yak to be driven up to high pastures. We trudged through a yersa at Konar, a deserted settlement of stone huts surrounded by a few rough fields. The frozen ground was scattered with pools of ice, the prayer wheel, a large gaily-painted cylinder, had ceased to respond to the wind and remained motionless. The wind howled as it tried to turn it.

The track followed the mountain wall, rising and falling along the rocky edge. On the far side of the valley I could see a similar trail stretching to the end where the white wall of Cho Oyu blocked up Nepal and marked the Tibetan frontier. We passed the odd person, an old man spinning black wool, a girl with a basket on her back filled with dung. We walked among grey moraines and crevices, cruel white peaks and screes of navy blue rock hurled against the side of the mountain. Even in this bleak and ugly place someone had scraped at the stony soil to make a few desperate patches of cultivation.

At Thare we found another collection of deserted stone huts, mostly windowless, but with the odd small hole patched with glass brought up an immeasurable distance. They had also gone to great effort to put up a little chorton and a mani wall which gave us protection as we sat and rested under beautifully-engraved holy lettering. I chewed a biscuit tasting of kerosene, Pemba picked his teeth and Nangpa went into his trance. Only a short pause; from Thare the track squeezed its way downward through a maze of rocks that had spilled from a glacier towards Nar, at the end of a two-hour descent stumbling in freezing wind among patches of snow and ice. As Nangpa kept slipping, his hoofs ringing on stone, threatening to go over, he appeared to be contemplating a demonstration of why yak steak was readily available in a country where taking life is discouraged. Suddenly, in a moment, he recognized where he was, and sensed a release from his labours on a familiar route at the end of which he knew that we would be stopping for the night. As if a brake had been released, he put on a burst of speed like a horse on the way back to its stables, as usual taking Pemba by surprise and leaving him whistling and screaming.

We came upon a small boy in a tattered brown coat dancing on a rock.

'Nar,' Pemba said contemptuously. 'I think we look out for potatoes.'

Nar was situated below some glaciers at the head of a valley which syphoned wind through wretched little houses indistinguishable from the stones around them. I sat shivering in a small stone enclosure above the river while Pemba went off whistling to himself, returning with two pop-eyed men wearing shaggy coats and identical baseball caps.

'Very good men, Boss.'

Their hut consisted of two black rooms. Everything was black, the sacks of potatoes, the potatoes themselves, the baskets heaped with wood and dung, the earth floor, the porous walls and the roof through which the wind howled. For once the fire was inadequate to keep up the usual Sherpa fug, and as usual, when I tried to light the primus to cook instant soup, the white magic failed. No one wanted cold soup.

'You eat with us, Boss.'

Potatoes were served in a tin basin on the floor. There were sacks of potatoes stacked against a wall, there was a loose pile of them on which we sat and, after eating a dozen or so sprinkled with salt, our hosts used potatoes for gambling with a dice and board. Hour after hour while my eyes smarted and stung with smoke, a man would toss up the dice and bang down a handful of raw potato chips, each worth so many rupees. Then the other would raise his call and count out another pile. Bang, shout, bang, shout. Bedtime loomed.

A simple test for accommodation is to lie down and curl up without hitting anyone. You may put your feet in another man's face or be conscious of his heartbeat or garlic breath, but there are limits, and the hut was far too small. Pemba had retired to the stable where he shared another stockpile of wood and dung with the wild men's yaks. I envied him. Inside the tent, inside the sleeping bag, I was chilled in my kapok trousers, thermal underwear, two sweaters, Gortex jacket, balaclava and scarf.

I could not feel my feet and the tent was stiff, frozen solid as an igloo. There came a prolonged crackling as someone outside struggled to unzip the flap, and a wild head and a dirty hand with bitten nails appeared with a tin cup of smoky tea. When I peered out the two men were there waiting, together with Pemba who had no coat or gloves and shivered in his cotton shirt.

'He say you owe money for potatoes and tea.'

'Tell him to come back later.' The time was half-past five.

'They want money now. They go to Namche to buy food at market. They go now.'

Thirty rupees put the tea and potatoes in the champagne and caviar class. The two men skipped away with their yaks, while Pemba took a ration of frozen potatoes over to Nangpa who had spent the night in a small enclosed field and may have been as cold as I was.

We went off from Nar in the grey light of early dawn in silence except for the wind and the clattering of stones under Nangpa's feet. Just below the settlement a few planks had been pushed over the baby Dudh Kosi, a brook that would gather strength from glaciers and melting snow so that in only a few miles it would become the familiar white torrent. All round was the roar of cataracts falling over rocks. Beyond the river the track ascended another morain where Nangpa halted. I had a good rest while Pemba twisted his tail; he was nearly badly hurt by a swipe of horns followed by a vicious kick.

'Whaa . . . whaa . . . ' Nangpa bellowed before moving on, climbing out on to a stretch of level land above the narrow funnel of the valley. Like the mongrel offspring of a Siamese cat, he had inherited the distinctive voice of his forebears – the moaning, grunting note that almost more than anything else evokes Himalayan travel. Ahead of us was nothing but the wall of Cho Oyo guarding Tibet. The sun had come out. An hour ago I had felt like a preserved mammoth, but now it was as warm as a Mediterranean beach in summer. I stripped off extra clothes and then took a photograph of Nangpa and Pemba standing together in the wilderness. Nangpa went galloping away, scattering baggage over rocks and snow.

'You shouldn't have done that, Boss. Zopkiok not like cameras.'

Gokyo comprised half a dozen yersa huts converted into tourist lodges standing on the shores of a frozen lake with a background of mountains, the same old friends. Colours were sharp, aquamarine and white blending with the rubble of grey rocks. Directly facing the little settlement was a steep golden brown hill called Kala Pattar, Black Rock, which every trekker who comes here must climb if he is to have Number One view of Everest. Nangpa, given temporary freedom, spent his time gazing at his reflection in the lake. Dull eyes, shaggy mottled head. I still felt disgruntled at wandering through the Himalayas with a bullock.

Above the doorway of one of the rough stone yersa was the usual sign; there cannot be a Sherpa in Khumbu who does not know the meaning of WELCOME. Half the interior was taken up with tiers of bunks, and at the other end was a kitchen and open fire around which a dozen people were being served food by a lovely Sherpa girl. Within a few minutes I was enjoying an omelette with chapattis and chips. She offered tinned porridge, powdered milk and beer at fifty rupees a bottle. There were potatoes.

'Yak food,' said the irritable Israeli beside me peering into his bowl. But, like me, he had lived on potatoes for days, and we owed a mutual debt of gratitude to the common spud.

All day trekkers sat in the lodge around the fire as the girl cooked a continuous supply of meals. There was rice and dhalma, yak steak and stew, and all the eggs carried up on yak back. For variety she offered mountaineer's leftovers. Japanese octopus seemed to have spread all over Khumbu. There was Polish chocolate and a month's supply of ravioli in tomato sauce.

'The stuff accumulates, especially when someone dies climbing.'

At 15,000 feet, Gokyo, located at the last stage before the mountain barrier with Tibet, appeals to the more experienced trekker. Here the riffraff had been weeded out; it was no place for softies. The talk was of lateral moraines, Schneider's map and difficult passes. Two Germans had just crossed over from Lobouje on the Everest side.

'Don't attempt the Pass if there is any cloud in the mountains.'

'It is always wise to bring a local guide.'

I sat next to a small middle-aged Englishman who ignored the cold and wore an open-neck shirt and shorts. He had scored rather more points than those who stuck to the usual Bangkok–Bali trail. Outer Mongolia . . . Turfan . . . the Yangtze Gorges.

The Sherpa girl, who was about nineteen, had learned a little English, almost entirely to do with food.

'I give two eggs . . . OK?'

'Two porridge . . . '

'Chapatti coming . . . '

'Six rupees very cheap . . . '

She worked away unceasingly in the smoky light, taking fresh orders. In between cooking she fed the baby that Pemba held on his knee. I had noticed that Sherpas and Tibetans have an instant rapport and, while her husband was away on his weekly descent to Namche to buy provisions, any visiting porters had a duty to help her.

People turned in around nine. Many kept awake because they had headaches or they were rendered sleepless by the coughs and wheezes and the voices droning away about prices and travel destinations. In the morning I could see a line of bright anoraks, yellow, orange and blue, moving up the coffee-coloured hill. Everyone was going up. Here was another test of fitness and adaptability to altitude, a two-hour climb over slippery rocks, avoiding gravelly spills of loose stone.

'We do it for the training,' said the German, scrambling up in front of me. 'Ya . . . two times each day . . . ya . . . is good.' He patted his bulging biceps. He wore corduroy trousers buttoned down over his knees, thick woollen stockings tucked into massive boots and an Austrian hat with a feather. He was full of advice. 'Take plenty of rest . . . a man your age . . . You must wear those glasses so . . . the sun will scorch your eyeballs . . . '

The view was very fine indeed, the mountains all round and, below, the stone huts beside the lake with its rim of ice and a brown dot that was Nangpa. All around the Kala Pattar against the background of chill blue sky were sounds of wheezing and gasps for breath.

'Oh God, isn't it wonderful!'

'Wow! If I stand up here on this rock I'm over 18,000 feet high.'

'I wouldn't do that if I were you.' A woman's voice shrill and anxious. 'It looks kind of crumbly.'

'You're a nut case, Maxine. Let the wind blow you off and see if I care.'

'Don't talk so much when you're gasping like that.'

A party of Americans was perched all round the summit like a flock of brightly-coloured parrots. They had pushed their way to the best position right at the top, and they scarcely had room to move. They were on the look-out for Everest.

'Where the hell is it?'

Clouds were dancing in front of the whole range.

'That must be Makalu.'

'What about the one two along?'

'I think that's Lhotse.'

'She's gone too.'

Not a sign of the big one. 'Fuck it, anyway.'

I wanted to travel up the valley as far as I could towards Cho Oyu.

'Zopkiok tired, Boss, after climbing.'

'He's had two days' rest.'

'He need plenty potato and grass. Here very little.'

I said my mind was made up. Pemba had enjoyed a happy rest period sitting by the fire eating at my expense. Now and again he got up and did a little desultory work around the yersa, or checked up on Nangpa who was also receiving extra rations.

Grumbling, he packed up the various bags together with two sacks of hay, taking longer than usual doing the balancing acts with ropes and pulleys on the zopkiok's back. We set off walking up the valley to many complaints, stumping over rocks and boulders towards Cho Oyu which loomed ahead blocking out the horizon and sending an icy wind down on us as we arrived at another lake, frozen among rocks and snow.

'I think we stop here.' Pemba settled in a small field dotted with cushions of moss that Sherpas use for burning which was being grazed by some yaks, proper yaks, smothered in long black hair. Just ahead was the dusty grey moraine and glacier sweeping up to the mountain.

After putting up the tent I set off walking alone.

'I tell you, Boss, it is better we stay in Gokyo.'

'I want to see the glacier.'

'No good glacier.'

The greyish convoluted fringe of ice reaching into the heart of the mountain among great spills of ice and rubble proclaimed desolation. Every detail was on such a gigantic scale, Cho Oyu, a daunting steel-grey pyramid dabbled white, and the peaks to left and right forming a ferocious line of crests. I had been told that at one time yaks crossed this barrier into Tibet; they must have had wings.

When I returned to camp I found the place empty; there was no sign of Pemba or the zopkiok. Gusts of snow began falling out of an ash-coloured sky.

I sat in the tent with a headache which I knew instantly signalled the real thing. The other little twinges back at Thyangboche had not prepared me in any way for this wall of pain. Only yesterday I had trotted up to 19,000 feet without a care in the world, but now I was sick.

Pemba and Nangpa reappeared.

'He go walking with other yak and cause me much trouble.'

I felt a little less depressed, having spent an enraged half-hour visualizing Pemba back at the yersa downing yak stew. We sat in the tent while, ever optimistic, I encouraged him to work on the primus. Outside, the snow fell more thickly and I remembered the Dutchman and his frozen toothpaste. When Pemba managed to get a little spurt of flame going, we had a lozenge of tepid soup and two cold chappatis. My head felt as if it was being squeezed in a nutcracker.

Later I said, 'I can't see much point in staying here.' Pemba was lying on the other side of the tent under his old blanket – he had no sleeping bag – his cap pushed over his eyes. He was shivering.

'We go back, Boss?'

'I think so.'

He leapt up. 'I think that good decision.'

No camp was ever struck more quickly. Even Nangpa cooperated. Down came the tent, and in a few minutes all our bags were roped together on the zopkiok's docile back. We left that unimaginably beautiful site like an express train.

'You're back quickly, mate,' said an Australian at Gokyo. 'Altitude?'

'I think so.'

'Mark my words, it always gets you.'

All night the lodge sounded to unnatural coughs and retching, and people swallowed codeine in handfuls. One of the Germans who had crossed over from Lobouje developed a high fever, while the Englishman who had been everywhere and done everything was prostrate from headache and vomiting. He spent the next day silent in his sleeping bag.

'That Pom has really overdone it,' said the Australian. 'If he wants to climb Everest, he shouldn't try to do it in those bleeding shorts.'

[46]

The rest of us huddled over the fire coughing and holding our heads, being served tea and omelettes and potatoes by the Sherpa girl, full of smiles.

'Come back springtime,' she said. 'Flowers good then.'

CHAPTER 4

Thami

The return to Namche was pleasant and easy. We spent the night at Machhermo on the dusty brown tableland overlooking a valley filled with grazing yaks. This was the place where in 1974 a yeti killed three yaks and attacked a woman. Next day we trotted through Lhabarma and Dole, and seven hours later the familiar rooftops of Namche appeared. Nangpa broke into a gallop and nothing would stop him until he pulled up beside the lodge.

'He's very happy,' Pemba said, throwing off the bags. 'Gokyo bad for zopkiok.'

In Passang's lodge was a party of Americans who had crossed the Tesi Lapcha Pass all roped together. Then in the Rolwaling they had climbed a more expensive mountain than the one which Caroline was buying for me.

'Pharchamo? Only a 20,000 foot walk-up.'

Jake, their leader, was small, lean as a pencil and wore a wispy red beard. He sat drinking a lot of chang. 'You need experience. You need a good guide.'

'Remember that fall of rock?' said Kathy, who was exuberant. 'Those boulders came crashing down like hailstones. They missed us by inches.'

'Last year someone was killed. An American, too, poor lady.'

'You'll need plenty of ropes and karabiner pitons to fasten in the rock,' Bob said. He was another who didn't feel the cold and wore a shirt open to the navel. His arms were like steel bands.

'The golden rule is take no chances.'

'The ice has shifted.'

'Those falling rocks are terrible.'

'Yaks? You must be out of your mind. The only way to get them across the Tesi Lapcha is by carrying them in baskets.'

Nevertheless I planned to make a leisurely reconnoitre of the Tesi Lapcha together with Pemba and Nangpa. (Mother still needed the yak.)

'Not to cross. Too dangerous. Zopkiok and I go with you only to look.'

We set off on the day of Namche market, the weekly event that tied the

[48]

area together. People came down from the most distant villages and yersas to buy and sell provisions. I recognized one of the wild men of Nar, while Pemba waved to the husband of the woman of Gokyo. By the grey light of dawn the dusty terraces were filled with a multitude, while on the rock above weary porters squatted with their empty bags. Already tourists were making their way towards the antiques and yak skin blankets.

The track to Thami followed the course of the Bhote Kosi, a tributary of the Dudh Kosi through another high valley full of waterfalls and precipitous slopes closed off by the mountains leading to Rolwaling. Although Thami was far nearer to Namche than the landmarks of the Everest trail – others more fit than I could do the route in a day and be back at Namche by evening – it was a lot less popular with trekkers. There were no big mountains at the end, only the Tesi Lapcha and its showers of stones and the forbidden Rolwaling beyond.

We met plenty of Sherpas returning from market, sweeping past us, trying out their English.

'Where you going?'

'Your name please?'

'Goodbye.'

In front of us a team of four yaks carrying potatoes was being urged along with piercing whistles by two fat girls. Pemba tried to keep up with them, prodding Nangpa ceaselessly, at the same time giving me an idea of the remarks being shouted back at him.

'She say why don't I visit her in Thami. Do you think her pretty, Boss? Sherpa girl very free to love-making, not like Indians. I like foreign girls best. Last year I meet Australian lady. After trek she say why you not come home with me? I tell her why you not wait for me? I have family here. I have mother, father, sisters, brother. She say she get ticket and look after me. Very sexy in bed. Australian ladies very sexy.'

At Thomde we came to the headquarters of the Hydel Project which planned to bring electricity to the area. In the little office of the chief engineer, Mr Ganesh Bahadur Shortse, were a number of uplifting texts. Any Man who Rules Himself is an Emperor. Where there is no Sound in the Mind God's Voice can be Heard. Seven years working with the scheme had inclined Mr Shortse towards natural philosophy, if not resignation.

'Please listen to me,' he said, offering a cup of tea. 'Is there any other country in the world where all goods must be carried by porter for fifteen days? Do you know what is the nearest spot where trucks can reach us? It is Jiri, many many miles down below.' Bags of cement, nails, steel rods, conductors had to come up on porters' backs. Each man or woman could only carry fifty or sixty pounds up a track which often vanished under a landslide or met a river whose bridge had been washed away.

'I need help with God and also with man.' Mr Shortse gazed out of the window at the mountains. 'Please guess how many months in the year men can work up here.'

'Eight? Seven?'

'Five months. Only five months. That is all they can manage because of the snow. Years must pass before the Sherpa people may switch on. It is fine to have a turbine at Namche. But Namche does not represent all the region by any means.' He smiled wearily. 'You love Nepal?'

'It is a beautiful country.

'I wouldn't say that. We respect the guest as the god, but there have been very many bad changes. I tell you something. When you have no money you are very honest and innocent, but when you make money you become materialistic. I see it coming. The east goes to the west and the west to the east. Do you approve?'

I said something about possible benefits.

He raised his hand wearily to his head. 'I tell you another thing. Tourism brings disease. When you have all this free sex it soon loses its charm I assure you. The day is coming very soon when Sherpas will have AIDS. Perhaps it is coming tomorrow.'

Later he gave me directions to Laondo Gompa.

'You are a tourist. No doubt you wish to study Buddhism. Many tourists like Buddhism. Many hippies visit Laondo.'

'Why go there?' Pemba pointed to the speck over our heads. 'Much better keep to main path.'

As usual he was right. The track gyrated straight up in a series of skinny ribbon loops past a few juniper bushes which were having trouble with gravity. A climb like scaling the side of a building, a sense of overpowering inertia, and a long gasping struggle to reach a cluster of trees and some prayer flags fluttering on outstretched poles.

The gompa was a small red building balanced on the edge of a crag poised for meditation. It was like Thyangboche, only second best. A good smell of cooking came from the open window, a pall of bluish smoke went up from one of the flat rooftops, and a monk from the Canary Islands sent me to a room with a single English word carved over the door: TOILET. Then he showed me the main gompa building containing a large room with four big seated Buddhas facing the door. Placed in front of them was a photograph of Lama Subha who had founded Laondo fifteen years ago as an international centre for Buddhism. At present he was in Los Angeles.

A charming girl in lama's clothes greeted me with a smile. She must have been the world's most beautiful nun. She was the product of two different cultures, her father being Asian, her mother European. After attending a short course on Buddhism in Kopan near Bodnath in Kathmandu, and finding the experience deeply spiritual, she had come here. Others besides myself must have wondered impertinently why she should hide herself away. Dark eyes flashed. 'Why not? In Christianity there is a strong tradition of women seeking peace and enlightenment in this way. You are from Ireland. You must know this.' Could St Attracta with her monastic foundation and her swarm of bees have been as beautiful as this lovely lama?

I was shown a small cave where Lama Subha meditated and one of his books translated into English '. . . The world has a red sky, reflected from the jewel "ruby" . . . Its size is two thousand pak-tse wide and the name means cow enjoyments . . . '

We gathered in a small dining-room, eating momos as the sun filtered through the windows, and outside prayer flags flapped and dipped in the wind. How peaceful everything seemed. An elderly nun, the Lama Subha's sister, sat with an equally elderly Nepalese follower, the Canary Islander fondling the pi-dog he had rescued in India, and the tall beautiful girl in yellow robes. Perhaps if she came down from here she would turn into an old old woman.

Clouds boiled up from the valley and the sudden cold was accompanied by a rumble of thunder. It was time to leave Shangri-La. Pemba and Nangpa waited impatiently outside the gate. Snowflakes drifted down from the overcast sky as we hurried down from the gompa to the Thami trail. A woman filling her pannier with pieces of dung smiled at us, but Pemba did not have time to stop and banter when Nangpa changed gear and his pace became a miraculously quickened trot. Pemba ran after him yelling and in a minute they were out of sight. The wind freshened, the falling snow blotted out the mountains as the vanished gompa assumed a dreamlike aspect, a legend of holiness. Once again I was in the predicament of finding myself alone, this time in dense cloud accompanied by wind. Occasionally the wind would blow the cloud apart, revealing a flash of light on a distant mountain before everything returned to cotton wool. I walked for two hours in white darkness before reaching a stringy little bridge slung over a torrent. In a field beyond, a dog barked beside two women pounding the earth with mattocks.

'Thami?'

'Ah . . . ah . . . ' They held up their arms vertically and one of them nodded and clicked her tongue. For the second time that day I was subjected to a lonely painful gasping climb. Poor feeble body. I clambered to a grove of stunted trees looming out of the mist and a sign saying WELCOME with an arrow pointing out the track.

The wind blew the cloud away, revealing dusty fields laced by thin stone walls with mountains looking down. Two women were unloading yaks watched by an old lady sitting in a sunny doorway spinning a prayer wheel. A chained mastiff burst out barking at the sight of me, and beyond, tethered outside a door, stood Nangpa. Inside Pemba was installed in the upper room eating potatoes from an enormous tin can.

Firelight made highlights on the copper cauldrons and Thermos flasks, lit the Dalai Lama and the king and queen, and failed to reach the dark and smoke of the roof. The hearth fire is sacred; it has taken time for trekkers to learn not to spit, pee or throw rubbish into the flames. An old man skinned a bowl of potatoes, adding a touch of salt and popping them into his mouth with as much relish as if they were grapes. I watched the woman of the house cooking in her elaborate costume, long grey dress with a red jacket, striped apron, fringed scarf and pounds of jewellery; it was like bending over the pot in evening dress. A transistor played all night.

At daybreak the big mountains of these parts revealed themselves. Teng Kangpoche and Kwangde, both over 20,000 feet, but not big enough to attract the trekkers the way the giants did. A snow-topped wall closed off the end of the valley and glaciers seemed to be falling through the window. I trudged around Thami looking for someone who might hire me yaks to cross the Tesi Lapcha. I tried the old man who lived beside the Hillary School who had once been a guide and had crossed the path many times. But now he was only interested in opening up his precious potato pit which lay buried under the sand beside his house.

'He say now too difficult to take over yaks, and how much money you pay?'

He scorned the going rate of sixty rupees a day which I mentioned. Our appearance did not promote the confidence that goes with a well-equipped mountaineering expedition. It was the same elsewhere. Pemba went round with me offering shrill advice. 'You not get good guides and yak here . . . ' 'Woman say very dangerous . . . no one goes to Rolwaling . . . ' 'I tell you, Boss, everyone remember dead American lady.'

He agreed to bring Nangpa on a cautious reconnoitre of the route along the valley leading to the pass. We first came to the gompa, one of the largest monasteries in the area, famous for a rumbustious and colourful spring festival. The lama who showed us round produced a donation box and a book filled with donors' names and the sums they had given. On the prayer wheel outside the gate someone had written the single word NO. Thami would never do as well out of trekkers as Thyangboche, but not for want of trying. Another lama ran to spread a piece of red cloth on the ground and take out a selection of antiques from a bamboo basket.

Beyond the gompa the valley narrowed and the mountains closed in. Which was my peak? Pemba had never heard of it.

'Perhaps they give you wrong name. Plenty mountains to choose from. Government people need money all the time. They take name out of drawer.'

In addition to the Tesi Lapcha into the Rolwaling, another famous pass crossed the mountains from Thami, the Nangpa La, which in the old days had been an important trade link between Nepal and Tibet. The long glaciers heralding its approach at either end had deep grooves worn into the ice by the passage of countless yaks coming to and fro bearing burdens over a route which before the Chinese take-over had been at 19,000 feet, the highest pass in any trade route in the world. Tibetans used to cross it frequently, not only bringing their merchandise but to attend religious festivals at Thami.

In Namche I had met a Tibetan who had escaped this way into Nepal.

'We fight Chinese for months. One time the horse that I rode was shot. When we reach Nepal animals all dead because there is no food.'

The frontier had been closed for many years. Just beyond Thami at a checkpoint two soldiers sat outside a hut knitting. Beyond them was a restricted area.

'Tibet?' I pointed to the mountain at the end of the valley. One of them finished a row, looked up and nodded. They made no move as we ambled past them. On this clear sparkling day when distances seemed to shrink I thought how easy it would be to keep going. Even Nangpa could cross into Tibet, past the last lonely gompa in Nepal with its small courtyard and a line of gilded Buddhas gazing through an open doorway. Perhaps when Caroline arrived we would just hitch our bags on any animal and keep on walking towards the final white crest of mountains.

We were back in Namche ending what the guidebooks describe as a side trip, good acclimatization experience before tackling higher elevations. Nangpa galloped down the final stretch as if longing to see the last of me. Payment was made. 'Goodbye, Boss.' The denim track suit and baseball cap, together with the piebald bullock, vanished out of my life. *Partir, c'est un peu mourir.*

CHAPTER 5

Yak

A letter awaited me from Caroline which had taken ten days to get from Kathmandu to Namche.'Nepal is late,' said Mr Pemajon. The missive had been carried up hill from far away Jiri in the same way that cement bags were hauled up to Mr Bahadur Shortse and his electrical project. My postcards to Ireland went down on porters' backs. Wish you were here. Greetings from the Land of the Yeti.

Caroline was incisive. 'I have been advised *against* Tesi Pass – it involves ice wall, due to major slide – this needs crampons and ropes . . . also at this time of year much danger from falling rocks . . . strongly advised against! Therefore I am not getting mountain. Have been told of great route up and over to Tinggri (in Tibet) – a friend just done this without visa, no checks . . . great route and traditional yak trail. Alternatively go by southern route – do this without permit. Have been talking to people who have lived here for years – they say just go. If you feel very strongly about the mountain let me know by letter or radio message.'

And yet . . . I received another leisurely delivered letter from a contact in Khumjung. 'I am quite well here and how are you. What do before we are trekking to Rolwaling. I search for good Sherpa in my neighbours. One man he have been to Rolwaling across three times and he know every way, and when do you go to Rolwaling you write to me.'

Another contact in Thyangboche promised a riding yak. Plagued with indecision, I waited for Caroline who arrived precisely at the time she had indicated, preceded by two children carrying her colossal baggage. Items in her luggage included Tiger Balm and tapes of Beethoven, Count McCormack and Edith Piaf to play on her Walkman.

'I must have two days' rest and complete solitude.' She scorned Passang's lodge with its restless trekkers. 'I've been lent a house. A friend had given me the code numbers of the lock on the door.'

She sought out a small traditional Sherpa building which had been rented by her friend Brock. Brock was a celebrity in Namche, a blond American with Viking moustache known as The God of Light. He had been responsible for installing the first turbine and bringing electricity to the town. While Mr Shortse struggled with the Hydel project, Brock had succeeded. The first night no one had believed that anything would happen, in spite of the parade that preceded the big event. People stood outside waiting for the miracle which came suddenly as all the windows in the rows of little houses were lit up simultaneously. Now electricity was a commonplace in Namche where the video film playing twice weekly at the cinema helped to change attitudes as much as the incoming tourists.

Brock was the man mentioned in Caroline's letter who had travelled unofficially in Tibet, and had made the crossing from Tinggri over the Nangpa La down into Nepal to the place which I had contemplated a few days ago. He had followed the old yak trail gouged out of the ice.

'He's quite disparaging about his achievement. Said there was a bit of ice. They had to cross a couple of glaciers which gave them a few problems, and apparently there were a few tight moments. Actually, he said he wouldn't like to do it again.'

She had gone on her sightseeing trip to Lhasa. 'The Hong Kong visa worked. They took it all right.'

After she had recuperated with the aid of Beethoven's output of symphonies we left Namche for Thyangboche in search of a riding yak.

'Of course I can ride. I've hunted with the Kilkenny for years.'

I told her about my experiences with Pemba and Nangpa.

'Surely, Peter, the difference between a yak and a zopkiok is obvious? Remember that we are doing this trip together, and it's no use telling me after the event that you mistook A for B. I want to survive the journey in one piece.'

She employed two more little boys to carry her baggage and mine. They climbed ahead under their loads. 'You don't know how strong these Sherpas are. Why do you suppose they are used on Everest?'

We followed the familiar route up the Dudh Kosi valley among the trekking groups, the biggest mountains in the world floating high above us. We came to a teahouse with a tempting display of antiques arranged on a low stone hall. A plump American was trying out a trumpet, red-faced and triumphant as he achieved a burst of farts which echoed over the valley. Caroline was tempted by a piece of horn shaped like a spout.

'It's obviously phallic – they probably used it for drinking urine. I know someone who would love it.' She bargained shrewdly with the sales lady, watched by an admiring little knot of Sherpas.

She walked much more slowly that I did, moving with a non-stop plod, always keeping going even up the steepest hill.

[55]

'You should breathe through your nose. It's no use just running on and then gasping.'

'I feel fine.'

'There's a lot of dust about, which is why I always wear a face mask. And look at your nose and hands – no protection at all from ultra-violet rays. Of course it's entirely your own decision if you want to wreck your skin.'

At Thyangboche there had been an epidemic of gastro-enteritis. The few unspeakable lavatories provided by the monastery were generally abandoned for the healthier outdoor scene with panorama.

Not only had we our water filter, but also pills. Caroline said, 'I think its important that even with boiled water we should pass it through the filter. It's amazing to me how slapdash people are.'

'You sound like an Englishwoman.'

'I am just as Irish as you aspire to be. The first rule travelling abroad is never trust the local water. If you don't believe me look around.'

In the big room at the lodge, inert shapes lying in sleeping bags one above another in tier bunks. The groans were continual, while every now and then an invalid would struggle out of his bag and make a dash for the door carrying the precious roll.

Possibly because of our precautions we escaped infection and spent two healthy days at the monastery. Some fine yaks had been recommended and a message had been sent up for them to come down to us. Meanwhile time passed pleasantly. I talked with Janbu, a guide who acted as chauffeur-nanny to endless trekking groups.

'Which nationality do you find the most difficult?'

'The French without question. They want to wash at every stream and they are impossible in their demands for cooking.' I had heard similar complaints in West Cork.

He took off his reflecting dark glasses and blinked at the room full of sufferers. 'Everything in Nepal now depends on knowing the right people and contacts. Of course that is how I obtained my job. You may think that I make a lot of money, but I get little more than an ordinary porter.'

I mentioned the changes.

'If you ask me about the benefits to Sherpa people I tell you that tourism only brings cheating and pimping, love affairs and carnal arrangements.'

'Do local people object to foreigners climbing to the summits of mountains?'

'The whole world knows the picture of Tenzing Norgay standing a few feet below the top of Everest in order to keep her untouched. That does not matter any more. Now mountains are big business and you have to book them like a wife.' He put back his glasses so that I saw two images of myself in front of his eyeballs. 'When the Americans landed on the moon the Sherpa people were horrified. They thought the heavens were desecrated. No doubt we will see the tourists up there.'

I was stopped by a young lama with shining pop eyes like blackberries. I think he waylaid a lot of people.

'Can I help you, please? I want to practise English.'

He was twenty-three years old and had been educated at the Hillary School at Khumjung. He brought me to his small mud-walled house overlooking the compound, which had been built by his family who lived at Namche. In his room containing a couple of benches and an open fireplace he cooked his meals, read and made his devotions. It seemed a limited life.

'I am happy.' He smiled as we sat drinking tea over the fire. His brother, who had climbed Everest, visited him regularly, and every now and again he was allowed to go to Namche and see his family. Coming here was his own choice, one that he did not regret. There were thirty-two other lamas in the gompa, as well as some adolescents who had taken the Rabodsung vow. Also a small school.

'Do the visitors bother you?' You could see lines of tents from his window..

'I do not mind. But they have so much money in order to climb mountains. Here people are poor.'

We sat translating his lists of English words. The day before an American woman had given him a romantic magazine. 'What is ardour? . . . hard-on? . . . he kissed my tits? . . . erection?' But most of Thubten's books were about Buddhism and meditation. He showed me *Path to Enlightenment* which was written in English. I turned to the section entitled 'The Agitated Mind and How to Treat It.'

A. Breathe in through the right nostril and out through the left three times.

B. Breathe in through the left nostril and out through the right three times.

C. Breathe in and out through both nostrils three times.

'Does it work?'

'Of course. Excellent for sleeping. You must practise seriously every day and no more mountain climbing or trekking. These things are of no value. What is important is the soul.'

[*57*]

Another young lama, Phurba Sonama, was a painter. He had turned his cell into a studio, where in addition to thangka images of seated Buddhas and Bodhisattvas he painted pictures for tourists of mountain peaks, lamas in furry hats, yaks and the gompa itself. I bought a spidery little view of Thyangboche, showing the gompa, the chorton with a golden barber's pole and umbrella, a tourist lodge with a tin roof, Everest topped by a pink cloud painted to look like a plume of feathers and three yaks.

'I would like to go to the west coast of America,' Phurba said as we drank tea surrounded by rolled-up paintings. A passing trekker had promised him an exhibition in Los Angeles and he was looking forward to the adventure.

'Is it difficult for you to leave?'

He shook his head. The monastery did not mind, there were no special permissions to be obtained, and all he had to get was the American visa.

The days are long gone since a Viceroy of India was refused to enter the secret kingdom of Nepal. Since Curzon's time Thyangboche shrouded by its trees, a short flight and walk from Kathmandu, has been breached easily enough by the West. There will be many more trekkers in the area when the central government manages to cut a road nearer to the Everest region. Up here just under the arc of heaven, in the face of the abodes of gods and goddesses, everyone knows that all foreigners are millionaires.

'Are you richer than the King?' a Sherpa was asking a Texan who was handing round photographs of his private plane.

'I don't know. But where I come from we'd rather have aeroplanes than culture. They are a lot more useful.'

Next morning many trekkers had disappeared and in the lodge the Sherpa hostess was lying stretched out on the ground while her child searched her long black hair for nits. The plaintive American woman whose headache was the big one, the dirty young New Zealand pair, the loud French party, the maverick German climber with hair like Struwelpeter, the blonde heavily made-up English woman whom everyone had called Honey Child had recovered and moved on upwards. Honey Child was the only trekker I saw who wore a skirt. Some trekking manuals recommend skirts instead of trousers for women – easier to squat in. There were still a few squatters out on the ridge. An Australian took another crap, holding a pair of binoculars in one hand through which he was looking in the direction of the trees.

'Blood pheasants, mate.' Or did he say bloody? 'They are tame because no one hunts them. There are meant to be scores of them lying around in the bushes. Have you any paper? Bugger it, leaves will have to do. Some fucker pinched my roll.'

I left him in his misery and returned to the lodge to find the yaks and their owner had arrived. Here was a rare moment of satisfaction and accord for Caroline and myself.

I couldn't get over how much bigger and hairier they were than Nangpa had been. The shaggy hair was the thing. Their long furry tails reminded me of the double-bodied fox stoles worn by women in the 1930s. It appeared that only one could be ridden, the black one with the white tail which had been specially trained as a riding yak and was extremely valuable. Riding yaks are getting very rare. Its name was Sod.

The other yak, who was called Mucker, could only be used to carry baggage. Mucker had an alarming white face and was much cheaper to hire. He cost sixty rupees a day, while Sod was two hundred.

'Outrageous!' hissed Caroline. 'Ask him does that include his food?'

It didn't. 'Very expensive and hard to find,' Janbu, my go-between said when I complained. 'Ang don't want to come. He is doing me big favour.'

Ang Tenzing had walked down with his family. He wore the usual track suit and baseball cap and a grim expression which never softened. His frown came from the worries of looking after difficult and valuable beasts.

The harnessing and loading was a long process accomplished with the usual display of temperament. Mucker twitched, groaned, ground his teeth, stamped his little feet, lashed his tail. I thought of Gregory Corso's poem, 'The Mad Yak.' I wonder if Mr Corso knew that all yaks are mad, and his poem might have been more accurately titled 'The Madder Yak'? Loaded up, Mucker had the familiar look of dejection.

> Poor uncle, he lets them load him.
> How sad he is, how tired!
> I wonder what they'll do with his bones?
> And that beautiful tail!
> How many shoelaces will they make of that?

Mr Corso caught the mood of yaks well. Another poem about *bos grunniens* by Hilaire Belloc may be better known but it contains numerous inaccuracies. 'As a friend to the children, commend me the Yak. You will find it exactly the thing . . .'

In addition to our baggage Mucker carried two sacks of hay that towered above his back so that he had the proportions of a galleon. Sod had a small leather saddle and a rope through a ring in his nose. There was no question of a bridle or halter or reins. Both yaks wore the usual bell attached to a collar.

Caroline suggested that a bicycle bell would be a useful addition, clinging to Sod's horn to clear a passage for our way.

'I'm quite serious. There should be some means of telling people you are coming besides those miserable little tinkerbells.'

I agreed to ride Sod first. Ang held the ringed nose and Caroline watched from a distance.

'If he turns his head put your leg up across the saddle so that he can't horn you.'

My legs almost touched the ground. In spite of my low seat I was surprisingly comfortable as if I was sitting astride a furry blanket. Like Isabella Bird's first yak which she rode in Tibet in 1889 on her well-worn Mexican saddle, Sod had a back that 'seemed as broad as an elephant and with his slow, sure resolute step he was like a mountain in motion.' In front of me jutted a massive head and cabriole horns framing a view of a snow mountain. These horns were polished and black with pointed tips.

'Don't kick or pull the rein until you see how he goes.' The voice evoked a moment of the past when Miss Duggan was putting a class of small boys through their first riding lesson. Walk on!

But after twenty yards Sod came to a halt.

Ang shrieked. 'Peter weigh too much! He too big! Caroline better!'

I protested, thinking always of the two hundred rupees a day, but he was shrill and insistent. Caroline soothed me as she prepared to mount. 'He'll probably change his mind. Remember that Sod is a Sherpa heirloom.'

She untied half the baggage on Mucker's back to find the small collapsible rubber pillow she had bought in London. She placed it across the saddle and jumped up with effortless grace, giving the impression of having ridden yaks all her life. After much readjusting of Mucker's load we set off, Sod taking the lead with Mucker and Ang following while I trailed in the rear.

The track passed the main gompa compound and lines of tents where trekkers emerged to cheer Caroline who was stylishly turned out. She wore a bright ethnic sweater made by Tibetans in Kathmandu, lightweight boots, and baggy trousers. Over the purple scarf tied tightly around her head was a bush hat from the side of which jingled the bunch of keys that locked her bags. A white Chinese face mask covered her nose and mouth and a pair of black silk gloves covered her hands. There was plenty of time during our slow progress for whistles and catcalls.

'Give it to her, cowboy!'

'Good luck! Rather you than me!'

'I wouldn't trust one of those animals with my life.'

'Watch out for those horns.'

'She's a beaut!'

Caroline waved back politely as we set out through the trees down to the Imja Khola. Sod ambled along with a gait that was almost languorous, and our passage continued, peaceful and slow, with an occasional indication of a nasty nature.

'Damn it, didn't you see him trying to horn me?'

'Yaks hate the smell of Europeans. You shouldn't kick him so much.'

Watching her, I observed some of the difficulties. The main problem was of control. The rider could only turn the animal in one direction by pulling the single rope tied to the ring in its nose. Kicking or urging it in another direction with the knees brought an erratic response that made you wonder if yaks were really as sure-footed as chamois, the way all the books describe them.

Once across the river, in spite of Ang's sour face and prolonged objections, I mounted. I found that I enjoyed yak riding. My progress, so near the ground that it was like being on a moving cushion, was comfortable and springy and very very slow. They tell you that a yak goes at a steady three miles an hour. The view crawled past as we climbed in slow silence past the snowy tooth of Ama Dablam, moving up a narrow track with a drop beside me back to the cascading water. This was not so good, and it took an effort of will to put all my trust in Sod's determination not to go over the edge.

Caroline took another turn as we descended towards Pangboche and the inviting prospect of a teahouse. I was walking in front, thinking of nothing more important than a cup of white tea and an omelette, when I heard a crash behind me. Looking back I saw that Caroline and Sod had vanished. My first thought was that they must have fallen into the river, to be carried by the current back along the way we had come. But there was a yell from some bushes high over my head.

Without warning Sod had veered off the path and galloped up the cliff at an angle of about eighty degrees. Caroline had tugged hard at his nose ring, but he hurried on, and without any means of control beyond the useless rope she had been carried to the heights until she came into contact with the branch which had knocked her off cleanly.

Ang dropped Mucker's rein for me to retrieve and ran up the vertical almost as fast as his precious animal to find the miscreant somewhere near the clouds peacefully licking some succulent grasses. In due course we trooped down to the teahouse, everyone on foot. After Ang had safely secured the yaks we were able to enjoy a well-earned rest and a cup of tea among German climbing boots, and Gortex jackets spread out for sale.

We continued on our way, taking turns in spite of the danger, to ride our expensive yak. We were following the Imja Khola towards Dingboche and Chhuking. As Cho Oyu closed off the trail beyond Gokyo, this route made its way towards a point where movement to the east was effectively blocked off by a whole lot of mountains pushed together like impacted dragon's teeth. Here were Lhotse, Ama Dablam and the rest curtained with serrated ice cliffs. Around here we found less evidence of the main body of travellers which kept to the Jacob's Ladder between Pangboche and Thyangboche. For a time, as we plodded along beside minarets of snow and ice by a silver morain, we were alone, a feeling that was unnerving.

Whenever it was my turn for a spell on Sod, Ang would complain. 'Too big for yak . . . no good!' His protests would continue in between his whistles, and every time he came up to seize hold of Sod's tail behind me and twist it he would wail:

'Too big! Too big!'

Yaks can stand high altitudes, but they will not tolerate long periods of work or cover too great a distance in a day. Modern yaks in Khumbu are spoiled with extra rations. Elsewhere they have to find their own feeding apart from the odd potato. Traditionally they travel slowly and conserve their strength to graze. I remembered an account by Professor Tucci of crossing western Tibet on what virtually amounted to a forced march, leaving a trail of exhausted and dead animals behind him. With a load on hisk a yak averaged about ten or twelve miles a day, but Sod was aiming for a lot less. Mucker had some excuse – his ship-of-war appearance was enhanced by his erratic gait as if he was tacking against the wind. His burdens were huge, and I was quite sure that I didn't weigh anything like the load that wavered on his back. But Mucker was not to be treated with the same reverence as the riding yak, and both Sod and Ang were determined we would not get far.

Himalayan literature is full of adverse comment on the 'unpleasant and helpless feeling' induced by yak riding. Explorers have mounted wooden saddles, sat cross-legged, grasped the rope leading to an animal's saliva-sodden nose, tried to guide it and suffered accordingly. The old Tibetan hand, Colonel Bailey, commented how the yak 'who has been steadily plodding along at two miles an hour can burst into an almost Olympic sprint without any previous warning'. Isabella Bird struggled to get along mountain trails on an animal which regularly lunged at her with its horns just like Sod. Was this a reason for the decline in riding yaks? Why weren't their horns burned off as calves? That used to be done in Turkestan and parts of Tibet as a precaution against 'loss of temper or lack of friendliness'. Looking at the head in front of me, shaking its weapons and personal ornaments to the accompaniment of showers of saliva, I could see it would be difficult to dehorn a mature beast. Perhaps horns helped with balance, as an animal tripped along narrow ledges and across bridges, like the pole of a tight-rope walker. Perhaps it hadn't occurred to anyone in the same way it had not occurred to them to install chimneys. They put up with yak horns in the same way they put up with smoke in their houses.

Here was another wilful beast getting its way. I grew tired of listening to Ang's complaints and allowed Caroline to take over the riding altogether, as we proceeded in what became an accustomed marching order, Peter walking ahead, Caroline behind sitting on Sod, who moved well for her when he was not trying to get her off his back, and Ang and Mucker walking in the rear. Mucker looked calm; his tranquil white face blinking ahead of the luggage on his back belonged to a patient beast of burden, but he possessed a wicked yak's heart.

I walked faster than the rest, and for most of the time was far ahead of the procession. Behind me every now and again a little drama would take place. Caroline would wave her arms like a windmill. 'I want to take a photograph. Hold the rein please.'

With mutters of 'No good!' Ang would drop Mucker's rope for a moment and come forward and seize Sod's. Sometimes this worked well as Caroline clicked her camera in peace. But very often Mucker would stray. He would wait until attention was diverted and then slide off on his own, leaving the trail with an absent-minded air that suddenly changed to determination as he galloped up a mountainside bearing his burden towards some overhang with a drop of several hundred feet. Ang would go off in pursuit yelling and throwing stones. A good many of these would miss and come clattering back down the slope. If we were really unlucky one would hit us, or, worse, Sod.

We moved in fits and starts until the evening, when we reached Dingboche, a place of stones, small stone houses, stone-walled terraces and stony fields beside the roaring river under the mountains. The first little stone building we came to, consisting of a kitchen-living room and a back room full of bunks, greeted us with the notice SHORTSE VIEW

LODGE. This establishment had just been set up by a young Sherpa who had retired from working as a porter with mountain expeditions. In 1979 he had climbed Everest with a Yugoslav team, reaching Camp Four. This was his first year as hotel-keeper. He did all the cooking, while his brother, who was deaf and mute, carried endless supplies up from Namche. Most Sherpas can turn their hands to anything. The menu card, written out in fastidious English, offered special milk potatoes, dhal, yak steak and the things his brother had brought up that day. Apart from the potatoes, everything had come up.

We sat eating with an American and his Japanese girl friend. From the moment that Ang had finished feeding the yaks and released them to graze, he began devouring quantities of food. A three-egg omelette vanished in seconds, followed by a Sherpa fry. Then a pot of chang and some tea. Then another omelette. Then more chang.

Caroline said, 'You'll be sorry you didn't take my advice. The arrangement of hiring the yaks should have made him responsible for his own food. That's quite normal.'

Occasionally the Sherpa host would throw another precious log or handful of dung on the fire, and there would be a short blaze of light to answer the gusts of wind outside pummelling the little door and window. The American and his girl held hands and crooned. It seemed indelicate not to let them have the small back room to themselves. Ang had already curled up by the fire, as I suggested to Caroline that we should try out the tent.

Before it got quite dark I pitched the little green globe in a small enclosure behind the lodge. Back home Gillian, who knew about sleeping-bag romances like the one in *For Whom the Bell Tolls*, had been nervous of moments like these. I had tried to reassure her by reading extracts from Peter Fleming's account of his testy relationship with Ella Maillart as they crossed Asia together. Caroline knew Ella Maillart well.

She had a good many zip-bags carried up on Mucker, each one with an essential part of her equipment, hand cream, face cream, lotions, medicines, tapes, meticulously-folded clothes. Her double sleeping bag was warm and luxurious; the rubber cushion used on Sod's back became a pillow.

'Do you have to have all this baggage – it takes up so much room?'

'I need it. Can't you put your boots outside? They smell.'

'Aren't you cold?'

'No. Please don't disturb me. Can't you see I'm reading?' In addition to her torch which she hung from the apex of the tent, she wore a special reading lamp strapped around her head like a miner's lamp. The batteries in my own torch had already grown weak. As I shivered on my side of the tent – Dingboche is over 15,000 feet – I watched her huge shadow on the green tent wall looking like a praying mantis.

Next morning I swore that nothing would induce me to sleep in the tent again. 'Please yourself' Caroline said. 'I was very comfortable.' The American and the Japanese had had a good night. Ang was on his second breakfast.

We did not travel that day. Caroline stayed in the lodge, the yaks were off colour and Ang could eat ten meals before I returned from my little side-trip. Having learned nothing from my experiences beyond Gokyo, I left them beside the fire and went off along a track leading up to the end of the valley and a small settlement called Chhuking, a frontier post where trekkers made a last stand against the Himalayan elements.

A pair of yaks was pulling a plough, preparing the ground for potatoes. Ploughing with yoked animals is a relatively recent innovation in these parts, and until the 1930s all ploughing was done by men. As late as 1937 the anthropologist, von Furer-Haimendorf, saw teams of four men dragging ploughs across the fields.

No one knows exactly when and how potatoes came into Nepal some time during the last century. The two most likely sources for their introduction are bungalow gardens in Darjeeling and the garden of the British Embassy in Kathmandu. They spread quickly; Sir Joseph Hooker found potatoes growing near Kachenjunga in 1848.

A hundred years ago the population of the Khumbu area was a fraction of its present size, and the potato has been held largely responsible for the four-fold increase. Something similar happened in Ireland before the famine. The new food supply not only reduced mortality among Sherpas, but encouraged immigration from Tibet.

Potatoes thrive in the light, sandy soil of Khumbu and yield a far greater harvest than the old traditional Himalayan staple, buckwheat. Until the 1950s dried sliced potatoes were exported to Tibet; now, since the border has been closed, Sherpas send their surplus to other parts of Nepal, even to the terai. Crops can be grown at many levels on the mountains, so that if one fails others may survive. But the demands of tourism result in a shortage of manpower to plant and harvest additional fields; nowadays nearly all the agricultural tasks are done by women.

There is something miraculous about the potato. Oddly I was reminded of the west of Ireland, seeing little fields surrounded by stone

walls and cottages with smoke pouring through the roof similar to Con-
nemara cabins a century ago. A few differences – the big mountains, the
stench of latrine manure.

I reached a scattering of houses surrounded by a wasteland of stones
where a bitter wind ruffled the hair of grazing yaks and blew through the
cabins. The tiny yersa settlement of Chhukung approached by a track
that lost itself among stones was not a place that invited habitation, let
alone hospitality. And yet an old man stood by an open door carrying two
big blackened pots in a basket, a couple of children were playing leapfrog
in and out of boulders, and on one of the stone huts a valiant woman had
written a notice WELCOME TO ISLAND VIEW HOTEL. At my
arrival she immediately began boiling up tea.

Mountains glowered, the formidable south face of Lhotse to the north,
Amphu Lapcha flanked by fluted ice walls blocking the horizon to the
south, the east face of Ama Dablam to the south-west. Sheer rocky spines
and tough-looking glaciers loomed a few yards away. At this very
moment, my hostess told me, a party of Americans was clambering on
Island Peak, a little 20,000-protuberance, so named by the Shipton
expedition of 1952 because it was entirely surrounded by glaciers. Soon
she was expecting another party to come along – Frenchmen.

'It is not policed.' She meant that the mountaineers were taking their
chances and were climbing illegally, having neglected to pay the government the required peak fee. It wouldn't be very expensive to climb Island
Peak – little more than Pharchamo would have cost. Still a penny saved is
a penny earned and, as long as mountaineers are not accompanied by
hundreds of porters and keep themselves small, there seems to be no one
to observe them, let alone stop them.

After a jam omelette cooked over her fire, I climbed a moraine up a
buttress and then went horizontal along a razorback ridge. Soon the
Island View Hotel had shrunk to a spot indistinguishable from surrounding rocks and I was standing on a broken edge gazing into space.

Sherpa's Law Number Two propounds that the higher you get the
better the view and no doubt the best view of all is from the summit of
Everest. Here the crest of Island Peak was directly overhead, and around
it was a dolorous frozen realm of tumbling ridges and glaciers blocking off
most of the sky. Dante's *eterno rezzo*, eternal shade. Francis Younghusband
found a mystic beauty in such views and wrote, 'It is only a century ago
that mountains were looked upon as hideous, yet now they are one of our
chief enjoyments . . . and often in reverie on the mountains I have tried to
conceive what further loveliness they may yet possess for me.' For once I

did not agree with him; I felt myself with the real old-timers who would think a view like this was a place of horror.

Down at Dingboche snow was falling on two yaks tied to a plough stirring up a patch of frozen earth. In another field men and women dug away with their hoes as the blizzard swept over them. Thick dark woollen dresses and cloaks, old felt boots, crazy fur hats, smiling faces. Rasping wind and driving snow.

The lodge was crammed to the roof with trekkers, two Israelis, Americans, Germans, English and a French girl incessantly playing a guitar. It was as if a bus had driven up and deposited them.

Chekhov wrote in his notebooks; 'I long to be exiled to Siberia. One could sit somewhere by the Yenissey or Obi river and fish and on the ferry there would be nice little convicts, emigrants . . . Here I hate everything . . . this lilac tree in front of the river, these gravel paths . . . ' Everyone wants to escape from the lilac trees. Paradoxically the search for grandeur and solitude results in communal living of a kind that would never occur domestically. An Israeli had the end of his sleeping bag in my mouth, a talkative American placed his head on my knee, beside me the French girl protected her virtue with her guitar. The big problem was getting up and going outside.

'For God's sake . . . some people are trying to sleep.'

'The Irishman has the runs.'

The wind had dropped. In the distance a bar of dawn light shone behind a mountain making it glow, and all around were stars. There was no sound from the little tent where Caroline slept aloof.

By seven o'clock everyone crowded around the fire. An American held up a bottle of rakshi and sniffed it as the innkeeper looked on.

'I want you to know that this bottle should contain seven or eight glasses. Right? Only fifteen rupees at Namche. You charge twenty. At least see to it that we get the full amount.'

The French girl was consulting her Schneider map, the Israelis were eating tinned porridge in between picking dirt out of their nails. By eight o'clock it was quite warm and the sky was clear. The best time of day. Caroline emerged from the tent legs first. Sod and Mucker were given hay and potatoes and Ang's face showed a meagre contentment as he settled down to breakfast.

The innkeeper stood by the fire ticking off items eaten by the Germans. 'Four porridge . . . two omelette . . . one Sherpa stew . . . six white tea . . . ' Calculations were done on the honour system, guests writing down what they had eaten, and the cost taken from the menu. I never saw a Sherpa query a bill.

As we left the main track and climbed past a lone chorton above the village, a helicopter flew past in the direction of Everest. Climbing Everest was a seasonal occupation like planting potatoes. This year the government had raised the peak fee, but still there was a queue of international teams prepared to pay the price. Everest was millionaire country.

Caroline rode Sod whose pace was infinitely slow as each weary footstep threatened to be his last. A veteran of the Transport Corps taking yaks to Tibet in 1904 has described how 'with vast internal rumblings, glowering eyes half-closed and expressionless, and an inveterate habit of grinding his teeth while he rolled along at a reluctant one and a half miles an hour, the yak nursed that hidden and groundless grievance against all mankind . . . The infectious depression to be got from half an hour of his company was enough to make you go out and howl at the moon.' Sod's gloom was bottomless; at the slightest excuse he would drop his head towards the ground. If Caroline wished to turn left, he went right, or backwards, or forwards or just stopped. The yak always knew better. How different from the behaviour of her own dear hunter back home in Kilkenny.

We were entering what is generally regarded as the final and most dramatic sequence of the Everest trail. Far below the ridge on which we were travelling so slowly we could see the hospital at Pheriche which treated AMS sufferers. The tin roof shone in the empty brown valley like a star.

At midday we stopped at the end of the Khumbu glacier at Duglha which consisted of two small teahouses. A Sherpa sat darning his trousers on a wall on which was painted in futile white letters KEEP THE EVEREST TRAIL CLEAN. Caroline dismounted and the yaks were led across a small wooden bridge. 'Milk or black tea?' asked the woman who came out of the View Hotel Restaurant, as matter of fact as if it was on a motorway. We sipped white tea, Ang ate some bowls of dhalma and rice and the yaks were given a bucketful of slops.

The trail went straight up, and soon the View Hotel Restaurant and the Himalayan Lodge were reduced to dots. There was nothing easy about this climb; every few yards I stopped gasping with thoughts of the shining tin roof of Pheriche. Behind me the two yaks followed step by step, showing more sense than usual, Caroline on Sod's back displaying her good seat to a couple of circling choughs.

We came to a sad place, a line of chortons commemorating Sherpas killed in accidents on mountains, including seven killed during the Japanese skiing expedition to Mount Everest in 1970. The casualty rate among Sherpas is far higher than that of foreign mountaineers. Porters have to negotiate icefalls and glaciers a number of times during one expedition, lugging up supplies, while in many cases the foreigner who is paying them only has to do the same route twice, proving his courage and endurance going up and coming down. Often it is the most enterprising and promising young men from villages in the area who are victims of the lust to put a flag on a mountain top, and the loss to Sherpa society is terrible. The casualty list has grown since the first attempt on Everest in 1922 brought about the death of seven Sherpas in an avalanche below the North Col. Since 1953 over a hundred Sherpas from the Solu-Khumbu area have perished in mountaineering accidents. From here the nearer you got to Everest, the more you saw monuments to dead men.

Beyond these first chortons we came out into another stark view of rocks and boulders where a bluff of land below us fell into a plain of red shale with mountains beyond. It was not the best place to decide to take a turn on Sod's back, but the climb had been exhausting. The yaks stopped, Caroline dismounted, Ang complained and Mucker disappeared. One moment he was there with Ang beside him spluttering as usual. 'I tell you, Peter too heavy . . . ' The next . . .

We went to the edge of the path and peered over where Mucker had rolled down the slope. Far below a forlorn white face gazed up amid luggage and scattered bags of hay. He may have been bruised, but he had bounced like rubber. A long time passed in the midst of desolation while he was caught and dragged back to the trail and the luggage was retrieved, reloaded and retied.

We trooped into Lobouje, Caroline back on Sod, Ang leading Mucker by the nose, the wretched animal showing not even the trace of a limp. Back in 1953 when Sir John Hunt had established a rest camp during the first ascent of Everest, Lobouje had been almost at the world's end, a couple of yersas in the trough between the glacial moraine and the mountains. Now the yersas had multiplied to become tourist lodges and guesthouses, while all over the moraine tents had been pitched full of weary travellers suffering from headaches and racking coughs. In general older people are less likely to get AMS because they take things easier than the impetuous young and plod along like yaks.

More than thirty years after Hunt's expedition Lobouje was still used regularly as a recuperation base for mountaineers. We paid a visit to a

Norwegian team which happened to be climbing Everest, a tough-looking lot of Vikings with golden beards and skin the colour of chestnut conkers.

'Hello, Arne,' Caroline said.

Arne, the leader, told us that there might be an attempt on the summit during the next few days, and during that time trekkers who visited Base Camp would not be permitted to stay and put up their tents. But an exception would be made for Caroline.

'Of course, come along any time. You are always most welcome.'

Caroline said, 'I have lots of Norwegian friends.'

The landlady at our lodge tried to coax us into a choice of tinned sausages, tinned peaches and a grisly assortment of Japanese delicacies. 'For Sherpa tsampa number one food,' Ang said, but that was after he had devoured two bowls of yak stew. Although tsampa was okay, it had the disadvantage of being cheap.

This was another night of dithering communal sleeping when even Caroline rejected the tent and came into the heaving warren where sleep was snatched amid coughs and the sound of yak bells outside. In the morning Everest fever gripped everyone. Except for the Canadian couple who crouched near a large rock with another painted notice: KEEP THE AREA CLEAN. PLEASE BURN AND BURY ALL GARBAGE. The woman was diligently lighting a little fire only a few yards from a great pile of refuse left by other trekkers.

'I always carry my garbage with me. Even the turds. We try and behave here just the same as back home. I think it is disgusting the way people carry on.'

Her husband agreed. 'If this was Canada they would be fined a maximum of five hundred dollars.'

Many trekkers had moved on but some remained to watch Caroline prepare to mount Sod in a moment of grand theatre. Today he nearly killed her. Hardly had she mounted when he was off with a violent lurch, breaking into a gallop. One moment she was mistress of her fate, the next she was being bucketed along by a bolting yak. When he threw her, she found herself in the classic lethal hunting situation with her boot caught in the noose of rope which acted as a stirrup. With her leg and foot stretched upwards and her head and body rumbling along the ground in Sod's wake, it looked as if she was going to be killed. Then he stopped.

I had the eyes of a dozen gaping trekkers on me as I ran up. 'Are you all right?'

'Don't be so bloody stupid. Get my leg out of the rope.'

Whether God was watching over her, or whether Sod had just run out of steam was immaterial. Apart from a few scratches and a swelling round her ankle where the rope had cut into her, she was uninjured.

'Stupid oaf!' She had plenty of energy left to berate Ang who had been lighting up a cigarette instead of holding the rein. Then she gamely insisted on remounting. There was no more trouble, and Sod walked on slowly and imperturbably through the rocks as if he was trying to make up for his awful crime.

Around him the grey shingle off the Khumbu Glacier looked like a giant slag heap. Here in this particular stretch of wilderness there was no trail, and the only method of finding the way was to follow the little heaps of stones put up as markers. At one of them we came across the body of a man. A small, well-built Sherpa wearing windproof jacket, jogging trousers and heavy boots was lying stretched on the ground, his eyes tightly shut, his mouth open.

'Should I wake him?' I asked.

'He take rest,' Ang said, peering closer. 'He famous climber. He climb Everest three time.'

We looked at the celebrity with more interest. He opened his eyes and gazed round blankly.

'Too much chang. People give me too much chang. Ooh . . . Aah . . . ' he clutched his head. He was fêted wherever he went. Other Everest heroes have had a similar problem.

'Are you staying here?'

'No, no. Today I must go to second camp to join other team.'

'You should be resting.'

'Not possible. We Sherpas strong people like tigers.'

As he walked along with us he would sit down every few minutes and groan. To get drunk is a sin for monks, but not for laymen. Finally we went ahead, leaving him holding his head in his hands. Somehow before the day was out he was expected to climb the Khumbu icefall and glacier.

CHAPTER 6

Base Camp and Back

Gorak Shep was the end of the line – all change for Everest. Beyond the meagre converted yersa huts – one called Yeti Lodge – were screes of rock heralding the Khumbu glacier, and somewhere behind them we would find Base Camp.

After reviving with tea I spent the day under a boulder engaged in the familiar Himalayan pastime of admiring the view. Directly behind me was a second brown hill called Kala Pattar, the twin to the Kala Pattar at Gokyo. But the view at Gokyo had been nothing like the miracle before me now. I could only marvel at the way the whole world of the Himalayas reached a crescendo here, with Nuptse and Lhotse pleated like ruffs, not to mention the grand old lady herself with wisps of cloud around her dark triangular summit. Occasionally I heard the rumble of an avalanche and saw white smoke flaring down a mountain side.

We slept in a Sherpa version of the Great Bed of Ware, a wooden platform at the end of a hut which managed to accommodate a couple of dozen bodies. Late at night I woke among the snoring sleeping bags and saw the stars through a gap in the roof, nearer and brighter than I had ever seen them before. In the morning the first thing I laid my eyes on after waking was Mucker's white head framed in the doorway. He was hungry, Sod was hungry, Ang was hungry, and their meals, together with our porridge and expedition tinned pears, came to sixty rupees. Prices rose with altitude.

From another hut emerged a group of immaculate Spaniards, all wearing identical clothes, matching jackets, trousers and even gloves. After them came some fair-haired, fair-bearded hearties burdened down with rucksacks, set to climb the Kala Pattar. The other Everest ritual which we intended to do, travelling to Base Camp, took much longer, and was regarded as a more serious enterprise. Ang certainly thought so.

'Not good for yak. No grass. No food.' But he agreed to bring his yaks to Everest, even though hay around these parts was spun from gold.

The final part of the route following the Khumbu glacier was announced by a mortuary slab commemorating dead Sherpas. The hills of gravel were sooty grey and everywhere frozen needles of ice stuck out from the moraine.

'We ride going up . . . we walk on flat,' Caroline told Ang, who complained with justification. The yaks were behaving like angels. Crunch, crunch went their footsteps across the glassy ice with its bands of light, pale green, arctic white, sapphire and winking ruby mixed together with kaleidoscopic changes. The ice curtain shrouding the glacier shifts constantly with the seasons and the movement of the glacier itself. We were only conscious of the perpetual jewelled changes of light as we followed a track into the heart of the glacier past hidden streams and pools of ice between the fingers of the moraine that had to be negotiated.

'I wish he wouldn't keep doing that,' Caroline said as Ang bullied Sod around a crevasse, all the time urging on the yaks with his tuneless whistle. They didn't seem perturbed by the idea of vanishing down a gaping hole, and even appeared to be enjoying the walk. The worse the terrain became, the more flamboyant their manner, as if they wished to demonstrate their skill in movement. We rode and walked alternately until after a couple of hours we came to a frozen patch of water which could have been a stream or lake. It had to be crossed. The distance was only about fifty yards, but there was no way of telling the thickness of the ice or the depth of the water.

'Let the yaks go over first,' Caroline said. 'I've no intention of drowning.'

Suppose the precious riding yak, the tremendous rarity which gave Ang the status of a millionaire, was to injure himself or perish? If I had been Ang I would have turned straight back to Gorak Shep, but he meekly lined them up to face the crossing as we sat down to watch. What about our luggage perched on Mucker's back? Generally the two animals followed each other nose to tail, but now Ang's technique was to give them each an encouraging wallop and set them racing across the ice. Sod went ahead, and there was a nasty crunch as ice splintered. I covered my eyes.

'He's out!' shouted Caroline like a racing commentator. 'For a moment I thought he was gone.'

'What about Mucker?'

'He's after him!'

Even if yaks' manners and temperament are to be deplored, there is something endearing about them that makes people smile. The two comical furry animals hoarsely grunting to each other were skidding across the green surface, Mucker with his load, Sod's bushy tail held up behind his back like a cat's. Yaks are best. We gently tiptoed after them.

On the far side the glacier turned sharp right, and the final part of the route to Everest opened up to a vista put up by a grand master of theatrical design. All the rocks and silted debris of the moraine vanished, and in its place were glistening spires of ice that stretched ahead as thick as a forest. Once we were in among them the light changed to a pale ghostly green. For a long time two yaks and three people stumbled through this forest of huge green stalagmites until we reached a short escarpment. When we were at the top we could see the tents of Base Camp enclosed in ice; the Khumbu glacier fell above our heads in white frills.

It should have been a moment of jubilation, but we were quarrelling.

Caroline had insisted on riding against Ang's advice. Ang, Mucker and I strode ahead, leaving her and Sod to follow.

'Didn't you notice me making signals?' she asked furiously when she caught up with us at a spot looking down on the view. 'When I make signals, I expect you to stop and wait.'

Ang scowled. I had also noticed Caroline waving her arms, but she did this so often when she was riding, that I hadn't taken any notice either. It was half-past three and already the day had been very long. Ang stirred with rage. He was usually taciturn, but now our grand entrance into Base Camp was definitely marred by signs of hostility. He dawdled behind us, and when we reached the main group of Norwegian tents identifiable by their national flag which hung together with the flag of Nepal, he looked much more bad-tempered than usual. Worse, he wanted to go back.

'No good here.' He looked round and pursed his lips. Ominously he refused to unload our bags from Mucker's back.

Caroline had already gone off to find her friends. A few yards away was an American camp with its Stars and Stripes, for the Americans, too, were about to climb Everest by a different route. Both camps had brought their own mini-culture along, specifically labelled, RADIO STATION, BERGEN BANK. From a tent labelled COOKHOUSE came an appetizing smell of Western food, something like hamburgers – why did it smell so different from yak steak? Up here in the sharp cold I felt a sudden longing for a change in diet, for something other than instant soup or potatoes or the massive choice of Sherpa menus. Various big men in climbing gear were drinking coffee and munching biscuits in the sun. The tents were interspersed with lines of prayer flags and little chortons, while here and there stone corrals containing stacks of folding plastic chairs had been built so that men could sit and sun-bathe protected from the wind.

Caroline returned with the Nepalese PRO who accompanied the Norwegians. The news of the impending arrival of the Irish party had preceded us, and he was helpful.

'Please put your tent anywhere.' He pointed to rocks and boulders thrown up by a gigantic geological upheaval.

Leaving Ang with the yaks we skirmished around, and soon concluded that the famous Base Camp had little to offer in the way of camping sites. Base Camp is not actually a specific site, just a location at the foot of the glacier where different expeditions have chosen to erect a series of shanty towns. The atmosphere was like a miners' camp without the saloon bar. Naturally we found that anything in the nature of a good place to pitch our tent had already been taken. What was left was a wedge of ice right beside the glacier disguised by a sooty sprinkling of rocks where after much rooting around we chose a narrow spit of level land overhanging a garbage heap.

Caroline said, 'Just clean the place and I'll get Ang to bring along the tent and equipment.'

I nudged some sacks of trash and rusting tins. A number of choughs which up here have acquired the habits of crows were hopping about checking for discarded food. Choughs are amazing birds who think nothing of soaring with the climbers; Sir John Hunt noticed one strutting about on the South Col at 26,000 feet. At Base Camp there was plenty of food for them to search out among forty years' accumulation of rubbish and they were very much at home. A lot of people have visited if you take an average of three porters to every mountaineer, and everyone has left bits and pieces. Tenzing Norgay buried a bar of chocolate, a packet of biscuits and some sweets at Everest's summit as an offering to the gods. Down here some dark demon rejects the accumulation of sacks and tins. The average tin can takes a hundred years to disintegrate; a plastic six-pack cover four hundred and fifty years. That is at sea level; up here they are indestructible unless sometime the glacier comes down and covers everything.

Caroline reappeared looking very worried. 'He says he won't come.'

'What's the reason?'

'How should I know? I'm sick of arguing . . . you deal with him.'

At this demoralizing moment we were saved by the Nepalese PRO who, hearing of our problem, immediately came bustling down full of official good cheer and a wish to help.

'What is the trouble please?'

Ang, who had been watching us mutely, sprang into a torrent of

Nepalese abuse. At this altitude even the smallest row takes on the aspect of a major confrontation, and he was in no mood for a small row. I had never seen anyone angrier. They argued on until Caroline interrupted.

'Listen. If it's any help, I'm awfully sorry. I didn't mean to offend him. I just don't like being left behind, that's all. O.K.' There was a good deal more argument before Ang still wearing his scowl was persuaded to mutter 'O.K.' as well. They shook hands.

'He say no food for yak here,' the PRO explained. 'Better he return to Gorak Shep and come back here in two days.'

If Ang was prepared to take the yaks slipping and sliding back over the ice, that was his business. We gave him two hundred rupees, and before leaving he even helped to put up the tent. 'Big deal,' said Caroline.

There was excitement in the Norwegian camp since two of their people were perched on the big mountain and hoped to reach the top next day. An event like this was the culmination of years of planning, involving a financial outlay that would keep every man, woman and child in Solu Khumbu for months.

'They will rise at three o'clock and perhaps reach the summit by nine o'clock,' the Base Manager told us as we listened to bleeps and whistles of static through the small transmitter which occasionally conveyed a muffled Viking voice from up above.

'The weather prospects are not so good,' one of the support team looked up at the ice fall. From down here you couldn't actually see Everest at all, and it was a strange feeling to sit drinking coffee aware of the men above our heads posed in their icy starting positions. By five o'clock it was quiet with everyone back in their tents, and the Sherpas gathered in the cooking tent, preparing themselves a vast meal. Whatever money could provide and human ingenuity could produce was being used for the publicized assault, another national ego trip. The yellow cross of Norway wavered on its blue background in the dusk; after all the years and the scores of climbers who had topped out since Hillary and Tenzing, to reach the summit of Everest would still be a major achievement.

We sat in our little tent, so much smaller than the rest, fiddling with the primus, watching the gushes of flame go up to sear the green roof. When the water refused to boil, we consumed half-cold noodles just before a climber from a neighbouring Snowbird came our way with the gift of some cookies and a warning. It seemed that the water we had scooped up from a crystal glacial stream bubbling out of ice and rock contained plenty of nasties which were difficult to boil to death. Pollution had come to Everest years ago with the early climbers and their attendants – since then people at Base Camp have been suffering attacks of stomach trouble for three decades.

The night spent beside the detritus of dirty mountaineers was made excruciating by sharp stones rising beneath the ground sheet, and the roar of avalanches. Caroline slept adequately in her cocoon. By eight o'clock the cold had gone and the sun had begun to heat up the rock. From our lowly position looking up the icefall the distant peaks were like unattainable celestial abodes. Down here Base Camp, like Dante's Hell, was too hot or too cold.

Caroline managed to get some water from the Sherpa cookhouse which had been well boiled, and we had the luxury of tea. We lay among the rocks watching the Norwegians and Sherpas pass another day in the warmth. A group of Sherpas played cards, a Norwegian shaved outside his tent, one of the few to do so, and from the radio tent came a burst of static to remind us that this was not an ordinary day. Among the half-naked figures lounging in the sun, you could feel the tension of waiting.

Things were a lot more relaxed in the American camp a few yards away where an assault on the summit still lay in the future. Another acreage of tents, enclosures and prayer flags was surrounded by similar impedimenta, ice axes, air bottles, coils of nylon rope, canned food stacked in the snow. Someone had contrived to make a solar shower out of a plastic bag.

'Hold it there!' A photographer was taking pictures for the expedition book of a Sherpa pretending to play a shining steel ice shovel like a guitar. The shovel manufacturers, who also supplied the ice axes carried by two climbers standing on a rock ledge waiting to pose, were among the sponsors of the team. Another sponsor's product, a computer, was arranged on a bank of snow, displayed for the camera in fierce sunlight.

I photographed Caroline in her T-shirt proclaiming the giant telescope at Birr. It was hard to find a place to pose without a backdrop of garbage.

The Americans were taking the more difficult route by the Col, while the Norwegians hacked their way up the more familiar glacier towards Hillary's 'impressive but not disheartening' approach to the summit. The two routes, almost beside each other, seemed equally dangerous, the Col with the precipice up which the Americans had to climb and winch their gear before making the final assault, and the glacier studded with sixty steel ladders. As I stared up at this icy froth, two Sherpas suddenly emerged as if by magic and passed by. The journey down the ice had taken them two hours.

If there was rivalry between the two nations, it didn't show. The morning passed leisurely in both camps as if the teams were sunbathing by the Mediterranean. By the afternoon the glare off the stones and rocks drove them back to their tents, with thoughts of the pair trying to make it to the top. The climbers would have to pass by a corpse, someone who had perished up there a few expeditions ago, and could not be retrieved. Frozen, inaccessible, but not invisible, the cadaver remained there, a spectral sentinel, and anyone going by would see it.

We learnt that the current attempt on the summit had failed because of bad weather. The pundits were right. 'Second team have chance,' said the PRO.

Next day Ang arrived back with the two yaks looking sleek after two nights' rest and plenty of food. We set off on the way down. I looked back at the mountains, the four giants, Pumori, Lhotse, Nuptse and Everest in its cloud, and decided that the difference in their heights was meaningless.

Coming back to Lobouje we could see with fresh eyes how we all tarnished the great landscape. Here was another group setting out for the Kala Pattar; on neighbouring Pumori a Japanese team was making for the summit before attempting four other major peaks. We were told of a surfboard enthusiast set to skim down Everest's side. Outside Lobouje we came upon a small Sherpa porter bending under the weight of a harp. Behind him strode a woman wearing an embroidered jacket on which was stitched in large gold letters FIRST HARP ON EVEREST. Without a word they passed on their way.

The small clinic at Pheriche was run by a young American doctor who was studying the effects of high altitude on local people and newcomers. Outside his consulting room some of his patients were sitting in the sun looking like ghosts.

'We try to scare people by giving them lectures. Did you know that death can follow as quickly as six to eight hours after cerebral high altitude hits you?' Of the five or six patients who came to him every week one would be in a serious condition.

'Of course you are going to get sick in Nepal wherever you are,' Dr Goldberg told us cheerfully. 'If the altitude doesn't get you, dirty plates or bad sanitation will. The least you can expect is Kathmandu crud.' Caroline showed him her precious medicine, but he wasn't impressed. 'Just plugs. They won't do you any harm, but equally they won't do any good.'

From Pheriche the track descended into the main valley leading back to Thyangboche. We had only gone a short distance when Dr Goldberg came rushing after us carrying a walkie-talkie in his hand.

'I've just heard some bad news. A Japanese climber on Lhotse has

developed cerebral oedema. Can you help us?' We looked bewildered.
'It's very dangerous for a man in his condition to walk, and we were
hoping that you could lend us your riding yak.'

Caroline hastily dismounted. Ang glowered.

'Don't worry. There will be extra payment.'

As we watched Ang and Sod slowly retracing their steps, the nature of
the enterprise, perhaps saving a man's life, gave us a new respect for the
yak's versatility. We might have known better.

Before Ang departed on his mission of mercy, he found a local boy to
lead Mucker. From Pheriche the track skirted down to the Imja Khola. As
usual I walked ahead and Caroline, the boy and Mucker followed slowly.
Looking back I noticed Caroline making her signals, and a little later she
caught up.

'Where's Mucker?'

At first I wasn't too alarmed. Here was another enchanting place with
the trail running above a deep ravine, the murmur of the Imja Khola
below and the great mass of mountains straight ahead.

'He's fallen over. There . . . can't you see him?'

We were at the edge of the precipice over icy blue waters newly melted
from glaciers higher up. In places a bank of shingle broke the surface, and
far below I could make out the shape that had haunted me all over the
Everest region – the white dot of Mucker's face. So much for the legend
about yaks being as sure-footed as chamois. Too late I remembered how I
had been warned against taking one animal on its own, since their
temperament demands a permanent companion wherever they move.
Without a friend a yak is easily distracted. But was Mucker a madder yak
than most?

> They are waiting for me to die;
> They want to make buttons out of my bones.

Was he more indestructible? I saw the white triangle move and there was
no doubt that he was still alive. This was no ordinary tumble downhill like
his last accident; he must have fallen like a stone, a drop of at least a
hundred feet. Could Tarzan have lived through the experience? I
wouldn't have believed it if I hadn't seen the before and after. I suppose he
survived because he fell into the water.

Caroline was the first to find her voice.

'Quick, get down there. All my film is in one of those bags.'

'Don't you care about Mucker?'

'We aren't here on an animals' crusade.'

I could see that the yak had dragged himself out of the river and stood on the spit of gravel still piled high with baggage. Water streamed off the lumpy orange burdens on his back and ran off his skirts. When he was eventually retrieved by the embarrassed boy who was supposed to be in charge of him, he seemed none the worse.

In the evening we reached Pangboche, the oldest village in the Khumbu area, settled around four hundred years ago from Tibet. A little juniper wood surrounded the ancient gompa, and directly facing the far side of the valley rose the distinctive fluted columns and double arrowhead of Ama Dablam.

We found Ang's house, a two-storey building set in a nest of fields running down to the gorge. Ang's mother made us welcome, greeting us as honoured guests and sitting us in the long narrow principal room while she prepared a lavish meal over the fire. Shelves backed with shining patterned brass displayed rows of crockery and Thermos flasks. The shrine was in a back room, and everywhere around the house you came across reminders of climbing expeditions, since the family, like so many in this region, was closely involved in mountaineering. Ang's father had been on Annapurna, and he himself had been to Nuptse the year before with a Franco-Nepalese team, reaching Camp Two.

During the night he arrived back from carrying the Japanese. At first the sick man had been supported on Sod's back with two other Japanese walking on either side holding him and Ang leading. But, after Sod had displayed a bit of temperament and had been deemed useless, the invalid descended to Pheriche in a sling on Ang's back while a Japanese led the animal.

> . . . commend me to the yak . . .
> It will carry and fetch, you can ride on its back,
> Or lead it about with a string.

'Not good.' But Ang's discomfort was forgotten in his pleasure at reaching home and having two yaks, a considerable portion of his family wealth, safe and sound. We glossed over Mucker's accident, and I doubt if the boy said anything. Although Mucker looked chipper, you couldn't tell if he had ruptured a spleen or punctured a vast lung.

At home Ang turned into a different person. In the morning he smiled and laughed, and there was nothing he didn't do to make our stay in his house comfortable. We had a huge breakfast of curried eggs, Sherpa style, served with an expedition tin of Korean rice, followed by the luxury of hot water to wash in. Later we were taken for a tour of the gompa, a beautiful place whose tangkas and images were exquisite in contrast to the yeti's head kept in a box, a nasty thing with parchment yellow skin and a few brownish hairs stuck on top.

Although Ang didn't want to go back with us to Namche with the yaks, his mother's intervention made him change his mind. She wanted an outing herself down to the big smoke. In a few minutes the baggage had been loaded up on Mucker and we were on our way, Caroline and I in front with the yaks, then Ang and his mother who was weighed down with two bags of hay. She must have been about seventy years old. Passang carried nothing, needing all his energies for whistling and throwing stones.

'Sherpa custom,' he said when we remonstrated.

How pleasant to be back on the road and travelling towards Namche. Ahead was Thyangboche crowning its wooded hill. In the short time we had been up to Base Camp spring had come. The slopes were sprinkled with pink primula and blue iris; the buds on the plants we had seen on the way up had opened, and as we climbed the hill to the gompa azalea and rhododendron bloomed on either side, the pink rhododendron looking like stylized rosebuds on medieval tapestries. The yaks seemed even more disgruntled than usual, sniffing suspiciously at the flowers; they were leaving their natural habitat of snow and ice to travel towards a decadent flowering forest made for other beasts.

The lodge at Thyangboche was filled up with muscled Australians and their girls; at breakfast they sprinkled their omelettes with tomato ket-chup which they had brought with them. We followed the familiar trail where trees had turned a bright green in the warm spring light. A haze covered the mountains, the air smelt of resin and everything in nature seemed a harmonious whole.

From Khumjung, set in layers of potato fields, we followed the leg up through the trees to the Everest View Hotel with its empty rooms. As we ate tinned soup and omelette we were joined by an American climber who had been in the area twenty years before.

'It was so much better then without all the elaborate expeditions. You might see a solitary Englishman casually climbing half a dozen peaks.' He was travelling to Gokyo to make a reconnaissance for an attempt on Cho Oyu.

The hotel manager came bustling up to tell us that the big mountain had just been climbed by the second team of Norwegians.

'Mr Bonington, he also top out.' We knew that Chris Bonington had been at Base Camp. We toasted him in Coca Cola, feeling satisfaction at the achievements of old men.

The American climber said: 'If I top out on Cho Oyu I have a piece of crystal with me to appease the mountain gods.'

In front of every house in Namche old women sat in the sun beside pots of geraniums praying or carding wool. On wooden poles and bent bamboo sticks greying prayer flags that had seen the long winter through were being replaced in fresh colours.

In a tent directly above the lodge a puja ceremony welcomed the spring with two lines of squatting lamas reciting mantras before the enthroned figure of the Rimpoche of Thyangboche who had come down for the ceremony. Amid the scent of burning juniper the droning voices competed with the wind flapping the canvas and the occasional clash of a cymbal or rap of a drum. After three days' prayers everyone in Namche crowded into the tent carrying gifts of food and kafkas to receive the Rimpoche's blessing of water sprinkled from a small silver ewer out of which protruded several ends of peacock's feathers.

Pemba was holding his own small festival in his house. Wearing a brown silk robe and an outsize Stetson, he prayed and chanted as the warm spring sunshine flooded into the room. He planted some rice seeds in a bowl of earth before we sat and drank tea with his family. How long and cold the winter must seem, and yet Pemba declared that he preferred the out-of-season months when for a time Sherpas were back with their past.

Ang was paid off, and the relationship between the hirer and the hired, so long, so intense, so full of emotion, drama and tension, came to an end as abrupt as death. You could not call it friendship, but there was some sort of mutual respect and satisfaction. I liked his mother.

Goodbye, Sod, goodbye, Mucker. Going to Lukla, we hired a reliable old zopkiok to carry our baggage down along the Dudh Kosi through the forest.

PART TWO
TIBET

Peter, Ang and Sod – Khumbu Glacier.

Caroline and Sod – Khumbu Glacier.

Khumbjung – Outside Hillary School.

Peter, Sod and Mucker – Khumbu Glacier.

Everest View Hotel.

Tibetan yaks.

Potala.

Gyantse – Great Pagoda.

Gyantse – Solitary monk.

Saka – Preparing fields for spring planting.

Peter in Tibet.

CHAPTER 7

~~~~~~~~~~~~~~~~~~~~~~~~~

Visa

In Kathmandu Caroline collected her mail. 'Look what I've got – your Tibetan visa.' First the good news – there were strong rumours that Hong Kong visas would no longer be valid at the Nepal–Tibetan border. Up until now foreigners were allowed to use them because of a loophole in the law – they were valid for the whole of China, and Tibet was technically a part of China. But the Chinese wanted to regulate visitors more closely. They did not want a string of impoverished trekkers, but wealthy tourists bearing loads of hard currency.

Everyone we asked agreed. 'Hong Kong visa no good.'

'Forget about them, the border's closed. The Chinese have got wise, and are turning back everyone.'

Still we persisted against all advice. Caroline had a friend, another one of the new Tibetan entrepreneurs who have made a significant contribution to the Nepali economy over the last twenty years. He and his family manufactured carpets, sending them back to Tibet among other places.

'We have a Land-Rover going up to the border tomorrow taking some carpets and seven lamas. If you wish you can join them. They are very nice fellows.'

The Land-Rover collected us next day beside the gompa at Bodnath where it picked up the lamas and a nun for good measure. Bulbous shaven heads shone in the sun like lumps of old leather as we twisted and trundled northward along the new Chinese road. We travelled all day until evening, when we reached a steep valley. Small villages with little terraced fields around them lay clear of the rocks, while a river poured its way down like a spurt of beer released from a bottle. The valley narrowed to a gorge; overhead the sky was blue, but down here everything was in shadow.

Deep in the gloom was Tatopani, the Nepalese customs post, a scrapheap of a town full of flimsy huts. We got down from the Land-Rover which instantly vanished. Everyone left us, the seven lamas, the nun, the driver and his long rolls of carpet strapped to the roof of his vehicle. We

[*85*]

were left on our own to be followed by some ragged children and dogs pausing to sniff garbage. A cold wind blew down from Tibet.

We camped in an inn, a derelict place with mud walls, a few benches and very little food – another foretaste of Tibet. Bed was the draughty dormitory upstairs with no glass in the window, no lights and sacks stretched across holes in the floor. Two strangers joined us; I could see their silhouettes in the dark. In the morning they turned out to be a couple of cheerful Nepalese who found Caroline an object of great fascination. She did look striking, lying back wearing her bandana and black silk gloves, like a picture I had once seen of Edith Sitwell posed like a recumbent ecclesiastic on top of a tomb.

In the gloom of the morning we could see how the place had been hurriedly thrown together to accommodate workers on the new road camped all round in squalid little huts made of matting. We waited for hours, despairing of leaving the dreary scene until suddenly the Land-Rover with lamas screeched to a halt a few yards from where we sat in a coffee house of almost unbearable filth.

Once more we were climbing up the gorge where men and women were breaking stones with hammers, building culverts and carrying baskets of earth under the supervision of Chinese engineers in blue uniforms and round straw hats. The occasional old-fashioned lorry with a rounded snout painted olive green rumbled past. We crossed the still-unfinished skeleton of Freedom Bridge which divided Nepal from Tibet. It had been completed some years ago, but then had broken up during heavy monsoon rains. On the far side of the gorge a waterfall splashed down and higher up were patches of cleared land and a few stone huts. Through vapoury mist mountain peaks glistened in the sky.

We reached the border town of Zhangmu, a contrast to Tatopani with its brand new lines of flat-roofed white houses and a large building with a flag waiting to receive visitors. We drove through the entrance on to a concrete ramp where a Chinese soldier stood waiting.

Caroline said, 'I'll do the talking.'

We hung around reading the large pictorial display outside the custom building showing pictures of achievements that had taken place since National Liberation. Time passed; I watched two more soldiers and a girl walking down the road carrying steaming bowls of rice. The lamas had long passed through the far end of the building and vanished. Two more officials in Mao suits sauntered down the road, their arms entwined like lovers.

Caroline said, 'They don't get proper sex until after thirty. During the

Cultural Revolution that sort of thing was not allowed, but now it goes along with the Responsibility System.'

A girl in uniform approached. 'Please sign visitors' book.'

The small office was spotless with a comfortable sofa and chairs, a large map of China and Tibet, and a bowl of plastic flowers. After we had completed forms declaring amounts of money and duration of proposed stay, Caroline went to the little window that overlooked us carrying our passports. Although I knew she had lived in China and spoke the language, it was still a pleasant surprise to hear her burbling away. I remembered the opinion of the missionary who considered mastering Chinese was a task for people with bodies of brass, lungs of steel, heads of oak, hands of spring-steel, eyes of eagles, memories of angels and life spans of Methuselah.

The two officers in their smart blue uniforms were also impressed, but not impressed enough.

She called back, 'They say the destination is not marked in.'

'What does that mean?' I knew well enough. Hong Kong visa no good.

The young man with the opaline face as round as a moon shrugged his shoulders. A soldier brought us cups of tea with lids on to console us.

We were not the first travellers to be denied entry into the secret land, nor would we be the last. As we stood forlornly beside our baggage, another Land-Rover drove up from the Nepali side. Beside the driver sat a bushy-haired African dressed in a kaftan.

'Hi, man! You going to Tibet?'

Joseph came from Mauritius and was on a world trip. He also had a Hong Kong visa; a journey to Tibet was a side visit. 'A crazy place, man.'

We watched him go up to the window and hand his passport to the same bland-faced official. After a few minutes it was returned politely. How infuriating it would have been if they had allowed him through.

'Hey . . . this is the latest visa . . . who do they think they are? I've paid good money to hire this jeep, man!' The Chinese officials could have been idols or stones.

Joseph's bad luck was a stroke of fortune for us, since we could share his jeep back to Kathmandu. Now that he was returning he did not seem to worry. He had made a big effort to get over, and okay, the visa was a piece of crap and there were other places to see. He was heading towards the stews of Bangkok. Hour followed hour as we sat bunched in the back nibbling some tasty cookies he offered us while the familiar road slithered past. At seven we were back at the Kathmandu Guest House, not feeling well; we were dizzy, the world turned in circles and my legs had become putty. The cookies had been laced with marijuana.

Next day we had headaches and shattered hopes. But by midday we had evolved a plan which was utterly illegal. It centred on the fact that there was very little wrong with our passports, just the lack of a name. The officials at Zhangmu had told Caroline that they needed a destination written in by their embassy in Kathmandu. The words 'Good for Lhasa' would be sufficient.

Possibly the dope helped us along. 'Why don't we get George to doctor them?'

George was a Hong Kong Chinese, one of a select group of foreigners at the Kathmandu Guest House whose mysterious comings and goings aroused envy among those tied to plebeian group treks. The dreaded independent travellers, immune to package deals, hated by the agencies, included some exotics who were pointed out with awe. A man with a black spade beard was said to have travelled around Dolpho. A German girl who went barefoot had spent the winter in a distant gompa with her Nepalese lover. There was the German who had walked through Cambodia, and the two Finnish girls who had hitch-hiked across Afghanistan. There was George. He and a few carefully selected companions had a scheme to bicycle into Tibet on inflatable mountain bikes with eighteen gears.

George's Chinese calligraphy was exquisite. We persuaded him to help us without much trouble, perhaps because his own plans were as daft as ours. We lent him a pen and the operation took a minute. He examined his handiwork with pride. 'I think that should do. I've written in 'Good for Zhangmu and Lhasa'.

'Wonderful!'

One day later we were on our way again in a Land-Rover which was decorated with a board on which was painted HARRY'S JOURNEY. It was an anxious time and we didn't speak much as we drove past skeins of paddy fields with the occasional group of trekkers trudging down the road bearing their rucksacks. We drove through the familiar mountains, through the gloom of Tatopani until HARRY'S JOURNEY was moving into the People's Autonomous Republic of Tibet. With each hairpin bend the idea of presenting our forged visas seemed less good.

Once again our bags were tumbled out and the same soldier looked on. Once again I watched Caroline go up to the same window and talk Chinese. I could see that a different official was peering at George's ideograms. For some time nothing happened and there was just the cheep of voices and unexplained silences. Then an officer came out and directed our baggage to the main hall to be examined.

We quickly paid off our driver, and then we were sitting on a bench in the empty customs hall on the correct side of the border.

I was suffused with such a warm golden feeling that I failed to notice a jeep roaring up containing four senior army officers. They assembled inside the office, talking and occasionally looking out of the window in our direction. The place smelt of disinfectant; minutes passed. Then an official appeared and handed back our passports. We were free to go.

Next to the customs was a new hotel waiting for the expected hordes of tourists. We had seen the manager two days ago strolling arm in arm with his friend.

'Good evening. You wish to spend night?'

'That sounds fine.' I looked at the comfortable chairs, the spotless disinfected passages and a group of Chinamen in blue Mao jackets waiting to serve us. With a good meal in mind, we went down to the kitchen which was full of women in white surgical robes where we found there was nothing to eat at all.

Caroline said, 'I despair of you, Peter. Perhaps you think that getting through the customs was a piece of cake. And who did all the talking? We can't possibly stay here. You realize it will only take a phone call to the embassy in Kathmandu to make someone realize that something is wrong with our visas. Anyway, I asked – a bed in this place is thirty pounds a night.'

After a jar of tea we left carrying our bags. There are no porters in the People's Republic. Although we had pared down everything, the loads were immense, Caroline's rucksack, zip bags and camera equipment, my large rucksack and the unwieldy duffle bag marked mendaciously ANNAPURNA EXPEDITION containing the tent, food, medicine and other useful things. A few steps filled me with bad thoughts about all the weary miles ahead.

Beyond the hotel the road turned up the hill in a series of dusty loops away from the neat line of customs house, hotel and bank to where the rest of Zhangmu was jumbled together in a collection of huts just like its sister town down the road on the other side of the border. We hoped to find a lorry and put a distance between ourselves and the frontier, but we immediately faced problems. In Nepal people still enjoy meeting and helping foreigners, but here we found any attempt to enter into a commercial travelling arrangement met with no, no, no. Staggering under our bags, we climbed the hill to more houses, barracks, and more lorries packed with timber or soldiers staring down. No lifts. Higher up and at the town's end were two lorries whose backs were covered with tarpaulin, indicating a long journey ahead. Once again Caroline tried fruitlessly to negotiate a price. It began to rain, then to hail and the road turned to mud.

'We must find a bed. We'll have to try again tomorrow.'

Just before dark we managed to obtain accommodation in a room full of broken beds, empty except for a Japanese couple huddled together on a stained mattress trying to keep warm. Wind poured through cracks and the roof leaked, making puddles on the floor. We were charged the equivalent of two pounds a night; it was not worth a penny more.

Stomach trouble compounded my misery and during the night I had to leave my dirty bed countless times to stumble past the creaking door out into the rain and wind to crouch in mud. In the morning I felt like a ghost, my stomach a sieve, pains racking my body. Caroline gave me a couple of her pills.

We struggled from the hut with our luggage into the steep shanty town where wisps of malodorous mist hung above the gorge and clung to the pea-green jackets of soldiers. Soldiers were all over the town, strolling about in the damp, a multitude of bright green uniforms, baggy blue trousers, boots and red enamel stars on peaked caps. Here on the frontier the People's Army seemed unoccupied and bored. Not everyone by any means was working on the road; there were no proper shops to go into or cafés or other garrison amusements. A ceaseless procession of lads in green walked up and down the corkscrew hill, pausing to look down into the forests of Nepal. There seemed to be mighty few Tibetans.

I searched out the driver who had hinted the night before that his lorry was leaving, and he might, just might, take on extra passengers for huge sums of money. But he and his companions were fast asleep. Carrying our bags down the spiralling street once again, we felt increasing despair.

Two cars swept around a bend on the way down to the customs post and we had time to glimpse some Caucasian faces. Abandoning our bags we ran down the hill in pursuit. At the hotel we found two Italians covered in dust and a young Scottish couple.

The Scottish pair told us how they had rented their van with great difficulty in Lhasa in order to see more of Tibet. The problem had been the driver. Throughout the journey he had ignored them and taken no notice of any requests they made. During every repeated breakdown of his tin-can vehicle he had infuriated them with his rudeness. He gave an extra dimension to the concept of rudeness.

Anthony's clipped Scot's vowels came through clenched teeth. 'If you've ever really hated anyone, double that again, and you'll get some tiny indication of the way I feel about that bastard!'

The Italians were continuing their journey down to Kathmandu. 'Thank God we leave Tibet! Thank God we go to Nepal! Thank God!' But miraculously Anthony and Jean were returning to Lhasa since their exit visas only permitted them to leave Tibet through China. There were eight seats in the van.

'You realise it's not very comfortable. Bump, bump until your ass is splitting.'

'Oh, we don't mind!' We arranged to meet in an hour.

When we returned with our baggage a crowd had gathered round the van, and in among the spectators Anthony and the driver were facing each other and shouting. In his hand Anthony waved the distributor cap he had torn from the engine. 'He's a bastard!' The roar was an octave deeper than the driver's Chinese cries, 'Bastard! Now he says he must have special permission to bring us back.'

'Why'

'You can speak Chinese, for Christ's sake! Tell him that unless we go now I keep the fucking distributor!'

The driver spoke to Caroline in the tones of a hoarse budgerigar. 'He says it is forbidden to go back.'

'Then I'll break up his fucking car!' Anthony was hopping up and down. 'I'm not letting him get away with this after all we've suffered! He can go to the police or whoever. I don't mind! I don't mind, I tell you! He's not getting his machine back.'

Caroline began loading our luggage.

The row ended abruptly. The driver consented to go back to Lhasa with his passengers, Anthony returned the distributor, the crowd wandered off. To my amazement and great joy we were driving up the hill past the shacks of Zhangmu. I remembered the mantra that Nhuche had composed before I left Kathmandu invoking success on my journey. He told me that its mystifying refrain 'Lalasu Thochhe' meant 'Yes, Sir . . . Thank you.' It had set us on our way, but would it help us any more? My stomach rumbled and I had a sensation of frailty like the man in Cervantes' story who believes he is made of glass.

CHAPTER 8

Journey to Lhasa

I sat beside the driver who crouched over the wheel in his padded Mao jacket and green cap muttering and grumbling to himself. Behind sat the Scots, then Caroline and behind her a late entry into the van, the Japanese couple who had shared our grim lodgings the night before. From the moment the van started the man began to take readings from a barometer as well as the inevitable photographs, clicking through the window, click, click almost as often as the wheels went round. Every time he aimed his camera, the girl wrote down the shots in a book.

Tibet greets you with wind and silence.

First came snow-covered mountains and then the perpetual wide empty gravel plain. There were no houses or trees or people. Everything was caught in an intensity of landscape and sky. The light changed constantly so that the colours of the plain fluctuated from chocolate brown to brilliant pink and red, while above the sky had a hard enamel sheen. A few waterless ornamental clouds were dispersing. An ochre mountain suddenly became striped like a tiger, a patch of shimmering shale would vanish as you looked.

I thought of all the other travellers for whom Tibet had offered a magical escape, seeking like Sven Hedin 'mysterious Tibet, the forbidden land, the land of my dreams'.

The eerie confrontation with space is something experienced by all newcomers. Robert Byron felt the instant startling change: 'Here was no gradual transition, no uneventful frontier, but translation in a single glance from the world we knew to a world I did not know.' It's still like that.

Here are facts about Tibet from a geography book, *The Chinese People and the Chinese Earth* by K. Buchanan:

'Over much of Tibet the general elevation exceeds 12,000 feet, the frost-free period is less than fifty days, and in no month does the mean temperature exceed fifty degrees Fahrenheit. Most of the area is a waste of frozen desert, with patchy shrub and grass vegetation. Its population is sparse and largely nomadic with the life based on herds of goats and yaks. Agricultural land is confined to the lower valley around Lhasa.'

China is the shadow. Yet the distance between Peking and Lhasa is one thousand, seven hundred and fifty miles as the crow flies.

We were climbing higher into space, and every so often the radiator of the van belched clouds of steam. The driver would stop, search out a frozen pool of water, open the bonnet and administer a few sharp douses over the engine as one might smack a naughty child. We came to Kose, set in the burnt gravel plain with a few strips of green, a rusty corroded landscape where the only life was the movement of black thumbmarks that were grazing yaks. A large mud tower stood quite alone in the gravel, while high on the hill were other scattered ruins and some sort of walled citadel coloured bright red perched on an overhanging escarpment above them.

Here the Japanese got out and left us. All the time they had been in the van they had been taking photographs and collecting information like squirrels storing nuts for the winter. Nothing escaped them, the speed of the van, rate of ascent, altitude, bird life, blood pressure. They bowed politely as we waved goodbye and went off to photograph the backside of Everest.

We travelled all day through wilderness with dust filtering in through doors and windows. Wearing her face mask, only a nose and angry eyes showing, Caroline looked as if she was frightening away evil spirits. The Scottish pair had similarly concealed their faces, and I was learning that climatic conditions here dictated that we should dress the part of gunmen in a Western. Covered up like that made it hard to talk. Outside, we were passing some hills, bare as the rock of Aden, as Spencer Chapman saw them fifty years ago. I fell asleep and woke to shouts. Anthony was tapping his head with relish.

'Now you can see what I've had to put up with!'

'We want to take photographs!'

'What are we paying you for, you bastard?'

'Don't get excited!' Jean said.

'WHO'S GETTING EXCITED?'

'Tell him to stop!'

'Talk to him, Caroline – you know the fucking language!'

Caroline said in Chinese, 'When we get to Lhasa I will report you to the authorities.'

I felt a little sorry for the driver, who subsided and pulled the van to a halt. We got out and looked to the west edged by a slab of the Himalayas with Everest among them standing out clearly against the bright blue sky. From this side the range looked diminished compared to the towering mountains above the great convoluted valleys we had explored with the yaks, for here the table land seemed to touch their waists. There seemed nothing to stop you walking across the plain and down the ladder to India.

In the evening we reached the check-point at Tinggri where I was interested to see that the soldiers merely looked at our names and returned our passports without comment. We might have been day trippers. I had not quite shaken off the dream of arriving the old way with lamas in their thousands outside their gompas and the air resounding with the braying of horns and rustle of prayer flags. Present-day reality was a flat-roofed compound, the prototype of dozens of similar staging posts scattered all over the country consisting of four lines of low mud-walled rooms arranged around a main yard full of lorries.

The driver left us to grab a room and order himself a good meal. Why should that set us all off in another rage? Altitude, altitude! Four hungry, furious foreigners glimpsing him sitting contentedly at a deal table picking away at little dishes with his chopsticks were provoked to another row about food and accommodation, a row which became fiercer with the arrival of a concierge in khaki uniform holding a bunch of keys. Anthony shrieked, Caroline screamed over prices, Jean and I nodded in agreement. We should have been ashamed of ourselves.

'She wants the equivalent of six pounds a night!'

'That's quite ridiculous! The normal price for this sort of place should be about two.'

'Oh, let's just accept.'

'Don't be so feeble, Peter. Can't you see it's a matter of principle? If you let them get away with this sort of extortion, heaven help other foreigners coming this way.'

Caroline won, hitting the concierge with her Chinese like a soldier with a bayonet. We were brought to an empty hall where a man in chef's uniform dished out ladles of supper through a hatch. After we had eaten the concierge reappeared, and to the accompaniment of much key jingling we were led to a small dormitory furnished with six iron beds on which were placed rolled-up coverlets and bolsters. Wash basin, towel, candles and a large Thermos of hot water were provided by the state.

At daybreak we were woken by martial music. It was the first time that I had heard this particular way of saying good morning, get up, but Caroline had endured it before, and the Scots had had more than enough of it. The squeaky urgency of the non-stop marching rhythm vibrating around the little room and rattling the window panes set Anthony on a familiar round of curses. Occasionally there was a break in the tape for voices to shout out instructions about exercising. We used the water in the Thermos for a vestigial wash, urged on by an ear-splitting combination of shrillness and decibels coming in from outside where the air pulsated with marches and then operettas pouring out of loudspeakers placed at intervals along the dusty streets.

The sleeping compound was in the new Chinese enclave, cut off from the Tibetans, a colonial outpost kept as rigidly separate as the cantonment and the bazaar in Imperial India. There were no gardens, and the houses, built in People's Republic Ramshackle, one-storey high with tin roofs, lacked any feeling of permanence. Above them on a hill were some ruins, the first Cultural Revolution ruins that we had seen. Somewhere behind the Chinese town clustered Tibetan Tinggri, a military outpost before the invasion, where a monk and a layman had jointly and ineffectually supervised detachments of picturesque soldiers in this border area. Nepal was very close. If I had continued travelling with Pemba and his zopkiok from Thami across the Nangpa La Pass, I would have followed the ancient trade route over the glaciers to reach Tinggri on the other side. Brock, the god of light, had come down the other way.

We did not see much of Tinggri because the driver treated our request to visit the Tibetan town with contempt, spinning us out onto the main Lhasa road where there was next to no traffic, a lorry every few miles or so, and the odd horseman kicking up dust. Soon I saw my first real Tibetan village, placed under a crumbling ledge of golden rock, almost indistinguishable from the surrounding landscape. Small brown houses were arranged in layers, each crowned with fluttering pennants and flags, each with its own little courtyard. The windows and doorways were splashed white and the only signs of life were women collecting baskets of dried sticks and turds stored on rooftops.

From now on at intervals we would glimpse clusters of flat roofs on which firewood and dung were neatly piled, where prayer flags flopped above doors and windows were edged with whitewash. Out on the dusty road we passed shepherds wrapped in sheepskin coats surrounded by their flocks, who swivelled as if they were watching a tennis shot while they followed our bumpy progress. Foreigners were still rarities, and we did not yet make an impact on this stern empty landscape.

Everywhere there were ruins, some recent, others a part of the scene long before the recent bout of destruction. Many resulted from the decline of population which had been a trend during the century preceding the

Chinese invasion. Impossible to guess their age. Some were roofless, clustered together on the plain. There were great mud-walled spouts that resembled the open-necked furnaces leading to Hell in the paintings of Hieronymus Bosch. Others clung to the summits of small brown hills, ancient fortresses that looked towards the Himalayas designed to guard Tibet against foreign intrusion. Today the pitiless wind blew through them. At one spot I counted half a dozen clusters of abandoned buildings within a few miles.

In the afternoon we reached the edges of the Tsangpo valley, the fertile arm that runs across southern Tibet which would become the Brahmaputra after it had made a great thousand-mile sweep into India. Here the views wavered, as the empty spaces and distant aspects of cloud-covered mountains changed into fragile evidence of something a little more domestic. There was an unexpected sight of spring in the groves of sprouting poplar and willow which were the first trees we had seen, while in stony fields men and women were busy preparing the ground for planting. Behind them smoke from rooftops rose straight into the sky – the wind that comes at midday had not risen yet.

Most likely the crop would be barley, the staple diet, although here in this fertile area potatoes and legumes are grown. They say that in the absence of rats a stored harvest will last for a hundred years, while meat will keep in the dry air for a year.

The yaks were fine-looking creatures which Caroline and I examined with the air of connoisseurs. It was not merely a trick of the light that made them seem larger than our old friends in Nepal. Tibetan yaks are larger. These were all huge with a sable quality to their long black hair that set off the crimson banners sprouting from their heads which were in fact dyed yak tails – the things that used to be exported to India to make holy fly-whisks. They wore collars from which fell lines of brass bells and occasionally cowrie shells dribbled with the spume from their noses. We drove past another pair and another of ornamental yaks, black or spotted, hung with decorations, red plumes waving on their backs, moving with the bulky ceremony of oxen. I remembered how the Dalai Lama used to be escorted on a sacred white decorated yak to and from Ganden monastery. Ploughmen in saffron chubas, fur hats and dangling earrings followed behind their animals pushing a wooden scraper among the stones, and behind them, women in long black dresses and coloured aprons similar to the costume worn by Sherpa women threw seeds out of enamel bowls. Now we passed a man who was harrowing, mounted on a wooden board and holding on like a charioteer behind two lumbering spotted beasts. The ground was dust-dry, a tableland that seemed to be composed of ground-up bones, and these agricultural activities seemed to have a measure of faith and theatre.

The ornate scenes of husbandry, the trappings of the animals, the clothes people wore perpetually brought to mind scenes from a Book of Hours. The clear light could have been created by Flemish painters with their egg white. It was strange how this desert evoked nightmares of Western artists like Bosch and Blake, whose horrors of hell and famine were set in places far more like Tibetan landscapes than the background to the writhing hells depicted on Tantric murals.

The similarities to medieval Europe have been commented on by many observers. Fosco Maraini compared pre-Communist Tibet to France and Burgundy six hundred years ago, with the predominance of monks, the uniformed ranks of the nobility, the structured religion with its extremes of hell, the squalor and the beauty. The confrontation with communism was bound to be brutal; the new zealots could not approve the outmoded harmony and feudal equilibrium which they set about destroying. There could be no sympathy for the lifestyle evoked by Maraini with its 'medieval feasts and ceremonies, medieval filth and jewels, professional story tellers and tortures, tourneys and cavalcades, princesses and pilgrims, brigands and hermits, nobles and lepers; medieval . . . divine frenzies, minstrels and prophets.' So much to vanish within half a dozen years of his visit; and today, looking eagerly for vestiges of a brilliant and squalid past, we found them first in the hardships of the countryside.

We halted at Lhatse where we bought cold dumplings from a woman who appeared in the compound carrying a basketful. On to Shigatse, where another quarrel blew up when the driver refused to take us to the Tashilhunpo monastery which is the seat of the Panchen Lama. From the modern town with roofs of tin we could look up and see a crescent of golden rooftops climbing the hill. Down below in a roadhouse full of soldiers spitting out sunflower seeds, we crowded round a small wooden table and wrestled with chopsticks, dabbing at rice and struggling to pick up lumps of yak meat. In between trying to hold on to salty cabbage leaves without dropping them on the filthy ground, we continued to vent our spleen on the driver.

'I'd like to wring his neck!'

'He's being paid double the amount we agreed in Lhasa.'

'I bet you he's putting everything he gets from Caroline and Peter into his own pocket.'

'Do you remember when he wouldn't stop to let us pee?'

Our hatred was weird. We took no notice of the glittering gompa on the hill or the drabness around us. We only stopped bad-mouthing the driver to observe the disgruntled air of the woman bringing us more bowls of sloppy food from the kitchen. Caroline said, 'It's the same all over China. There's no incentive to work.'

When we left Shigatse the sun had gone and the air was suddenly bitterly cold. Then it snowed, slanting flurries descending on the flat roofs and dusty trees, the half-finished new blocks of houses, whirling around the golden monastery up above. Outside the town, snow covered the burnt vistas and sweeping gravel plains, falling over empty lakes and mountains and scattered peasants working in their fields.

Two hours later we reached Gyantse, the second largest city in the country, whose Jong and monastery were once show pieces of Tibet. Gyantse had been the scene of the climax of the Tibetan expedition of 1904 when an Imperial force under the command of Francis Younghusband had opened up Tibet to English influence. The capture of the Jong at Gyantse ended a bloody campaign tinged with shame because the Tibetans were so brave and so easy to kill. A VC was won, gallant Gurkhas participated and Tibetan resistance crumbled.

Apologists for China like to remind Westerners of the slaughter of Younghusband's invasion. Today the Chinese soldiers in their green drabs wander about a place where Sappers and Pioneers, Johnny Gurkhas, officers and sahibs marched through on their way to Lhasa where they claimed victory and held a race meeting beneath the Potala.

Nearly thirty years later Robert Byron came this way and met a man who left the army and stayed on, a Cockney called Martin living in Gyantse. Martin sang 'She's only a bird in a gilded cage' and dreamt of burying his second Tibetan wife and retiring to Peacehaven in Sussex.

In his youth he had faced soldiers who fought like no one else in the world. Edmund Candler, the *Daily Mail* correspondent who accompanied the Lhasa expedition, wrote of the Tibetans' 'elan, their dogged courage, their undoubted heroism, their occasional acuteness, their more general imbecile folly and vacillation and inability to grasp a situation'. He paid tribute to 'the men who stood in the breach at Gyantse in that hell of shrapnel and Maxim and rifle fire . . . met death knowingly and were unterrified by the resources of modern science in war, the magic, the demons, the unseen imagined messengers of death.' Their lamas fought with them; afterwards bullet-ridden, shaven-headed bodies were found. The ground was frozen: the dead remained unburied and preserved in the sterile air. A witness observed how 'the sorry human debris . . . left perforce unburied on frozen shingle . . . were there months later when we passed on our way home. Fingers shrivelled, lips retracted from white teeth, but otherwise normal human beings – asleep.'

In the 1960s the Khambas fought the Chinese in similar spirit against similar odds.

There are other sad memories at Gyantse. One of the greatest of Tibet's monasteries was savagely diminished during the Cultural Revolution. A few buildings remain, the modern traveller does not realize quite how few, until he has seen old photographs of the elaborate series of buildings which once rose one above the other like golden eggs on the dragon's back hill, the colour of crushed strawberry. So Byron noted when he wrote how, viewed as a whole, the complex 'gives an impression, not only of movement, but of unity and organic strength'. There were eighteen temples clustered around the rock of Gyantse and now there are just two, together with the great stupa, the main temple, and the pagoda of Palkhor Choide. This destruction has been so neatly tidied up that you simply cannot make out the grandeur that has gone, with all the broken walls carefully scraped away. Reduced by fury, the religious city is a fraction of its original acreage, and what is left is shored up for tourists and a few pilgrims.

I walked up the hill to watch the evening shadows creeping over the plain bordered by the frill of mountains guarding the frontiers with India. Down below I could see some horsemen riding down the main street on thin ponies kicking up dust; behind them were farmers in donkey carts loaded with sticks and sacks of grain. There was no trace of the snow that had engulfed us at Shigatse; it had all melted in a blast of afternoon sunshine. Above me there should have been a fortress, but it had vanished as if a sea had washed it away. Below was what remained of 'the divine territory of Gyantse . . . land that is a mine of wisdom . . . ' The pagoda glinted, a powerful building in ziggurat style with tiered galleries, staring painted eyes beneath a golden dome, and the thirteen golden rings that represent the stages of advancement to Buddhahood.

We stayed in a guesthouse that had the distinction of being purely Tibetan. Behind the upstairs gallery decorated with latticed woodwork were communal bedrooms and a large room for eating and relaxing with wooden tables and benches on which young soldiers, filling in time from barrack duties, sat wrapped in tobacco smoke slapping down cards and mahjong counters. They played like maniacs in the gloom, banging the counters and calling out numbers in between hawking and spitting and drinking bottles of beer.

In the kitchen a number of cauldrons full of soup and lumps of dark-coloured rice were guarded by an old woman from a number of children who kept jabbing their hands into the food and running off screaming. They kept a wary eye on us until our plates were in front of us and then lunged in our direction. Dirt clung to them in scales like armadillos; ropes hung from their noses. They surrounded our table and waited; after I had toyed with my fried potatoes and greasy onions a small boy seized my plate, emptied the remains into his woollen cap and gulped it down. Others imitated him; they persisted, using their hats as scoops or bowls for snatching handfuls of rubbery potatoes. Anything left neglected on a tin plate for an instant with only a slight hesitation was torn from the table by hungry dirty little fingers. Occasionally a soldier would get up and chase them out of the room, but they would return. They put you off eating, and soon we had all handed over our half-eaten dinners to settle back and enjoy a Thermos flask of rancid tea. It was my first experience of this horrible beverage; I had not yet learned to filter the mud-coloured liquid through the lumps of grease by drinking it very fast. Outside, music was switched off all over Gyantse as loudspeakers wailed their satisfaction for another day's work done.

The same broadcast sounds woke us next morning, and even Caroline, who had woken on countless similar Chinese mornings, winced. Saying that the altitude made the noise worse, she drowned it out with Beethoven. The newly-awoken made the morning grab of the Thermos flasks which stood in their coloured ranks guarding against the hardships of the ordinary day, providing water for drinking and washing.

The driver was almost pleasant now that he was on the last leg to Lhasa. He made no headway into the hearts of his employers.

'I wonder what's got into our friend?'

'He's afraid we'll complain to his boss.'

We left Gyantse and its nest of fertility and headed north through mountains towards Lhasa. A few miles on we slowed down behind an army convoy, a long line of identical green lorries with tarpaulin hoods packed with soldiers. They were following the English path of conquest. At the Kro La Pass forty-seven miles north-east of Gyantse the Tibetans had been massacred in a painful encounter where the English lost four men, Edmund Candler lost his arm, and fifteen hundred Tibetans were killed. In spite of his wound Candler felt sorry for the 'cheerful jolly fellows . . . their struggle was so hopeless. They were brave and simple, and none of us bore the slightest vindictiveness against them.'

With the expeditionary force came yaks galore. Here was a reasonably modern army – this was three years after the Boer War – supplied by mules, ponies, donkeys, bullocks, sheep wearing little saddles and yaks both Nepalese and Tibetan. The Nepalese animals, mostly zopkiok, were almost wiped out by disease and by eating aconite in a valley on the way up from Nepal. The few left were butchered. Tibetan yak died largely because there was not enough grazing and they were subjected to forced marches. Before they perished they made history.

Among the leisurely pages of Imperial reminiscences in *Blackwoods*, an officer of the Transport Corps writing under the pseudonym 'Pousse Cailloux' recalled his experience with yaks in Tibet. 'Great, ponderous, slow-moving beasts, proof against cold and wind, carrying dependent from their underparts a great sagging mass of tangled woolly hair wherein stones, bits of straw and stick, and, you would say, even birds' nests . . . combined to form a swinging mattress whereon the beast subsided to sleep; head and horns carried low, tail vast and bushy, the wool of which alone would have been enough to stuff three pillows; and, between the two, a mass of disgruntled depression.'

The men of the Transport Corps put their minds to the prospect of wheeled traffic on the Tibetan plain and thought of the light, two-wheeled *ekka* of the Punjab, a few dozen of which were dismantled and hauled up across the passes from India. The yaks were harnessed to them and dragged the first wheeled transport in a country whose use of wheels had hitherto been confined to prayers. A yak's carrying capacity is two and a half times that of a mule, and apart from the fact that they died, they proved to be satisfactory pack animals.

We wound through the mountains down to Yamdrok Yamtso, the Turquoise Lake. Tibetan lakes are generally described as turquoise, and certainly, in their drab brown settings, the startling South Seas blue stands out. I don't know if Yamdrok Yamtso is more turquoise than the rest, but the colour had a sheen as if there was a light at the bottom. The lake, whose name means 'the upper pastures' from the elevated district nearby, is shaped like a scorpion, a fact the British discovered when they mapped it. They noted the water tasted saline, the circuit was about a hundred and fifty miles and it took two weeks to go around on foot.

We skirted the bright blue water edged with a sandy beach as white as coral which curved through the mountains, its shores quite empty. There were no fishermen or boats, nothing except for a couple of primitive villages and thousands upon thousands of birds. And some yaks grazing the boggy perimeter. It was dead calm now in the morning, but later on the wind would start, and at any time it could whip up a sudden ferocious storm. That is true all over the country, and all lakes are considered dangerous for boats. There is no tradition of fishing or boating apart from river ferries, but this is not only because of the weather, but because water is sacred and fish are sacred. The Chinese have ideas of changing out-moded superstitions and have decided that Yamdrok Yamtso will do admirably for foreigners to waterski on. There are plans for a marina where people will be invited to come and fish if wind and scruples about deeply-held religious beliefs are not too much of a problem.

We climbed up to the Kamba La Pass at fifteen and a half thousand feet which overlooks the valley of the Kyi, the tributary of the Tsangpo that flows by Lhasa. Below the highest point, marked with chorten and prayer flags, somewhere off the highway, were the ruins of Samye, Tibet's oldest monastery, founded in the eighth century, another memory of black and white photographs. Over the pass was another river valley with planta-tions of trees, lines of poplars showing lime-green leaves and the wind brushing silver willows. The Kyi, the last barrier from the south, 'a river as broad as the Thames at Windsor', according to Younghusband, used to be crossed with old ferry boats which had curved prows in the shape of horses' heads. There was also an ancient suspension bridge of which four rusty chains survive, but it has been replaced with something capable of taking lorries leading to the airport road.

On the far side we stopped at a commissariat for a meal. The concrete hall had a counter running down one side where lengths of garish cloth were offered for sale, together with straw hats and a few tins of pork and mandarin oranges. This was our first glimpse of the staples that would keep us alive for weeks, just about the only items of food on sale in any government depot in the country. Presumably they were for home con-sumption, since we were served reasonable chop suey and rice, sitting alone in the gymnasium-sized space at a shaky metal-legged table. Out-side, trestles were set up in the dust where Tibetan traders were selling packets of sweets and nuts and coloured pictures of Chinese leaders. Groups of soldiers wandered around spitting sunflower seeds, and a film of golden dust covered everything.

Further on banners and placards with uplifting slogans made a bland welcome. This section of the road was still under a feverish bout of construction to get it smart in time for the celebrations later in the year which would mark the twenty-fifth anniversary of National Liberation. Along the edges on both sides were lines of tents, while the road itself was a scene of Pharaonic activity with Tibetans and Chinese conscripts in caps studded with red stars all raking, carrying stones, beating stretches of earth and shouting at lorries which had stuck, wheels spinning in the mud.

Like the Romans before them, the Chinese are amazing road-builders. I have seen them carving out the hills of North Yemen and have driven on the Karakoram Highway linking China and Pakistan where the road has been pushed through savagely inhospitable mountains. In Hunza a plaque commemorates 'those martyrs of the Frontier Works Organization who laid down their lives in constructing this highway'. About four hundred people died there. But in Tibet road-making has had few problems. Back in 1904 an engineer noted that Tibet was 'the most perfect country for road building: immense level plains, no gradients and a small rainfall'. The trouble was the Tibetan: 'practically all he has to do is to remove the stones to one side and a splendid road is made; but for that small amount of energy he is unequal to'.

The Chinese have supplied the energy. Before National Liberation everything had to be carried up to Lhasa on the backs of animals. The first lorry reached Lhasa on December 25, 1954. (There had been a telegraph link between Kalimpong and Lhasa laid by English sappers after 1904.) Today the road between Lhasa and Shigatse has reduced the journey from a week to a day, more or less. Between 1954 and 1977 more than 18,000 kilometres of road have been built in Tibet, and they are still at it. The labourers are 'volunteers'. A good way of shaking up the old social system was to get the work done by members of the old ruling classes – so the exiles say.

CHAPTER 9

Lhasa

For many travellers, including myself, to see Lhasa has been a lifetime's ambition. They have shared the resolution of Madame David-Neel, the determined French lady who was the first woman from the West to reach the capital. She came illegally, like so many of us, disguised as a beggar carrying a revolver beneath her rags. 'I took an oath that in spite of all obstacles I would reach Lhasa and show what the will of a woman will achieve.' Her arrival did not disappoint her. 'As we advanced the Potala grew larger and larger. Now we could discern the elegant outlines of its many golden roofs. They glittered in the blue sky, sparks seeming to spring from their sharp upturned corners, as if the whole castle, the glory of Tibet, had been crowned in flames.'

The trouble about the modern approach is the distraction of Chinatown. The Potala's flowing walls rose above the concrete Chinese dragon, the noble bulk sullied by the factories in front and the new housing estates spawned all over the green river basin. Now and again you caught a glimpse of other landmarks, reminders of the best of the old life. Hemmed in by drab new buildings, the Norbulingka Palace stood among trees within its walled garden. In the past every spring a procession of mounted noblemen and lamas set off from the Potala to this summer palace of the Dalai Lama, their god king wrapped up in their midst, moving along the route now covered with jerry-built blocks and shacks. I could see the Drepung monastery, once the largest monastery in the world, perched on a hill looking down on the chipped and dirty concrete and the acres of tin.

It was not our business to condemn what we saw – the efforts of the People's Republic to bring housing and industry to an uncomfortable place. Why should Lhasa have been spared the universal urban sprawl? These dismal suburbs were no worse than those of any substantial Chinese city. If the Dalai Lama had managed to bring Tibet into the twentieth century without the aid of the Chinese, would the development of Lhasa have been more sensitive? The new surroundings of Kathmandu are ugly as well. It was my fault for coming here with the illusion that the old picturesque feudalism had at least survived visually. I had only myself to blame for my depression as the van bumped over giant potholes and craters past soldiers bridging a landslide with shovels. By the time we had reached the main street, I was more conscious than usual of feeling tired and dirty, as well as being in a state of shock. The only thing to cheer me was the prospect of parting with the driver sitting beside me growing horns and a tail.

One final row occurred before we said farewell, when Caroline foolishly offered to straighten out matters for Anthony and Jean and retrieve any money that was owing from the company that hired out the van. While they were all crowded into the little office, I stepped out for my first view of Lhasa at ground level. The new main street that runs under the Potala was filled with lorries and horse-drawn carts as if it could not make up its mind whether it belonged to the old pre-motor age or to the new. A herdsman wearing a thick posteen coat, the wool the same dirty yellow as the sheep before him, his felt boots patchwork red and green like the Pied Piper's, was driving his charges oblivious to blasts from horns. On the pavement men squatted selling biscuits and clothes, while others sat with sewing machines and cobblers' awls. A horseman came jogging along on a black pony. A blind old woman in a long striped woollen dress and woollen bonnet crouched spinning a silver prayer wheel.

You couldn't blame Caroline for feeling cross. Her special skill meant that she was in demand by every Big Nose in difficulty.

'I'm sick of speaking Chinese for all of you.'

She put on her mask again; the driver flinched, the Scots stormed out of the office. We had been travelling for three days and needed a good night's rest.

Until recently all foreigners were quartered under an official eye in government guesthouses which were kept very expensive. Visitors were processed by guides and interpreters and anything outside what was considered legitimate areas of interest was forbidden to them. With boomtime tourism approaching, these restrictions have been eased. We found ourselves in Snowlands, one of the newer and cheaper guesthouses that cater for the new egalitarian class of tourist. A large four-storey building surrounding an open courtyard, it was situated at the edge of the old Barkhor area near the Jo-Kang monastery. The Jo-Kang, referred to by old travellers as 'the Cathedral', one of the most holy places of pilgrimage in Tibet, still stands in the centre of the old city, which is small, only two and a half miles in circumference within the concrete fringe.

There were no luxuries at Snowlands. A woman took our passports amid the usual frisson that the border authorities at Zhangmu might have realized that we had deceived them. Another woman, clanking with keys, took us along to our dormitory where guests were furiously washing filthy clothes in plastic buckets. We went off in search of dinner. Caroline led me back to the hotel where she had stayed two months ago, a much more lavish place, where you could hire a room of your own. Since her last visit there had been changes, and the spacious bedroom where she had slept was now divided into three in order to take more tourists. Down in the basement was a restaurant like a catacomb lit with candles, where assorted foreigners were sitting at wooden tables being served from a big open kitchen crammed with cooking pots. After you had chosen your bits and pieces the cook took them all together and heated them up in a giant frying pan. Smaller plates and smaller helpings than the month before last, Caroline said. We ate and ate and I drank a great deal of Chinese beer. We had a little quarrel, nothing too strenuous, since I felt an enormous sense of well-being.

She said, 'I know what's wrong with you. A lot of people who come here first time take to their beds immediately because of altitude.'

I got up and thumped the table. 'Nonsense, I have been to Everest. I have the lungs of a yak!'

Next morning the deep blue of a Tibetan sky was showing through the window; I was in Lhasa. Down in the courtyard women were washing clothes around a pump, while from the street came a sound of singing as men and women threw bricks to each other on a construction site.

I went walking among the handful of traditional houses grouped around the Jo-Kang stretching down to the river. Tibetans congregated in bright clothes, showing evidence of what has been described as a 'convivial serenity alongside a more solid religiousness'. It was moving to see a line of ugly shaven-headed ash-covered young men stripped to the waist (with little relic boxes strapped on their backs like the powder-boxes old soldiers used to wear), prostrating themselves along the dusty thoroughfare entranced by what they were doing. They progressed and prayed in unison, rising and falling with the precision of a corps de ballet, and no one was in the least put out.

The striving for perfection disages the impact of change which can be ignored in the passionate quest. Thubten Jigme Norbu, the Dalai Lama's brother, wrote how 'the only truth that is worth anything to anyone is the truth in which he believes with his heart as well as with his mind, and toward which he strives with his body . . . Perhaps the greatest ignorance of all and the greatest cruelty is to try and force others to see the world as we see it.'

Outside the Jo-Kang, another golden roof, a man was chiselling sacred scripts on stone while the pavement was thick with prostrate figures. A group of nomads strode by, the girls in long dresses and lead-heavy jewellery with a confidence and grace that reminded me of Aran women.

Other things in Lhasa were new and ugly. In Lhasa as elsewhere much has been destroyed.

You should try and see things the Chinese way. Imbued with zeal, fired by age-old hostility for Tibet, the Chinese failed to be convinced that the Tibetans had anything worthwhile in religion, literature or architecture. Everything they found conflicted with socialism. While they were smashing up things in their own country, a mad contempt for the stately anachronisms of the old Tibetan theocracy was logical. Now they are sheepish about their immediate past and admit it was a mistake perpetrated by disciples of the Gang of Four. In homage to tourists they are restoring the more important temples as 'cultural centres'. They have spent over four million pounds, but it does not go far to repair what has been destroyed. There are also some efforts to recreate the past. Near Snowlands, a new plaza Tibetan-style, infinitely easier on the eye than other new buildings, was being hurriedly rebuilt in a pastiche of the old traditional architecture, which like the airport road would be part of the celebrations for the twenty-fifth anniversary of National Liberation.

You can have no clear idea of what has been going on from a few tourist impressions. You can only feel the sorrowful changes from the reactions of those who knew Lhasa before, like Heinrich Harrer who returned in 1983. 'Time and again I would stop on my walks and ask myself: Is this really the city in which I spent so many happy years?' The newcomer can only seek out the vestiges of those elements that combined to make Lhasa unique. The double intensity of light made colours glow and take on importance; the blues were bluer, the reds redder, the yellows yellower with a shocking radiance like a painting by Van Gogh. I thought again of how colours and landscapes here take on a dreamlike quality that constantly evokes the imagination of Western painters. In the market place Tibetans were selling their sacks of potatoes, jars of hard-boiled eggs, lumps of butter, barley meal and bags full of pieces of smoked yak meat. In addition many had something out of the past to sell to the foreigner. An old woman would take the amber and turquoise necklace from round her neck and offer the chunky beads for sale. A woman cut off the leather strap at her waist holding her horoscope, a little brass dish encrusted with miniature rats and horses and other astrological data, which she sold to me for very little. We were hungry for silver sheathed knives, amulets, figures of the Buddha, teapots, prayer wheels, jewellery; old Tibet would dribble away in our holdalls.

Buses drove out full of foreigners with cameras to watch sky burials and record low-caste undertakers ripping up bodies, splashing blood all round, crushing bones to powder and mixing them with butter before making come-come noises to the vultures to swoop down and snatch the bite-sized pieces. When the birds got nervous of onlookers, the locals made embarrassing demonstrations with stones and knives. Now the Chinese had ideas of tidying up the bloodstained spot where the undertakers did their work and constructing a viewing platform with telescopes for a distant inspection so that the vultures would be kept calm and happy. So far Tibetans do not bury people unless they are criminals or lepers.

I visited the squalid grid of Chinese streets and another government store, its shelves almost bereft of food. Mandarin oranges. In the old days when lamas and nobles gave feasts they made a point of offering delicacies from China, dried slugs and shark's fins imported through agents in Calcutta. I went to the post office to fulfil a lifelong ambition and send messages from Lhasa. The postcards said, Greetings from the Roof of the World. The Potala is a precious relic of Chinese national culture and is the crystallization of the wisdom of the Tibetan people.

The Norbulingka Palace is set in a large pleasant garden surrounded by huge half-mile walls. I was sorry that the Dalai Lama's car was not on display – the Baby Austin that bore the numberplate Tibet 1. But the garden flourishes, very like an English garden up here at 12,000 feet. We were too early for the dahlias, roses, phlox, petunias, hollyhocks and marigolds that bloom late in summer; even the fruit trees were not yet in blossom – apples, apricots and peaches which do not have a long enough season to bear fruit.

We viewed the exquisite thangkhas on show in the Norbulingka Palace which date back to the twelfth century. The girl who showed us round, too young to remember suffering, was enthusiastic and happy. So were Caroline's friends. She took me to a studio where a Chinese and a Tibetan worked together as official artists. As we drank beer, we inspected their pictures which were imbued with social realism. Farmers were happily liberated from slavery and harvesting girls looked resolutely towards the east. A soldier seemed a bit odd and elongated, but that was because he had been painted in the manner of El Greco.

'We would be grateful if you would send us books on modern art.' They were tired of the harvesting stereotypes and longed to learn more about artists in the West. Would they have found inspiration from Dali, Blake, Van Gogh? Meanwhile they learned from the fragments all round their little studio, pieces of old sculpture and carving they had picked up from sites that had been dismantled by iconoclasts. They gave us each a leaf-shaped votary tablet made of clay and funeral ashes, stamped with figures of deities and left at some shrine by pilgrims. They were happy and earnest, and moreover, Chinese and Tibetan, they were good friends. The Tibetan was a Muslim, a member of a community that has been in Lhasa for centuries. We had a lengthy ceremonial tea at his father's house, a friendly place with a little courtyard and a main room decorated with a picture of the Ka'aba at Mecca.

It was hard not to feel that as foreigners we were a form of pollution. I had seen what had happened in Sherpa country and remembered Robert Byron's comments on India in the thirties. 'It is a question of the moral effect of the first train, the first motor car or the first aeroplane. If a swarm of strangers arrived on us from the moon, furnished with aerial torpedoes at moderate prices, and then converted the summit of Everest into a hive of industry we ourselves should feel inferior and wish to reform our way of life in accordance with the new methods.'

Byron was predicting the triumph of the West. Here, in Tibet, should we feel guilty about the impact of our presence or go on blaming the Chinese for everything? So far the West has made little impression, since so little of its influence has been filtered through China. It could also be argued that a foreigner is usually a very welcome guest who can do something to satisfy the curiosity which Tibetans have about the world outside. In return they have an unusual rapport with strangers, which anyone who has met them outside Tibet as exiles has experienced.

I put off visiting the Potala for a couple of days to lessen the deep sense of disappointment I had felt seeing it in its ugly framework. That was unnecessary; it retains its glory. Its shape has been described as Babylonic. The sloping rhomboid, suggestive of a man standing on a rock with his two legs apart, has its origin in an architecture that imitates mountains. It is more than a building; that is far to weak a word to describe the walls and golden rooftops rising out of the plain. It seems more a work of God than of man, something with the impact of a volcano. The flights of steps that ripple up and down its sides evoke features of the

Himalayas. I wondered if the maniacs of a dozen years back had any idea of pulling it down.

The place is classed as a museum, and you pay an entrance fee fearing that you are entering a dead palace embalmed by the state. But the acreage swarms with pilgrims who have travelled here from all over the country, and, since religion persists, they come prostrating and mumbling prayers. Isabella Bird compared the chanting of lamas' voices to the purring of an ancient cat. I watched an old lady scurrying through the Dalai Lama's private rooms, praying as she went, tossing money to every Buddha. There were a few tourists – a Dane with a microphone was squatting beside a prostrate pilgrim dressed in Western clothes, taking down his prayers on a tape recorder.

Apart from the Dalai Lama's apartments which were painted in saffron tones, every other wall was covered with whitewash which sparkled like phosphorescence and relieved the windowless semi-darkness. There are said to be more than 1000 rooms, 10,000 altars and the gilded tombs of eight Dalai Lamas. Huge holy places have a particular atmosphere. The great dark recesses and the innumerable chapels with their frescoes, the lines of statues, had something in common with the interior of a Spanish cathedral. There were statues everywhere, stuck in dark rooms, some enormous, fifty feet high. Some were swathed in kafkas, others sur-rounded by brass butter lamps, Buddhas in every attitude, Bodhivistas, demonic deities, gods balancing on one foot, some peaceful, some toothily savage. It is impressive now. In the old days it must have throbbed with power and prayer.

Before the Chinese began their programmes of re-education, humilia-tion and killing, there were 25,000 lamas living in the three big Lhasa monasteries, of Drepung, Sera and Ganden. Now around 300 elderly men remain. As elsewhere a lot of the surrounding buildings have been destroyed, like the Great Western Gate that stood below the Potala and hundreds of temples and chapels with their reliquaries. (A sight to see a century ago was the little zoo containing a poultry yard to which only cocks were admitted. Madame David-Neel counted: 'the celibate birds number at least three hundred.')

There is even less butter. 'Thank God I am not a lama,' an English subaltern was heard to declare in 1904 after he had been overcome by a suffocating reek of candles and butterfat. Today the Chinese have ordered a reduction in the number of butter lamps here and at other big temples, so as not to offend tourists who have expressed a dislike for their footy smell.

[*110*]

A faked visa instils dread in the most sanguine traveller.

'When they see we have been allowed through the Nepalese frontier they will smell a rat. It must be obvious to anyone that individual tourists coming up from India or Nepal are not allowed in. Can't you get it into your head that we are only here on borrowed time?'

The period that Caroline had lived in China had given her a dread of any higher authority.

'At least we must get visas to enable us to re-enter Nepal.'

This proved to be surprisingly easy. We paid a visit to the Nepalese Consulate which stood among trees at the western end of the city. The day was hot, the Consul was sleepy, and Caroline displayed a powerful combination of pushiness and tact. A few words on the beauties of Kathmandu and the superior attractions of Nepal to anything we had seen in Tibet lulled and charmed him. We left with handshakes, our passports containing the precious entry stamps, our bogus visas ignored.

Caroline was jubilant. 'That means we can get back into Nepal anywhere, since he hasn't written down any particular frontier crossing. All we have to decide is where to go.'

Next day a notice appeared on the board of Snowlands asking for volunteers to travel to Nepal by bus along the route we had taken with the Scots and the devilish driver. This particular outfit looking for passengers appeared to be as impudent as we had been, travelling cheaply with the vaguest of destinations – perhaps to one or two places without permission, perhaps an exploration of the Tibetan side of Everest.

'Remember your ideas about Kailas and Manasarowar? Why not just abandon the bus at the Tsangpo and travel west? We could hitch lifts on lorries.'

In for a penny, in for a pound.

Kailas is the holiest place in the world. As far as we knew, no Westerners had visited it for more than fifty years.

In a woolly way we looked at its location on a map which showed it to be quite near to India.

I said, 'After we've seen it, why don't we just walk out?'

'Those dark smudges are the Himalayas.'

We sought help from Bradley who had been all over Tibet, breaking a good many more rules than we had. In the independent club, with the recognition that the heroic age of Tibetan travel was over, there was a desperate urgency to see as much as possible before tourism took hold. It was the same motivation that I despised when I saw it among mountaineers.

Bradley seemed to have travelled to most places, swopping passports and visas with impunity. He had passed through western Tibet, although he had not got to Kailas. Having thrown up a good job to go wandering, he fitted into the age-old tradition of eccentric English traveller. The motive for his journeys was the exploration of 'the early stone routes of man'. Wherever he went, he spoke English loud and clear.

'I make it a rule never to learn a foreign language.' He peered at us over his thick glasses. 'Far too much bother. Do you realize that there are a hundred and thirty different dialects in Tibet alone?'

He was lying on a dormitory bed suffering from Lhasa tummy. He was delighted to be of help. There were two recognizable roads to the west. The old southern route that skirted the Nepali frontier, and eventually reached the old trading post that used to be called Gartok, had been used by the early explorers before any sort of road existed. The Chinese had turned it into a proper road and in addition had built a new road which took in a big northerly loop before descending on a provincial town called Shiquan He or maybe Ali. When you were planning journeys in those parts the constant name changes drove you mad. Another road linked Ali to Kailas.

'You want to watch out for checkpoints,' Bradley said, looking up some old notes. 'At some towns its better to go round them altogether in order to avoid security.'

'What about food?'

'Mostly there's nothing. Take everything you want to eat. And your own medicines of course.'

Caroline carefully wrote down all the names of towns and villages. Very few of them were on the map.

'Did you know that Kailas is regarded by devout Buddhists as the centre of the universe? That should make things easier.'

For those who were unused to sacks of smoked yak meat, Lhasa was not a good place to buy provisions. I watched Caroline go into shops and after a few minutes come out again shaking her head. Flowers on every window sill but next to no food inside. We bought up the complete supply of instant noodles, tinned pork and oranges displayed on the spare shelves in the government store. We collected some remanbi or official People's Currency at the official rate and changed it into black market currency. Perhaps the bargaining was more risky and complicated than it needed to be because the money-changer was deaf and dumb, playing his fingers like piano keys.

[*112*]

On the last evening at Snowlands a New Zealand girl who was travelling on our bus threw a birthday party. Music came from foreign tapes played on a recorder, and some Tibetans came in to watch what must have been a novel experience. Foreign boys and girls were shuffling and twisting away to the pulsating din. They included two girls who Caroline said were Lesbians in Tibetan clothes, the Austrian who was organizing the bus, and an American who dressed as a lama in saffron robes and coloured boots. Tibetan ladies sat startled in their stiffened aprons as he whirled in front of them showing off beads, boots and robes. There was also a proper Tibetan lama, from the Dalai Lama's retreat at Dharmsala, and he, too, was going to venture on the bus. The music roared, the dancers gyrated, a birthday cake got from heaven knows where was handed around to the accompaniment of Chinese beer and chang, and everyone got drunk. The Tibetans giggled as they sat and watched the first consequences of the officially decreed tourist invasion.

The outside world had arrived with a stamping and pounding of bodies and posturing around the little room. The dancing continued into the small hours when I went to bed past the long queue of hunched figures waiting outside the only lavatory. 'I wouldn't go in there,' said an Australian woman coming out looking like a ghost. 'It's worse than Kathmandu.'

Our disco was impromptu, but elsewhere in the holy city there was a proper commercial disco called 'The Roof of the World' located in the basement of a house close to the Jo-Kang. Later in the year it was closed down for rowdiness after a fight with knives when someone died. Western decadence or too much beer in the rarefied air?

CHAPTER 10

~~~~~~~~~~~~~~~~~~~~~~~~

Bus

A few hours after the party, on Friday, May 9 at five o'clock in the morning, a small group of foreigners huddled around the doorway of Snowlands. The sky was full of stars whose sparkle gave some outline to the buildings in the street beyond the ring of light supplied by the bulb in the porch. Occasionally we could make out the shapes of stray dogs moving in search of garbage.

'Has anyone seen Yogi?'

Yogi was the amiable young Austrian who had brought us together with the promise of a bus. Plans had been worked out and we had all agreed on the fare, but we were sceptical as we stood stamping to keep warm, nursing hangovers and beer-ravaged stomachs. No one could recall ever seeing a bus on the Lhasa streets.

Cold and sleepy, we waited for an hour as the stars vanished and dawn began to light up the sky to the howls of the dogs. You would think the Chinese would have got rid of them entirely. Sometimes you saw a pretty little shi-tzu, hairy as a yak, but most were fierce and nasty. Every traveller who visited Lhasa up until the Chinese invasion moaned about dirt, beggars and dogs. Thomas Manning, the first Englishman to reach the forbidden city in 1811, saw 'avenues full of dogs, some growling and gnawing bits of hide which lie about in profusion and emit a charnel house smell; others limping and looking livid; others ulcerated, others starved and dying and pecked at by ravens'.

Time passed, and in 1936 Spencer Chapman had much to say about swarms of beggars with obtruded tongues and upraised thumbs whining for alms. But it was the dogs which really got him down, 'one of the most disgusting and pathetic sights in the city'. They would never do for the Chinese who set about getting rid of them with the zeal with which they attacked flies back home. (Of course they had no problem with flies in Tibet; the absence of them in the face of so much filth reduces some ghastly health hazards. There are no swallows or other insect-eating birds.)

The Chinese began their dog-elimination campaign in sensitive days when the problem was to refrain from offending the sensibilities of their Tibetan brothers with regard to the taking of life. The solution was to round up all the dogs and pen them in corrals and leave them. No one actually killed them; they either starved or ate each other. But there must have been animals that had escaped the dragnet and multiplied; soon it would be time for another round up. The feelings of tourists had to be considered.

There was a sudden roar as a very old bus made its appearance and pulled up beside us. The driver got out, followed by his young wife and a smelly old man dressed in sheepskins. The bus was a mystery, and where it came from we had no idea since Yogi was secretive about his enterprise which he claimed was the first one of its kind. The vehicle had a scrapyard air of antiquity combined with neglect. The metal body was lined with wood; broken seats had been hastily thrown into lines, the door was held shut with a piece of string, and a big mound of a gearbox stuck with gears like knitting needles took up most of the front section of the aisle. The rest of the aisle and much of the available dingy space was occupied by bits of broken metal, coils of wires and cans of petrol and water. We stormed on board, pushing and punching our way since it was immediately obvious that the best seats which retained something pertaining to a springy undamaged surface were up in front.

Caroline wore combat gear, face mask and black gloves, and the keys in her hat jingled like sleigh bells. 'Quick, quick, don't let them throw you about.' We won ourselves seats behind the lesbians and barricaded ourselves in. It wasn't the best spot to.have chosen, because it was much too near the old man in sheepskin. The smell turned out to be mostly yak butter and we were to savour it for many miles. Chuka was a herdsman from somewhere on the roof of the world, who was working his way from his pastures in the north to the monastery of Sakya to present a large lump of his very own butter wrapped in yak skin to the monks.

Now he poured petrol from a can into the tank on the other side of the aisle, while Lobsang, the driver, stood very near smoking a cigarette. Up front Lobsang's wife wrapped herself in numerous shawls and sheets and prepared to be sick.

We drove off through suburbs, past the grey shapes of new houses, a barracks and the scaffolding surrounding the 400-bed Lhasa Hotel where visitors would be expected to pay the equivalent of £75 a day. The enterprise was wholly Chinese with 3000 imported Nanking workmen being paid oil rig wages to build it in a year. Tibetans were considered incapable of doing the job, an insulting conclusion considering the Potala was nearby. Everything, windows, air conditioners, carpets, lifts, was being brought up by truck from China. No doubt it would do better than the Everest View in Khumbu.

Down some new streets to the river and the plain where eighty years ago the English force set up their race course and built a judges' box for little ponies to race past. Here Colonel Younghusband wearing his best topee greeted the Chinese Amban, another of the endless meddlers in Tibetan affairs. The whiskered British soldiers in their topees and khaki had something in common with today's flotillas of tourists. They visited the Potala and neighbouring monasteries, gloated at sky burials and bought lumps of turquoise – even then much of it was fake. How justified the Tibetans had been in their cruel xenophobia, and no doubt this present-day load of travellers deserved torture. Most of them had come into Tibet by way of China or Turfan. The busload consisted of:

1 Austrian organizer
5 tough New Zealanders
5 Brits
1 neurotic American
2 well-heeled Australians
1 nervy Frenchman
2 grim Danes (1 sick)
2 intrepid Irish travellers
1 Tibetan monk on his way to Dharamsala
1 herdsman/water carrier/trader/butter carrier (Approximately six pounds of yak butter)
1 assistant whose main job was to suck petrol
1 Tibetan lady – wife of driver (sick)
1 driver – Lobsang

The route followed a bumpy track along the river bank over what would soon be the new tarmac airport road. Already soldiers and Tibetan comrades were hard at work with shovels and baskets. As the bus roared on everyone became happier. The girls in front hugged and kissed each other.

A few miles after crossing the river the engine began to smoke. As the bus came to a halt Lobsang's wife, who had been moaning for some time, lurched to the door and undid the string in time to be sick outside. Chuka was delegated to go and look for water, the boy assistant spat and sucked petrol from a can with a plastic tube, while Lobsang tinkered with the carburettor.

The passengers got out and left him. We all walked along the road which wound up to the Kamba La Pass through brown barren hills. Sometimes a line of Kaifung Liberation lorries and petrol tankers would pass us, the uniformed drivers peering down blandly from their cabs at the rich foreign devils. At the top of the Pass we gave a cheer as the bus caught up with us, and it seemed that Lobsang and Chuka had mended it by stuffing pieces of rag into an oil leak. We climbed aboard again without worrying.

'Everything is now OK,' Yogi said.

Thirteen hours later when we limped into Gyantse, greeted by evening opera choruses from loudspeakers, we had long lost any sense of optimism. There had been the lengthier breakdown at Yamdrok Yamtso where views of the turquoise water had palled, the pause for an hour under a mountain buffeted by an icy devil's wind, and another interminable halt in a stretch of wilderness. It was plain that there was something more fundamentally wrong with the engine than mere plugs or feed. Yogi was sad.

'Perhaps she gets us there if we stay in Gyantse one day. I ask Lobsang to find a new part for the engine.'

We spent the night in the same inn where we had stopped on the way up from Nepal, among the same gambling soldiers and the children who once again emptied the remains of our meal into their caps. In the morning music resumed from every post and corner, shot through with crackles, howling all over the ancient town. The Tibetans have their traditions of music, measured out on drums, cymbals, long trumpets and bugles. Fosco Maraini wrote: 'In Tibet trumpets and bugles more or less correspond with our church bells. Like church bells they can fill a whole countryside with something that is more than just sound, a physical vibration in the air that has powerful emotional overtones.'

Now all the solemn religious rhythms are blotted out by tinny opera and takeaway marches. 'The East is Red' blared forth. During the Cultural Revolution it began and ended each day all over China. But you don't hear it now in Beijing and the more sophisticated central areas, where the custom of playing it largely died out in the late 1970s. It survives in remote regions which are always resistant to change, even drastically imposed change.

While we waited for the bus we could see more of Gyantse, one of the

[*117*]

largest towns in Tibet, but still little more than a handful of houses overlooked by the remnants of the monastery and the Jong.

'The English destroyed that,' a Chinese soldier told Caroline, eager to demonstrate that his own country's behaviour was not unique. After the English receded the Jong was rebuilt. Now it looked impressive from a distance like the Rhineland castle to which Robert Byron compared it, vast walls clawing up a ridge. But more recent destruction has made these walls paper-thin with light shining through.

Dust blew down the narrow streets. 'Bye bye' was the new greeting when they saw foreigners – no more sticking out of tongues except by very old people. Pots of geraniums stood outside windows, children danced around us, old women in long black dresses squatted by a stream cleaning pots. We looked for more supplies. At one time the bazaar held within the monastery walls – mostly razed – was an important centre for the wool trade, carpet-making and the distribution of brick tea. The tea came from China – the British found that the stuff grown on Indian estates did not brew into the beetroot-dark tanin concentration preferred in the greasy Tibetan recipe. Bricks of tea still come from China, and we saw them for sale looking like pieces of turf. We succeeded in buying some rice: like Madame David-Neel, we would take the most meagre of rations as 'we did not intend to indulge in refined cooking'.

Gyantse guards the approaches to India and the route to Lhasa. For a time earlier this century an English trade mission was maintained here under the protection of its own small polo-playing garrison. The mission, one of two – the other being Geer in west Tibet – was among the fruits of conquest. Members stayed at the 'Fort', a solidly-built two-storeyed house where they had trouble passing the time. Colonel Bailey used to wake up each morning wondering what he would kill that day. No nonsense about reverence for life. Gyantse was considered a dirty hole with a terrible winter climate that got on men's nerves. No English women were permitted to stay there with their husbands.

At the entrance to the great pagoda we were greeted by a very old lama sitting in his small room. There was hardly anyone else in the spooky deserted galleries and side chapels crammed with the same frescoes and statues which Edmund Candler had condemned as 'gilded images, tawdry paintings, demons and she-devils, hideous grinning devil masks, all the lamas' spurious apparatus of terrorism – outward symbols of demonality and superstition invented by scheming priests as the fabric of their sacerdotalism.' The voice of the Puritan had much in common with the disgust of the image-breakers urged on by the Gang of Four. The lamas are reduced from 500 in the old days to about a dozen bald crinkled old men.

While we were wandering around the labryinthine rooms and passages, a Chinese delegation got lost. It vanished into a dark interior and a door accidentally closed behind it. I could hear the delegates scurrying around behind the door, knocks and voices squeaking like mice. When someone managed to prise the door open, they came tumbling out into the light rubbing their eyes. There were a couple of girls, one with a camera, two men in Mao jackets, and a young man in a tailored suit who liked foreigners. He caught sight of me staring rudely, and came over at once to shake my hand.

'I am Mr Tung from the Foreign Office in Lhasa. How are you Sir?'

He was on a tour of inspection of the monuments that remained after the Cultural Revolution and he seemed delighted to find someone like myself wandering around.

'OK, you please come with us and I will show you everything. Your name, please, and country?' I told him while shaking hands with the rest of the party.

'He is Irish – good. Now we take photograph.'

We trooped off to the light outside the main door where the girl with the camera snapped away as I stood arm in arm with my new benefactor. 'You are my friend,' he kept saying as more photographs were taken of me with my arms around one or other members of the delegation. (What on earth did they do with them?) Everyone was smiling. Then all together we walked back through the great halls smelling of old butter while statues of Buddha looked down on us. In one shrine an ancient lama sprinkled us with water from a silver ewer. In another a shaven old man chanted to the clash of cymbals surrounded by paintings of the tortures that faced the damned.

Tibetans love hells. They recognize thousands of them, of which there are sixteen specific regions, eight hot and eight cold. There is one for incompetent doctors, where the victims are clumsily dissected and cut to pieces, only to be reunited and revived so that the process can be repeated. I picked out a suitable hell for the man who had sold me my sleeping bag.

Mr Tung said, 'After National Liberation these people very poor and backward. Now we give education and things get better.'

He took me to the library to inspect stacks of scrolls with carved wooden covers which had survived the despoliation of the monasteries when similar ancient covers were turned into parquet floor, while the manuscripts inside made handy inner soles for boots. 'Paper – the beautiful fascinating primitive paper of Tibet with irregular fibres as big as veins,' in Fosco Maraini's words, was trampled by sweaty soldiers' feet. Religious books were also used as paving; there are stretches of new roadway where they have been hammered into the ground.

'This culture is dead,' said Mr Tung when we emerged from a final group of dark buttery chapels full of demons rolling their eyes and showing their teeth. 'But now our policy is restoration. We look after old buildings. In Lhasa you see Potala? Very good. Now many tourists come to visit.' He pointed up the hill. 'English people destroy Jong. We restore.' Another photograph. 'Please smile.'

Later Caroline and I walked out to a denuded hill where the religious clutter had been swept away to a vast dilapidated barn with a padlocked wooden door and tiers of little windows. It seemed to be abandoned, when we noticed someone beckoning from an upstairs window. There was a side-door into a dusty hall beyond which another door led into a room full of decaying paintings. A Buddha, a patchy Bodhisattva, a demon or two, Yamantaka the Terrible, blue-faced and loaded down with skulls.

No one about. We went up a ladder to a corridor with numerous small empty rooms leading off. A rat scuttled across the gaping wooden floor. We inspected room after empty room, until we came into one where an old man sat in a darkened robe copying down mantras onto a piece of parchment paper with the careful flourishes of a calligrapher. He told Caroline that he was the head lama of this empty building.

He took us to a small room which had furniture – a few Tibetan chairs and a painted lacquer altar on which were placed an alarm clock and a photograph of the Dalai Lama.

'I met the Dalai Lama in England,' Caroline said, and he smiled with such pleasure that it seemed impertinent to have had the inestimable advantage of meeting his spiritual leader while he was confined here, sitting and praying alone. He must have been middle-aged when this monastery was full. So much gone, and yet he seemed happy living by himself, offering prayers and looking out of the small window with its view of the plain swept so clean of buildings that had bustled with the ferment of religion, rimmed by snow mountains. Tibetan Buddhism, developed in a harsh environment, is imbued with stoicism and resignation. What has taken place in the last thirty years is a pinprick in the cycle of human suffering and rebirth.

We piled back into the bus before daybreak. Lobsang had mended the engine, so he said, Chuka was crooning over his butter. Everyone else was morose as we headed in the direction of the Bhutanese border. The stars faded and the sun came out, the slanted dawn beams lighting up the remains of old castles perched on rocks above the plain. The wind whipped up yellow dust, and by the time we reached Gala two break-downs later we were all covered in it.

Before anyone knew what had happened, we drove into the middle of a large army camp where lines of green lorries were parked, the sort we had seen everywhere moving all together on every dusty road. Beside them was a number of the bulbous tankers in which precious petrol is carried all over the country. I don't know who was more astonished, the group of dusty dishevelled tourists or the Chinese. Various officers came out to gape at us and took Lobsang away to a mud hut.

'Why do you suppose he stopped here?'

'He probably wants to find the right way.'

'You always think the best of people, Peter.'

'Yogi, what the hell does he mean by coming here?'

'I do not know.' As usual Yogi seemed on the verge of tears. Try not to worry. Time to wander on a green plain with mountains at its edge. It was still bitingly cold in the month of May, but the air was full of singing larks. A hoopoe, other birds; none of us were ornithologists. Always the birds of prey overhead. And another scene of husbandry with women digging or scattering their basins and baskets of seeds, and teams of richly-decorated yaks covered in nosegays and red pennants. The hills and mountains changed colour like a vast chameleon, and the Gala plain was tinged pale green. I lay on the grass with the scent all round under a blue sky that seemed solid.

Lobsang came out after two hours, by which time we were wondering if he had been torn to pieces. When he shooed us back on board, we found to our dismay that his long talk with the military had discouraged him from continuing on the southern route to Everest. We drove back as fast as possible to Gyantse. It was bad enough having to retrace our route without having to endure a dust storm.

A strong wind blew across the plain throwing up a golden cloud which tore down the road, ignoring closed windows, filtering in through numer-ous cracks in the bodywork until everything was covered in a golden film. Particles of dust rattled round the interior, burrowing into clothes, strik-ing behind face masks, hitting hair, lips, throats, making our beards stiff. Lobsang stopped and wrapped a towel round his head, and only Chuka the herdsman lit a cigarette and took no notice. Plenty of weather like this in north Tibet. After the worst had passed Lobsang resumed the same furious speed until the Jong of Gyantse reappeared on the skyline. Here Yogi finally managed to get rid of the hysterical American woman.

We drove on to Shigatse over the flat panhandle separating the two cities, where the bus broke down often enough for us to have a worm's eye inspection of the rich heartland of Tibet. We saw nearly as much as old travellers on foot or horseback. A halt heralded by stuttering jerks as the engine ground to a stop. Another search for water to dowse it. A group of men riding donkeys passing slowly, gazing with astonishment. Another breakdown; the sight of our first tractor and some indication of modern agricultural methods. Then Shigatse, greeted with ironic cheers.

Coming up from Nepal we had seen little of Shigatse because of the antics of our driver, but now we could wander about at leisure. The Jong, which had resembled the Potala, has been totally demolished, and so had the 'cloister town' Sven Hedin described, 'at least a hundred separate houses very irregularly built and grouped, joined in rows or divided by narrow lanes'. At the turn of the century there were more than 3800 monks living in the vast compound.

The gilt-topped monastery of Tashilhunpo gleams over the modern town, its roofs shimmering in a series of golden waves. Like many Westerners we came with a prejudice against Tashilhunpo because it was the headquarters of the Panchen Lama, reincarnation of the Dyanni Buddha, and China's ally. No doubt this made our reactions subjective. Was the fat lama standing at the main gate really so sour-faced and brusque as he demanded an entrance fee? Everywhere, warning hands seemed to stop us.

Others, too, were stopped, a small group of tourists out of a Landcruiser marked MARCO POLO EXPEDITION. These were official CCT tourists, for Shigatse is at the tail end of a number of the really classy tours to China that take you well beyond the Great Wall. Although we told ourselves they had paid untold wealth to be here, they looked as scruffy as we did. A little Chinese lady guide was shepherding them, calling out in Americanized English. 'The gompa closes for lunch. You will have to hurry to see everything. Taking photographs inside is not permitted.'

In the government store at the far end of a series of long shelves, empty except for packets of instant noodles, Caroline spotted some clothes. Soon she was clad from head to toe in a chuba, an ornate dressing gown with sleeves wide enough to take a Pekinese. 'How do I look?' She strutted around, watched by an admiring group of Chinese, looking like a black heron with striped blue feathers. The chuba is part of Tibetan life, a barrier against weather which can be made out of wool, silk or even sheepskin. It is adapted to the abrupt daily changes of temperature as sun turns to snow and the midday wind gets up. When it is cold the wearer can be wrapped up, hood and all, like a monk; when the sun shines hot in the thin air the chuba can be let down so that a man can strip to the waist. An old adage about chubas:

> May not the edges turn up;
> May this felt be as strong as the dark brown
> Spotted forehead of a wild yak.

We dropped off a Dane who felt too ill to travel. 'See you in Kathmandu,' called out his companion optimistically as we got into the bus once more and drove out into another empty brown land of scattered willows, sparse houses and mountains shining ahead. We were making for Sakya, a journey that should have taken three or four hours. Nine hours later we were still on our way.

Sometimes the engine billowed clouds of smoke, sometimes it coked up, and on one of the most lengthy breakdowns it exploded with a rattle of vital parts. Down on the ground, watched by his assistant, his wife, Yogi and a score of impatient travellers, Lobsang struggled for hours. Most times he appeared to fix the problem with his teeth, emerging from his bouts beneath the chassis gripping an important piece of metal in his mouth. On the empty plain a driver must be his own mechanic, and Lobsang could expect no help from his passengers, not one of whom knew a thing about how to make a·bus go. As we hung around, sighing with exasperation, admiring the view, we failed to appreciate what must have been a mechanical ability of genius.

Long after dark we reached Sakya and a wonderful dormitory with candles and the luxury of iron beds. Some women gathered in the shadows to watch the strange sight of assorted foreigners trying to get to sleep, and sleep we did, oblivious to the fact that we were not allowed in this town at all. Perhaps the authorities allowed us to stay because the hour was so late. The reason we had come seemed solely so that Chuka could deliver his butter.

Sakya was closed to foreigners. Tourists with official permission stopped at Shigatse which was ready to receive them and give them a processed welcome. But the CCT vans would not come to Sakya until the ruins had been cleared away. Our unexpected arrival appeared to stun the people in charge. One distraught official did think he would try and stop Caroline taking photographs of ruins from a rooftop, but when she snarled at him in Chinese he retreated like a puppy before an angry cat.

There were several acres of ruin. The great monastery survived with a maze of wrecked buildings beside it. At Shigatse, Gyantse and even Lhasa, the destroyers never took the main temples to pieces, but confined the destruction to the dismantling of peripheral buildings. Elsewhere you could only guess about the destruction by invoking memories, reading travellers' accounts or consulting old photographs. There is no evidence of what went on. But here at Sakya the shocking stretch of broken walls and rubble was still spread over the hillside and the plain, the remains of a great monastic city. Yet again, after the perimeter had been knocked to pieces, the core of the religious foundation was preserved. In all these places it was the Tibetans themselves who dismantled the trappings of the old religion under the direction of the Chinese.

Sakya was founded in 1071 by Konco Gyepo on a site where the earth was grey – *sa-kya* in Tibetan. This was the monastery that obtained special favours from Kublai Khan at the time when the Mongol Emperor was searching for the best religion to give his people. He summoned to his court representatives of various faiths, Buddhists, Muslims, Nestorians, and had a contest for performing miracles. The abbot of Sakya was the only one who was able to raise a cup of wine to the Emperor's lips without touching it. As a result the Mongols adopted Lamaism and for a time Sakya had special temporal powers over Tibet.

The monastery that survives at Sakya is an immense austere building, half grey, half red, girdled with a painted white strip. In one of the two great courtyards closed off by high wooden doors an old man with padded arms and knees, the pads worn thin by prostrations, lay stretched on the ground, while inside the main hall a lama was blowing a conch shell and giving his blessing to the men and women filing past. This was a different sort of cathedral, not a collection of dark shrines smelling of incense and butter, but a hall filled with shimmering colour and light, a place where you felt that life's events had less to do with man than with some higher power. While we made our namstes to the gilded figures scattered round the walls and the master scholar Kunga Nyingpo perched over the altar wearing a red and silver Mongolian hat, in the centre of this chanting hall young monks were squatting on immense bolsters like woolsacks of yellow silk, intoning mantras. The sound of their voices rose and fell like waves. A forest of painted red pillars at least sixty feet high made from tree trunks reached up to the roof, and under this big canopy Tantric Buddhism flickered. The monks had been left to themselves for the decade since the destruction.

Among the murals along the side we spotted two paintings of Kailas, the holy mountain which we hoped to reach. In another shrine we saw a photograph of the Head Lama of Sakya who was in exile in India. Our friend, the lama from Daramsala, knew him well. He considered that we were fortunate in seeing Sakya before it was cleaned up and the tourists were invited in. In spite of the presence of these young monks, he was deeply depressed about the future of religion in Tibet. When we passed out of the main gateway, there was the old man, still moving along, his hands protected by blocks of wood.

'You will soon see the last of that.'

The ruins were haunting. For a long time the Chinese were proud of the destruction which they considered to be evidence of progress.

On the bus the butter had gone; Chuka had left us to take his gift to the abbot. There was general relief in not having to brace ourselves each time before stepping into that smell. Lobsang continued his heroic and epic struggle to keep us on the road. We drove off at speed with everyone muzzled against the dust. At our first breakdown a storm raged and the dust billowed in. The way continued across another gravel plain with telegraph poles marking out the distance. On our second breakdown we got out and sat under a floating rainbow over another staggering emptiness, and it was easy to understand the Tibetans' appetite for religion.

After Lhatse Caroline and I planned to leave the bus and head west. A few miles away was the Tsangpo where we hoped to get a ferry; once across, perhaps a lorry. It seemed most uncertain; how tempting to continue with our companions into Nepal. Suddenly the old vehicle seemed like an ark.

The last morning, hours before dawn. The journey to Nepal was long, and Lobsang was eager for an early start. We got up in the crowded dormitory where we all performed our usual race, trying to pack belongings by torch-light before rushing out to get a good seat on the bus. There was nothing to eat or drink. When we checked the provisions which had been so hard to buy, we discovered that the potatoes and hard-boiled eggs bought in Lhasa had gone rotten. So much for the preservative qualities of the dry air.

CHAPTER 11

Lorry

Just outside Lhatse the engine began spluttering, an all too familiar sound, signalling a sudden stop. We sat in the dark without speaking while Lobsang made desultory attempts to clean the carburettor before climbing back into his seat and falling asleep. Time passed before he stirred, managed to get the bus going, drove on for a few hundred yards, and then stopped beside a dusty side road.

Heads fuddled with sleep looked up.

'Good luck.'

'Rather you than me.'

Voices faded, the string of the door handle was tied up again, and the bus moved on. The noise of the engine, still spluttering, died away. Would they ever reach Nepal? We never saw the bus again or heard from any of our fellow travellers.

We stood in the dim morning light with our pile of baggage.

'Can you see the river?'

'It must be somewhere close.'

I could just make out a line of mountains behind Caroline's back. She was wearing her chuba; we were cold, and we needed all our powers of concentration not to feel panic.

We carried our mounds of luggage down the lane, and sure enough, there was the river shimmering in the dawn. The luggage felt like lead. I reminded myself that we were not carrying anything like the amount of stuff most old travellers took. No mass of scientific instruments. Richard Strachey crossed western Tibet with a small theodolite and a lot of boxes for drying plants. Sven Hedin took something like a complete laboratory. We could do with some of his porters and yaks. The Indian pundits, brave spies for the Government of India, travelled light with doctored rosaries to measure their footsteps. Madame David-Neel only carried one small tent with no ground sheet, some clothes, two spoons, an aluminium bowl, a revolver and a travelling case containing a long knife and chopsticks. But she was supposed to be a beggar.

So here we were in the middle of Tibet sitting down beside a sacred river. We began to quarrel.

'If anyone comes along, you do the talking. Don't tell me you can't speak Chinese. Try some of the Tibetan phrases from the book. It's time you took some responsibility.'

We waited in silence. A steel hawser spanned both banks, and, on the far side about a couple of hundred yards across, we could see a few houses. Here was the Tsangpo which would become the Brahmaputra, the son of Brahma, one of India's great rivers. Its source was under the holy mountain in the region we hoped to reach, where four holy rivers, the Indus, the Sutlej, the Ganges and the Tsangpo-Brahmaputra, all rose in the sacred neighbourhood of Kailas. The Tibetans, who make most things holy, associate the rivers with sacred animals, the lion, the elephant, the peacock and the horse. I couldn't remember which animal sponsored the Tsangpo. At 12,000 feet above sea level it is the highest river in the world. Before the coming of the ferry it used to be crossed in coracles made of yak's skin stretched over a frame. Downstream well over a thousand miles away it completed its giant curve to the Indian peninsula and reached the sea at Assam.

After an hour a young cyclist appeared.

'Here's your chance to practise Tibetan.'

The phrase book was elementary. 'Des yak du gay?'

'What did you ask him?'

'Are there any yaks here?'

He sped away in panic, leaving us waiting on the river bank. The sun crept up slowly and the tendrils of mist melted away. I could see a few figures stirring on the far bank and heard a dog barking. We munched a piece of stale Lhasa bread. In front of us the river which gave life and fertility to this rich and populated area of Tibet drifted brown and sluggish.

Two hours later a lorry appeared and the driver got out to stretch his legs. He was a middle-aged man wearing civilian clothes. Caroline hurried over, and I watched them arguing away.

'It's no good. He works for some cooperative and says he is not allowed to take passengers.'

'Did you offer him enough?'

'I think he's frightened. If you think you can do better . . . '

In a mood of depression we watched him return to his cab.

One result of his unexpected arrival was the ferry winding up. The box which we could see on the other side turned out to be a sort of boat with an engine that activated the pulleys and steel hawser.

I said, 'They've got something like that on the Blackwater at Villierstown. They use it to take the hunt across.' Unimpressed, Caroline made another attempt to make the lorry-driver change his mind as the ferry crept over.

Triumph. 'He'll take us.'

For the first time I had a sense of freedom enhanced by our escape from sitting on the river bank. For some tranquil moments we had no problems as the ferry slipped across calmly. Besides our lorry driver, Norbhu, there was one other passenger, an elderly farmer in a tattered brown chuba carrying a wooden plough and leading a yak.

North of the river, we had only driven for a few miles before Norbhu stopped at a small house belonging to a friend for a taste of Tibetan hospitality. We were shown into a room with an iron stove in the middle, a shelf with a line of Thermos flasks and cushioned seats all round the walls which were completely covered with pictures. None of them had to do with religion; instead Chairman Mao was huge, benevolent and garlanded with silk as if he was a tankha. The cult of Mao continues among Tibetans long after their sophisticated Han brothers have changed their minds and taken his picture down. Having spent a couple of decades persuading Tibetans of his worth, the Chinese have a problem in re-education. Mao replaced the Dalai Lama as an icon, and so far no one else has come along.

On one side of Mao was a patchwork of bright certificates showing that our host with the big almond-shaped smile was a model worker. On the other were posters of Chinese leaders, generals on rearing horses with ribbons and medals on their chests like smocking, and behind them mountain landscapes covered in big flowers. They had an old-fashioned air which summoned memories of the era of Passing Cloud cigarettes or the mountains and streams that were worked into advertisements for good whiskey on bevilled mirrors.

Caroline said, 'That sort of thing has completely gone out in China.'

Two men, both with red hair in a plait, one with the startlingly wrinkled face that people here acquire after decades of exposure to wild weather, smiled across at us, while the woman of one of them brewed tea on the stove. Meanwhile Norbhu picked up a bone covered with half-cooked meat that lay among others arranged neatly on the couch beside him. It was evidently the leg of a sheep because a little cloven hoof hung off at an angle. The red flesh must have been good, as he tore hungrily at the fibrous meat. Good manners required him to finish it completely – my dog Bonzo couldn't have done a better job. While he gnawed away we tackled purple broth and sour butter, and the old man who watched us, checking that we got it all down, produced a leather bag filled with tsampa. The trick was to pour a little into your silver-lined bowl and mix it with the tea, forming a paste that was almost palatable after the butter disappeared into it.

In a harsh environment the Tibetan diet reflects a craving for fat and protein at variance with religious beliefs. In one of Sven Hedin's detailed footnotes he gives an ideal nomadic feast – 'a bowl of goat's milk with rich yellow cream. Yak kidneys, fried a golden yellow in fat. Marrow from yak bones toasted over the fire. Small, delicate pieces of tender juicy meat from the vertebrae of the antelope, laid before the fire and slowly browned. Antelope head, held in the flames, with the hide and hair on it till it is blackened with soot . . . '

A final gulp of tea and tsampa, a final exchange of fraternal smiles, and we were on our way leaving the lonely little house buffeted by the wind. We drove on through tawny brown country north of the river set with an occasional lake like a blue glass eye. This was an ancient route, once a rough track that was part of the most elevated highway in the world. The road-making was perfunctory, with the dusty track almost indistinguishable from its surroundings. In places someone had built a little pile of stones to indicate the way forward, or a dip was filled in with rocks, but the road had done nothing to change the landscape which was still wilderness where the sky and the land met each other in a burning collusion of wind and vibrant colour.

The wind blew constantly, sending dust to cloud the windscreen and ping against the sides of the vehicle as we moved through the same biscuit-brown land, empty for miles and miles, and then a few tents and shepherds and little sheep like crumbs on a carpet. The emptiness was oppressive. The lakes had ceased, and now there was no water, no vegetation. Once we passed a thermal spring, steam rising out of rocks and pools of bubbling water. In the distance a mountain peak glimmered in the sun, then vanished.

After the bus, sitting in the comfortable little cab was wonderful. Like everything else in Tibet the lorry belonged to the past, a more recent past conjuring up wartime images of supply lines coaxed along by the voice of a B.B.C. news-reader. The Chinese motor industry is home-grown; before 1949 when it began all motor vehicles were imported, mainly from the USA. There has been no development in design. Naturally the vehicles are utilitarian, iron Ox tractors, Red Flag tractors, jeeps and these Liberation lorries, old-fashioned like the posters of generals, reliable and weather-proof. This model had been constructed to withstand wind and distance; everything worked, the divided windows in front that cranked open, the separate headlights, the few basic instruments on the dashboard that combined to turn it into a moving oasis.

At nightfall we stopped at another friend of Norbhu's who lived in an equally tiny house that beamed a welcome in the wilderness. We were given rice and tinned pork washed down with tea, and afterwards Norbhu and his friend smoked cigarettes under more generals on rearing horses. Outside the wind howled, really howled, inside the little room lit by the flickering stove was warm and comfortable. Laws of hospitality, the first to go when tourism comes, still prevailed here. Our host gave us breakfast – stinking tea is a terrible way to start the day – and after a battle of smiles refused to take our money.

We set off towards Saka where we hoped to find another lorry, although Norbhu was not hopeful. He told Caroline that parts of the road were broken, and there was little reliable transport.

We drove through another sandstorm as the roaring wind covered the plain in whirling dust that blotted out the sun. Half an hour later we emerged into a bright blue sky, bumping along another vast chipped gravel plain, which turned into stripes of colour as the sun hit it. Bands of black, white, pink, gold, purple. A mountain in front had a touch of snow. Along the way was one solitary huddle of chocolate-brown nomad tents with goats and sheep guarded by ragged figures resigned to wind, hail and sand. Then suddenly a barracks. Here was Saka, a large dusty square the size of a college quadrangle filled with men, mainly soldiers, staring. Norbhu threw down our bags, took our money, and, having dumped his illegal passengers, was off as quickly as possible, away from one of the new army towns that guarded the frontier. Dust from his exhaust was the last we saw of him.

'Get a room quickly! Take the bags!'

Around the square were bleak lines of mud apartments. A woman took her keys and opened up one which smelt of urine with quite a lot of rubbish scattered on the floor. Behind us a dozen faces peered in, watching Caroline.

'Shut the door,' she said, 'I can't stand the little buggers.'

But among them was an officious young man with a dreaded accomplishment – he spoke English. He was dressed in a blue zipper jacket,

track trousers and rubber-soled jogging shoes that in these parts are a sign
of modernity and authority.

'You have permission? Passports?'

For a time we pretended we had not heard the little voice like a mouse
nibbling burnt toast that came out of the crowd. We undid our sleeping
bags and laid them on broken filthy beds. He pushed past the spectators,
came in and coughed.

'I am Foreign Affairs branch of Public Security Bureau.'

When the passports were handed over, he flipped the pages to the
forged visas and examined them with the concentration of the short-
sighted.

'Who say you come here? This frontier area. No foreigner. I find out
from higher authority. Please stay.'

We watched him strut across the square towards a small office followed
by the crowd of Tibetans who appeared to have satisfied their curiosity
about Caroline. He had left our passports behind.

'Let's get out of here.'

We emerged from the small room which had an unpleasant
resemblance to a cell, shook off Caroline's remaining admirers, and
removed ourselves to a neighbouring hill. Below us beside some nomad
tents women herded goats; apart from them the only movement came
from the spires of smoke rising from the tents and from packs of dogs and
flocks of black birds seeking out rubbish. Even the children had vanished;
it was siesta hour. Apart from the new barracks the place was as Major
Ryder saw it in 1905 when he rode through on his way to Kailas. 'Saka
Dzong has only a dozen or so houses, very dirty, the neighbourhood
(height 15,119 feet) being like every other Tibetan village a dust and
refuse heap.'

We had to move on rapidly. From here we could see the southern route
to Kailas stretching in the direction of Nepal, but, if we took that, we
would come upon more checkpoints and alerted officials. The much
longer northern route would be safer; the map showed that the turn-off
must have been somewhere along the way we had driven that morning.

Caroline went off in search of another lorry, while below me the world
started to move again. There was a building that I had not noticed before
where people in face masks and white coats were entering which must be a
hospital. The Chinese record in medicine and in encouraging barefoot
doctors in Tibet has been praiseworthy, and they have transformed health
care since the terrible medical practices of thirty years ago. In those days
Tibetans knew nothing of operations apart from the lancing of boils. No

instruments were used in obstetrics. Heinrich Harrer and his companion, Peter Aufschnaiter, were terrified throughout their years in Tibet in case they had an attack of appendicitis. The Chinese discouraged the taking of lamas' faeces as pills and tackled the problem of venereal disease – they estimated that when they first arrived eighty percent of the population suffered from venereal problems. The scourge of respiratory disease has still to be overcome, and the incidence of TB remains high.

This is one part of China where you are not punished for having too many children, but rewarded. The Chinese give population figures for 1957 for Tibet as 1,270,000. Previously there had been a decline in numbers attributed not only to poor health and infant mortality, but to the fact that a quarter of the population were celibate monks. Since then an unknown number have been killed or have gone into exile. But a rise of two percent annually is now claimed, and a precise Chinese population figure for Tibet in 1982 gave 1,892,393.

Caroline reappeared, running up the hill waving her arms.

'There's a lorry going in twenty minutes and the driver will take us.'

We retrieved our luggage from the dirty room and carried it as non-chalantly as possible down to the main road. There was no sign of the Public Security Bureau man. But a long hour passed. Then a welcome roar and another green lorry identical to the one on which we had travelled from the Tsangpo. Except that now we would not have the privilege of driving in the cab; we would travel in the back, open to the sky. We lay among sacks and accumulated baggage, keeping our heads well down as we were driven out of town. I could see the zinc tops of the barracks where, inside, an official in a blue zipper jacket was very likely putting away his chopsticks before ringing Lhasa.

We did not go very far, just a few miles back along the road we had originally come on to a place called Raka. Birds of prey circled over another compound empty of vehicles, a well in the middle and the usual square of small rooms.

My thoughts were still in Saka where the Public Security Bureau man would have found out that we had vanished. He had hundreds of soldiers around him doing nothing, and it seemed very probable that he would organise a pursuit. In such an exposed and empty land it would be easy to find us. Caroline did not agree.

'How many times do I have to tell you, Peter, that in China no one will take responsibility. They pass the buck. We've moved on out of his orbit and he's not going to worry about us now. We are someone else's pigeon.'

We acquired another cell. Two beds with their coverlets, a broken-down stove, half a candle and a large Thermos flask. I list these small details again because all over the country these lorry stops are similar. If you have been to one you have been to them all and experienced what seems to have become an immutable way of life. They differ only in their degree of cleanliness. They link with a very old tradition when every Tibetan town had an obligation to put up travellers and every camel stop in Central Asia had its quadrangle offering accommodation, frugal comfort and shelter against the desert. Apart from the change from animals to vehicles, they remained remarkably similar with their lack of heating and electric light, and only the central well in the centre of the square providing water.

The tough little man who ran this Holiday Inn lacked a suspicious mind. It helped that he had never seen a foreign passport before, and he appeared to be satisfied with us. He cooked our noodles over an open fire while we waited at a rickety table, and a lot of nomads wearing blackened sheepskin coats over trousers and pigtails dangling down from under rakish fur hats sat and grinned at Caroline.

They had plenty of time to hang about and watch the gorgeous Big Nose. We were marooned in Raka for five days.

We had our new plan worked out. We would hitch a passing lorry going on the northern route; after a quarrel we agreed on a division of labour. I would watch for it and flag it down, then call for Caroline who would rush forward and talk to the driver.

There were no lorries at all on the first day, one on the second which was crowded out with passengers, while on the third day the only vehicle was an army jeep bristling with Chinese officers which I avoided hailing. Most of the time Caroline lay on her bed, away from admiring Tibetans, listening to tapes, while I wandered around listlessly.

Outside the compound was only the harsh lunar plain, smooth and empty, stretching away to an assortment of distant mountains which, for a Tibetan horizon, were comparatively meagre. Overhead were always birds of prey or carrion; beneath them the smaller birds they sought sang constantly. Whenever I walked out across the gravel towards the nomad tents in the middle distance, I would see big hares bounding away. There were other little gopher-like animals the size and shape of guinea pigs, which must have been mouse hares. A lizard would flick its tail, a shrivelled old woman sat outside a tent nursing a lamp, a couple of toddlers whose filth aroused unexpected feelings of revulsion staggered about throwing stones. One day I came upon a stream edged with ice where I frightened two large golden ducks with white heads that dashed away over the desert. There was never any rain. The morning clouds were empty of moisture; perhaps to the Buddhist mind they were an omen of the vanity of human wishes.

The worst thing was the wind. Regularly by midday it began blowing, and it increased until you had to fight it, together with pelting particles of dust, in order to stand up. Charles Bell, who knew Tibet as well as any foreigner, described the wind exactly:

'You wake on a clear morning . . . the air is calm, the frost is keen, in the sky not a cloud. It is indeed good to be alive. But by eleven o'clock a wind rises. Two hours later it has deepened into a gale, which sweeps across the wide, treeless uplands of Tibet. As you ride across the plains, your heads bowed to the storm, you are frozen to the marrow and begrimed with dust. Soon after sunset the wind may abate, but sometimes it continues to whistle through half the night.'

It was my first prolonged experience of a landscape with a degree of desolation that made it unreal. We were at about 15,000 feet and wherever you looked you saw the same flat scree of rocks and shingle with the sharp ridges of hills rising in the thin air, and rising out of them like a dream the distant snowy crests of mountains. A visionary world where the intensity of light and colour responded less to anything similar in nature, but to a deep inner experience. There was a link with this landscape and the great Buddhist shrines I had seen where the flames of butter-lamps illuminated dark interiors and gilded Buddhas stared out of the dark.

On the fourth day a spanking new Toyota Landcruiser drove into the compound. Once again it was full of senior officers who wore resplendent uniforms like bandsmen with plenty of gold braid and red piping. There was no way of avoiding them, but to our surprise they turned out to be Tibetans and extremely friendly. One woman officer was a doctor who spoke a little English.

'We can give you medicine,' she said, appalled by our appearance, while the general or colonel nodded in agreement. Their jeep was a sign of affluence and power in a land where motor transport was a rarity. They brought along their own cook and provisions in a lorry behind which was also full of followers – a squad of tall swaggering men in wine-coloured cloaks, felt boots, earrings and wide-brimmed hats, all carrying daggers. Around one man's neck I noticed a picture of the Dalai Lama, the first I had seen for some time.

We tried to cadge a lift. It would have been a lofty way of travelling, speeding through any checkpoint in the company of the top brass. But there was no room among the uniforms and the cloaks and daggers; both the Landcruiser and the lorry were tightly packed with people. Next morning we watched them all drive away, the officers wrapped in furlined coats.

Another bad day passed. Caroline listened to her music, I read Cervantes and walked about. A dog attacked me.

'I don't blame it,' Caroline said when I limped back. We quarrelled; we had almost run out of food.

'The haste of Europeans has no place in Tibet,' wrote a traveller who took a year to reach Lhasa. 'We must have patience if we wish to reach our goal.'

During the frosty night, as I lay in my sleeping bag trying to keep warm, I heard a roar and four lorries turned into the compound. Outside, an avalanche of people descended into the cold. Torches shone in the dark and scores of men were dashing across the illumination of headlights. There were shouts, the dog lunged, snapping his teeth, and the girl who did the washing came into our room with the news.

Caroline leapt out of bed and put on her chuba. 'You stay here, I'll talk to them.'

By now I was used to the routine. We would be refused, either with an excuse – most times no room – or without. Chinese drivers perfect rudeness to a fine art.

But once again Caroline demonstrated her powers of persuasion and found a driver who would take us for fifty yuan. There was no problem with the baggage, but once more we would have to sit in the back. The convoy intended to leave at four in the morning which meant only a few hours' sleep.

Of course we hardly slept another moment. We were up and ready well before our fellow travellers, and our driver had been partially paid. The rest would be given to him when we reached his final destination at Gertze more than 600 kilometres away.

We squashed in the back with half a dozen other passengers. A man's head was jammed against my knees, and beneath me a piece of metal stabbed my back. After five days at Raka it was a pleasant sensation.

These lorries belonged to a cooperative in the west to which they were bringing seed potatoes and other provisions from Lhasa. This had been their first trip to the big city, and now they were returning. It had been a matter of chance that they had decided to spend the night at Raka, and we might have waited a long time more for a lift. Passengers are not officially allowed to be taken on, but in a land where transport is so limited the rule is generally ignored. Like other drivers, this one appeared to welcome his windfall, especially since foreigners could be charged at least double the normal rate.

After sunrise the lorries began racing each other through blinding clouds of dust. Shouting insults, the drivers felt compelled to use suicide tactics to get ahead, charging across the plain, and only screaming to a halt when some unforeseen obstacle loomed. A large wooden churn for making tea dropped on my head.

The misery of travelling across Tibet in the back of a Chinese lorry is considerable. Imagine a small cramped space packed full of groaning people, kerosene drums, pieces of machinery, wooden planks, plastic cans of petrol, sacks of potatoes and sharp things like spades and axes all tumbling about. Imagine a pitted, dusty road on which a wild driver is going at sixty miles an hour behind a comrade who is throwing up dust, which pours down your throat to combine with your thirst. You are unable to move or see anything outside through the yellow clouds unless a fortuitous gust of wind blows it aside for an instant. Occasionally one of the other travellers sends a well-aimed globule of spit in your direction – not from malice, since even here amid the discomfort they aim a wan smile at you as well. Otherwise there is little movement as they sit about seemingly dead, wrapped in their own personal hell of suffering. A soldier in dark glasses sits on a potato sack nursing his head in a demonstration of how Chinese posted here have altitude sickness to deal with. An elderly Tibetan, his body covered with bits of grimy sheepskin, squats beside his two daughters who are stretched out, their heads wrapped in tasselled green scarves, their big eyes swivelling as they stare at the foreigners.

The convoy turned north along the 'New Road', a scraping on the empty landscape with little definition except for the ruts of previous vehicles or the occasional cairn marking some direction in this immense solitude. Dust wrapped our lorry, but occasionally it was blown away for fleeting impressions of the passing scene, a nomad encampment with tents battened down against the wind, a hot spring with streams of vapour rising out of the rocks into the freezing air. Luminous colours fluctuated in the changing light, an ochre mountain suddenly becoming striped like a tiger, a patch of shimmering shale or a little blue lake gleaming and vanishing.

I lay in my sleeping bag with the face mask I had bought in Lhatse slipping down over my nose. It had become quite black on the outside, and a lot of the dust made its way past, making my mouth and throat taste of gravel. I was wearing all my clothes and still felt cold. Caroline looked more comfortable, muffled up, earphones conveying Beethoven above the wind.

At noon the convoy stopped among rocks to make a meal. This was an opportunity for the drivers to examine their vehicles. One wanted water, another had developed a slow puncture and the spare wheel had to be racked down from its position beneath the chassis. Then a carburettor was giving trouble and an engine needed persuasion to start. Each driver had his own starting handle, and at intervals on the journey you would see one or other of the four men cranking their wonderful lorries as if they were winding old grandfather clocks. Or an engine might overheat. It was fairly common to see forlorn people beside their stranded transport watching clouds of expiring steam.

In a country devoid of garages or even people, each driver was responsible for his own lorry, and because of the bleak nature of the terrain they usually moved in convoys. When there was a breakdown everyone stopped, and it says something for the nature of these old-fashioned machines where everything mechanical is of basic simplicity that you rarely saw a vehicle that had been totally abandoned. At night in the caravanserai engines were stripped and lovingly assembled, each driver attending to his darling like a dresser robing a star.

We sat down Chinese fashion for lunch. Behind us was the unchanging barren plain, in front a jagged line of snow mountains. As always the horizon was defined by snow peaks. 'Mountains like spires, fracturing with cold,' William Moorcroft wrote when he saw them. Ample provisions from Lhasa, tins of meat, rice and vegetables, were cooked on a species of blowlamps; everyone took out their own chopsticks. The dozen people were a mixed group of Chinese and Tibetans, the Tibetans being the ones who were not wearing uniform and huddled by themselves eating tsampa. One Chinese, taller than the others, wearing an officer's fur-lined coat came and sat down besides us.

'Why do you come here?' he asked in English. 'Have you visa?'

We both nodded vigorously.

'Ah. Where are you going?'

'We think to Ali.' Caroline put on her disarming smile. 'We wish to see more of Tibet. It is so beautiful.'

This statement dumbfounded him. He put down his chopsticks and gazed at us for about a minute.

'But there is nothing here. I would like to see California. I have read about it in many different magazines.'

He was an interpreter who had learnt his English in some Chinese

[*137*]

academy before joining the army and being posted to western Tibet; it was like going to Siberia.

Lunch hour over, the interpreter gave up his privileged position in the cab to join us as we bowled along in the back, covering our faces against the dust. It was too noisy for conversation. Hours passed. The old Tibetan had taken out his prayer beads, while his daughters lay groaning among the sacks.

We stopped beside a stream, and everyone climbed out.

'We go fishing,' the interpreter said.

The sparkling mountain stream wound through a wasteland of sand and rock with an unexpected pale green edging of thin grass on each bank. Four men walked downstream for a hundred yards or so and then ran back. Suddenly there was a spout of water and an explosion.

'This river very good for fish.'

Boom! Up went another stick of dynamite. When the ripples had died away all the Chinese pulled up their trouser legs and waded around in the freezing water picking up corpses. By the end of the fishing there was a bucketful of trout, soon to be gutted and fried in a pan by the blowlamp.

Both Caroline and I had been reared in places where dry fly fishing was a sacred rite. The previous year I had reverently tried to pull some fish out of Lough Mask, while Caroline spun a rod on the Dee. Now we were unsporting enough to eat our fill with our hosts. Only the Tibetans did not join us.

'Silly people,' said the interpreter. 'How can they progress with such old-fashioned attitudes?'

Veneration for life, evolving from the central doctrine of reincarnation and the belief that life progresses from the lower animal world to the human level had kept this river full of fish. Tibetans might gnaw and kill yaks and lambs, but they did not like to kill little things with souls. They were pragmatic: one slaughtered yak equalled the souls of several fish or birds. So every lake and stream was crammed with fish, while the plains and mountains teemed with hares and gazelle, and the sky overhead and the marshes beside the lakes were filled with unshot birds.

Water is particularly sacred. Spencer Chapman, lamenting that he was unable to fish since he was on an official visit, commented that 'as water is the purest element, so the body of a fish may be the temporary resting place of some holy lama whose hope for immortality one would not willingly jeopardize'. Heinrich Harrer has a moving account of the Tibetan's attitudes towards life and death, describing how an ant at a picnic was gently saved or the catastrophe of a fly falling into a cup of tea.

[*138*]

'In winter they break the ice in the pools to save the fishes before they freeze to death, and in summer they rescue them before the pools dry up. These creatures are kept in pails or tins until they can be restored to their home waters.'

In the old days no one would dare fish in Lhasa. In the whole of Tibet there was only one place where fishing was allowed, a spot where the Tsangpo ran through a desert and there was nothing else to eat. The people of that region were looked down upon like slaughterers and blacksmiths.

The trout were very good.

We moved on in darkness, the interpreter once again sitting in the cab, and after twelve hours of driving, interspersed with picnics, we reached a little settlement called Cuoqing – at least that was what it sounded like. Lights in the darkness, a small compound with other lorries and a line of huts. Drivers tinkered with engines. Outside the square, a young moon shone down on the empty plain turning it aquamarine.

Everyone vanished. It was as if the earth had opened up and devoured them. Caroline eventually routed out an old man who had been left behind like the lame boy in the Pied Piper.

'He says they've gone to the cinema.'

For the next two hours we hung around in the cold. All the rooms were shut and locked and there was no way we could get a bed.

'Typically Chinese,' Caroline said as the entire population of Cuoqing enjoyed a video whose music was relayed through loudspeakers out onto the moonlit landscape. Where there was electricity there was noise. There had been films in Tibet for many years; Heinrich Harrer built a projection room for his young pupil, the Dalai Lama, who particularly enjoyed *Henry V* with its medieval knights, similar to his own courtiers. Earlier, in 1936, Spencer Chapman had arranged a film show which included movies of Charlie Chaplin, the Grand National and the Jubilee Procession.

It was almost twelve o'clock when the music was switched off and a few dim figures emerged into view at the end of the square. Lights began to shine in windows. In one room we tracked down the interpreter just as he was going to bed. We reminded him that we were strangers in a strange land, we were extremely tired and would be so grateful for his help.

'Ah. You wish to sleep here? That is not possible. There are no extra beds.'

We wrangled for another full hour before a door was unlocked and we were shown into a room containing four beds. Smells of tobacco smoke

[*139*]

and urine, the musty nature of the standard quilt, failed to make the prospect of sleep uninviting.

Next day the troupe left the gravel plains and climbed into a land of towering mountain peaks and immense dried-up valleys. We were up at 19,000 feet for lunch, eating another picnic heated on the blowlamp. Just above where we stopped a shepherd and his daughter were erecting their tent in a waste of gravel before a mountain background. Their dogs barked at us, massive brutes that were tied down during the day and were only given their freedom at night. It must have been lonely and tough in this world of snow and rocks; the two of them watching their flocks in a routine unchanged since the days of Abraham. They sat outside the tent, beside a stream edged with jagged pieces of ice, watching us scoop meat and noodles and vegetables with our chopsticks. They watched when, after the meal was over, one of the drivers took out a revolver and everyone shot at an empty tin placed on a rock. They watched spellbound as the lorries roared away; all the time there had been no communication or greeting.

During the journey to Gertze the revolver came in handy as the Chinese kept stopping and shooting at anything that moved. They shot mostly at hares, tame little animals that sat watching us, twitching long silky ears. They stopped and aimed at a herd of gazelle. They hit nothing, unlike Captain Rawling eighty years ago. 'We saw and shot numbers of Tibetan partridge, ramchikor and Tibetan sandgrouse, giving us a momentous change to an otherwise monotonous fare of mutton.'

Pinioned in the back, we continued glimpsing the passing scene through dust – a woman herding sheep, searching for spiky tufts of yellow grass, a deep blue lake with a band of mountains rising steeply on the far side. For the last few miles before Gertze the lorries had another race, throttles full down, horns blaring, insults screamed like the cries of Iroquois braves, fists waving.

At four o'clock the lorry stopped and the interpreter got out stiffly and walked away.

We were in Gertze, home town and final destination of the convoy – hence the race to the finish, which had been the climax of a long journey to the big city and back. The old Tibetan unwrapped the sheet from around his head and sat up like Lazarus revived, while his daughters ceased to clutch each other and collected their belongings. Time to pay off the driver, already busy unloading the assortment of ship's chandler supplies he had transported from Lhasa and taking it to a large galvanized store built beside the barracks. Gertze was a frontier-style town with some official buildings within its mud walls, nomads without, camped on the edge of the desert surrounded by their animals. The place was big enough for officials and queries about permits. Instinct to seek out a room and a bed was quelled. Caroline sought out another lorry travelling west, and with her touch of the miraculous immediately managed to find a driver who said that he would be leaving early next morning. Watched by a man spinning a prayer wheel, and a couple of idle nomads, she struck another bargain – so many yuan now, the rest when we reached Shiquan He.

To avoid suspicion we made a stupid decision to spend the night in the back of the lorry where we would be out of sight. Once again everyone had gone to the cinema. Lying in the cold amid the reek of petrol, half crushed by some lumps of machinery destined for a new electrical plant away to the west, we listened to the strains of Strauss and Chopin on the loud-speaker. After the film was over a number of people found us and came and had a look, climbing up on the back to stare at us eating biscuits until Caroline's glare made them retreat.

Our behaviour was inconsistent, since we had spent five nights openly at Raka without arousing comment. There was nothing to stop any of the people watching us now from reporting us. Oh, for a nice little urine-smelling bedroom with an iron bed!

'It's no worse than being in a small boat,' Caroline said next morning as we watched the shocking pink dawn. 'My father was in the navy.'

The driver had said that he planned to leave early, but by seven o'clock he was still shunting backwards and forwards around Gertze collecting people and things. A load of long wooden planks was shoved on top of us, some sacks and tins of petrol, and then half a dozen passengers, including the interpreter who sat up front. The lorry drove into a camp where scores of soldiers gathered round to have a look at us with blank stares that put you in mind of the terracotta army. And then mercifully we drove away.

The highlight of this day's travel was a stop in another small canton-ment where I was able to buy a dozen more tins of oranges. At one time it snowed, soft white flakes spilling down on us from an overcast sky, increasing the coughing and retching around us. Most of our time was spent on defending an oasis of comfort; with so many people and so little room to move, space was contested like a gannetry, and any incursion into someone else's territory was met with a kick.

We lay in our sleeping bags, very cold, hardly moving for stops and starts and pauses to cool the radiator. By the time we reached Gaiji eighteen hours later memory receded. I retained the impression of another starry night and a crowded dormitory where Tibetans were chewing legs of raw mutton covered with long black hairs.

In the morning I woke and lay listening to the sounds around me – bubbling throats, wheezes, rattles, heavings, gaspings, dry barks and long harsh series of early-morning evacuation from the lungs. Every Tibetan appeared to have a respiratory problem as people coughed in lorries, in their sleep and at every moment of the waking day. By six o'clock the sun had come out and it was already quite hot. I sat in the doorway eating the mouldy remains of Lhasa bread, the alternative breakfast being half-chewed bones, watching the lines of snow mountains in the distance that seemed to float above the dusty plain. Two soldiers were pulling up a bucket from the well in the middle of the compound, the big creaking winch letting down a long leather thong and bucket into the depths to draw up the precious water for cooking and washing. A hen ran across the yard, a litter of small black pigs came out from beneath the wheels of a lorry. The soldiers carried their bucket across the dust to some mud cabin. There was a potent sense of exile. I had been reading Tolstoy's account of a Russian garrison, and, just as his soldiers felt themselves cut off from all sense of civilization on the rolling steppe, so did the Chinese feel isolated in modern Tibet. Their families were far away and the nomads they encountered reminded them of a barbaric past that had no place in the brave new world back home. Tibet is officially regarded as a hardship post with six months' leave every two years.

At ten o'clock, watched by numerous idle Tibetans, a group of Chinese women wearing straw hats, blue trousers, coloured aprons and face masks began dusting and sweeping the rooms. It was time to climb back onto the lorry.

From Gaiji to the lorry's final destination of Shiquan He, also called Ali, was only a hundred kilometres. Back in Lhasa Bradley had warned us that Ali was the provincial centre of western Tibet, a large town with a security check where he had been stopped and experienced a lot of trouble.

'If I were you, I'd stay somewhere outside and get around the place without being seen.' With our developing paranoia this seemed good advice.

We bumped along in choking dust on the New Road, another indentation where lorries passed the occasional cairn. Somewhere in the desolation the lorry stopped and a moment later the face of the interpreter appeared squinting over the back of the lorry.

'The driver wishes to be paid now.'

'We'll pay him at Ali.'

'Ah. That is no good.'

'It's what we agreed.'

'Ah. It is better to pay now.'

'You deal with it,' Caroline said. 'I hate being interrupted in the middle of a symphony. Tell him to go to hell.'

I got out, the better to argue. The driver and his two mates glowered at me impassively from the cab, and according to the interpreter were demanding twenty yuan more than the agreed price.

'We're not paying until Ali.'

'He say no go.'

'Tell him I will report the matter.'

'Ah. We are not bound to take foreigners.'

'In my country we treat foreigners better.'

From the back came Caroline's voice. 'Greedy bastards! Not a penny more!'

'If we don't pay they'll dump us here.' All around the bald plain stretched away empty and desolate.

We paid up. I tried appealing to chivalry. 'You could at least offer the woman a seat in front.'

'You are in China now and we treat you the same way as any Chinese.'

'You're just uncivilized.'

The interpreter paused. 'I cannot understand why foreigners should wish to come to such a country.' He looked at me pityingly and furrowed his brows, huddled into his sheepskin-lined army coat and walked away. To a certain amount of sniggering at the sight of enraged and hysterical foreigners I climbed back in among the coughing passengers and dusty sacks.

We had one more stop beside a pleasant stream.

'The Indus.'

The last time I had seen the Indus it had been an immense grey flood in Pakistan. Here it was sylvan. The interpreter took off his boots and washed his feet in the sparkling water.

'Bet you a tin of Mandarins you won't push him in.'

Behind him six Chinese were defecating along the side of the road. Their faces were rapt; a bird sang overhead.

CHAPTER 12

Ali to Kailas

Although the correct name for the town was Shiquan He, and it was marked thus on my map, everyone called it Ali after the province. We had repeatedly asked to be let off at the perimeter, but drivers seldom listen and this one may have felt some glee in dumping us in the main street where a crowd collected to watch us throwing out our baggage before the lorry moved on.

Ali seemed big. The dusty streets, half-finished factory blocks and rows of new tin-roofed houses built at the foot of a hill represented the first real town we had seen since leaving Lhatse hundreds of miles away more than a week before. Army lorries, the only traffic, charged up and down, throwing out dust. A soldier came over and joined the crowd while Caroline was scolding a ragged man who took a finger out of his nose to stroke one of her zip-bags. At four in the afternoon the heat was mal-evolent as the sun flashed down from the dark blue sky.

The way out of town was across a new metal bridge over the baby Indus and along a road that led straight out into the silent plain where the wind streamed over floating mirages of water – blue water, the bluest mirages I have ever seen. We would have to pass a large official building, and wherever we pitched our tent it would be exposed to public view.

Because we had so much baggage, we took it along in relays. I picked up the heaviest and began walking with buckling legs, but the effort to keep going, combined with lassitude induced by heat, meant that I could only go a few yards at a time. At one of these frequent stops I suddenly picked up delicious smells of cooking coming from a small building. With an appetite sharpened by a diet of mouldy bread, instant noodles, tinned oranges and the odd trout, I forgot about Chinese jails.

The restaurant was a small dark room crowded with people, many of whom were gambling, and all were shouting. From a loudspeaker over the kitchen door came the scream of music. Chinese soldiers and Tibetans sprawled over their benches drinking pint-sized bottles of beer waiting for the young girl in the white coat to come staggering out with more steaming plates of food which she slammed down on rough wooden tables.

When I flopped down beside a group of tousle-haired Tibetans who were smoking and drinking beer, I was handed a bottle of beer which tasted better than champagne. Caroline joined me and translated the menu which was written in chalk on a blackboard like a Paris bistro. Soon the girl was bringing us a pale amber soup with something like dried grass and pieces of dandelion floating on top, pork and cabbage, boiled rice and chunky radishes sliced in bright yellow sauce.

The next ten minutes passed in a delirium of unexpected pleasure. I drank some more beer. At some stage I looked across at Caroline.

'You're not eating?'

She shook her head. Earlier I had been conscious that the roar of music had suddenly ceased after she had taken off her face mask, stalked out into the kitchen and shouted an order.

'I can't stand that dreadful noise.' The shouted conversations, the gambling and ringing laughter continued without musical accompaniment.

'If they want to break their eardrums, they'll have to wait.'

Now I noticed she hadn't touched the pork. 'Have some rice.'

She collapsed in a heap over the table.

One moment she had been directing the terrified little waitress to get clean plates, and the next she could have been dead. I examined the dormant figure slumped among scattered pieces of meat. It took a few minutes to revive her, and help her to her feet. Everyone stopped eating and talking, their attention switched to the two helpless strangers shuffling past. Outside I discovered a small room behind the restaurant filled with rumpled clothes and containing a sleeping alcove. With the help of the waitress, Caroline was propelled in there, where she lay comatose.

I should have gone off immediately in search of a doctor. A bit of folk medicine and some needles stuck in her might have done wonders. I hesitated; could we wait until tomorrow morning? 'Caroline?' She appeared to be unconscious. Occasionally the door would open and someone would stalk in and shine a torch in our faces. I gave them big smiles.

We lay for some time, and I fell asleep to be woken by two men moving around the room with candles.

Caroline stirred. 'Tell them to go away.'

But they wanted to go to bed, and this was their bedroom – at twelve o'clock at night they were entitled to their sleep. Protesting, we got up reluctantly and tottered outside. Even at this hour the restaurant was filled, mainly with soldiers who were gambling with the sounds we had heard at Shigatse – thumps and shouts coming from cards being banged down and their sequence being called out.

People were very kind, taking us into a nearby house where there was a room filled with empty beds. Someone brought over a Thermos of tea from the kitchen.

In the morning I was awakened by the sound of Caroline getting up. At first I thought she was about to be sick, but then I could see in the dim light that she was packing bags.

'How are you feeling?'

'I'm all right.'

'Why don't you sleep on and take it easy?'

'You don't seem to realize, Peter, that at any moment the Public Security may come.'

The woman who had brought us the tea and appeared to own the beds on which we had slept, did not seem worried about us after we had paid her. We left with all our bags, our idea being to remove ourselves as quickly as we could out of town and try to hitch another lorry. Once again we carried our bags in relays backwards and forwards yard by yard from the street and its lurking dangers.

Only a few hours ago Caroline had been alarmingly ill. 'Are you really all right?'

'Quite well, thank you. Hurry up.'

A long time later we were sitting down on a rock beside the road with our baggage around us. Ahead was the usual sort of view, a limitless expanse of gravel with a distant smudge of mountains. With the first warm glow of the sun came the crash of music as all the loudspeakers in Ali were switched on at the same time, and a male chorus immediately began singing some piercing reminders that only sluggards and other criminally-minded people lazed in bed. Soon we could see groups of people exercising and moving along the road in our direction. We watched spellbound as they approached, throwing out their arms, kicking and tossing their limbs.

'Do you think we should hide?'

'Where?'

At the end of the road was a small broken-down wall, and it would have been feasible for us to have hidden ourselves and our bags behind it before the keep-fit enthusiasts arrived. We did nothing.

The first man to reach the spot where we sat, dressed like all the others in a tracksuit, was vigorously flapping his arms in time to the music. Soon the rest had caught up, coming to an abrupt halt at the sight of us.

Caroline said, 'I'm not speaking Chinese. If you ignore them, they'll get bored and go away.'

They weren't a bit bored. Word got round, and soon some school-children turned up from the large building we had passed and joined the crowd. Here, high on the plateau, one of the subjects they were taught was English.

'Hullo, Mister, how are you?' A small girl produced a phrase book and we sat in the sun going over the words. 'Who are you? Where are you going? My name is Mr Yin. I am very happy to meet your mother.'

At nine o'clock the music stopped and everyone vanished.

For most of that day we waited around for lorries. By eleven o'clock the wind sprang up throwing whirlwinds of dust across the plain, while the sun beat down from the indigo sky. The main street of Ali had become a vacuum sucking in the heat, and nothing moved except the occasional mad dog. A few lorries passed, but didn't stop. One was taking soldiers to some army compound, while another was filled with workmen carrying picks and shovels. Then an army jeep sped by. At one moment we saw in the distance a long green convoy like a centipede, each truck following the next in a long dusty line northwards.

'Probably returning to Kashgar,' Caroline said. 'That's where they get all their fruit and vegetables.'

From the map I could see that Shiquan He/Ali was a junction for a number of strategic roads. One led towards Ladakh and its capital, Leh, beside Kashmir which, as the pariah kite flies, was only a short distance away across a couple of mountain ranges. The road where we were sitting would go in the general direction of Kailas, while the road northward took the convoys into the heart of Chinese Turkestan.

At first, after being cooped up in lorries, it was a pleasure to stretch and luxuriate in the sun, but pretty soon relaxation gave way to anxiety. We sat all day. At dusk we went back to the restaurant, dumping our baggage under the eye of a kindly old shepherd with a wish to please. We left him sitting among his sheep and our zip-bags contentedly spinning out thread from a lump of wool.

It was not very wise to go back, but Caroline had recovered enough to consume egg plant soup, squirmy noodles and even drink some of the dreaded beer. Around us the same soldiers played cards and shouted out numbers. One of them sloshed a bowl of tea over his unfinished meal so that no one else could eat it.

[147]

'Typical demonstration of social behaviour from the average Chinese communist.'

We went back to our position on the empty road where the shepherd still sat spinning. It seemed safe to put up the tent in a little hollow nearby, a long struggle since the hard gritty surface demanded that every peg to hold essential ropes had to be hammered in. There was a frost and there was the problem of dogs whom we could hear howling all around us. Robert Louis Stevenson described the tortures of lying awake in the dark with nothing to protect you against these unwelcome intruders but the flimsy canvas tent: 'At the end of a fagging day the sharp cruel note of a dog's bark is in itself a cruel annoyance; but to a tramp like myself he represents the sedentary and respectable world in its most hostile form.'

The howling dogs of Ali were not in the least sedentary, and at some dismal hour we were both sitting up in our sleeping bags wondering if they would attack.

'I doubt it once they've smelt your shoes.' (The boots that had let down the British army had been left behind in Kathmandu; they had done me fine, but were a little heavy. Now I was crossing Tibet in a pair of runners.)

The howls came nearer. 'I wonder if they could be wolves?'

'You deal with them, Peter.'

At six next morning we struck tent, the dogs having vanished. In due course we were once more sitting by the road watching the light change colour as yet another dawn took hold as spectacular as the aurora borealis. We ate some biscuits we had bought the day before. Ali had plenty of supplies, although nothing very varied – more noodles, more tinned oranges, and some stuff that was identical to Spam, part of the time warp. Once again the morning music started up, followed by reveille from the school. The same joggers bounded our way, the same children emerged with their English text books.

Then a single lorry appeared at the end of the road and drove slowly towards us. I watched it without enthusiasm or hope, another green truck with a tarpaulin cover in the back and up front the engine casing pulled back to allow a stream of cooling air. I signalled, and to my surprise it stopped; what was more remarkable, it was empty except for the driver.

He had driven here with another truck from Kashgar, a journey of four long days. He had another day to go, his destination being Geer, which would suit us very well. He was a Tajik, and his Mongol face with high cheekbones looked quite different from the features of Tibetans and Han

Chinese. Within a few minutes of meeting him a price was fixed, our bags were thrown in the back and we had squeezed in beside him.

Ali was behind us, Chinese bureaucracy, the school, the barracks, the silver-roofed houses. At last we could drive towards the mountains in the south, the nearest of which were painted startling reds and yellows, the distant range much higher and much more impressive than any we had seen in western Tibet. These were the main ramparts of the Himalayas whose snow peaks and glaciers marked the boundary of the high plateau; behind them lay the drop down to the sub-continent. But the silver of the Himalayan snows was still far off; meanwhile we were crossing another crusted brown plain past browsing sheep and goats, black tents, dogs and nomads, all standing out in the vapourless air microscopically sharp.

Even by Tibetan standards the road on which we were travelling was diabolical. When we stopped and waited for the radiator to cool, our driver compared it unfavourably to roads in Kashgar. When we climbed back on board and drove along, we heard much about his native region, the abundance of fruit, vegetables and flowers he had left behind, the railway, the splendid hotel. Comparisons seemed unjust between that rich central Asian oasis of fragrant fertility and the plain around us where there was almost nothing to support life. We drove by a couple of lakes, their rims crusted with salt that had a sparkle subtly different from snow, another empty waste and a group of nomad tents camped among stones.

As birds dipped and wheeled over the bonnet of the lorry the driver burst into song. He sang in a high voice with a Russian-style chorus that brought to mind campfires at night and the endless blue expanse of the steppes. Life is good in old Kashgar. I remembered groups of Tajiks in striped silk robes picnicking under trees and all around them the scent of flowers mingled with the smell of melons; their plump faces and contented expressions as they swallowed grapes or bit into over-ripe melon flesh. How different this wilderness must seem where every blade of grass was a rarity. The driver went on singing. He sang hour after hour while we sat back enjoying the luxury of the cab and the magnificence of the approaching mountains which would soon dominate the plain. They stood one behind the other, sharply etched against the sky in an immenseness where men did not seem to have a role to play.

We lurched and bumped along, stopping every few minutes as the radiator boiled over, when it took all the driver's patience to let it cool before starting off again with a sudden surge of speed and a whirlwind of choking dust. Even the nomads must have found this place forbidding. Tents were few; I remember passing a couple of stone huts with an old woman outside huddled in a patterned cloak, sucking her thumb. Above, two shepherds, biblical in their chubas, were trying to find nourishment for their animals among cold grey rocks.

Coming into Geer in the late afternoon we passed the bloated carcase of a yak. Some Tibetans muffled up against the cold stood beside it watching us. The driver stopped singing.

'That is what I mean about Tibet. You cannot teach people like these how to behave.'

We found a room in the courtyard, pushed out the faces peering in, and settled down to wait for further transport. It was hard to believe that the familiar little compound with a fragmented mud wall to keep out the elements was once Gartok, the trading capital of western Tibet, the highest town in the world. This small grubby line of rooms was on the site of an important trading station ruled by two Viceroys called Garbons, situated strategically above the Indian and Nepalese frontiers.

After the English invasion of 1904, Younghusband sent people to explore western Tibet which was still so unknown that the four officers were asked to look out for any mountains that might surpass Everest. They did not care for Gartok. 'We only halted one day . . . In that time we had seen more than enough of it. We were unanimous in looking at it as one of the most dreary inhabited places we had struck on our journey.' Later, a second British Agency was established here, the other being at Gyantse. Gartok was not a popular posting.

As Geer, it still made you despair. But we were saved almost instantly by the arrival of two army jeeps followed by a truck full of men who wore Western clothes and could speak some English.

'Where do you go, please?'

'Kailas. We are hoping for a lift.'

'Ah.'

The party, which included a Tibetan woman with a small child, turned out to be a professional team which had been sent down from Lhasa to investigate this remote corner. There were two geologists on the look-out for gold and minerals, and a film-maker.

A few minutes later we were bundled into the back of one of the jeeps on our way to Menshi Menang, another 200 kilometres further on. More remarkable, Caroline had persuaded our benefactors to make a detour next day and drop us off in the vicinity of Kailas.

Travel in west Tibet is so haphazard that we might easily have been subjected to a lengthy experience of life in Geer, just as we had spent five days in Raka. We had escaped through luck and a good deal of kindness.

These jeeps were just as crowded as the army jeeps that had driven into Raka and found no room for us. But here at Geer our benefactors put themselves to the utmost discomfort to find space for two foreign hitch-hikers. The jeeps, utility vehicles, manufactured by the hundred thousand back in China, designed with a similar disregard for the pains of long-term travel as their American counterparts, were already crowded with people and baggage. Recollections of our recent journey from Ali with the singing Kashgari evoked memories of luxury as we bounced along; somehow we had been fitted in with four other passengers in the back where the dust that evaded the barrier of the small perspex window pelted us painfully.

These Chinese made me ashamed of my general dislike of their fellow countrymen. They made me reflect on the good things China has done in Tibet, the introduction of health care, roads and reform of an ancient system of government which for all its medieval passion and splendour was in many ways grotesque. What benefit did China gain out of annexing Tibet? The financial strain of trying to revive a depressed feudal economy must be awful. They had acquired general opprobrium from the rest of the world, a delicate and explosive frontier with India, a large nuclear testing site and the enmity of generations of Tibetans.

There was the zeal for improvement. The two geologists squashed beside us were enthusiasts for the Wild West scenery, the lines of snowy mountains, the stony plains changing colour as they caught the light, the lonely landscape with the occasional solitary group of black nomad tents.

But we were going to a more fertile land. We came to a small river where one of the jeeps and the lorry got stuck in a quagmire of mud and reeds. Across the stream was another small encampment with a woman engaged in the usual pastime of spinning a prayer wheel, men gazing into the distance. But around them yaks were grazing, together with a large flock of sheep, and they were eating real grass, not the little fringes of green baby's hair bordering lakes and rivers which had been the only signs of fertility for a thousand miles. Into this gentle oasis came our vehicles, engines shrieking, people shouting, wheels spinning; and finally, with a couple of lurches, we were free.

We drove on through prairie country, until we reached Menshi Men-ang, having travelled for sixteen hours since the moment at daybreak when the Kashgari had picked us up outside Ali. As usual our first reaction was to seek a bed, but we had not taken into account the hospitality of our hosts, who invited us to share their meal, a feast of cartons filled with food from Lhasa heated up on an oil stove by one of the drivers. The group was regarded as an important delegation, and every-thing was done to make their lives easy, to the extent of warm water and towels appearing for their comfort, rather than the usual Thermos.

Beer was passed round as one of the geologists set his tape recorder to play Strauss; the strains of 'Vienna Woods' and then 'The Blue Danube' sounded sweet as we picked titbits out of cartons with our chopsticks. The other geologist compared his camera with Caroline's, nodding his head in appreciation. Hers was so much slicker than his own, a bulky Seagull made in Shanghai which had taken him years to save for. We stuffed ourselves with rice, strips of grilled yak steak and curried vegetables. A stamp album was produced and exhibited amid apologies for a lack of Irish stamps. We relaxed under the tranquilising influence of food, hospi-tality and friendship. The man in the blue padded Mao jacket washed his hands in a ewer brought in by one of the staff. The others were lying back on cushions smoking; the music changed to Schubert.

'Why do you go to Kailas?' asked the man in the padded jacket. When we explained our wish to visit the sacred destination of pilgrims, there were sounds of approval. These people representing the new generation after the Cultural Revolution were among the few Chinese we encoun-tered who appeared to be genuinely interested in Tibet. In particular the geologists were enthusiastic about their work and presence here, and the unexplored mountains that offered an immense challenge.

The chances of their finding gold together with other minerals were high. Tibet has an age-old tradition of primitive mining. The gilded roofs of temples and gompas proclaim Tibet's gold, sacred buildings which pilgrims saw as Madame David-Neel saw the Potala burning with sacred fire.

Next day we continued to travel towards the wave of mountains. Perhaps as a sign that we were approaching holy places, we noticed increasing signs of life, hares, little deer scurrying over the stones, and small birds dipping their wings and playing like porpoises around the noses of the jeep. Pairs of eagles soared overhead; herds of sheep and yak increased in size.

The jeep stopped and the driver pointed to a glistening white cone. 'Kailas.'

To reach the holy mountain, the focus of what has been called the greatest and hardest of all earthly pilgrimages, we had travelled west-wards for sixteen days across a series of desolate and noble landscapes. Lorries and jeeps had made our journey simple in comparison to the hardships of other pilgrims.

In the Skanda Purana is written: 'There are no mountains like the Himalaya, for in them are Kailas and Manasarowar.'

CHAPTER 13

Kailas

When we looked at the circle of orange-coloured hills grouped around the snow-covered lignam, Kailas seemed an intimidating distance away. First there was a river to be crossed, then a baked clay corridor, then the mountain. One of the geologists casually mentioned the existence of a pilgrim resthouse.

'I do not know where,' he said, shrugging his shoulders, but adding that the driver might know. He meant the driver of the lorry, and he had to wait for an hour for him to catch up. He confirmed the news, before we drove on a few miles to a dusty track. We were deposited, together with our baggage, beside sloping ground covered with small prickly bushes. A couple of miles away, the line of red foothills met the ground, half-concealing the dome of Kailas which glinted in the sun above them.

The holy mountain of Kailas is unique in its phallic symmetry. Its shape, which has been compared to temples in South India, is one of those rarities in nature, a perfectly regular form, four sides of a crude style facing the four corners of the compass as sharply defined as if they had been chiselled by an axe. Traditionally they are said to be composed of crystal and different jewels, but in fact the mountain is geologically significant as the world's highest deposit of tertiary conglomerate. In other words, it is a giant mound of cemented gravel.

Remotely placed near the world's largest snow barrier among the headstreams of four mighty and holy rivers, the Ganges, the Indus, the Brahmaputra and the Sutlej, the two sacred destinations of pilgrims, the mountain of Kailas and the oval lake of Manasarowar beside it, present in geographical fact the images of natural harmony that are essential to Tibetan and Hindu philosophy. The union of balancing and opposing forces, earth and water, male and female, are here for the pilgrim to see. The image of the mountain, reflected in architecture all over South Asia as far away as Indonesia, evokes the idea of the world Pillar, and suggests the symbol of the Mandala. Kailas was holy for the old followers of shamism with their wild gods; it is holy for Buddhists and it is holy for Hindus.

Shiva, the creator and destroyer, is a god of mountains, and Kailas which he shares with his *shakti*, the goddess Devi, who represents the female aspects of Shiva's qualities, is his special abode and Paradise. The Tibetan counterparts of Shiva and Devi, the four-faced demon Demchog and his consort, Dorje Phangmo, also have their home among the snows of this eastern Olympus where beliefs of Hindu and Buddhist alike are fused in perpetual holiness.

The sacred mountain spire loomed in the distance behind a row of splintered orange hills which seemed sharp as sharks' teeth. The sun was blindingly hot. Caroline took up one pack and I carried the others, dropping them along the way in clusters. We moved very slowly along the track.

After a few hundred yards Caroline said, 'I think I'll go on. You bring up everything.'

I watched her bound away towards a little building surrounded by an encampment of huts, behind which the dome of Kailas showed over its guard of foothills. I followed on slowly with a back-stitch gait, carrying some baggage forward, going back for the rest and taking that beyond the load in front. After about an hour I reached a rough road where groups of women carrying enormous loads were striding along, and a lorry went by crammed with nomads who looked like Red Indians. These were pilgrims. Then a pretty girl caught sight of me and came rushing down to pick up some of the bags and toss them easily up on her back. Further on I could see Caroline standing outside the gate of a walled enclosure that surrounded a low building. She was talking to two men.

When I at last came to the gate I was met by a Tibetan and another Oriental, a plump middle-aged man in a bright blue jacket and yellow cap. The Tibetan was Dorje, who ran this guesthouse for pilgrims. The other:

'I am Dr Kazuhiko Tamanura, Professor of Tourism from Doshisha University, Kyoto, Japan.' Kazi, as we came to know him, smiled and shook hands, dismissing the girl who had carried my bags with a few sweets.

Dorje helped us bring the bags inside and assigned us a room. He was in charge of this very ancient pilgrimage centre, originally built by a king of Bhutan for the benefit of pilgrims from outside Tibet. Controlled by the Bhutanese for centuries, Tarchan was independent of the Gartok Viceroys, and remote and far away, ignored any directives from Lhasa. The lamas who ran it were called Dashok, and they seem to have had a certain style. When Colonel Sherring visited Tarchan in 1905 everyone in the place was drunk; twenty years later, when Colonel Ruttledge journeyed here across the Western Himalayas, the Dashok still appeared to be drunk.

Before 1981 the pilgrimage had been suspended for a twenty-year period, during which any manifestation of Buddhist ceremony was forbidden. Now religion was acceptable once more, and back in China fifty million Christians were allowed to go to church again. Here in western Tibet, after the eclipse of the Cultural Revolution, the resthouse had been rebuilt specifically to accommodate Indian and Nepalese pilgrims. A trickle had already journeyed here across the Himalayas during the three years since the parikarama and festival of Kailas had been resumed, but until this year no foreigners from the West had been here for at least thirty-five years. This year a number of outsiders had made the journey to Tarchan:

One American, who hired two jeeps and drove here from Lhasa. He got official permission by paying thousands of dollars to China Travel. Remembered because he only drank beer.

One Austrian who also paid thousand of dollars to China Travel.

Dr Kazuhiko from Kyoto, Japan.

Two impoverished Irish travellers.

The room we were assigned was simple – no washbasin, no beds, just sacks filled with dried pellets of sheep dung. But it was our first room since leaving Snowlands in Lhasa that didn't smell of urine, and on the whole it was clean. Caroline had a fit of housekeeping. The mud floor was washed and brushed out, the sacks of sheep shit were arranged to make mattresses for our sleeping bags, a clothes line was erected. At her end of the room she made a primitive table out of a plank and a couple of rocks on which she laid out her face creams and washing things, her Walkman, books, camera films and tapes in neat piles.

'I can't stand dirt.'

At my end things were less tidy.

'How can you live like that? You really are at home in a country where people never change their clothes.'

In the evening the Japanese professor entertained us. First he gave us a glass of Japanese whisky, and then out of a large cardboard box he took packets of dried seaweed, prawn chips, dried vegetables and strips of processed beef which he heated on a gas burner.

'Perhaps you like green tea?' he asked as various Tibetans crowded round the door to have a look. Kazi was a member of the Chinese-Japanese Friendship Mountaineering Expedition which at this very

moment was engaged in climbing Memonani, a peak in the Gurla Mandhata mountain range which we could see from the guesthouse. Twenty-
five Japanese and Chinese were out on the slopes of what would be for a
very short time the second highest virgin peak in the world. The Japanese
had worked for almost twenty years to get here; negotiation was sweetened by staggering sums of money, paid for, so Kazi assured us, by the
richest man in Japan.

'You see, we must each pay twenty thousand dollars for the permission.
We also give four new Japanese Landcruisers as a big bribe. The Chinese
are clever people and climbing mountains is political. If we reach the
summit – and there are many problems, plenty of dangerous blue ice on
the way – everyone will be pleased. Already a celebration dinner is
planned in Beijing. Very good for Japanese–Chinese trade.' The food we
were eating, so similar to what was on offer in the Khumbu area, was part
of the expedition's general supplies. Around his room were stacked pieces
of equipment donated by Japanese industries, offering a dazzling display
of Nippon technology, expensive cameras, sound equipment, jostling with
gadgets I didn't recognize. This was stuff that had been left behind; there
were plenty more aids to modern mountaineering up on Memonani.

Before we retired Kazi lent us an extra gas stove and that night we
enjoyed a cup of tea.

Caroline said: 'Don't use two bags. If you remember to use them
carefully, one bag is ample for two cups. We aren't millionaires.' The
sheep dung pellets felt like plastic chips.

It was strange to get up without the feeling of 'Oh God, can we find a lorry
today?' At Tarchan there was no prospect of officials strolling around in
green jackets asking awkward questions.

There was peace. Being so close to Kailas – called Tise by Tibetans –
was a source of wonder. When you looked out you could see the fretted line
of snowpeaks. Sir Thomas Holditch observed how 'the chief obstacles to
Tibetan exploration have been the mountain barriers which surround the
plateau, massed together like a series of gigantic walls. They rise in a
region of unbroken silence like gigantic frosted fortresses until their white
towers are lost in the sky.' Behind the peaks on the far horizon were
Kashmir and Ladakh, Nepal and the Indian plains.

Directly in front of Tarchan the prow of Memonani shone white in the
sun, and below the Gurla mountains among which Memonani starred
were the lakes of Manasarowar and Rakas Tal, associated in holy unity
with Kailas. Manasarowar, in particular, is sacred, and the pilgrim who

reaches its shores acquires immeasurable merit. For the Hindu it is as good a place to die as anywhere along the Ganges.

For the first time since entering Tibet our lives took in a settled pattern. In the morning I would get up and collect the glacial water from the stream that ran down through the pilgrim encampment from the nearby mountain. Upstream, above the encampment, naturally; there followed a long process of filtering and boiling. The boiling was presumably cosmetic, since boiling point was low, and tea was never quite hot enough. Caroline had fixed up the ground sheet from our tent to be hung over the window by night, but, when we took it down by day, onlookers would instantly gather to look through and watch us wash clothes, cook, read and quarrel. Caroline wandered around in her chuba like a convalescent in a cottage hospital.

Behind the pilgrims' resthouse were the remains of the old gompa surrounded by tents with the cone of Kailas shining behind its back. One morning I investigated the old building which for centuries must have been the only solid habitation for scores of miles that had a roof and walls. Until the resthouse was built in 1982, this important centre for pilgrims had been allowed to decay. I walked through the small bare rooms where the lamas had lived and prayed and got drunk, where shepherds now camped down with their meagre possessions . . . a few battered tin pots, or a tea churn with a long elegant brassbound stem. A sheep peered at me from a doorway and an old woman wrapped in a bright Aztec patterned shawl was cooking over a fire. She smiled and said something, but I couldn't stay; the smell of burning dung and damp earth and years of unwashed communal life was overpowering. I felt as if my head was on fire and each short breath made me gasp. In the next dark room a rickety ladder led upwards, and in seconds I was out on the roof, breathing the rarified cold air, looking down on the shimmering golden plain with its two lakes and the background of the Gurla mountains. Behind them I could see more lines of mountains, the Himalayan barrier which was like so many breaking waves.

The lamas had gone. Would the Chinese let any trickle back for the sake of the pilgrim trade? People give you different figures. One estimate has about 120,000 monks in Tibet in 1959 and 2,711 monasteries, many of which were destroyed during the upheaval because they were centres of rebellion. After the fighting many were razed for building material before the further destruction of the Cultural Revolution. At present, nine monasteries with lamas remain in the whole of Tibet.

Perhaps things would change with the new tolerance. Here was

Tarchan rebuilt and functioning as a hostel. This was its third year. Most of the rooms would remain empty until the end of June or the beginning of July when small contingents of Indians and Nepalese would come this way after the passes were free of snow. Tibetan pilgrims did not aspire to stay indoors, but camped all around outside. At this time during the first weeks of June Tarchan accommodated, beside ourselves, Kazi, Dorje, Dorje's aunt and another old lady with cracked blue-tinted glasses and a face as wrinkled as W. H. Auden's, who almost qualified for Holditch's severe estimate of Tibetan looks: 'The life they lead on these sublime heights has wrinkled them exceedingly, the old people being especially hideous.' Witchlike, she was followed everywhere by a small brown cat.

Dorje, a small, sinewy man with a cast eye, could just remember the old unchanged Tibet, warts and all, before the Chinese swept in. He fled into exile in India, where he learnt English, returning to his own country in 1970 to look after his sick father. During the Cultural Revolution his ability to speak English was regarded with the greatest suspicion.

'They said I was a spy.' He did not enlarge on his personal experience of persecution during the years when thousands were killed in a period of unprecedented violence, and much of the social and cultural fabric of Tibetan life was destroyed. The memory is recent, but like so many other Buddhists Dorje displayed a lack of bitterness almost incomprehensible to Westerners; the passive acceptance of suffering is an intrinsic part of the Buddhist path to perfection.

'It is not that we do not care. But our beliefs make us realise how little time we spend in this world.'

'And those who died?'

'They have their reward.'

By day most activity was centred around the small yard crammed with pilgrims' belongings – piles of bags and bound pieces of sheepskin, firewood, posteen coats and supplies of herbs gathered daily for medicinal purposes and left to dry in the sun. In the old days Tarchan was a centre of trade, as well as a pilgrim hospice. Just north of Kailas are important salt deposits, and the whole area used to have a thriving wool trade. We had assumed that sheep caravans travelling between Tibet and India and Nepal had ceased, but we were to find that we were mistaken.

All around us were nomads with their animals. In the early morning I watched them milking their sheep before letting them go free on the mountains, absorbed by the daily spectacle of hundreds of bleating ewes and the gaudy clothes of those who tended them. Getting the ewes into parallel lines for milking, facing each other, heads interlocking, took time and expertise. A description of 1906 shows that the method has not changed. 'These latter are tied neck to neck in a long line, so closely together that movement is impossible, alternate animals looking in different directions, and the women go up and down the line with great rapidity.' Later, when the sun got up people and animals vanished into the hills. A man or woman with a staggering amount of sheep would fade away, expressing a potent force of freedom. The Chinese have had little luck with cooperatives in Tibet.

Often Kazi would invite us for a meal. Why wasn't he on the mountain with the rest of the Chinese–Japanese Friendship Expedition? He was engaged on important research on pilgrims. While his colleagues were busy on their virgin peak, he was a star turn down at Tarchan, as he made a detailed study of the pilgrims and their motives for coming to Kailas. He walked around armed with notebooks, sketchbooks, index cards, typed questionnaires and flipover counter-check lists, tape recorder and Polaroid camera.

The Polaroid was part of his irresistible interviewing technique. After he had questioned his pilgrim, he immediately photographed him, giving him a free coloured print, while keeping a second picture to be filed with his notes. Sometimes he handed out cigarettes, a pen or pencil. Most people had never seen photographs of themselves before. All day long the little courtyard was filled with eager interviewees, monks and shepherds, nomads and merchants from Lhasa, mountain men with their families, who had come from all over the country to the spiritual heart of the Himalayas and the centre of the universe. The pilgrimage to Kailas was the fulfilment of a life-time's ambition, which the coming of Communism had not diminished, and Dr Kazi was one of their rewards.

Dorje was essential to Kazi as interpreter. Squatting together, they would begin their day's work. The Japanese had a shy diffident manner, which put the pilgrims at their ease as Dorje translated. You could see them beginning to enjoy the questions.

'Please ask him the colour of his tent – is it white or brown?'
'White.'
'How many sheep does he own?'
'Sixty.'
'Has he heard of Japan?'
'No.'
'Why does he come here?'
'For the future life.'
'How many days did he travel from his home?'

'Twenty.'

Kazi noted everything down, earnings, the food the pilgrims ate, whether they could read or write, probable age. Occasionally he made a mistake.

'You must not ask if he is married,' Dorje said. 'That is unlucky.'

When everything was written down the Polaroid was produced, the moment everyone was waiting for. Often it was the signal for the pilgrim to go off and change into his best clothes. Here were four young nomads with their wives, swashbuckling figures in embroidered hats and cloaks, two brandishing ornate daggers which intensified the impression of cavaliers. In the old days almost every man carried a sword or a gun. The wives in long black dresses, their hair braided to the height of mantillas, stuck out their tongues and giggled. A tall youth displayed his new cloak edged with fox fur, an old man in a shaggy chuba appeared dazed as he held the little piece of card and watched his figure slowly emerge. And so they came day after day, all morning and during the hot windy afternoon.

Then Kazi decided to do the parikarama around Kailas in the steps of his compatriot, Ekai Kawaguchi, who circled Kailas in 1900.

There are three paths of pilgrimage around the mountain. Most pilgrims take the widest and lowest. One tour is adequate, but many do three or thirteen a particularly holy number. Those who complete twenty-one parikaramas are considered worthy to attempt the middle circuit high across the four faces of the mountain. There is a higher route still, only attainable by those who have achieved an advanced state of Buddhahood, culminating in the hundred and eighth circuit, which is said to ensure Nirvana.

One circuit would do for Kazi. We watched him depart with his two porters and return two days later exhausted, to receive our congratulations before collapsing in his room.

'It was so difficult. I am not used to such things, and you can have no idea how dreadful was the track.'

We planned to follow his example. Originally we toyed with the idea of going around on a yak like Sven Hedin or Ekai Kawaguchi, even though this meant less merit. I would have thought it would have added an added measure of penance. There were no riding yaks available. Dorje's was far away grazing on a mountain. 'Everyone knows my yak.'

He found a young brother and sister who were willing to carry our bags. Pusu Seren Urju and Pusu Chorten were a handsome pair with apple-red cheeks indicating high quantities of red corpuscles in their blood, who found working for foreigners hilarious. Their laughter was uproarious as we showed them our rucksacks, bags, tents, provisions, all to be taken along. First the girl was loaded, and then the boy, everything tied on and balanced by straps across the forehead.

As we left the courtyard Kazi was back at work, three pigtailed nomads standing in front of him waiting for the magic moment when the camera appeared. Outside the guesthouse another lorry crowded with pilgrims roared up after a journey from somewhere far away which must have involved a penitential degree of discomfort. They climbed down laughing and smiling; the sight of Kailas over their heads in the sun was the glorious indication of journey's end. They had little in the way of baggage or food. There were men and women, old men and old women, and babies wrapped in sheepskin. In June it could still snow, and every night water froze solid; summer was short like life itself.

We followed our porters, strapped and bent down with our bundles, as they led us round the edge of the hills. The girl, wearing a fringed scarf that covered her head, a furry jacket and long dress, carried my rucksack, the heavy green army bag and her own rug. Her brother's load was much lighter.

Pale yellow flowers bloomed among the rocks, and, as the sun came up behind our backs and warmed us, the light picked out details like a probing torch. A mani wall of stones, elaborately carved with sacred texts and figures of Buddha, had stood there over the centuries as a reminder of our transitory existence. A hare twitched his ears as he saw us pass, and others bounded across the grass, tame as dogs. Reverence for life, the philosophy that Albert Schweitzer shared with Buddhists, ensured that this morning the tame hares around Kailas had their place in the Buddhist cosmology. (Not everyone feels this way. Hares are incorporated in the Sino–Tibetan cuisine, and numerous English travellers have shot and eaten them.)

The waterless air conveyed the sun's rays in relays as it hit the plain, changing it from green to golden brown, coral pink and gold. The colours evoked Blake and his natural world to which hares belong. We walked in a silence which in Tibet has a quality of its own. 'A four dimensional space silence,' Fosco Maraini called it. 'There is the yellow ochre silence of the rocks, the blue-green silence of the ice-peaks; the silence of the valleys over which hawks wheel in the sun; and there is the silence that purifies everything, dries the butter, pulverises the bones and leaves in the mind an inexpressible dreamy sweetness, as if one had attained some ancient fatherland lost since the beginning of history.'

We came up to a young man prostrating himself along the route. It would take him about twelve days to complete the circuit, following the prescribed rules for covering the ground. There is the way to stand and lift your arms, the way you pause and pray and measure your length. The distance around Kailas is about fifty kilometres, much of it over snow and rocks and stones. He wore the uniform of prostrating pilgrims, the protective sheepskin apron and wooden blocks strapped to his hands. Beyond him we caught up with two more men making the same progress, and we would pass many more.

All morning we followed the traditional route towards Kailas, a dusty trail marked out with little piles of stones and chortons stuck with blue, white, red and yellow flags. Pilgrims were walking and praying around each one. At midday we turned our backs on the plain at a place where another chorton covered in tattered flags marked the first important point of the circuit. It stood at the foot of the circle of high buff-coloured hills that had seemed red or orange when seen from a distance guarding Kailas; now the holy mountain towered in front of us.

At 22,000 feet Kailas is a modest peak compared to many Himalayan giants, but its shape is striking and unmistakable. It has been compared to a chorton, the handle of a millstone, a great lignam. 'The eastern face is crystal, the south is sapphire, the west is ruby and the north is gold,' one legend said; another claimed it was clothed with fragrant flowers and shrubs. Sven Hedin was more prosaic; he considered Kailas 'a tetrahedron set in a prism'. At some periods during the summer the ridges on the south face, catching unmelted snow, are seen to record the holy mark of the swastika.

Rather than trying to capture the ecstasies of pilgrims, it is safer to record the impressions of strangers. 'It is incomparably the most famous mountain in the world,' Sven Hedin wrote, 'Mount Everest and Mont Blanc cannot vie with it.' An earlier lone traveller, Henry Strachey, catching sight of Kailas's snows in the summer of 1864, considered it the most beautiful mountain he had ever seen, 'a king of mountains, full of majesty'.

A hot wind stirred up the dust as we walked towards a gorge that opened out from the rust-coloured rocks with Kailas above our heads. Two horsemen were riding towards us, the hard wooden saddles of their ponies placed on embroidered saddle cloths; their plaited manes and tails were tied with pink bows. The riders, wearing fur coats, fur hats and high decorated fur boots, spurred their mounts beside a stream known as God's River, trotting on what appeared to be bright green grass. But when we came closer and the ponies were urged past us, the green dissolved and, like other spectacles in the thin air, turned out to be hallucinatory; all I could see were specks of burnt foliage among the rocks.

A little further on we came to a huge wooden pole covered with coloured yak skins whose streamers tumbling from its head gave it the look of a giant maypole. In a land without trees, the sight of such a giant which must have been carried up painstakingly from the forests of the Himalayas was a startling herald to the entrance of the gorge. Inside, the path followed a dark, cold valley; above our heads one side was crossed with moving shadows, while the other sparkled in light where the world of snow and ice began above the crests of stone. Occasionally there was the thunder of an avalanche, the crack of falling rocks, a distant puff of snow and a long silence. Beside us the murmur of the little river continued undisturbed, a burble like monks praying in the dark.

We joined a group of pilgrims camping under a mani wall glistening with butter spread over the years. Two men and their wives, one with a parcelled baby, welcomed us and offered us tea. They had lit a small fire using the same sort of pellets of sheep shit on which we had been trying to sleep for a week. The smallest and most ordinary things would keep them alive on the parikarama, ground-up barley meal taken from a leather bag, rancid butter swirling in the bowls of luke-warm brick tea which they shared with us.

After we had swallowed tea and tsampa in the cold, the family went ahead, while we continued more slowly among the stream of pilgrims who walked and prayed, spun prayer wheels, or carried poles or staves, usually with prayer flags tied to the tips to help them over the rocks. There were also a number of Nepalese pilgrims carrying umbrellas. Now we reached another chorton where pilgrims stopped and prayed, circling it in the prescribed clockwise direction. Here was the family who had given us tea going round briskly, baby bundled on his mother's back, reciting their mantras and religious texts while we gasped for breath. This chorton had an imprint of Buddha's foot, the next one along decked with flags contained the bones of a holy man, and now we were passing a cave revered as a place of particular sanctity because it was once the abode of an ascetic. It may well have been one of those where in the old days lamas were walled up for a grim bout of meditation.

We continued to follow the track beside God's River, our porters trotting many yards in front, occasionally stopping so that we could catch up. Along the way groups of pilgrims travelled with us, many passing us, others stopping to pray or picnic, the occasional dogged prostrator inching his way up the dark valley. Above us was still the steep line of corrugated brown peaks that guarded Kailas, and from time to time the holy mountain would emerge from a cauldron of clouds with snow running down its shoulder like a Christmas pudding. Once Caroline stopped and took out her paintbox to sketch the dome in the freezing air before it vanished again in swirling mist. The effect on passing pilgrims of seeing a recognizable image of their holy mountain was electrifying. They stopped, stared and muttered; one elderly nomad, his face scorched by sun and wind, snatched up the still-wet watercolour and reverently touched his forehead with it.

At noon we camped beside the frozen river bed. Kazi's stove didn't work.

Any benign and profound thoughts about holy places and the nature of pilgrimage and faith evaporated in a high altitude fit of rage. All over the Himalayas I had been demonstrating either the failure of Western technology in the face of challenge, or the paucity of my travel budget. But I had thought the Japanese might have come up with something more efficient. We watched water remain sullen, leaving rice half-raw, while the busy little flame of our porters' turd fire a few yards away mocked us as it cooked their tsampa.

No need to linger. Beyond the river the track twisted in a gentle bow and the valley widened as we started to climb towards the Dolma Pass. Among the weeping spires of ice and frozen waterfall, we came across a large herd of yaks, big Tibetan yaks with fringes over their eyes and rivers of hair falling down to tiny protruding legs. Some were golden, others spotted or dabbled with white, but most of them were black as ebony. What did they live on? Moss, perhaps, lichen? There was nothing visible for them to graze on in this wilderness, certainly nothing in the way of grass. 'Pousse-Cailloux' of the Army Transport Corps watched yaks grazing in empty country on their way to Lhasa. 'Smooth your hand along the table. Bare. Just like that.' He had great admiration for 'an uncouth beast of burden which in some primeval fashion, seemed to be able to pick up a living off the bitter barrens across which we were slowly advancing. Watch it for an hour when turned loose to "graze". At the end of the time you would swear a solemn oath that its diet was stones and shingle. As a matter of fact, it seems to be able to dig up with its great fore-feet a subsoil saxifrage moss of sorts, a thing which must be almost chemically concentrated nourishment to support such a vast and hairy bulk.'

How spoilt Sod and Mucker had been compared to their cousins snatching meagre grazing beneath Kailas. Big as these yak were, wild yak would be bigger. My ambition to see a wild yak was not fulfilled – unless, I torture myself, somewhere on our journey a herd or an individual might have passed in view of one of the lorries in which we rode. There must be some left. Western Tibet used to be famous for its herds of wild yak, drong in Tibetan. They are massive animals, standing six feet high in the withers with a reputation of being as ferocious as lions. Given the temperament of domesticated yak, that must be true. Drong have been hunted to the edge of extinction, since, unlike their domesticated cousins, they failed to qualify among Tibetans for the licence to live. No doubt the Chinese have taken pot shots at wild yaks; there is no estimate of surviving numbers. Heinrich Harrer saw herds during his escape; earlier, Colonel Bailey described a huge herd he saw grazing near his camp in the region of Geer. 'I saw what I think was one of the finest and most impressive sights in my life. As soon as they smelt a man, the whole herd lifted their heads, waved their big bushy tails over their backs, and as though drilled, galloped off.'

We were climbing at over 18,000 feet, moving very slowly alongside all the pilgrims, every now and then passing someone flat on his stomach. At one of our numerous pauses for breath Caroline encountered an old lady resting, wrinkled like a relief map of the Himalayas.

'She's exactly your age,' Caroline said.

I recalled Po Chu-i's thoughts on being sixty. In Arthur Waley's translation:

> Between thirty and forty one is distracted by the Five Lusts;
> Between seventy and eighty one is prey to a hundred diseases . . .
> I am still short of illness and decay and far from decrepit age.
> Strength of limb I still possess to seek the rivers and hills.

Among the men Sven Hedin brought with him on his trans-Himalayan expedition was an old man of sixty-two who was so keen to travel 'that he had the forethought to pack up a shroud that he might be buried decently if he died on the way'. It was comforting to remember he had survived.

By dusk we had been walking for almost twelve hours; the gleaming sides of Kailas were directly above us and it was very cold. In the old days there used to be four monasteries along the route, 'like jewels in a bracelet', to shelter travellers – three were near the summit of the pass. But up here nothing remained to welcome pilgrims, and we were lucky to erect our tent inside the shelter of what seemed to be a run-down yersa situated beside an abyss. A camp site for ascetics – no prospect of keeping warm as icy winds rattled the tent's sides. Outside were the porters; from time to time we heard a song or the hum of a mantra.

'For God's sake, shouldn't we ask them to come in?'

'How do you think they can possibly squeeze in beside us?'

It was true that the tent was crowded out and with the best will in the world there was no room for two other bodies. We were not breaking any rules. A traveller who came here in 1848 explained the procedure:

'We carried two small tents eight or ten feet in length, one for our own use, the other for the Bhotias; and if it is asked how our sixteen men shall get into one such tent, it must be explained that there is an aristocracy in the heart of the snowy mountains – and that the underlings were expected to lie wholly in the open air day and night, which they did without any apparent inconvenience.' A hundred years on, Professor Tucci mentioned how Tibetans slept out in the open wrapped in their robes and woollen blankets.

But 19,000 feet up at the summit of the Dolma Pass? Brother and sister were softly praying outside. Their prayers may have kept them warmer than I was in my sleeping bag. 'Perfectly adequate for sub-zero conditions.'

At dawn Kazi's stove failed us again before we resumed climbing. Our porters appeared none the worse for wear. Nor did the pilgrims who climbed with us, without visible sign of camping gear.

The sun ascended slowly as we walked in Indian file, our porters moving steadily in front of us, towards another snow field, behind a group of pilgrims which included our hosts of the day before. The baby's fur-wrapped head stuck out of a sack, alert black eyes looked back at us from a small crimson face. The crowd of pilgrims was becoming denser, and more and more were prostrated on the wrinkled icy surface of the pass.

Caroline wore chuba and face mask, although why she needed a face mask at 18,589 feet was a mystery. It was midday and we had reached the very top of the pass, where a large pillar of black stone decorated with flags cut the skyline. The Dolma Rock marked the culmination of the pilgrimage. The shining polished appearance of the bottom part of the monolith came from butter smeared on the sides as far as human arms could reach. Numerous small objects were embedded in the grease. In the old days a pilgrim would smear a bit of butter on the stone, pluck out a lock of his hair and slap it into the butter. According to Sven Hedin, the stone resembled 'a huge wig-block, from which black locks of hair flutter in the wind . . . . Teeth are even stuck in the chinks of the Dolma Rock, forming whole rosaries of teeth.'

Today's offerings were a lot less grisly, just coins and bank notes, a few sweets and nuts, a piece of chewing gum and a photograph of the Dalai Lama. Would I revive an old custom by leaving my own teeth there?

We were in a state of immense exhaustion, as mountain sickness increasingly claimed us with shortness of breath and a headache that made me feel that my skull was much too small to contain my brain. For a long time we sat gasping, watching the column of pilgrims pass, praying and touching the great rock. Behind us, far below, other figures were waiting patiently in an endless line like the famous photograph of the Klondyke.

Somewhere hidden in the snowfield was the holy lake of Gaurikund which remained frozen all the year. Later in the summer when the snow retreated and it was uncovered for a few weeks, the faithful would break the ice and place a little water on their heads. Now they could only wait their turn to greet the holy pillar with reverence. We watched a group of shaggy men carrying spears as they prayed and touched the great lignam. Then a family group, then more nomads and their women – all those we had seen arriving at Tarchan on foot and in lorries from vast distances to conclude their pilgrimage with a journey of immense hardship. The sight of so many trudging through the snow, waiting to make their devotions at the shining black, butter-smeared, flag-hung rock standing in snow and ice was sublime. When Sven Hedin saw a similar line of pilgrims eighty years ago he observed how 'they feel no weariness, for they know that every step improves their prospects of the world beyond the river of death'.

We were the intruders, myself and Caroline with her camera and sketch book. No doubt the next thing would be a film crew. I wondered how much longer Kailas would remain isolated from outsiders and non-believers. Would foreigners travel this way in the numbers that wandered under Everest, to mingle with the great queue of the devout below us?

Time had fled and we had recovered enough to begin the descent from the pass through another steep slippery valley of snow and ice. A line of pilgrims was holding hands to try and stop slipping since there were no aids to safety, no guides or ropes or handholds. I watched men and women of all ages, arm in arm, slithering down the bone-breaking ice. My contemporary was there, being helped down by her daughter, a handsome young woman wearing long earrings of coral and seed pearls. Slowly, slowly we made progress down the slippery trail, and then Kailas was behind us with all its ice and mystery. We came to a different world, a windy valley free of snow through which a stream bubbled over rocks.

With muted green, brown and grey colours predominating, it resembled a glen in Donegal except that yaks were grazing with the sheep, and there was not a blade of grass to be seen. The bright greens that shone with a quality of stained glass could only be mistaken for grass at a distance – when you looked closely you found lichens and moss growing all over the rock.

We stopped to eat and once again the gas burner lost out against dung fires as women in their long dresses went searching for fuel. Yak turds were king-sized, sheep pellets smaller and harder work to gather. Dung-collecting is part of the daily round, and at any nomad encampment you can watch people moving about slowly looking for argols (a much prettier word than turds). The yak provides not only meat, milk, butter, cheese and wool, but also fuel. In a country without trees, the large yak dropping is important for making a fire, and the very survival of many nomads would be in doubt without the yak standing by. Père Huc, the Lazarist missionary father who travelled in Tibet in the early nineteenth century, described how 'when one is lucky enough to find half concealed among the grasses an argol recommended for its size and dryness, there comes over the heart a tranquil joy, one of the those sudden emotions which create a transient happiness'. Today at the foothills of Kailas they were much in demand, but there seemed to be enough for all; soon blue pillars of smoke rose all round us for the last meal of the pilgrimage.

The final stage back to the resthouse took a further three hours. Snow was falling, and some shepherds, immobile as snowmen, stood and watched us pass in the blizzard. We went down round the last bluff and hill towards the familiar plain.

At the point where the valley opened up to the plain we found a small derelict gompa whose sole inhabitant was a very old lama with whom we drank tea. This was the only holy building left on the parikarama; the monasteries of Juntilphu and Nandi Phu with its offerings of matchlocks, swords and shields and a pair of elephant tusks, and Diripu, which were all situated near the summit of the pass, have been destroyed. Juntilphu and Nandi Phu had been maintained by the same Bhutanese authority that controlled Tarchan. Although this one remaining temple was a bleak little place without thangkas, shrines or gilded Buddhas, it appeared to have a future – workmen were repairing it after the long night of the Cultural Revolution.

We reached Tarchan in the evening when the rays of the setting sun were touching the distant mountains; snow peak after peak was caught in the light before vanishing suddenly in darkness. We passed a herd of sheep marching across the hills throwing up dust, each animal carrying two small woollen bags strapped to its back. Then Tarchan came in sight.

The parikarama of about twenty-eight miles had taken us two days.

'I was worried about you,' Dorje said. 'Such an old man walking the round.'

CHAPTER 14

Spring Festival and Manasarowar

We felt a sense of achievement, having joined a select group of foreigners who have made the parikarama of Kailas. They include:

Ekai Kawaguchi, the Japanese Buddhist, who toured on a yak in 1900. At the sight of Kailas he was inspired with 'the profoundest feelings of pure reverence and I looked up to it as a natural mandala, the mansion of Buddhas and Bodhisattvas. Filled with soul-stirring thoughts and fancies, I addressed myself to this sacred pillar of nature, confessed my sins and performed to it the obeisance of one hundred and eighty bows.'

Sven Hedin, the ambitious, emotional, wrong-headed Swede. He may have ended up as a discredited, lonely old Nazi, but the travels of his youth were stupendous, and his account of his journeys in Tibet is still an inspiration. He went round Kailas in 1907, also on a yak. 'I saw the silent procession, the faithful bands, youths and maidens, strong men with wife and child, grey old men, ragged fellows who lived like parasites on the charity of other pilgrims, scoundrels who had to do penance for a crime, robbers who had plundered peaceful travellers, chiefs, officials, herdsmen and nomads; a varied train of shady humanity on the thorny road which after interminable ages ends in the deep peace of Nirvana. August and serene Shiva looks down from his paradise, and Hlabsen from his jewelled palace on the innumerable human beings below who circled like asteroids in the sun, round the foot of the mountain.'

Colonel and Mrs Ruttledge. We had thought that Caroline might be the first European woman to walk around the holy ice mountain, but Mrs Ruttledge, who travelled to Kailas with her husband in 1926, beat her to it. Her feelings about making the circuit do not seem to be on record, but her husband, Hugh Ruttledge, who had come to Tibet to investigate complaints about the trade between Tibetans and Bhotias, wrote up his experiences in the *Geographical Journal*. His style is clipped and precise,

[*170*]

lacking any mystical content. After commenting on the state of drunkenness among the lamas at Tarchan, he noted the variety of the pilgrims who stayed there: '. . . full of interesting types – nomads from the north, pilgrims from Khan and the Chinese frontier, some distant tradesmen . . . beggars of all descriptions and three devoted Hindus from the Central and United Provinces – recently robbed and miserably cold and underfed.' (Other travellers noted how pilgrims who arrived penniless at the mountain took to banditry to keep themselves going.)

Colonel Wilson accompanied the Ruttledges to western Tibet, but circled the mountain at a different time. He had the impious notion of climbing the sacred lingam. He and his porter, whose name was Satan, saw a white ridge and a possible route. 'Sahib,' said Satan, 'we can climb that.' But the Colonel lacked time for the difficult ascent. 'Above, the mountain was almost perpendicular, while below was a pitch black abyss of incredible depth and steepness, quite the most awesome place I have ever looked into. The sides were partly slatey black shale and partly snow black with dust and debris . . . I think that neither of us would have placed a foot on the treacherous surface for all the precious metal and stones of which the mountain is said to be made.' Moreover: 'To make matters worse it began to snow, and suddenly without preliminary warning of any sort came a brilliant flash of lightning and a shattering crash of thunder immediately over our heads. Truly the gods were resisting our intrusion.'

Bhagwan Shiri Hansa published his account of a pilgrimage around Kailas with a rich introduction by W. B. Yeats. Yeats wrote of how 'thousands have circled [the mountain], some bowing at every step, some falling prostrate measuring the ground with their bodies – on another ring, higher yet, inaccessible to human feet, the gods move in adoration. Still greater numbers . . . know that a tree covered with miraculous fruit rises from the lake at its foot, that sacred swans sang there, that the four great rivers of India rise there with sands of gold, silver, emerald and ruby, that at certain seasons from the lake . . . springs a golden phallos . . . In this mountain, this lake, a dozen races find the birthplace of their gods and themselves. We, too, have learnt from Dante to imagine our Eden, our Earthly Paradise upon a mountain, penitential rings upon the slope . . .'

The Bhagwan emphasized the difficulties of his pilgrimage. Part of his troubles arose from his dislike of Tibetans: 'Credulous by nature . . . mean, cruel, and unscrupulous, ignorant even of the common courtesies of human dealings.' The parikarama was terrible. At Gaurikund lake, 'everywhere there was snow and ice, snow and ice. My lips became green and blue with the severe cold; my nerves seemed ready to burst, and respiration extremely difficult.' He complained of 'bitter cold, piercing winds, incessant snow, inordinate hunger and deadly solitude . . . The body becomes numb and unable to bear the pangs. Snow covered me up to my breast, and till after midnight I was fighting desperately with my mind.'

Unimpressed, the *Geographical Journal* gave the Bhagwan a generally bad review. 'By way of encouragement to the prospective buyer, the publishers state that Mount Kailas is almost inaccessible, and that only Hindu adepts who have attained a very high step of spiritual development make their pilgrimage to it. In sober truth the mountain can be reached by any man with a reasonably sound pair of legs and a stout heart in about a week's travel from the Indian frontier.'

Perhaps the last European to make the circuit before we did was Herbert Tichy, a twenty-three-year-old Austrian much influenced by the travels of Hedin, who came to Tibet in 1936 dressed as an Indian 'and not a very grand one either. My hair was long and matted, my turban a dirty grey and my shirt, which I wore like all Indians outside my trousers, was for the most part anything but white.' He made the parikarama with two Indian companions, taking striking photographs of pilgrims. 'It is impossible with words and almost with pictures to bring Tibet close to other people. One would have to relate all the vibrations of a thousand thoughts . . . that one has experienced in the presence of the scenery.'

Even our porters were pleased that we had achieved the greatest of earthly pilgrimages. For the whole time they had been with us there had been no acrimony. I felt a sense of my own inadequacy; how can people who endure so much always remain friendly and cheerful?

Spring was being celebrated at Kailas. The great garlanded pole we had seen at the head of the gorge marking the beginning of the parikarama would be replaced to the accompaniment of all kinds of different rites. For Dorje the most important thing about the festival was that it was taking place at all. For seventeen years from 1966 to 1983 it had been prohibited, and a whole generation of people had grown up without taking part in its ancient rituals.

For the next few days he organized the arrival of the thousands of pilgrims who descended on Tarchan. He was everywhere, directing mothers with crying children, or sorting out a group of nomads carrying daggers, their chubas peeled back to reveal tough torsos, who strode into

[*172*]

the courtyard making demands in harsh grating voices. Every few minutes another pilgrim group would descend from the lorry to be told where to pitch their tents or find water and other provisions. Many stored their possessions in the courtyard which became fuller by the moment with old coats, woollen blankets, decorated rugs and yak-skin bundles.

Besides sorting out pilgrims' problems Dorje arranged the ceremonies for the third festival since the long lapse. He had invited along a young lama who had made twenty-two circuits of Kailas and hoped to do at least a hundred. Apart from being a priest, Karma Tsatar was also a doctor of Tibetan medicine, which by all accounts is peculiar. He could not escape from Kazi who produced the questionnaire the moment he arrived. Age, interests, why he wished to visit Kailas, his reasons for becoming a lama. He cooperated with detachment and humour and got the polaroid portrait showing a smiling shaven-headed young man in a long yellow sheepskin coat.

'What is Kazi going to do with all that information?'

'Someone will write a paper about Kailas or pilgrimage in western Tibet or nomadic tribes or the survival of Buddhism under Communism. With academics nothing gets wasted.' Caroline had studied for a PhD.

From early morning we could hear the lama Karma Tsatar chanting away in Dorje's section of the guesthouse which had been rearranged. Dorje, the two old ladies and the calico cat crowded into the front room while the small room behind was converted into a temple. In spirit the lama's presence reminded me of a priest coming to do the Stations in a farmer's house back in Ireland. The cupboard acted as an altar, a flickering butter lamp balanced on an empty cocoa tin and a small drum hung from the ceiling. The lama sat crouched against a wall, reciting mantras, seemingly oblivious to the pilgrims perpetually crowding in. When he finished one page, it was taken out and replaced by another, and in spite of his zeal in reciting there was a pleasant casualness about the scene. If a man came in during the prayers and talked to him in the middle of his reading, he wasn't at all put out. Someone would be passing around chang, while next door the old women endlessly pounded churnfuls of tea. For an hour or so we crouched on the floor sharing offerings of little cakes made in the shape of Kailas and painted bright red. There were plates of nuts and sticky sweets, thimblefuls of barley grain and a sickly-sweet drink served in a silver-rimmed skull.

The next day we all set off for the ceremony of erecting the new maypole. We were travelling along the same route we had taken towards Kailas two days before together with Dorje and a small party which included the Chinese geologists who had arrived at Tarchan the night before.

The morning was windless and perfect, the sky deep blue, the mountains white and golden, the plain tinged with sapphire and emerald. The colours of the landscape were echoed in pilgrims' clothes for everyone was wearing their best and the strong clear colours were attuned to their surroundings. Much in evidence were long shocking-pink dresses, embroidered cloaks and dresses and wonderful hats, some lined with fur and perched on women's heads like embroidered cushions, bonnets of snow-white wool and stiff Gretchen caps. Among the men was a great variety of cowboy extravaganzas in black and brown with immense brims that had the effect of dwarfing the proud wearer's face until it resembled a nut or a berry.

Dorje was wearing a long gown of chocolate-coloured silk and had brought along a camera, a relic of his Indian days.

'We must take three photographs of everything', he said, focusing on some pilgrims circling a chorton. The figure three, representing the trinity of Buddha, Sarma and Sanga, was auspicious. To Caroline it seemed a waste of good film.

From every direction groups of pilgrims were walking towards the gorge. As we rounded the last hill we could see scores of tents in front of us. Father Huc compared similar tents to huge black spiders with long thin legs, their bodies resting on the ground. Some were little conical erections with spears for tent poles, others were more elaborate and rectangular, and looked like Noah's Arks. Flags were everywhere.

So much of the picturesque quality of Tibetan life has disappeared, the robes of higher officials, the mulberry silk gowns, the embroidered under-coats, the wide-brimmed papier-mâché topees lacquered with gold, the yellow woollen hats shaped like legionnaires' helmets – such formalized frivolities have given way to pea-green uniforms. But here was a glimpse of a fast-vanishing world.

It was a time for prayer and enjoyment for pigtailed nomads, yak herders, shepherds, lamas, nuns, battered old men and women and plenty of giggling girls, many wearing make-up, since pale complexions are desirable. Both sexes were loaded with jewellery, silver necklaces set with egg-sized lumps of turquoise and the warm chestnut of amber beads. Flintlocks decorated with coral and silver balanced from girdles: portraits of the Dalai Lama hung from pilgrims' necks.

A good many of the horsemen carried spears and old guns. When Richard Strachey visited Kailas in 1846 the scene he witnessed was very like the one being recorded by Dorje and Caroline's cameras. The things men carried were similar, purses, pouches, knives, guns, while the women wore then as they do still 'a tremendous châtelaine which seemed to contain all conceivable objects ever invented for the use of a Tibetan household'. Only the slouch hats for which the Himalayan people ultimately owe a debt to the Boers, and then to the British Army which adopted them for a time, had not been introduced in Strachey's time. People still carry the brass or silver reliquary boxes which he said con-tained 'maybe charms or maybe their Penates in the form of a clay figure of Buddha and blessed by the Grand Lama at Lhasa'. Although these boxes are religious objects, we found pilgrims were just as willing to sell them together with their prayer wheels and jewellery as had people in the streets of Lhasa.

A line of ponies and yaks was being driven up, the ponies mincing along, the big black yaks lumbering, followed by nomads in fur-lined coats and coloured boots, their left arms swinging free as they swaggered along. A yak caravan loaded down with sacks and poles had just appeared from around the hills, the animals giving out their familiar grunts, the drivers shouting with delight now they had arrived. Caroline in her mask was attracting constant stares and comment. An old lady came up and patted her chuba, now she was circled by a group of beautiful girls in silk dresses and striped aprons, their faces painted and rouged, strings of shells around their waists. Other girls wore lines of little brass bells that rang out as they walked.

The great pole lying on the ground, eighteen times a man's length, was being dressed by groups of pilgrims. Two men sat outside a tent sewing together coloured prayer flags donated by the devout, including a string that had been brought up by a party of Nepalese. Others decorated the shaft with strips of yak hide, a blacksmith hammered away at the huge metal chains, men and women walked around it praying, and a lama blessed the work by throwing handfuls of rice over the stump.

The intention had been to raise it during the afternoon, but by five o'clock after a couple of attempts and much praying, nothing had hap-pened. Although teams of men and women had done some preliminary heaving at the chains, the carpenter who was overseeing the work wasn't satisfied. Then the wind got up and the crowd in its holiday clothes was enveloped in yellow dust. As people wandered around from tent to tent, a row started when a horseman plunged into the middle of bare-shouldered pigtailed nomads, to be pulled from his pony by some angry men carrying spears and holy texts. Time passed; two Japanese Landcruisers drove up

[*175*]

containing members of the mountaineering team which had just succeeded in climbing Memonani, together with the first ever Chinese television team to come into this area of western Tibet. Suddenly a microphone
was thrust under my chin.

'You are from where?'

I admitted to Ireland, but otherwise answered questions with a Gaelic
shrug.

The television crew consisted of big burly men wearing tracksuits
emblazoned HIGHER PERFORMANCE GORTEX, most of whom
appeared to be urban Chinese from Beijing and Shanghai. Now that
religion was respectable, it was possible to entertain Han comrades back
home with picturesque views of ceremonies in far-flung corners.

'What do you think of Tibet?' I asked the soundman who was unpack-
ing microphones and other equipment.

'Not like.'

Cameras whirred, a lama was interviewed, Tibetan brothers and sisters
in exotic costumes very different from the uniforms of the cities were
caught on film. It was well for them to capture the past that had been
despised; already there were portents of things to come among the pilgrims – from time to time beneath an embroidered robe you would catch a
glimpse of light-weight shoes and jeans.

The pole-raising ceremony did not take place that day, and as evening
approached the cameras were packed away. We walked back to Tarchan,
where the resthouse had become inundated with Chinese. In addition to
the cameramen, a couple of journalists and the geologists, a mysterious
Mr Su had arrived, who, we learned, worked for the government in
neighbouring Pulan. For the first time since our arrival we began to feel
vulnerable.

The night was hellish after the Chinese switched on a generator whose
humming killed all ideas of sleep. Perhaps to make up, they offered us a lift
in the geologists' jeep next morning. As we banged our way over the rocks
back to the site of the ceremony, I could make out through the small
window which didn't open groups of pilgrims going a pleasanter way by
walking in the sun.

Once again preparations were being made to pull the pole upright into
position by its four chains. At first the ceremony seemed to be proceeding
smoothly, and by ten o'clock the carpenter had given his signal for the
teams standing at the end of each chain to begin pulling. As the cameras
recorded the event, the huge tree trunk, bigger than a telegraph pole, was
raised foot by foot over the heads of the crowd. From every tent and from

every corner the people watched this vernal emblem of their religion rise into the western skies under the holy mountain for the third springtime since the ceremony had been revived. A group of lamas were chanting prayers, men and women prostrated themselves and a lonely shepherd, watching the event from the top of a rose-coloured rock, stopped whistling to gaze across.

And then everything went wrong. After the seventeen-year gap those who had been accustomed to overseeing the smooth running of the tense ceremony had gone, and, although the pole had been raised without incident for the past two years, the actual mechanics of leverage had still not been worked out with confidence. Enveloped in skins, streamers flapping, a yellow-painted basin at its top, the pole stood upright for twenty seconds; then it began to totter. Perhaps one of the teams was pulling its chain too hard. Before anyone could call out there was an almighty crash and it came down, missing me by a couple of yards. There it lay, splintered in two.

Miraculously, no one in the huge crowd was killed. A woman, slightly hurt, was surrounded by well-wishers while the lamas chanted mournfully outside a tent. The gaiety was extinguished. What had gone wrong? Many reasons were given. The chief lama was said to have hurried the prayers. Perhaps the failure was a portent of irrevocable change signalled by the presence of the cameras and by our own intrusion. Like the American plane which flew over Lhasa during the war, we may have represented a blasphemy that had to be punished.

For the rest of the day the crowd waited around anxiously while the broken halves of the pole were tenderly lifted into place and the carpenters began to splice the pieces of wood together, working at the join in the same way as an old sailing ship damaged in a storm is fitted out with a jury rig.

While waiting, we were invited into tents for tea and tsampa, snug and comfortable interiors, hospitality that put strangers at their ease. A fire in the centre, smoke making its way to the small vent in the roof, always the small shrine attended by butter lamp and picture of the Dalai Lama. Often the tent pole was a pilgrim's spear or javelin. An old couple in one tent, faces cleft with age. Children in another, with the good manners and grace of noblemen. A herdsman came into another and tried to sell Caroline the chunky turquoises he took from around his neck. ('Too expensive. I have experience of Lhasa prices.') Another cup of tea with a lama and his friends. He was dressed in a long saffron gown and wore a pigtail curled on his head like a bun. He had a bad leg; with a smile he pulled up his gown for us to see the livid flesh, and receive a dab of antiseptic cream from us. Stoicism is still needed in a land without medicines. Beside his travelling shrine he had a box full of Buddhist insignia from which he took a towering ceremonial hat more marvellous than any we had seen yet, trimmed with fur and decorated in gold braid. Caroline took a photograph of him blowing a trumpet against the white cone of Kailas.

Another tent, the smiling host and hostess stoking up the fire with a handful of sheep shit, dispensing basins of tea with the odd hair floating on top and offering us a bone. We became adept at hesitation. Another invitation, another smoky interior with altar, icon and smiles, a cosy dung fire, a briquette of tea, more bowls of swill to be surreptitiously emptied behind a mat or cushion and then insistently refilled. One traveller has compared the taste of Tibetan tea to water in an oriental harbour. Peter Fleming seasoned it with vinegar and Worcester sauce.

Just before dusk the broken pole was spliced. Now it rose again under Dorje's direction, and this time there was no mishap and everything was properly secured. But the joy and excitement of the festival had gone with the sense of shock and dismay and the silence when it fell.

As we walked away from the gorge, the pole with its prayer flags was being circled by the crowd, while the light fell behind the mountains. Other pilgrims were moving in prostration or setting off on the parikarama. The festival was a particularly auspicious time to make the round, and one circuit now was the equivalent of thirteen made at another time.

Back at Tarchan we encountered some Nepalese pilgrims who had crossed the barrier of snow mountains. Unlike Tibetans they were fully equipped with mountaineering clothes and camping gear.

'We take bus from Kathmandu,' Mr Kurong their leader said, 'then we walk. I bring food, tents, everything. In western Nepal there is nothing. Very difficult. My wife get very sick.' Most of the time she lay groaning in the small tent Mr Kurong had brought along while he remained in the best of humour. A stout, jolly man, he owned a small shop in Kathmandu that sold trekking equipment which his son managed while he made the pilgrimage.

We asked, 'How long would it take to reach the first Nepalese town after crossing the Tibet–Nepal frontier?'

'About three days.'

'Can you buy food?'

'There is none.'

'Would it be possible to hire horses or yak?'

Mr Kurong shrugged. 'Perhaps you may have good luck.'

When we made our itinerary in Lhasa, we had concentrated on reaching Kailas without looking beyond that moment. Now our plans for leaving were vague and our map was almost empty of place names. Many of the ones we had been able to mark in suffered from the usual changes in nomenclature that make Tibetan map-reading a traveller's nightmare. Maps had hardly improved since Madame David-Neel's day. 'They are of but little use to the traveller, if indeed they can be of any use at all. The names on them seldom correspond to those one hears from natives. The rivers and mountain ranges are not really in the places they are shown to be, and a number of them are completely imaginary.'

Most of our information had been obtained from Bradley lying on his sickbed in Snowlands Hotel. 'Pulan. Near frontier with Chinese customs and checkpost. To be avoided. Tinker. Walk one day. Nepalese customs. No resthouse. No food. Darchula. Walk three days. Tent and food necessary. No yak. Mahindarnagar. Two days' walk. Resthouse. Bus via India.'

The next day we got a signal that we would have to move on when the geologists invited us into their room for lunch. Halfway through the noodles and the affable conversation one of them produced from his inner jacket pocket the essential travel permit for western Tibet and asked if we had similar ones. There was an exchange of smiles as Caroline put on a brilliant display of not quite understanding what he was saying. He put away his document and picked up his chopsticks again, having given us a kindly warning.

Kazi had been away, high up on the slopes of Memonani. When he returned we decided to take advantage of his long-standing invitation to pay the mountain and its conquerors a visit. Enveloped in the prestigious Friendship Expedition we might be overlooked, and we even thought that we might return to Nepal by way of Lhasa, groupies of the victorious mountaineers.

But Kazi said, 'I am afraid that the Chinese have decided it is not possible for you to join us. They give no explanations. That is the Chinese way.' It appeared that, for all the friendship and the victory, the Japanese were having their own troubles with officialdom.

Kazi gave us a memorable farewell feast, dipping into his provision boxes for instant cake and instant noodles, instant prawns, the last of the crackly seaweed and a bottle of whisky. Japanese whisky is to whisky what military music is to music – not quite the same. It did not combine well with the spirit which Dorje produced from the resthouse store, something called Chinese White Wine which had the kick of poteen. I lay in a giddy daze with a hammering in my head like mountain sickness listening to a girl's voice singing a Japanese love melody on Kazi's tape recorder. Later I recovered enough to enjoy Kazi's presentation to Dorje of a *Guest Book for the Pilgrim's Guesthouse*. This was the first of its kind in which we all wrote our names and Caroline added drawings. Kazi wrote, MOUNT MEMONANI JAPANESE CHINA FRIENDSHIP EXPEDITION, and under a drawing of Kailas added:

'All that is beautiful is sacred. To Mr Choying Dorje. You are a religious, dedicated and respected guide and excellent interpreter. I will never forget your collaboration for my research. Thank you. Kazuhiko Tamanura. Doshisha University. Kyoto, Japan.'

Although we could not visit the camp on Memonani, Kazi agreed to drop us off next day at a village close to Manasarowar where we hoped to hire horses and tour the lake. Meanwhile Caroline had managed to beguile Mr Su, the government official from the administrative capital of Pulan, and persuade him to give us a note asking the police or anyone in charge for their help. Her foresight meant that, in addition to the Nepalese visas we had insisted on obtaining in Lhasa, we now had an important scribbled piece of paper signed by a bona fide government official which was the first legitimate piece of authorization we had acquired since leaving Kathmandu.

'What happens when he finds out about us?'

'There's no need ever to see him again.'

In the morning we were ready with all our bags. But the small uniformed Chinese driver in charge of the Landcruiser looked us over and refused to take us even as far as the next village.

'I tell him you are my friends, but it is no good.' Kazi almost wrung his hands as he pointed to Japan's friendship present with its rows of empty seats. 'I tell him you only wish to go a short distance. He says no. Only official people allowed in Landcruiser.'

Caroline said, 'It's the leader mentality. Now perhaps you can appreciate, Peter, what it's like to live in China.'

So it was back to the waiting game. We had to hope that another lorry carrying pilgrims might arrive in Tarchan and we could bargain for a lift. Our position was difficult, but Kazi's soon proved to be worse as news of his departure spread around the tents, and a crowd assembled, besieging the poor professor in a last desperate attempt to get their photographs taken. Men and women were pushing and shaking his arm to get his attention.

Our porters loading up at Kailas.

Kailas – Prostrating pilgrims.

Kailas – Pilgrim.

Kailas – Pilgrims.

Kailas – Pilgrims.

Chinese marksman.

Tarchan – Preparing food in the courtyard.

Spring festival, Kailas – Raising pole.

Spring festival, Kailas – Nomad tent.
Pack sheep and goats – Tibet-Nepal border.

Caravan – Tibet-Nepal border.

Farewell to Tibet.

'Only one more photograph please!' I heard him shout in English as three braves bounded up and stood in front of the camera. 'I cannot take everyone.' Time passed and a couple more rolls of Polaroid were used up. By midday the kindly man had had enough. People were still pursuing him, striking extravagant poses, but his tolerance had worn thin as he put the camera away.

'I tell them no more. They do not understand.' Caroline had been taking photographs too, or trying as best she could, since she was completely ignored. Her camera had no instant magic.

At last Kazi's bags and equipment were packed inside the Landcruiser. Dorje had climbed aboard; as friend and associate of Kazi he was to attend the celebrations. Over the last weeks the Tibetan and the Japanese had combined in a smooth partnership. They had communicated and interpreted through English, the language for which Dorje had been persecuted a decade ago. It was ironic to think that in modern China more Chinese were now learning English than the total population of the United States.

Dorje had put on his best silk gown embroidered with lotuses and significant characters. During the lengthy goodbyes Kazi gave us the gas stove we had borrowed for the parikarama, an extra cylinder and surplus food. Then the rapt crowd watched the professor climb in, gazing with the enthusiasm of fans saying farewell to a favourite star.

We waved, but nothing happened. The vehicle did not move. I could see the driver arguing with Kazi, raising his voice and pointing at Dorje's profile behind him.

Kazi got out, almost in tears. For such a mild and gentle man he looked not only distressed but very angry.

'Now driver says Dorje may not come. He says he has no authority. I tell him that Dorje is my colleague and interpreter for the last month and without him I cannot do my work. He still say no. What is the reason?'

He tried more persuasion, but the driver was adamant. No authority. Mention of the invitation to the official party made no difference. Orders had come from higher up, and for the sake of Japanese–Chinese friendship had to be obeyed. Dorje climbed out, and stood beside us in his robe as we watched Kazi being driven off alone in Japan's friendly gift. He had remained calm during the exchanges, although he and, by implication, his fellow Tibetans watching the departure, had lost face by this show of petty dominance. But most onlookers were more annoyed by the departure of the Polaroid.

Dorje refused to be put out. 'Perhaps tomorrow they will change their minds and send a car for me.'

By contrast fortune was kind to us. We only had to wait a couple of hours before a truck arrived with pilgrims and the driver agreed to take us to Hor, the nearest village to Manasarowar. Dorje helped in the negotiations.

'I have told him to bring you to the man in charge who may have horses so that you can ride to Pulan.'

With great sadness we climbed into the cab. We had been here for three weeks, and during that time Tarchan and its surroundings had become intensely familiar. We would remember the resthouse with its dusty yard stacked with pilgrims' belongings, the ruined gompa behind, the huddle of tents, and Kailas always framing the view. I remembered that Dorje liked the winter best of all, when during the bitter cold Tarchan was cut off by snow for months.

'Then I can study in peace. No one is here. I cannot tell you how lovely it is then. Kailas is white and everything looks like the pure white silk of prayer scarves.'

I watched Tarchan vanish behind us, the pilgrim tents and sheepfolds, and the small place of refuge where we had spent happy weeks. Dorje stood by the gate and waved.

The distance to Hor was only around twenty-seven kilometres over a golden plain rippling down to the two lakes, Mansarowar and Rakas Tal, one round, one in the shape of a crescent moon. Our first stop to let the engine cool down and ragged children stare at Caroline was at a small settlement with high-walled enclosures like something out of *Beau Geste*. Around and about were a few dirty tents. Beyond the rocks and the sand that blew up thick as custard and the dingy prayer flags rattled by the wind were patches of bog that perhaps heralded the presence of the lakes.

This place was Barga, an official stop for pilgrims which has its place in the travel books. Before the road was built Colonel Sherring wrote how Barga was situated 'on an enormous plain. There is no apparent track anywhere, and the only course possible is to fix the eye on the desired goal – and woe betide the wretched traveller or pilgrim who does not know the country or confounds one range of hills with another exactly similar. A weary march and much fruitless wandering will be his reward, as so many pilgrims testified to us.'

Barga had two houses – 'one for the Headman, a glorified hut, in which peasants of our territory would scarcely deign to live – the other for official travellers . . . this latter was composed of pitch dark rooms, the only windows being tiny apertures bare to the outside air (glass being unknown) and full of every sort of filth.' The place has improved just a little.

Another hour's drive brought us to our destination at Hor, which was as welcoming as Barga. We were instantly surrounded by another jostling crowd; a child took up one of Caroline's bags and she snatched it back. A man came out of one of the mud-walled rooms wearing a Western-style jacket and trousers, the sign that he was an official. Caroline presented him with our paper from Mr Su and a host of problems – accommodation, horses to hire for travel around the lake, a guide. Followed by an interested crowd, we retired to his small office which was decorated with familiar portraits of generals on horseback among rocks and flowers. Beside the metal stove was a small table on which was placed the luxury of a tape recorder.

Over lidded pots of tea we were told swiftly that horses were no good for making the round of the lake, since there was no grazing on the other side and no hay on this side. Although he mentioned that this was the first time that foreigners had come to Hor, he was ready for us. He announced that, if Caroline wished to use her camera out in the countryside, the fee would be ten yuan a photograph. The idea of fees for photographs was taken for granted in Lhasa and other tourist centres – so much per gilded Buddha, so much per lama dressed in his robes – but this was the first time we had come across the rule in western Tibet.

'Outrageous,' she hissed as we were shown across the dusty compound past a group of men playing cards towards one of the few mud dormitories that did not have broken windows. Two ragged men were curled up on sacks, and a woman with a sick child sat in a pile of litter.

'Far too dirty – let's camp.'

And just a few yards beyond that village was the sacred lake beside a green meadow with the mountains beyond. There were two shepherds' tents and, apart from them, solitude and peace. The only sounds came from nature, the murmur of a small river and the cries of birds skimming over the water or feeding on the grass. Birds in their ten thousand with little to fear from hunters, ducks, geese, herons, dense flocks of waders in three or four sizes, and multitudes of screeching black-headed terns flying over the water. Big hares bounded in the emerald-green grass and everywhere larks were singing. The lush landscape was filled with herds of grazing sheep and yak with the occasional horse. A few miles off, the green oasis by the lake faded away once again into the sparse pasture that supported the nomad herds we had been watching for weeks; burnt stretches of rock and clay and the orange hills that rose before the distant dome of Kailas.

Manasarowar was in front of us, the oval lake lying tranquil, formed by the mind of god, the world's navel whose waters are like pearls. While Kailas is the holiest mountain in the world, Manasarowar is the holiest lake. For Hindus it is as potent as or more so than the Ganges. 'When the earth of Manasarowar touches anyone's body or when anyone bathes therein, he shall go to the Paradise of Brahma,' wrote the poet Kalidasa in the third century AD. 'He who drinks its waters shall go to the heaven of Shiva and shall be released from the sins of a hundred births.'

Bhagwan Shiri Hansa described the reaction of pilgrims who had journeyed many hundreds of miles on foot to this sacred place. 'We all bowed down and poured out our heart in worship. For fifteen minutes were were all under the chain, the spell of adoration, not a word passed our lips . . .'

When Sven Hedin first caught sight of Manasarowar he burst into tears.

I wished I could tell the birds apart. When Colonel Ruttledge was here he noticed bar-headed geese and Brahminy duck beside the lake. We were certainly seeing something like that, thousands of them, thick flocks, more birds than I ever remembered. Spencer Chapman found Tibet 'a very heaven for the ornithologist.' 'If, as I do, he recoils from shooting the birds he loves, he is saved by the sanctity of the place from the barbarous necessity of obtaining specimens for purposes of identification.' Among the birds he noticed around Lhasa were 'brilliantly coloured rose finches, two kinds of equally gay redstarts, desert chats and robin accentors. Beside the sandy stream we could see snipe, redshank, greenshank, and wood sandpiper together with several varieties of wagtail. In waterways there would be bar-headed geese. Brahminy duck, mallard, gadwall and teal, white terns, cormorants and goosanders frequented the river. Ravens and choughs . . . lammergeyers, Himalayan vultures, buzzards, kites and ospreys . . . fish eagles . . .'

Birds that I knew for certain were the larks that rose up and sang above us.

The fish in Manasarowar are particularly holy. When they are thrown up by the waves they are used for treating cattle, the exorcism of evil spirits and a general tonic for the sick. After being cleaned and dried in the sun a bit of holy fish is burnt and the smoke and smell inhaled by the patient. Of course no Buddhist will go fishing on the lake (nor will he take

[*184*]

a boat). Collecting water birds' eggs here is also forbidden, which is exceptional in Tibet where elsewhere a trade in swans' eggs has evaded strictures about life and death.

We camped peacefully that evening beside the calm lake. A group of shepherds came over to inspect us. Their tents, made from thick yak hair, were cavernous and held down like battleships with lines of ropes; in comparison ours must have seemed fragile as an egg. They felt the thin green material and stood around and gaped at Kazi's stove, which for once did not let us down and cooked the noodles. We sat on the grass as the sun set over Manasarowar in an orange ball and the mountains turned from white to gold until the last snowy peak shone like a star. Then the darkness drifted down and the only sound was the rustling of sleepy birds. Later, dogs began barking; we had not seen a dog all day, but now like spirits released only by night they filled the air with doleful wails.

In the morning the first skeins of duck began to fly low over the lake, while already at first light the herds of sheep and yak had spread out across the plain. More people appeared around our tent. Groups of villagers who stood riveted by the sight of our small domestic cares, Caroline brushing her hair, myself cleaning tin plates in an ice-edged stream. The waters of Manasarowar may be pearly, but in the dawn light it was the curve of Kailas that gleamed like a pearl in its setting of burnt hills.

Although the headman of Hor had said that we could not make the full circuit of the lake on horseback, he provided two thin steeds for a day's hire. They stood waiting for us in the yard, horses that had suffered a hard life before being fitted with high wooden saddles that felt like sitting on knives and very short rope stirrups that pulled up our legs like flat race jockeys. When I mounted I seemed to be doing penance for the whole suffering animal world. They were so enfeebled, they needed a guide to pull them along by a rope halter.

We left the village at a pace that made Sod and Mucker seem Derby winners, and our original idea of travelling around the lake lunatic. Perhaps they were the wrong colour. Chapman, after mentioning that there are certain colours for ponies more auspicious than others, writes that the most prized sort of animal was an 'ambler'; an ambler is what the Americans call a pacer, a pony that trots like a dog or camel, trained to move alternatively his two left legs and then his two right. Perhaps the creatures we rode were amblers; we never got to the point of trotting. After an hour of torture, disregarding the pleas of the guide, I dismounted and handed him the rope. Freedom never seemed more pleasant. Caroline followed my example.

We walked across a sand dune to the great blue pool of Manasarowar, and for the rest of the day wandered along the curve of empty strand. There were no houses or boats or people, just space filled with the sound of water and birds, mostly screeching terns. In places there were huge sand dunes along the shore, and by the edge of the water was a ridge of dark chocolate-coloured weed. It could have been any familiar sea shore, grey waves with terns weaving and calling and the chill of an ocean wind, except for that unique rippling light, and always, whenever you lifted your eyes, snow-capped mountains – ahead, the Gurla range with Memonani among them.

And the birds. Perhaps the numbers of birds owed something to the numbers of fish we could not see. Manasarowar is supposed to harbour golden ling, whatever that may be. In 1812 William Moorcroft saw 'an enormous large animal or fish like a porpoise . . . he kept a considerable time upon the surface, was of brown colour and had apparently hairs'. An outsize otter, perhaps.

Watching the rippling light on the water we witnessed the suddenness of the changing weather when at one moment the lake was calm and blue as turquoise and the next it had exploded into lines of black waves as a storm blew over it, blotting out the mountains. When Richard Strachey was here in 1846 the force of the wind tore off the ends of the measuring tape that his friend Mr Winterbotham had used. 'The waves roared as they rolled towards us breaking on long lines of foam that receded over the shingle beach, the broad expanse of sea green water.'

The fifty-mile circuit of the lake used to be as important a part of the pilgrimage to holy places as Kailas. For Hindus, Brahma himself made the lake, and pilgrims who came here are expected to follow the precepts laid down by the ancient Puranas, for like the banks of the Ganges the shores of Manasarowar are a good place to die.

But we found no pilgrims circling the sacred lake as they had been rounding Kailas. Perhaps after the long period during which religious practices had been forbidden the lakeside parikarama had not been resumed. Perhaps the time of year was wrong. When Heinrich Harrer camped near here he noticed the many pilgrims creeping around on hands and knees and carrying away jars of holy water.

Without inducement we had no urge to do the circuit ourselves, and ambled instead for some hours on what seemed a seaside walk. We realized that the headman of Hor was right and that horses – certainly not those horses – could not find sustenance beyond the fertile strip where we were encamped. The land turned once again to gravel and there was no grazing for the hardiest ruminant; the shores were totally devoid of human habitation. After the storm the slap of water continued on the shore and the air was shrill with bird cries. Nothing disturbed them; Manasarowar, rippling in blue light, was surrounded by an empty ring of sand.

CHAPTER 15

Hor – Pulan – the Nepalese Frontier

On our second evening encamped outside Hor, the headman invited us into his room to cook our meal on his pressure cooker, something new in this part of Tibet. While our noodles softened we listened to his tapes, muted versions of the noises sent out in other towns on loudspeakers for early morning exercise. 'The East is Red' was confined to his quarters; outside, the loudspeaker had yet to reach Hor and life in such a small place was still tranquil. We began to think we were settling down the way we had in Tarchan. 'English people! English people!' called out the children, primed by their text books. But their elders were generally too occupied with their peaceful lives to take any particular notice of us once their initial curiosity was satisfied. For once we lacked the usual audience, as people were busy cooking, gambling or herding animals during the long hot afternoon. As I waited for another outsize sunset, I watched a girl bringing in yak. Her technique was to use a rope as a catapult with pieces of oh-so-useful dried dung as ammunition. 'Crack!' went an argol at a woolly baby galloping after its mother. Her aim was unerring.

As the sun went down and the birds settled over the lake with their raucous cries, clouds began to gather, some black, others touched by the sun, echoing the gold and pink of the mountains. Line after line of them sailed up, filled with snow. We went to bed in spring and woke to midwinter. During the night, snow had gently covered the world. Outside the tent was a blinding white light and the ochre hills in front of Kailas had become a glittering white line. Snow lay on the grass and on the lake shore; the small river was completely iced over and the only sign of life was the dark humped shapes of yaks. The lake remained blue in its white setting.

We had decided to make for the Tibet–Nepal frontier, since, even discounting the blank spaces and inaccuracies of our map, Nepal was close by. Beyond the Gurla mountains was the frontier post at Pulan.

The headman announced that a lorry was leaving Hor that day. He spoke with an enthusiasm that suggested he had had his fill of foreigners.

Caroline bargained with the driver, the usual uniformed Chinaman who peed as he talked. Another tough guy – a hundred and twenty yuan for the five-hour journey to Pulan, the equivalent of two months' salary, and travel in the open back in the driving snow. No, we could not join him in the cab.

The snow came in fits and flurries as we lay in the back with a crowd that included a man who had a septic leg and sat propped up against a steel drum as if he was frozen. Soon Hor was behind us, and, turning south at Barga, we followed the narrow isthmus between Manasarowar and her sister lake, Rakas Tal. The sanctity of Manasarowar is counterbalanced by the evil associated with the sickle-shaped stretch of water beside her. At the same time, the shape of Manasarowar represents the sun and is synonymous with wisdom and compassion, while the crescent of Rakas Tal stands for the moon and enlightenment. One is good, one is evil, one is a bride, the other a groom; they are ying and yang. In Hindu legend the attributes of these lakes, both about forty-five miles in circumference, are similarly intermixed, mysterious and contrary. But Rakas Tal is an integral part of the cycle of pilgrimage. The Hindu scriptures give advice on how a pilgrim must offer water to the ghosts of his ancestors at Manasarowar, and bathe and worship Shiva in the name of the Royal Swan. After walking round the lake, he must visit adjoining Rakas Tal, do the parikarama of Kailas and bathe in all the neighbouring streams.

The link between the two lakes was particularly desolate. It was not just that there was no vegetation, it was the way the dry stone funnel of rock and sand fused the harsh ingredients of the country. There used to be a monastery here, favoured by the Dropkas, 'one of the dirtiest in Tibet'. Vanished. We looked back for a final view of empty beach beside the sacred inland sea of Manasarowar before approaching the bridegroom, Rakas Tal. The snow ceased as the sun shone on the sinuous stretch of water surrounded by high cliffs which had a cobalt blue glow that burnt the eyes. This 'clearest brightest blue' even goes beyond the turquoise of other Tibetan lakes; perhaps the steep surrounding hills funnel down the blue of the sky in thin atmosphere or it may have something to do with the fact that the waters of Rakas Tal are brackish – naturally those of Manasarowar are sweet.

There are a number of islands on Rakas Tal, including one near the shore of the Devil's Lake, where during the twenties and thirties of this century an Indian hermit took up his abode. In the winter local people took food to him across the ice, but one year the ice broke and they drowned. Nothing more was ever heard of the hermit.

[*189*]

Most travellers feel a spiritual uplift from the physical contrast between the lakes, with Kailas making a Trinity; added to which they know that the sources of four holy rivers are not far away. Lying in the back of the lorry with half a dozen Tibetans, snow flurries, dust and sand raining down on us, we felt no mystical experience. Now we were driving by the Gurla mountains and could see Memonani, their highest peak, and even make out the Friendship mountain camp up on a buttress of ice, a bleak spot surrounded by boulders and open to the winds. No wonder Kazi preferred to work with the pilgrims at Tarchan.

Others had attempted the mountain before the current expedition. In 1907 Dr Tom Longstaff and two Swiss guides made an assault and were only defeated a thousand feet from the summit in a performance which Herbert Tichy considered 'bordered on the miraculous'. The young Austrian, Tichy, also tried to to conquer Memonani in the pre-technology era. In 1936 he climbed with an Indian companion on a wearisome four-day slog before turning back at 23,000 feet. He thought Memonani easy enough by Alpine standards with a snowline that starts at 18,000 feet. Nevertheless they were defeated, not only by the climb, but by some Tibetans who spotted them and thought they were after the gold and silver found in the mountain range.

The lorry stopped at a mountain hut while the driver and his friends got out to quaff tea. We were ignored.

'I wouldn't mind if we were just hitching,' Caroline said when they ambled back at last. 'But we've paid them a king's ransom.'

More snow fell on us. We lay among muffled figures and worried about our arrival in Pulan with its customs and checkpoint.

The nearer we got to Pulan the more it became obvious that it held a noosehold on travellers crossing the frontiers of Nepal and India to the south-east. The town was an outpost standing at the end of the valley beyond the Gurla mountains at a junction of three rivers, one of which, the Karnali, is a tributary of the Ganges. It guarded the western approaches, and for hundreds of miles there was no other way south over the Himalayas. In the old days Pulan was Taklikot, another name change to discourage the traveller. In 1906 Sherring noted Taklikot's unique position for trade 'only one hundred and seventy miles from the plains, the pass is easy, and lastly the great wool country lying east of Manasarowar.' Even the railway down in India was only 210 miles away. All that was needed was improved communications between Tibet and Nepal and India for Taklikot to become an important trade centre. Eighty years later, the uneasy relationship between China and India, has meant that

Pulan remains a place of potential. The Chinese and Pakistanis might link up with a great highway, but there is still no proper road for motor traffic between Pulan and the frontier, and trade between Tibet and the south is still restricted to what can be brought up on the backs of men and animals.

After we had left the Gurla range behind, the countryside changed dramatically. One moment we were surrounded by snow peaks and in five minutes we were among groves of poplars and small terraced fields with burgeoning green crops. (But in winter this area must be as desolate as elsewhere. One traveller mentions how the Jongpen of Taklikot started a poultry farm which prospered in the summer, but in the cold weather the fowls' feet froze and they became crippled. You don't see hens in Tibet.)

In a landscape that was lush and green we were passing a small village, like those we had seen far away to the west, with flat roofed houses, prayer flags and stacks of dung. Then a small gompa with a curved golden roof looking down on the Karnali and the honey-combed cliff below it. The caves were homes for a number of people whom we could see standing beside their white-painted doorways rubbing their eyes as they came out into the light. We stopped at a flimsy suspension bridge guarded by lounging soldiers; above them some shepherds were guiding their flocks which grazed around clumps of violets growing among the rocks. The roar of the ice-blue river drowned out all other sound.

After dropping off some of the Tibetans and their bags, the lorry moved forward towards the outskirts of the town. Once again we were at the mercy of a driver; although we banged helplessly on the roof of the cab, he swept us into the centre, past a barracks with a decorated gateway, a line of official residences, and into a large compound where, to our consternation, Mr Su was waiting for us among neatly-trimmed flower beds, staring officials and senior army officers. The black leather jacket, sneakers and dark glasses were those he had worn when we met him in Kailas.

He greeted us shyly with every wish to please. 'Welcome to Pulan.' Handshakes after we had climbed off the lorry and retrieved the baggage. 'I was expecting you here, there is wash house and good restaurant. No problem.'

Carrying our bags, our minds filled with visions of corrective camps, we followed our mentor down a gravelled path between flowerbeds filled with geraniums and salvias to one of a series of chalets that brought to west Tibet the air of a Butlins holiday camp. The usual woman with the keys appeared, and took over from Mr Su who retired with smiles and the announcement that dinner would be ready in an hour.

We were in a bedroom that offered us the nearest thing to luxury that we had found in Tibet, a room which had its own basin, mirror and two comfortable beds with clean linen. It was a bewildering new experience to wash with a decent amount of water while Caroline unzipped her bags and went through her housewife performance. Outside, groups of women with yard brushes were sweeping, while a gardener worked among the flowers. China was in charge of a routine that was clean and ordered.

There was a discreet knock, and outside the door stood Mr Su with an older official wearing a tight buttoned-up blue tunic whose name was Mr Sung. He spoke no English, but smiled a lot.

Mr Su said, 'Mr Sung head of Security.'

We discovered that Mr Sung was head security chief for the area round Pulan. But he had only been here for ten days and had not adjusted to Tibet. Mr Su came from Xian where he had two brothers and two sisters. Mr Sung came from Shanghai where he had a wife and two sons. And now they were in Pulan.

'Not interesting. What is there to see?'

This resthouse, designed for the comfort of pilgrims coming up from India and Nepal, had only just been completed. 'Rich pilgrims.' As such they would pay the relatively high rates charged here.

We explained our problems. 'We wish to travel to Nepal.'

'Sure, When?'

'Tomorrow – if that is possible.'

'Sure. I will see to everything.'

But the inspection of our passports was an ordeal to come.

Meanwhile Mr Su and Mr Sung took us to the small shop where we were able to buy provisions for the journey ahead. A girl produced the usual noodles. biscuits and a pungent Chinese sausage like a shrivelled bar of soap.

'You can charge them more,' Mr Sung said in Chinese.

'A good seventy percent more,' Caroline said later. 'About ten quid extra.'

That evening we invited Mr Su and Mr Sung to join us for a meal. In the canteen – dining-room would be too elegant a word to describe the barnlike structure full of metal tables and chairs – we discovered a number of burly Chinese and Japanese mountaineers from the Friendship Expedition. Among them was Kazi.

He came over and joined us 'You go tomorrow?' Caroline smiled and nodded and he realised that we were in a very delicate position.

Appetising smells seeped in from the kitchen next door where we glimpsed chefs in white hats and coats bending over cauldrons. The arrival of our little party galvanised the staff into activity and waiters jostled to bring in a series of dishes that demonstrated the best of Chinese cooking, served in the land of tsampa and mutton bones. We feasted on bowls of thick egg soup, glazed sauces, creamy sauces sprinkled with herbs, and kebabs, strips of pork, bean curd, crinkled stalks of a nameless vegetable, dishes of boiled rice, fried rice, sweetened rice, noodles. Many of the ingredients of the feast must have been carried across the high plateau in lorries. There was beer and two fish cooked in their skins, complete with heads. Something like carp, they were delicious.

'Holy fish from Manasarowar,' Kazi said. 'I do not eat.'

Halfway through the meal one of the Chinese climbers left the great mound of food in front of him and came over to our table with an enormous egg which was a gift for Caroline.

'Eagle's egg!' The whole dining-room roared with laughter; no doubt this tremendous delicacy was a fertility symbol. The perfect gift for carrying in a knapsack. Caroline smiled sweetly at him, put it down on the table and continued to entertain Mr Su.

'I hope next year to bring the Rothschilds to Beijing. They are the sort of people who might well be interested in subsidising an industry.'

Mr Su's tired face gazed at her over his chopsticks with an awestruck expression.

'When I was in Beijing last November, I stayed in the Vice-Presidential suite.'

While she was describing the lavish sitting-room and bathroom provided for members of the higher echelons of socialist administration, the conversation came to a halt when a sallow-faced officer marched over to our table and had a word with Mr Sung who passed on what he said to Mr Su.

'Security now wishes to see you. I am sorry we stop good meal.'

At least we had reached course eight. With foreboding we abandoned the feast and followed the khaki figure back to our room where, outside the door, four more men in uniform were waiting.

'Passports.'

We sat on our beds while they crowded in and handed the passports around to one another, examining them page by page, first the message from the Minister for Foreign Affairs in Ireland, then the place of birth and *signes particuliers*, then the horrible photographs, then the pages with stamps.

'What is Harwich?'

'A port in England.'

'Ah. What is Dieppe?'

'A port in France.'

'Ah. Who give you permission to come here?'

Fingers crossed. 'The Chinese Embassy in Kathmandu.'

'Ah. Why you have Hong Kong visa for Tibet?'

'We understood that was correct.'

They departed, taking our passports with them. In spite of the comfortable beds and sanitized atmosphere we did not sleep well. Sometime in the night someone opened the door and switched on our light; there were shrill voices, footsteps, then darkness and silence.

In the morning we made our way to the dining-room to renewed feasting as tasty dishes were served up, pickled cabbage, spicy sauces and something in gelatine like sheeps' eyes. Around us the mountaineers were eating heartily as if they had never gone to bed, their appetites hard to satisfy after their exertions.

We were spooning gruel soup when Mr Su bustled in. 'Good morning, good morning. You sleep well?' He sat down at our table and lit a cigarette while once again Caroline recalled her privileged sojourn in Beijing. I was wondering if she wasn't overdoing it, when the swing doors burst open again to reveal another young army officer. There was something familiar about him, about the sharp glare with which he picked us out from the other diners, his slight stoop as he walked towards us, the gloating way with which he stood looking at us over the scattering of dishes. It was the interpreter.

The last time we had seen each other was hundreds of miles away on the road to Ali. I remembered the painful row as we stood outside the lorry in a stretch of wilderness and I had called him the most uncivilized man I had ever met.

'The Director of Police wants to question you.' He bit out the words with venom and I remembered the old adage about travel. In the East, want of respect is the precursor of danger.

We abandoned the breakfast and returned to the bedroom where the same group which had questioned us the night before was waiting. One of the officers was carrying a large parcel wrapped in brown paper.

Our passports were produced. 'I wish to ask a question.' A ratty little man turned to me and flipped a page. 'What is this?'

'It must be an exit stamp from Greece.' Evidence of a package holiday on Corfu.

'Ah. This?'

'Dover. A port in England.'

'Ah. Why do you leave Tibet by Pulan?'

Now it was Caroline's turn. 'You see, we got Nepalese visas in Lhasa.' I remembered her insistence on wasting precious time in Lhasa trekking out to the Nepalese Embassy.

'Ah.' The passports were handed back, and we couldn't look at each other. There was a long moment of silence before the man carrying the parcel began to open it. 'We would like to present each of you with a beautiful calendar of our country.' He spoke officially, watched by three smiling colleagues. The calendars, large as prayer mats, were unrolled to reveal bright pictures of Tibet. The Potala, blossom in the Norbulingka, a couple of mountainy places, a blue lake, a shaggy man on a shaggy pony, some girls in distinctive clothes dancing near a flower bed.

Caroline was the first to regain her voice and wits.

'You are most generous.'

'It is nothing.'

Many smiles and handshakes. No mention of baggage and currency. They saluted and walked out of the room.

In a state of euphoria we congratulated each other.

'It was the Rothschilds that did it.'

Maybe it was the Vice-Presidential suite. Maybe they thought we could obtain every Chinese in Pulan a visa for California. Most likely they were kind, friendly, hospitable and unable to believe that we had no permission to travel here.

We could start for the border right away, and Mr Su and Mr Sung had ordered us a jeep. Like visiting royalty we had to make our goodbyes. There was Kazi saying farewell all over again. Then the mountaineers, whom we found in their dormitory, all reading copies of *Playboy* as they lay on their beds passing the time.

'You are the two Irish travellers.' The richest man in Japan raised his eyes from the centre spread and gazed at us benignly. 'Now you go.'

Other heads nodded over the nudes as more smiles were exchanged.

Mr Su and Mr Sung told us they would accompany us all the way to the border. It was their duty. A small fee was agreed for the journey and, hardly believing our luck, we watched the jeep being loaded with our bags. After we paid our bill Caroline took group photographs of the best of friends. (The interpreter had vanished.) There was Mr Su, his dark glasses removed, grinning in his ritzy black leather jacket. Click. There were Mr Sung and myself with our arms around each other. Then we all got into the jeep with two Security men and the driver hunched up in front.

From Pulan the route followed the edge of the river, lined on either side with small terraced fields, while across the valley lines of snow mountains caught the sun. Since the road-makers had not been this way, the route remained more or less a path for track animals. Even with a four-wheeled drive the jeep found it very rough going, negotiating places where the track had been washed away or a vertical stretch of hill had to be navigated inch by inch in first gear.

'Tibet is very poor country,' Mr Su apologized for any discomfort. 'Much better in America.'

Although the jolts and bumps were painful and hard to bear, we knew that every yard took us further away from Pulan and its telephone link with Lhasa. An hour later we bumped to a stop in a small village with flat-topped houses surrounded by the usual high mud wall, set in a patch of greenness and fertility like nothing we had seen for months. This was Khojarnath which Dorje had described to us – it had an important gompa built by Indians, which Indian pilgrims to Kailas always made a point of visiting.

Even at this final stage of our journey the two security chiefs felt obliged to show off Tibet's heritage. Mr Su rooted out the lama in charge. 'Five yuan each to see.' He himself did not want to go in. 'People do not go to temples any more for prayers. Only to look and take photographs.' Both Mr Su and Mr Sung disapproved of anything to do with religion, man-ifestly a backward step into the past. On the whole they seemed to find little to enjoy in these parts. Mr Sung had a cold and Mr Su complained about the problem of the headaches that had afflicted him ever since he arrived. I remembered how Manchu officials a century ago regarded their tours of duty in Tibet as a thankless penance, usually a punishment for some massive misdemeanour.

The old lama to whom we gave our money seemed well used to tourists. Like every monastery in Tibet, Khojarnath is much reduced from the days when it used to harbour sixty monks and about a dozen nuns. At the beginning of this century a fire destroyed much of the interior, but the place was soon redecorated in the most gaudy style. Although the stuffed tiger, stuffed yak and antlers of a Sikkhim deer that used to welcome pilgrims at the entrance have been thrown out, the gay interior with red wooden pillars and giant statue of Buddha remains cheerful. There were echoes of Sakya also in a reminder of the pilgrims' destination; Sakya had frescoes of Kailas, while here on a piece of wooden panelling was painted a scene of Lake Manasarowar with a skein of duck above the water.

Mr Su and Mr Sung were waiting outside the main door. 'You like?' But Mr Su was not really interested in our opinion. 'Please, there is some small trouble. Jeep cannot go on.'

We hardly dared to ask. 'What's the matter?'

'Road no good. We learn from headman here. Better take horse – I have given orders.'

We waited, trying to appear unconcerned, inspecting the small market under the village walls where a few people squatted in the dust offering dull things for sale on pieces of cloth – plastic-framed mirrors, Chinese leaders, hair ties. Then the horse arrived, poor creature, another wretched skinny pony with an angry-looking old man dragging it along.

'Tibet very primitive,' Mr Su apologized as the man began to strap our bags over the saddle.

Goodbye, goodbye. Many thanks. 'One moment please,' Caroline said as Mr Su and Mr Sung were climbing back into the jeep. 'I suggest you write a letter for our porters, which we can show if we meet a checkpoint. 'Of course.'

'Thank you. Goodbye. We are most grateful.'

The jeep drove away. How nice Mr Su and Mr Sung had been, and how glad we were to see the back of them.

CHAPTER 16

Into Nepal

A cold wind blew up as we followed the horse down a narrow sunless valley with the river thundering at our feet and the promise of mountains ahead.

'Do you think that's Nepal?' I shouted above the noise of the river.

'For your sake, Peter, I hope it's not India. Remember what Bradley said about not having a proper visa? Years in a filthy Indian jail. Fortunately mine is okay.'

We had asked Mr Su the distance to the frontier. 'Perhaps two hours. Perhaps five.' He had changed the subject. Either he had not been there, or, like the man who had made our map, he had been defeated by this impossible landscape. How could you draw neat lines, mark frontiers and give tidy definitions to the vast empty world just beneath the clouds?

The track rose and fell over the rock, mile after mile. Mr Su was right, no jeep could have made the journey. The horse with our baggage had to be cajoled all the time, dissuaded from stopping and snatching at weeds. Its owner continued to look angry. We had been travelling for three or four hours and were descending towards the river and a long bank of shingle, when we noticed half a dozen men coming our way. One moment the world was empty except for our gruff companion yanking his horse along by a rope, the next we were surrounded by a group of chattering men, one of whom spoke the world's lingua franca.

'You are foreigners? How are you here?'

He was Nepalese, and had made the journey up from Nepal with two companions. All three wore track suits, as distinct from their porters who had pixie caps, jodhpurs and bare feet. They were pilgrims on their way to Kailas. When they heard we had come from there the whole group looked startled.

'Nepalese frontier closed to foreigners. Not possible to come this way.'

Caroline smiled. 'We read in the *Rising Sun* that the western border is open.'

'Minister talking nonsense. No foreigners here.'

Not a matter to take further. Instead we asked them the way, and they told us they had come up from Simikot which was the government headquarters of a province of western Nepal which we knew very well was out of bounds to foreign trekkers. But from here Simikot would be hard to avoid; in any case it had a small airfield where we might get a flight to Kathmandu.

Before the pilgrims went on we changed some of our surplus yuan into Nepalese currency. By using the black market exchange we had travelled across Tibet for few hundred pounds, doing very little for the Chinese economy. We watched them walking away in the direction we had come, the lines of porters with their conical straw bags whistling and singing to each other in encouragement under the heavy weights they carried.

A voice called back. 'Remember Nepalese nice people. We like English people.'

An hour later we reached a small village hanging over the gorge in a nest of trees surrounded by a few little fields. In front of us the valley had narrowed to what appeared to be a cul de sac, and the mountains faced us, rising straight up and threatening. Our porter began taking our bags off his horse with great haste.

'Go on,' Caroline shouted in Chinese, and then in English. 'Nepali border.'

He shook his head and our bags continued to pile up on the ground.

Some men and children came out to watch him escape. He was away; Mr Su's letter did us no good, and we would have to get from here to the frontier on our own. It was not far off, but the bag of provisions, my Annapurna bag and Caroline's heap of effects all had to be moved.

'I'm going on.' Sinking under the weight, I plunged ahead, Caroline following slowly. There were a few houses and then the path veered down steeply through rose bushes. Far below I could make out a thin line crossing the river which turned into a small wooden cantilevered bridge. That must be the frontier. On the far side a path led in a thin scratchy line up the hill to where another mountain peak gleamed in the sun.

'There's something wrong with me,' called out Caroline behind. 'I think I'm getting a heart attack.'

'It'll have to wait.'

I left her to her own devices and she managed to persuade two children to take her things.

Although we had received much kindness, it was still with a great sense of relief that I entered Nepal once again. No matter how much the Chinese try to project their new open policy towards foreigners, no matter how much they emphasise the improvements that Communism has brought, there is still the overwhelming sense of visiting an occupied country. But mingled with the relief was the regret. I remembered the space, the dust, the mountains, blue lakes and the people with their charm and courage. I thought of Kailas and the pilgrims in the cold, Manasarowar with its canopy of birds. I thought of Dorje settled in Tarchan for the winter with his aunt and her friend in the blue spectacles and the cat after the pilgrims had gone. Kailas with the winds howling around would be a dome of snow, linked by snow plains to the stretches of ice that were Manasarowar and Rakas Tal.

Sven Hedin wrote: 'As long as I live, my proudest memories, like royal eagles, will soar round the cold desolate crags of the Trans-Himalaya.'

Heinrich Harrer wrote: 'Wherever I live I shall feel homesick for Tibet. I often think I can still hear the wild cries of geese and cranes and the beating of their wings as they fly over Lhasa in the clear cold moonlight.'

Some months later Caroline received a letter from Kazi. 'When I was in Tibet I made up my mind not to come back again. However, when I landed at Osaka International Airport my heart was longing to go back again. Tibet has everything that we don't have. Dry land, pilgrims, sheep, tsampa, wolf (yes I met him on the way to Lhasa), Tibetan hospitality, even dirty clothes. Everything I am recalling the pleasant days at Tarchan. Especially those days are unforgettable. The most delightful days for us. Do you agree?'

I looked down on the ice-blue river cutting through the steep gorge. I was almost there. Nothing to indicate a border, not even a chain at the rickety little bridge, just a few tottering steps across the wooden planks with the river roaring its welcome.

'Nepal?' I shouted as one of Caroline's child porters lurched into sight. 'Nepal?' He nodded and thoughts of a Chinese prison finally faded.

Caroline crossed. 'I still can't believe it.'

'How's the heart?'

'I really didn't feel well, Peter, and I must say I got very little sympathy from you.'

We sat on a Nepalese rock and munched our last chocolate bar, feeling like gods.

I asked, 'What was your family's attitude towards this expedition?'

Her reply was Anglo-Irish, 'Oh, they thought it was quite all right since your grandfather christened my mother.' She scrunched up the wrapping and placed it carefully under a stone. 'What did Gillian think?'

'She was relieved to read that high altitude decreased the sex drive.'

'Huh. No need for high altitude to put her mind at rest.'

'She thought up what she said was the perfect title for my travel book.'

'What?'

'Travels with a Donkey.'

We had crossed in the late afternoon, and now we pitched the tent on a narrow shoal of shingle just above the river. This had seemed a lonely place when we viewed it from the Tibetan side, a thin eyebrow of rocks and vegetation backed by perpendicular cliffs. Now we found there were people squatting among the rocks, men wearing thick woollen coats and hats like pancakes flopping over their faces. They were Nepali drovers taking their pack sheep into Tibet, and like the Son of Man they had nowhere to lay their heads. They had no tents or equipment, just flimsy bits of cloth stretched over stones and little bags stacked in heaps that acted as wind-breaks. I had seen many similar bags stored at Tarchan, and I knew they were sheep packs. Each was made from coarse wool and stitched with leather ends designed to act as a saddle with two pouches strapped across an animal's back.

The nearest group of shepherds were bunched together in a circle on the ground gambling with dice and pieces of stone.

Caroline said, 'From now on you do all the organising.'

I approached the players, who were so intent on their game that they never looked up to give us so much as a glance. I remembered the Chinese soldiers I had seen in Tibet with their cards and mahjong; they had played with absorption, but it paled before the ferocious concentration of these Nepalese who were showing the preoccupation and abandon of true gamblers. A man with a round mongoloid face and sharp darting eyes was thumping a bid of three stones down onto the earth, while around him came excited cries and exclamations.

'Simikot?' I shouted. 'Porters? We pay good money.'

The player glanced up and vigorously nodded his head before continuing to gamble.

'He seems to understand. I knew that once we were in Nepal things would be easy.'

But the game resumed and we were ignored. When language barriers proved insurmountable Caroline had a technique of drawing out her message. Now taking a page from my notebook she sketched two men laden down with baggage.

'Fifty rupees each man one day!'

The same player looked up from his game again. 'Five hundred rupees.'

'Ridiculous!'

He shrugged and resumed playing.

In the evening we were rescued from having to abandon most of our luggage entirely by the return of the children who had carried down Caroline's bags. They were two girls who came back to see the foreigners put up their tent and parade their camping utensils. When they understood that we intended to travel in the direction of Simikot, they needed little urging to join us. They had relatives there, and no need for visas in this wild country.

So much has been written about the problems of entering and leaving. Madame Neel, after condemning 'the absurd prohibition which closes Tibet', ended her account of her adventures in ragged disguise with a grandiloquent appeal. 'The earth is the inheritance of man, and consequently any honest traveller has the right to walk as he chooses, all over the globe which is his.'

The Tibetans themselves have always argued that the secrecy and the centuries of opposition to people entering their country was never of their own making, but was forced on them by outside hostile powers. Now it is the Chinese who have begun to open up the country to outsiders, and the Tibetans hardly come into the decision-making.

We lit Kazi's burner beside the bridge on the border and contentedly ate the sausage we had bought at Pulan while we watched the sun sink behind the mountains. The girls, who must have been about fourteen or fifteen, came down again with some coarse blankets to sleep in, which they stretched beside a fire made from scraps of brushwood and argols. After Kailas I felt no qualms about their not sharing our tent. Later, listening to the roar of the river, I thought of the places I had seen – Gyantse, Shigatse, Sakya, all diminished, Lhasa, tarnished, but all places of beauty and mystery. And deserts, moonscapes, mountains, blue lakes. Kailas and Manasarowar.

We were woken by the sounds of thousands of scurrying feet.

Dazed with sleep, I poked my head outside. In the dawn light I could make out the two girls squatting beside their fire, trying to relight it with wet sticks. But something else was going on; slowly, like one of Kazi's Polaroid pictures, the scene became plain. An army of sheep was pouring down the mountainside towards the bridge across the river. Our small camp had become submerged in animals. More and more continued to thunder through.

As the light increased, I could make out how each sheep or goat – there were goats mixed up with them – was fitted with a pack saddle. Most likely, these would contain rice or grain, although I could see that some animals had small pieces of wood sticking out from the pouches. Only castrated animals can be trained to carry burdens in this way. A pouch contained a weight of freight of about fifteen pounds, so that each sheep carried roughly thirty pounds.

It took more than an hour for them to hurry past, thousands of bony bodies covered with rough wool, thousands of angular heads with curving horns. Through the foghorn of bleating I could hear the shouts and whistles of the drovers who were whirling around as the immense flock formed a pushing, moaning traffic jam at the foot of the bridge. On the other side, high up towards the Tibetan village, a continuous line of animals covered the narrow track in a moving grey ribbon.

At last they had gone and there was silence. We made tea and shared some biscuits. The sun was skirting the tops of the mountains, and Caroline was brushing her hair, each stroke followed intently by the girls. A little later, our party was increased by an old man who was almost to be our undoing. After the tent was struck and bags distributed, we all set off at a spanking pace, the man and two girls, each in a Mao hat emblazoned with a red star, scampering ahead.

After being asphyxiated in the back of Chinese lorries, I found something magical in making a journey on foot. How fortunate the old travellers were with their particular combination of hardship and achievement. Battling against formidable physical obstacles, facing danger and disease, could bring a sense of awareness and something like joy, which is hard for the modern trekker to achieve. Still, this was a fine lonely place, and if we were going to get anywhere we would have to cross a good many hills and a good deal of forest. The track rose straight up from the river into the sky, through tawny rocks up to the first drifts of snow. In spite of carrying no baggage, we were soon gasping for breath. Ahead, two of the girls were having a last look back at their home, the small village on the edge of a cliff above the thin divide of the river.

In another hour that particular river was behind us, and so was Tibet. We had reached a divide in the Himalayan landscape which was like stepping off a high terrace into space. Here was another world, of snow mountains as dramatic as those we had seen when we travelled near Everest. But no trekkers or tourists came to the Humla district of western Nepal where the travellers were shepherds, traders and other nomadic wanderers.

Now that the short summer season had begun, when the passes were free of snow, people were bringing their caravans of goods and animals up from Nepal into Tibet. This was a very ancient traffic. In the nineteenth century it was already old when foreign travellers noted how gold dust, borax and salt were carried down on the backs of animals while cooking utensils, pots, pans, earthenware and foodstuffs were brought up from Nepal. I had read that, when the Chinese moved in, much of this trade had ceased, and that the traditional nomadic life of the Bhotias who wandered between Nepal and Tibet had been drastically curtailed. But we were witnessing how the old ways had survived. We came out into a fold of mountains with another steep gorge falling beneath our feet, where looking up we could see a flow of people and animals descending in our direction. Another long sheep caravan took half an hour to float past us, each laden animal kicking up dust; ten minutes after they had gone by I could still hear the clang of bells and the shouts and whistles of the shepherds. Behind the sheep jogged some horsemen oblivious to the precipice that edged the track. Then, higher up, I could see approaching a column of yaks with valuable planks of wood strapped lengthways along their backs, the ends sticking out far beyond their bushy tails like bowsprits on old sailing ships. They, too, passed in dust, big shaggy Tibetan yaks balancing like tight-rope walkers – one false step would be fatal – an impression of flaring nostrils puffing out steam, massive heads lolling downwards, musky body scent, the creak of wood, and then they were gone.

Behind the yaks came another line of porters, small men in tattered white pyjamas so different from Tibetans with their thick furry clothes and pigtails. These men were bent double under the same massive wooden planks the yaks had been carrying, and climbing slowly step by step. Their ordeal seemed terrible.

Far ahead, another steep escarpment fell thousands of feet below. Although photographs of Himalayan trails may seem giddily dangerous, when you are actually walking along one, the danger of falling over the side somehow appears less. New instincts of balance take over like those of flies climbing up window panes, and much of the time your feet stick to the shaley surface without slipping. Higher up, where a rim of snow began and pools of ice had formed, we met more shepherds sitting under rocks having a picnic below the frozen wings of a mountain. They were making tea, each man supplying his own little bag of tsampa to be put in his cup. Somehow they managed to look cosy in the midst of the mountains, sitting in the open around their turd fire with an air of contentment. What was surprising was to find that once again in this remote corner some of them spoke a few words of English. They told us something was wrong.

'Your porters want to know what you will pay.'

'We agreed the price.'

'They say more money.'

The girls and the old man were watching us closely. Until now the whole expedition had been something of a lark, the girls sprinting on ahead, the old man following, our bags carried effortlessly up and down steep tracks.

'If they think they can blackmail us into giving them extra they're mistaken. They're trying it on.'

I tried not to think of the problems of dealing with our baggage on our own among these mountains. We cooked noodles and tea, while the Tibetans ate their tsampa and watched us silently. Nothing was said.

By midday we had reached a point well above the snow line where black clouds rolled over our heads and the air was winter. Here were more sheep. A sheep caravan moves along slowly – I believe that it averages about four miles a day. This makes for great difficulty in keeping the animals in some sort of formation without breaking ranks. The idea of dogs as herders has no place here, and the men who coax up and down the mountains hundreds of erratic beasts straying and snatching at ragged pieces of grass as they move along, channelled for miles along steep narrow tracks beside precipices, have a tremendous task. These drovers were returning from Tibet, bringing down sacks of salt as their ancestors had done for thousands of years with the same perils and misfortunes. I watched a man pick up a sheep carcase and throw it over a cliff away from the track like sailors consigning their dead to the sea. The body rattled over rocks and stones until it vanished, while another shepherd took out a small mouth organ and played a wheezy lament.

After another back-breaking climb we reached the head of a pass marked out by a chorton with strips of flag cracking in the wind. Far below us another valley, a gulf closed in by mountains. Wherever you looked the peaks clawed into the sky, wave after wave, with the Tibetan plateau a lost world behind our backs.

With the freezing wind blowing up and tearing at the flags, the pass was no place to linger, and we followed our porters who had galloped down the other side, our bags bobbing on their backs. As we went gasping down the track, suddenly instead of menacing lumps of rocks and snow and pools of ice we were walking among green specks of vegetation and bright yellow flowers. A herd of yaks was grazing on a mountainside, birds were singing, and a rivulet splashed beside the path. In a hundred paces it was spring. We had missed all the blue poppies and yellow roses of Tibet that do not blossom until late July. The flowers waited for us here. We had seen spring below Everest and lost it; now we found it again high up in western Nepal. The air had a greater warmth and smelt of pine trees; primulas and hyacinths grew at our feet.

Perhaps the thin mountain air increased the sense of well-being, sharpening smells, increasing the delight for the eyes. I was resting, sitting in the sun enjoying my charmed surroundings, so different from the wilderness which was the world of the Tibetan nomad. Suddenly the sun was blotted out by a shadow, and I looked up to see an eagle flying over my head. Around it were five others effortlessly sailing over the valley floor, taking advantage of swirls in the air with an ease I had only seen in gannets. One of them, a big brown bird which seemed as large as a hang-glider, swooped down and landed on a rock not far away – I could make out a yellow eye. Eagle? Lammergeyer? The Spanish call the lam-mergeyer *quebrantahuesos* – he who breaks bones. Did a bird like this one lay the egg that Caroline received as a present in Pulan? Here, more or less safe from guns, they were in the concentration that nature intended. Wouldn't eagles be more solitary? I was so entranced that I didn't notice Caroline coming down waving her arms.

'I'm not interested in birds when all our baggage has been stolen. I asked you to keep a close eye on the porters.'

'You're exaggerating. They've just gone on ahead, and anyway, what's interesting about our stuff?'

'In Tibetan terms it's worth a king's ransom. My camera!'

Shouting insults at each other we continued downward separately. I had no doubt that the porters would be waiting for us a mile or so along the track. If Caroline's paranoia led her to believe that they were going to sneak back to Tibet carrying our baggage, that was her problem.

We were reaching signs of human habitation, small green terraces running beside the track, a few walled enclosures, and once I noticed a wooden pipe used for irrigation. Then we came to a cluster of houses with thatched roofs standing on a bluff above the river. I had been keeping an eye out for two girls and a man, who should be easy enough to see. I went swiftly around the next bend in the path, but there was no sign of anyone. Behind me I could hear reproaches. 'I told you not to let them out of your sight! It's not my fault that you move faster than I do!'

I had watched eagles. I thought about passports, money, notebooks, her camera, my tent, and her camera, and remembered that dacoits were an accepted hazard of Tibetan travel. What was the name of the English-man who had twenty-one yaks stolen from his camp? 'It goes without saying that in Tibet every man goes around armed with a sword and gun, and if he cannot afford either, he fits up a stick to look like a gun.'

The valley widened out and there were numerous places where they could safely hide until we passed by in despair.

Then I heard footsteps and voices, and looking back I saw the girls in their Mao hats, together with the old man, all walking ahead of Caroline who followed like a prison wardress.

'Where did you find them?'

'Just as I said.' She gave me a freezing look. 'They were skulking behind a rock waiting to double back after we had passed. If I hadn't found them we would have been in a fine mess.' The porters appeared totally unconcerned, marching along laughing and joking with each other. I noticed that all our baggage was still tightly packed and no attempt had been made to open it. The girls still continued to carry it as we resumed our downward journey.

We came to another small thatched house surrounded by flowering bushes where a group of men were playing cards in a yard outside. Two of them wore khaki uniform, and it seemed that we had arrived at our first Nepali checkpoint.

'Yes, please . . . what do you want?' One of the uniformed men looked up from his cards. English again, and his command of foreign words seemed to give him and his friends great satisfaction.

'We have come from Tibet. Do you wish to speak to us?'

They didn't particularly. They were playing with the same concentration as the shepherds on the frontier, and we were an interruption. For a while they went on throwing down cards as if we didn't exist. Then: 'You are English?' said the man with the handsome bony face and clipped moustache who had won another trick. 'I listen to the BBC . . . Very good . . . You come from London. Buckingham Palace. The Tower of London. Windsor Castle.' He picked up another deal of cards.

There seemed to be no point in staying here since no one wanted to inspect our credentials. We had been walking for almost ten hours, and quite apart from feeling tired we were also hungry. We would move on and camp.

While we had been watching the play, our porters had taken off their loads and were sitting together in a conspiratorial group talking to each other. Now as we got up one of the girls went over to the card-playing group where she started to argue and wave her hands. The old man stood and watched, scowling, and at last there was a pause in the game as the conversation with the officers became more heated.

The traveller's constant problem. Old John Murray Guides and Baedekers are full of advice about dealing with guides and porters. No doubt Marco Polo had similar problems.

'They say more money. They won't go further.'

'We made an arrangement.'

'These people no good. Better you pay them.'

'No,' said Caroline.

All anyone wanted to do was to get back to the game. After much shrill chat, it was agreed that the porters would bring our bags down to the checkpoint at Yari a few miles on. There we would find a senior official to sort things out and argue over the contract of fifty rupees a day.

As we rounded the little hill the players were again immersed in their cards. At any other time we would have enjoyed the walk through puffs of spring blossom and flowers scattered on the turf and the accompaniment of burbling water and birdsong. We marched down to Yari, a cluster of houses by the track, where we found more soldiers, some policemen in buckled khaki, and a flagpole on a small terrace. No one knew what to make of us. A portly officer came out of an office and stared disbelievingly.

'Tell these people there is no way we will give them any more money.'

The Police Chief brought us all into his office where an ancient crank transmitter stood against a wall. We all crowded into the small room, our three porters, the Police Chief and most of his staff. Everyone was talking at once; the arguments were paraded amid a long exchange of translated abuse. The point was that the girls and the old man wanted more.

'Tell them I'm not the sort of person to deal in blackmail,' Caroline yelled, and I had rarely seen her so angry. The Police Chief trembled. Then all of a sudden she got up and pushed the Tibetans out of the door.

'I'm not having any more arguments. They have been fully paid, and anyway I'm tired.'

The door was firmly shut on the girls and the old man. We never saw them again.

Immensely impressed by Caroline, the Police Chief gave us tea and cakes, and later directed one of his men to help me pitch the tent in a field beside the station. It was a perfect site looking down on a valley full of sheep grazing among bushes of thyme and lavender and scattered flowers. On the far side the vegetation and tree line soon gave way to screes of rock, and above and beyond the sharp white line of peaks.

As we squatted in our little toehold over the valley, our tent caused a diversion for the policemen and their families who stood around us in the shadows laughing and joking and discussing life.

[208]

Western Nepal was a place of hardship. 'We are a poor country, a poor country,' intoned the man who had helped me erect my tent and now, together with the others, stood watching me cook – a novel spectacle that would not have aroused any interest in Khumbu. 'In Simikot no doctor. What shall we do?' Simikot was two days' travelling away. Did the poverty and isolation of Yari and the surrounding province confirm the theory that, although Nepal is one of the most subsidised countries in Asia, much foreign aid intended to bring medicine and education this way vanished somewhere to the east?

The same man told me that this was the territory of the snow leopard. 'Leopard no good. Come down in winter.' The beautiful endangered feline did not confine its prey to the bharal, wild sheep and tahr in the remoteness of the mountains, but sometimes sought easier prey in the form of domesticated animals.

I wondered how on earth half a dozen men could occupy themselves at Yari. (Were they tempted to hunt the leopard for his pelt? Laws and special trusts for its protection were far away.) This might be a border post, but the big police presence seemed little more than cosmetic – there could have been little in the way of official duties. Although this was a check-point for anyone entering or leaving Nepal, the only people who passed through were drovers with pack sheep, and no one took any notice of them. They were camped all around us waiting for the first light before resuming the mountain trail towards the frontier. As their fires smouldered in the dark, I watched a man going from camp to camp with a pan of salt to put on their food.

None of the policemen had been in Tibet. One said, 'Tibetans look happy, but they are sad people.'

'They were right to get rid of their temples and their lamas. We should do the same.'

All night I could hear the patter of rain falling on the tent and worried that the monsoon was here. But next morning the sky was still blue above the sound of bells as the sheep resumed their long journey towards Tibet. The sun was lighting up the snow peaks and the valley exhaled scents of herbs and flowers.

We asked if we could find more porters. Perhaps even a horse?

Like Mr Sung in Pulan, the Chief of Police at Yari had only taken up his appointment a few days before, having been posted to Yari from Nepalganj in southern Nepal. He was clearly depressed at the prospect of enduring life in such a remote place, especially since he had spent time in

Kathmandu, and already dreamed of returning to its queasy delights. No entertainments here, no civilized company.

'These people no good. If I tell them to do something for me, the next day they run off. I must warn, you were careless with your bags. You must always watch out.'

He told us that the trail to Simikot was difficult and very dangerous. There were falling rocks and landslides and every kind of wild animal – tigers and leopards in every tree. As a special favour he would try and arrange other porters, but he couldn't be sure of obtaining them.

'I send two of my men to get someone to help you. If they find someone, OK I give them instructions. If not,' he pursed his lips, 'things very bad.' We pictured ourselves surrounded by our bags and the roars of wild animals.

He sent off one of his men to try and find us a porter locally. No luck . . . 'These people do not even respect the police. I give orders and they do not do as I say.' He changed the subject. 'I have bad stomach.'

Caroline produced her pills, and soon found herself dosing everyone in Yari. The pills made everyone more disposed towards helping us, and suddenly the Police Chief took more positive action. A whistle blew and his men lined up shoulder to shoulder on the little terrace beside the flagpole.

'I will give you two men as far as the next village and they will take some of your baggage. Please divide it into four parts.'

Another whistle, and the line of men stood at ease while the sergeant walked down the rank and picked out two. His boss retired to his room and the dilemma of what to do with us had been solved without anyone having to inspect passports and visas.

The policemen, carrying almost everything, shot ahead rapidly while we followed towards another snow mountain, a barrier rising above the forest pine and juniper. We walked among jasmine, honeysuckle, flowering hawthorn, yellow dog roses, potentilla. There was lavender, peppermint and thyme. A cuckoo called.

We were walking down a pathway above the river through a country garden in early summer. There were enough flowers and flowering shrubs here to gladden any collector and fill every garden in the British Isles. There were sulphur-coloured butterflies and black and yellow swallowtails.

The policemen had disappeared. 'You can provide food and nothing else for them,' the Chief had said when we mentioned payment. It had been an order. They had been given their instructions, and there could be no question of them running away. But how to find them? In places the small track divided and wandered off, and we could easily part company with them for all time.

I had a dip in the stream, plunging into the ice-cold water of a deep pool with a flaky gold sandy bottom. We lazed for a while in the sun, before continuing beside the little brook which took strength and shape as it was fed by melting snow and glaciers from up above. Soon the trickling brook of a few miles back had become a torrent and we rested again beside a sand bank speckled with flecks of colour by hovering butterflies seeking moisture. Occasionally a yellow cloud or a blue cloud would expand. Dragonflies the size of birds lunged across the water.

There were trees all over the place, big deciduous forest giants all in the first flush of spring, carrying the pale limey green of early foliage or the distinctive bronze of young oak leaves. I suppose we had seen about twelve trees since we had left the Lhasa plain; now we had come into a forest which thickly covered the slopes and fissures of the river valley down to the water's edge. We had seen rhododendrons and azaleas full of little birds in Sagarmatha, but coming upon them in a place so much more remote and wild was a different experience altogether.

In places the main stream divided, forming islands with cataracts splashing between the rocks, and lower down we had to cross over a small wooden bridge balanced between two boulders. The trail became con-fused and split into numerous small tracks. But before we became totally lost we walked into a group of shepherds sitting in the shade of the shining green foliage of a walnut tree, their woollen packs stacked behind them, their sheep and goats scattered while they concentrated on their gamb-ling. Arcadia with playing cards. I recalled that such is the Nepalese passion for gambling, that they devote an annual feast day to it. Surely a Nepalese version of Monopoly would be successful – I devised one, using staging posts in Khumbu, with Everest in place of Park Lane.

A player looked up just for a second and pointed the way up the hill where the policemen had gone. We climbed after them through the pale green forest, the moss at our feet another series of luminous greens, every bush in flower, and everywhere birds, butterflies, dragonflies, bees, bee-tles and lizards. Larger animals kept away as they usually do in forests. Higher up we came to a terrace containing a long low building which turned out to be a school. This was Muga, one of the teachers gave us a delicious cup of tea, and here were our policemen. In Nepal everything seemed easy.

We pitched the tent in a small hollow full of wild flowers beside a stream that bubbled out of a well. The night was cold and we wore every garment we possessed. The tent smelled of thyme and mint.

'I bet Adam and Eve didn't have it so good.'

'They didn't have Gortex.'

By six o'clock as the first trickle of pack sheep were passing us, we were woken by their bells, men's voices and the patter of hooves. The burly drovers in homespun, a stick in one hand, a stone in the other, urged them on with whistles and hisses as, bleating and tinkling, they vanished up the valley towards the frontier. For how many more generations would they continue to travel this way?

The policemen stood outside the tent with a man and a boy they had recruited as porters to take our baggage to Simikot. The father dressed in cotton pyjamas and jacket was grinning; the boy looked about ten.

'These men very strong.'

The day was cool with mist rising over the river, and above the cloud cover a white mountain. We dismantled the tent and loaded up the porters. The boy vanished under luggage so that you could only see his legs; we referred to him as the Walking Rucksack. His father seemed impervious to weight. The policemen came too.

We hadn't gone far when we came to a low house built on a cliff above the river almost lost in bushes of orange, yellow and pink azaleas. This was our porters' home.

Soon we were squatting on the mud floor of a familiar Nepali interior with smoke trapped beneath a blackened ceiling. Here was the same welcome I remembered from Khumbu, as smiling women served up scoops of rice and pieces of goat meat with the texture of rubber. Afterwards we said farewell to the policemen who set out on the return journey to Yari.

Below the house the valley which we had been following for two days seemed to come to a stop in front of a wall of steep forested hills and a background of snow mountains. We realized that we had come to the entrance of a narrow gorge whose cliffs formed a funnel through which the water of the river roared so loudly that we had to shout. Another herd of sheep came towards us over a terrible suspension bridge, followed by two shepherds who appeared as if by magic through what appeared to be an impenetrable wall of rock. It was very hard to see how men and animals had come this way, but once we were over the bridge we found a sheep's path on the far side which rose dizzily upwards over cliffs and rocks. Then it descended to the river and up again, spiralling upwards to another thin ledge – along a bit, then down and around, and up and along and down, never more than three feet wide with a wall of moss and slimy rock on one side, and a drop on the other.

In front of us, walking and climbing places which would perplex sheep, was the Rucksack with the stick legs beneath.

'They are used to it,' Caroline said like a Victorian factory-owner. Once again we paused for breath while father and son continued sturdily ahead of us. I felt as people do when they ride in a rickshaw. Our porters were so much smaller than we were, and they were going up and down a three-foot-wide path carrying our burdens at a tireless pace, whistling through their teeth. There were many stretches of path where if they made one false move they would fall hundreds of feet.

Caroline said, 'Peter, isn't it time that you did up your shoe laces?'

There are not many river gorges among virgin deciduous forest left in the world. I had travelled through a place like this, thirty years ago, in Bhutan. I remembered a similar cleft in the jungle carved out by a river, the same roar of white water, the thick forest and flowers, and everything untouched and unsullied. I had not thought the experience could be repeated in the modern world.

Mist and spray from the river made the trees grow huge. The massive oaks, festooned in mistletoe, had trunks that would do for the roofs of palaces, the towering maples and chestnuts were draped in moss. In the higher places above the spit of spray we walked among junipers and tiers of pines reaching upwards to the snowline. But, if the trees were spectacular, it was the river that dominated this narrow enclosed world, giving it a presence and a life, the milky flood gathering speed and strength as it thundered its way through rocks.

Around midday we came to a village on a ledge where the river turned south. We had been walking for five hours, and I remember feeling a sense of awe that people could live in such isolation with the path that we were following their only communication with the outside world. Their lives were passed to the accompaniment of the roar of water louder than the human voice.

The river valley was all around us, flecked with green foam. Over our heads there were still white-capped mountains rising out of trees, and everywhere a muffled sound of running water. Terraces painfully carved out of the forest fell steeply in broken frills down to the river, each stretch of green barley dotted with women working in bright red dresses. Everything was stirred and put in motion by icy draughts of mountain air sweeping through the gorge. Grass bent double, the tossing trees and swathes of green corn were caught by the wind and moved endlessly. From far away came the crack and roll of thunder.

We stopped in a small square with a chorton in the middle. In the pretty villages of Khumbu the architecture was gradually being moulded by the demands of tourism, but here the village had taken centuries to grow out of the forest. The houses, hewn from the surrounding trees, were made from massive blocks of wood ringed by a couple of balconies which had the look of creepers and were linked by a series of notched ladders leading finally to the flat rooftop where a number of people were gazing down at us. Other were gathered beside the chorton. It was a shock to see how most of them were ill and undernourished. There were goitre pouches under thin faces, and here and there a set of features retarded by lack of iodine. Unsmiling children had stick legs and pot bellies. The scalloped fields round about that looked so rich provided insufficient harvest for the apathetic groups that were watching us go by.

That village was Yangar, and from there it was a short climb and descent to the next which was called Yalvan, a similar group of high houses with notched logs leading to terraces and galleries, carved pillar posts blackened by smoke and small dark interiors made from great beaded slabs of wood. Even the dogs and goats wore wooden collars. Similar paradisal surroundings beside roaring water, more dark-eyed, sick-looking children staring down at us. There are plenty of other remote places like these in western and central Nepal where food shortages threaten starvation and poverty is exacerbated by the difficulties of communication. For a large part of the year Yangar and Yalvan would be entirely cut off by snow and floods.

The Sherpa lands have been transformed, some would say degraded, by the onslaught of tourism. But, no matter how much their culture may have suffered, the Sherpas have enough food; they have medicine and education.

The trees around Yalvan's steep clearing had been left standing with nearly all their branches lopped off; no one had bothered to cut them down. A short distance away the forest reasserted itself, larger and more beautiful than ever. We came down to the river bank and cooked a meal in a parkland where all the trees were of specimen size. The depression induced in us by the poverty of Yangar and Yalvan could not last. The forest green elated and refreshed us. In only a couple of days we had left behind the wind-scoured Tibetan plateau and, although we had descended a considerable distance, it still seemed astonishing how the physical world could have changed so dramatically in such a small period

[*214*]

of time. No matter how stark and noble the Tibetan landscape had been, those gaunt stretches of wilderness were places for ascetics or saints or artists with a feverish vision. We found we were more attuned to succulent tones of green, bushes, flowers and trees. Above us a waterfall curved in rainbow spray with a couple of extra silver plumes watering moss and ferns, filling up dark golden pools.

'I bet there's good fishing here as well.'

We resumed climbing, another giddy clamber skirting the edge of a gigantic rockface that plunged back down into the river. We continued downward, always beside the water, and when we camped in the evening it was within sound of water. We put the tent on the path; there was just enough room to pitch it without it slipping away downhill. Our porters were joined by a third man, and they slept together under an overhanging rock blackened by smoke, a resting place traditionally used by travelling shepherds and nomads.

We slept beside the steep drop to the water's edge from where came the river's roar, drowning out every other sound. It had grown monstrous from the small ice-edged trickle in the snow to an irrepressible force cascading through the rocks. It made different sounds that became a chorus, some muted where it eddied and turned into a quiet pool, then again a low hum like a man greeting the first good day of spring, and somewhere where the valley narrowed a noise like a cry of pain.

Next morning a curl of smoke came from the ledge under which our porters had slept. There could be few places in the world where it was such a pleasure to camp and wake, watching the first glow of light stealing over the hills and listening to birdsong while drinking your first cup of tea. Caroline picked flowers, roses, honeysuckle, rock roses and fragrant herbs. Along with the sounds of water, the gorge was full of flower scents. Birdsong was inaudible with the noise of water. Down through the trees I could see the creamy torrents of the river breaking over the rocks.

Soon after we began walking, the gorge opened up and suddenly there were a lot less trees and a lot more people. We passed fields with women at work wielding scythes; we were down now in a place that was ready for harvest. The great shadowy forest was behind us, the land here was cleared in burnt-out patches and the weather was getting hot.

By now we were impatient for journey's end. 'Simikot?' we kept asking the old man who carried our bags, and he would point over the next range of hills. People and animals had changed. Instead of the pack sheep with their Roman profiles, now in the heat there were buffalo and Brahmini cattle.

[*215*]

We had accumulated other travellers who were going the same way. A bearded monkish man in a threadbare chuba walked barefoot behind us, a military-looking man with moustaches suddenly appeared from behind a tree. We sat and rested in a small village under a grove of walnut trees harbouring monkeys with furry black faces and bushy tails. On a rooftop some women were flailing corn with paddles; I watched their arms rising and falling and listened to the chorus of cicadas. The heat also seemed to rise and fall in waves. Men and women gathered to watch us as we sat perspiring, trying to keep cool and here again we could see signs of deprivation. In spite of the rich vegetation, the barley and newly planted paddy fields, the walnut trees, everyone looked sickly.

It was almost a week since we had left Tibet and stepped off the great tableland into the Himalayas. In Manasarowar it had been snowing, at Yari spring had lasted for a day before we descended to the heat of full summer, we had seen the sprouting green fields of barley then the thick golden heads of ripening corn, and finally we had watched the harvest. It was now really hot, and we walked through a vaporous soup of steaming air that clogged the valley in a wet sticky embrace. We rested and shared tea with some cattle people living here with their Brahmini bulls and cows on the edge of the forest. There was a look of India about the men in their loose-fitting white clothes and the women in their brilliant saris, and a different sort of jewellery to the Tibetans' and the hill people's – the heavy elaborate necklaces had given way to a lot more jingling of silver bangles and earrings. The sub-continent loomed.

We had been walking through one of the world's most magnificent surviving forests. Now as we approached Simikot we could see it being destroyed. Stretches of ruin where the primeval jungle had been gutted and charred into pools of grey ash covered the hillsides as far as we could see. At some places, where the bare eroded ridges stuck out from the trees behind, the next to be felled, the ground was still smoking.

The trail had risen again, and once more we faced the mountains at the end of the valley where a massive cul-de-sac was blocked by another pyramid of snow and ice. There seemed no way out. But once again when it seemed that we were doomed to turning back our porter found a path that wriggled up a neighbouring ridge. We were climbing into the shadows and, as the last strokes of sunlight faded, the sunlight was succeeded by the bright orange tongue of forest fires lifting up clouds of dense black smoke. Everywhere you looked the forest was being burnt; as we walked in the twilight the pall of smoke was supplemented by prickles of orange flame catching the crackling trees.

Then we came out on top of another steep rise, and down below were electric lights. Simikot.

We made our way there, stumbling down the hillside in the dark. We had left behind the river, the forest and the roof of the world with its remaining monasteries and black tents and conquering Chinese. In their bottle-green uniforms and Mao hats they were busy, busy making roads, improving health, constructing factories, building houses, pulling down the past, tempting tourists and organizing their colony. Poor Tibet.

An hour later we reached the outskirts of the town. I could see dim shapes of houses threaded through with muddy lanes and then a long stretch of grass which was the airfield.

'In our machine age,' wrote Fosco Maraini, 'rapid means of transport have deprived arrivals of all significance . . . But no one who has not experienced it knows what it means to arrive . . . after days and days of travel by the most primitive means of locomotion.' Maraini was coming into Gyantse nearly forty years ago. Peter Levi made the same point. 'To descend on a remote city out of the air without a slow arrival is to deprive yourself of any change of understanding where you are going.'

'Please come in,' said the young airport official. 'I fear we are not too comfortable.'

Four of them, together with a cook, ran the small airport. There was a plane coming in the following day and we could change at Nepalganj for Kathmandu. If we had come a week or so later the monsoon would have been upon us. Then the airport would have been closed down except for emergency flights and we would have had to use our feet. There would have been no other way. And it appeared that the problem of trying to obtain porters would have been horrendous.

'I think it would have taken you a month to the nearest place where there is a bus. We have no cars or buses or motor traffic here.'

No one could have been more hospitable than the airport staff at Simikot on whom we had descended without warning, putting them to great inconvenience. The cook prepared our remaining supplies and two of them insisted on moving out of their small bedroom for us.

At eight next morning Simikot's link with the outside world appeared as dots in the sky and a small crowd gathered to watch two small planes land in dust. Just as at Lukla way down east, the turn-round had to be quick, for by ten o'clock the atmospheric conditions made flying in the mountains impossible. Another farewell. We had paid off the Walking Rucksack and his father the night before and gave them our surplus stuff. Now they came to see us off and shake hands. After we got on board they lingered; I could see them through the small porthole window, the boy's head enveloped in my orange balaclava. The old man was smiling; he hadn't seen a plane before. Later they would struggle back upstream to their small house in the flowering forest above the ice-blue river.

Out of her window Caroline could see the Governor of Simikot in white jodhpurs appearing with a group of policemen and officials to greet a VIP who had arrived on the plane, oblivious to the unauthorized departing foreigners. Then the engines roared. The take-off was a hair-raising exercise which young Nepalese pilots manage with assurance. They fly these small planes through the mountains and foothills with a skill and experience which has to measure turbulence as the sun heats up the waves of mountain air, wicked cross-winds and monsoon showers that can strike out of a velvet sky. Among the peaks there is no level land to put a plane down. At one moment we were placed precariously on the shelf of land on which Simikot was built, the next we had shot over an abyss with a quick glimpse of roofs of baked brown houses and paths zigzagging up and down ravines. After Simikot fell away, there was nothing but bare mountains where the big trees had been cleared.

'I have a present for you.' Caroline opened up one of her bags and produced a bottle of Scotch whisky. She had kept its whereabouts a close secret for two months, and now judged that the right moment had come to drink it.

We slugged down a good deal, and the pilot smiled when she fell out of her seat.

She had also managed to bring the eagle's egg all the way down the mountains.

We changed planes at Nepalganj, a small town on the edge of the terai which has the reputation of being the hottest place in Nepal. After the cool of the Tibetan plateau the blasts of hot air were difficult to endure. We sat in the canteen watching a couple of pilots eating curry, sweat dripping down their faces.

In Kathmandu swollen grey clouds that covered the valley belched a welcome. Rain pattered on the corrugated rooftops of the Rana palaces, ran down the fake Corinthian columns and soaked the bright flowers. It poured on the rose-brick houses of the old city, the new garish villas, shoddy commercial blocks and lines of Indian-style godowns. It fell on the ferro-concrete monuments and fountains of the Tunde Khel, on the camellias and mauve bougainvillaea, on the bronzed helmeted head of Jung Badadur astride his horse, on the rickshaw wallahs crouched under

[*218*]

the flimsy hoods of their cabs where they sought shelter from the down-pour. A gilded dragon spouted water in front of a shrine.

'Monsoon early this year,' said the taxi-driver as a crack of lightning was followed by a roll of thunder. The windscreen wipers worked furiously to reveal glimpses of pools of water and stretches of mud.

In the Kathmandu Guest House I was pointed out like Dante with his singed beard back from Hell.

'You must have been in Tibet,' said the dhobi when I handed him a large bundle. 'I have never seen such dirty clothes.'

INDEX